In Green Sleep

In Green Sleep
A Tour of Duty

—◄○►—

A Novel By

JERRY ACKERMAN

iUniverse, Inc.
Bloomington

In Green Sleep
A Tour of Duty

iUniverse books may be ordered through booksellers or by contacting:

iUniverse
1663 Liberty Drive
Bloomington, IN 47403
www.iuniverse.com
1-800-Authors (1-800-288-4677)

ISBN: 978-1-4620-0244-3 (sc)
ISBN: 978-1-4620-0246-7 (dj)
ISBN: 978-1-4620-0245-0 (ebk)

Library of Congress Control Number: 2011903799

Printed in the United States of America

iUniverse rev. date: 03/23/2011

In memory of the forbearance of my mother,
Patricia Mary Paish Ackerman,
and with gratitude to my family.

Under this two-faced moon
we live with our fears
until they are old familiars,
or someone cracks the cipher
of our selves,
or walks the waters
of some northern spring.

Brendan Galvin

Prologue

—◄o►—

November 1966

Gray, almost transparent clouds drifted below him, sparse as trails of smoke, comings and goings, in shimmering blue light. I pointed out some images (remnants of ghosts? robes of the departed? long bearded prophets?), and we exchanged a few glances without saying a word. It seemed that his frozen eyelids told me he saw nothing profound, mysterious, or beautiful in the airy terrain. Or was it that the wonders of nature and the achievements of flight were nothing more than a dimple in a black hole?

What John Bluderin thought would not be stated in words. He avoided casual conversation, a trait that irritated his fellow soldiers. Yet the tiny beads of sweat on the borders of his trimmed, blond hair, the way he cupped his hands on his lap as if he were holding a chalice, and the pulsations stemming from his long distance runner's frame all told me he could be feeling the anxiety one has when a plane flies into downdraft, causing turbulence, and drops a few thousand feet.

"Your self-imposed exile into silence has already caused you trouble," I said. "I thought you would learn from that experience."

He looked at me, biting his lip. He knew damned well what I was talking about.

During advanced individual training, or AIT, in Fort Lee, Virginia, many of the soldiers there thought he was contemptuous—*uppity* and *haughty* were the words most commonly used to describe Bluderin— and they resented him. A few soldiers in particular disliked him so much that when rumors spread about an enlisted man screwing an officer's wife they pinned the deed on Bluderin. While no one could prove any truth to the allegation, the cuckolded officer, Lieutenant Justin Williams, had threatened revenge. He would see to it that Bluderin got what he deserved. The lieutenant had "connections" on *every* U.S. Army base, *no matter where it was located*, or so he said.

"You blew it when you walked away from Williams while he was still talking to you," I said. "When you had your back to him and waved good-bye with both hands, he was visibly incensed. His fists were clenched so tight I thought his fingernails were going to pop out, right through the back of his hands. You're lucky you weren't on military premises at the time. You could have been court-martialed for insorbordination."

The bizarre irony about this episode was that Bluderin had never been near Williams' wife. He didn't even know who she was, whether she was blonde or brunette, tall or short. His isolated behavior—*his refusal to socialize with other GIs in a spirit of jocularity or comaraderie*—had flung him into this ludicrous imbroglio.

The clouds disappeared. An endless veil of blue seemed to control his vision.

"Must be in the middle of the Atlantic," he said—*finally* speaking—and lit a cigarette. Inhaling what could have been a breath of fatigue along with smoke, he coughed and crushed it out. His reaction did not surprise me. The entire fuselage was dank with the stench of human perspiration and depleted smoke.

I listened to the subdued humming of the plane. The vibrations synchronized with the hiss of air, a sound I recognized as his somnolent breathing. He opened his eyes to see if there had been any movement. It had gotten darker. The obscurity in the air and the obscurity of the earth blended in a nightly fraternity.

"We should be arriving in Germany soon, early morning their time," I said.

Before we flew out of McGuire Air Force Base in New Jersey, he had said he had no idea where he was or why he was boarding this plane. I mentioned some prospects about our upcoming tour of duty. He offered no response.

He stretched his arms and shook his head. His eyes were dimly lit, silver then blue, flecked with red. His sad, vacuous stare overcame any other facial expression. It was because of a girl, he had confessed to me during our training at Fort Lee. There might have been other reasons for his austere taciturnity, but a girl was all I had to go on.

He had tried to describe her to me, alluding to her beauty, but his descriptions drew an unappreciative blank in my mind. I could not get a sense of her through him. To me, she was a wingless prayer in the mind's eye, an abstract reference made solely through his worshipping lips.

Ignorant of whatever qualities she might have, I saw only what a demoralizing influence she had on him. It was as though she had the combination to his psyche, opening up his romantic boyhood, dismissing it, and spilling out all of its contents into a devouring ravine. I learned that her name was Sarah, a girl he grew up with in Defiance, Ohio.

During one conversation in Virginia, he had said that he and the girl were like each other's missing half. His half, I saw, as the one missing. Without her he seemed to be without substance, a vacant presence waiting to be touched with the gift of unconditional love.

When the hard blow came—his rejection, the *Dear John*—it marked the moment when this formerly thoughtful and friendly guy regressed into a mood uncertain of any character. He became a stranger to me and, from what I could observe, even to himself.

His mental distortion was mild in comparison to other *Dear John* GI recipients I had known or heard about since my army induction. Several whom I knew personally committed suicide. Bluderin's suicide was more cerebral in nature, but whatever the outcomes, these deaths were all bellwethers that the concept of innocence was becoming extinct for his generation.

This story deals with John Bluderin and his philosophical voyage from self-infliction to an understanding of truth in a helpless universe. His animus becomes a mental current within my veins, circulating through my brain like minerals in blood.

Although I could feel little empathy for his losing Sarah (given the far more serious predicament of soldiers serving in Vietnam), I knew well the symptoms that followed his vulnerability—breathing that cannot survive without dreams.

After we landed and claimed our baggage, I watched him board the train that would bring him to his destiny. I imagined that his pilgrimage was going to be pathless, but not without purpose. As the voyeur to his subconscious and his Doppelgänger who could make himself invisible at will, I will vanish at this point.

One

◄o►

Although he had been ordered time and again not to, Specialist 4 Wiley Couch banged the spring-loaded door wide open to Specialist 5 John Bluderin's office and sprinted into it like a man on an urgent mission. He plopped an olive-drab satchel on Bluderin's desk.

Bluderin jerked back from the desk when he heard a shotgun blast, the sound the huge, thick door made when it closed itself. The crackled shot ricocheted all along the corridor and into other offices. It was not the sound anyone wanted to hear in a military building at Hardt Kaserne, especially one that was built like a bunker and once occupied by a battalion of Nazi infantry officers.

"Gotcha," Couch said, belching, patting his beer-belly with one hand and scratching the crotch of his pants with the other. He leaned over, pressing his forearms and elbows on Bluderin's desk. "Hand over the hashish."

The soldier's imposing presence was as exasperating as his diction. His thick head of dark hair—shone to a midnight blue—was always clean but unkempt and usually longer than military regulations allowed. His eyes, which were blacker than his hair, were pierced with pupils the diameter of pencil erasers.

Bluderin believed that Couch was forever under the influence of

5

alcohol and hashish. His constant smile was wide and wet, showing the considerable gap in the center of his upper teeth. Whenever he laughed, and he always laughed at his own quips, such as referring to himself as *Smiley Wiley*, the lower buttons of his fatigue shirt either tightened severely or busted loose from the pressure of his inflated girth.

Bluderin was accustomed to Couch's careless rhetoric and behavior. His coarseness seemed to be the only way for him to release his pent-up frustration with Bluderin, who (although three years younger than Couch) outranked him and was better looking. Bluderin's six-two, one hundred eighty pound physique—wired with hard, tight muscle—was softened only by his ash blond hair and cerulean eyes. The Führer doubtlessly would have approved of his physical features. However, Bluderin's acceptance of all ethnicities as equals would have landed him in brutal heat with the megalomaniac.

"What can I do for you today?"

Couch opened the satchel and took out a sheet of paper. He looked it over several times, apparently to make sure he had the right item.

"This thing needs to be retyped," he said. "I spilled some beer on it. Can you get Tyler or one of the other grunts to redo it and make around two-hundred copies? But I need you to check it out first, John. Last time I ran a memo the brass gave me all kinds of shit about my spelling and grammar."

Bluderin read the memo and, upon picking up an army pen intended for such purposes, began to make corrections. By the time he had finished, the memo looked stained in rivulets of blood. Even the tips of Bluderin's fingers were marked with miniscule blotches of red ink.

"I don't know how you do it, Wiley. Ten misspellings and a dozen or so grammatical errors in a hundred-word memorandum."

"They didn't teach me much about readin' and writin' down at the farm in Missouri," Couch said. "More or less picked up what I could, and it ain't much."

"Why did you come down from Göppingen? Just to have copies of this notice made?"

"The copier in Göppingen shit the bed again," Couch said, "and, as you saw, the memo is about a change in payday hours and location. I do not want to upset *Ma Fella Americans*, as President Johnson says, or my fellow GIs, by not keeping them up to speed on the new changes."

From previous discussions with him, Bluderin surmised that Wiley Couch had as much regard for his fellow GIs as LBJ had for Vietnam War protestors. Bluderin suspected that the reason Couch drove down from Göppingen was to spend some time in Schwäbisch Gmünd.

Wiley Couch was not a difficult guy to please. He thought that Schwäbisch Gmünd had everything, meaning great beer at cheap prices, farm girls he could bed down for the price of dinner, and a few regulars at a local Gasthaus with whom he could play cards or otherwise socialize. Like Bluderin, Couch enjoyed the advantage of being fluent in German.

Joining the army and being sent to Germany had been a windfall for Wiley Couch. Poverty-stricken when fresh out of high school, he now always had cash at his disposal and had improved his hygiene considerably. He recently purchased a 1956 Mercedes-Benz 220S black sedan. The gap in his teeth widened whenever he spoke of that possession.

"Like you, my friend, I have it made here, and you're doing better than me. Setting your boss up with a drop-dead gorgeous German broad certainly didn't hurt your standing."

"I must admit," Bluderin said, trying to withhold a smirk, "that the captain has been nice to me since I introduced him to Ingrid

Dannette. Sure makes military life easier, and Ingrid is a classic European beauty, don't you think? I wonder, though, how she and McCandley relate to each other. Her English needs to improve, while his German is helpless."

"Come on now, Johnny boy. You're always so goddamn polite and distant. Be real. You know the score. Fucking is a universal language."

"Like music and mathematics, I suppose."

PFC Joseph Tyler walked into the office, taking the memo from Bluderin and listening carefully to his instructions. Bluderin could not help but notice how diminutive Tyler looked when he passed Couch on the way out. At five-six, the PFC was a full head shorter than Wiley, and the circumference of Tyler's chest was less than a third of Couch's. The PFC's clean-shaven skull made the two contrasting images look even more emphatically like a portrayal of David and Goliath.

After Tyler left, Couch grabbed his satchel and pulled out a flask of Jägermeister. Guzzling a large swig of the liquor, he offered some to Bluderin, who waved him off.

"*Put that away.*" Bluderin said in a loud whisper. "You never know when the brass is going to make an appearance. In fact, McCandley could be here any minute. He needs to approve some documents before he lets me go on a three-day pass. Do you have to drink something with such a strong, licorice aroma? I hope the captain doesn't smell it. As it is, he'll probably reprimand me for letting the door slam shut. That's bad enough. Alcohol could make him renege on my pass and have you demoted."

Bluderin was anxious for Couch to leave so he could finish his work for McCandley and go to his apartment. Although no unmarried GIs were allowed to have a private residence, Bluderin had gotten approval from McCandley to have a "temporary private place, given the cramped barrack space, provided he can be contacted at any time." The fact was that Bluderin was going to be assigned, from time-to-time, to temporary duty (or TDY) covert missions, supposedly from orders out of the 8th Military Intelligence Unit in Ulm. A private apartment could be a necessary accommodation to fulfill some assignments. McCandley knew all about that, of course, but for the record he had to come up with some other "reason" for allowing Bluderin to have an apartment. So the TDY business was tucked into something vague—with not a word said to anyone—and with a pledge of secrecy.

Arranged by intelligence agents, Bluderin's private residence was located two blocks away from Gustav Erdmann's Gasthaus. Erdmann was designated to be a key communications point for TDY assignments.

For Wiley Couch, the Gasthaus, as an overall concept, was his main attraction in Germany, and Schwäbisch Gmünd had plenty of them. There were approximately a hundred and thirty in town. Couch's mission was to visit every one before he completed his tour of duty. The Gasthaus number was significant, since the population of the town was around forty thousand, not including U.S. military personnel and their dependents.

"Around one Gasthaus per one-hundred adult citizens," Couch had estimated, "and when you knock off the non-drinkers, it probably comes down to a Gasthaus for every fifty folks."

Bluderin realized that, as fluent as Couch was in German, he had a naïve appreciation for what the Gasthaus and similar public inns or taverns meant to the country's social demeanor. Gustav Erdmann had explained to him that, since the vast majority of German citizens had relatively small homes, especially in comparison to those in the U.S., the Gasthaus served as an extension of their homes, where people could socialize. Even those who never drank alcoholic beverages had a Gasthaus they frequented.

PFC Tyler returned with the copies. Bluderin checked the master copy one more time and handed the stack of copies to Couch.

"Thanks for recommending me for promotion to Specialist 4," Tyler said to Bluderin. "I appreciate it, and I sure could use the money."

"No problem," Bluderin said. "You earned it."

Joe Tyler was a quiet, devout Mormon from Jordan, Utah, married with a one-year-old daughter and another baby on the way. Bluderin admired Tyler's humility, his "clean living" style, and his straight-dealing sincerity. Joe had married early—at seventeen—and told Bluderin that his wife was the only woman he knew, in the Biblical sense, and the only one he would ever know in that manner. Bluderin once shared the ideal that Tyler was living, but it no longer suited him. A former Roman Catholic turned agnostic, Bluderin no longer held onto any ideals.

Couch almost knocked Tyler to the floor, mumbling *so sooory* as he placed the copies in his satchel and shook hands with Bluderin. Tyler quickly scooted out of the office upon avoiding the near collision.

"Thanks for the favor, man. If you want, stop by Josef's Gasthaus later today, and I'll buy you a drink. I'll be there, either playing cards or squeezing Helga's titties."

"Maybe, we'll see," Bluderin said, waiting for Couch to leave. *Josef's Gasthaus is one place I will avoid tonight*, Bluderin thought as Couch left. At least he made sure to close the door gently this time.

He finished typing the corrections to several small documents, then looked out the window before clearing his desk. The sun had melted the frozen enamel off a colossal oak, and an ever-so-slight hint of green filtered the air, as if it had come in from the horizon on a breeze. A gray castle, set on the crest of a grayish blue hill in the background, jabbed at the sky like a fist of thorns. Having an interest in art, Bluderin thought the scene looked like something Pieter Breugel the Elder could have painted.

Captain William McCandley stepped into the office. "I know you're anxious to begin your three-day pass, Specialist Bluderin, so let me look at the English version of the court martial proceedings with the supporting documentation and you'll be free to go."

"Yes, sir. I made the final revisions."

McCandley scrutinized the English version of the proceedings with an utmost sense of detail. He had a legal background and used it extensively on base, so he was making sure that Bluderin made no legal misinterpretation in his report. A man of nefarious detail, the captain was as fussy in his appearance as he was in his review of documents. His fatigues were impeccably pressed, and his eyeglasses were always crystal clear. He shaved twice a day, had his brownish gray hair trimmed every five or six days, and smelled of English Leather.

"The documents look fine, John. Bring them over to Tyler for filing before you leave. It will take a week before the German counsel comes back with any comments."

"Yes, sir, and as you requested, the staff has plenty to do in my absence."

"Speaking of the staff, I heard that they refer to me by a sobriquet. You better warn them, if I as so much as hear the term *Candy Ass* around here I'll have every one of them busted down to buck private."

"I have never heard the derogatory term you referred to," Bluderin said, knowing damned well that if he acknowleged having heard it McCandley would press him for names.

McCandley took off his glasses and squinted at Bluderin, who interpreted the gesture to mean that the captain did not believe him. McCandley's ego was larger than his intellect, but the man was no fool.

"I understand your situation. Just tell them what I said. On another matter, I have a personal request I'd like to ask of you. Ingrid has a niece whom she would like you to meet, unless you have a girlfriend we don't know about?"

"There is no girlfriend, sir. I'll be pleased to meet Ingrid's niece."

"Good. I'll let Ingrid know when I take her to dinner tonight. She'll be delighted. We both think you need to socialize more, to bring you out of your shell."

McCandley loved to wield his influence, to coax soldiers into doing things he felt they should do to improve themselves.

Bluderin was annoyed that Ingrid was trying to set him up with her niece. He imagined that she mistakenly thought she was doing him a favor in return for his introducing her to McCandley. However, he did not want anyone intruding on his preference to be left alone. Outside of his friendship with Howard James, an army cook who was a gifted artrist, he did not want to know anyone else in the army—*or anyone with connections to it*—on a more personal basis. It wasn't that he felt he was better than everyone else. There were numerous soldiers whose talents exceeded his and whom he respected. He just wanted to be free of the army's influence whenever possible. He certainly did not want to be coerced into a personal relationship being promoted by his military superior and instigated by his girlfriend.

McCandley picked up a book from Bluderin's desk. His light gray eyes looked at Bluderin with what seemed to be a quizzical expression. His forehead wrinkled and he scratched his eyebrows on the rim of his glasses as he studied the cover of the book.

"Where did you get it?" he asked, his voice bearing an inquisitive, almost suspicious, tone.

"From the library in town," Bluderin said. "Ingrid checked it out for me. It's a book about the history of Hardt Kaserne. I've been impressed with the massive, stone structures since I arrived here. Everything is so solid. I swear the complex could withstand an intense bombing and remain essentially intact."

"When was it built?" McCandley asked.

"The Kaserne was constructed in 1937 and originally named the Adolf Hitler Kaserne. During the war the Kaserne was used as billets for German Officers Corps cadets."

McCandley raised his well groomed eyebrows in surprise. "What else have you learned?"

"I found out that the Kaserne also housed French POWs during the war. When the war ended, the complex became a clearing house for refugees, DPs from all over Europe. Later, it was taken over by the U. N. Refugees Relief Administration and renamed Hardt Kaserne. I'm sure you know the rest of its history, that American troops began to occupy Hardt in 1951, populating it with a series of Field Artillery Battalions ever since."

"I'm glad to see you taking an interest in military history," McCandley said. "I wish other soldiers would do similar things, instead of getting drunk whenever they're off duty and behaving irresponsibly. You should write an article, a summary, about the base's history and publish it in the weekly newsletter distributed on base."

"Yes, sir. I'll draft it when I'm on pass and type it when I return."

Bluderin was amazed how McCandley could turn anything—even a simple reading of local history—into a job.

"Great. Maybe the article will help raise the morale around here."

Wishful thinking on your part, Bluderin thought. Nothing could boost the morale at Hardt Kaserne. The presence of the Fascist architectural military complex, filled with a swarm of soldiers in olive-drab, army fatigues, stood in stark contrast to the more gentile—or gentrified—architectural masterpieces of the town surrounding Hardt and Bismarck, the latter being an American-occupied military complex situated at the foot of the hill below Hardt. During World

War II, the Germans had constructed a tunnel from Hardt Kaserne to Bismarck Barracks. Under U.S. Army control, no one was allowed access to that passage out of the base other than selected officers and intelligence-related personnel. Hitler had instituted a similar policy regarding the tunnel when he was in power.

However, it was not the environment of Hardt Kaserne that lowered morale. The Vietnam War was the catalyst to that problem. Nearly all the GIs at Hardt who had been drafted, versus the ones who signed up voluntarily, hated being in the army and counted the days to their release. They were angry because the Vietnam War was the basis for their being drafted, a war they deemed both unnecessary and unwarranted, or dead wrong. While the draftees were relieved by not having been ordered to Vietnam, they also felt guilty about being spared the fate of draftees serving there. This contradiction added to their emotional confusion and distrust of the military, the army especially.

Bluderin looked out the window in his office and saw two GIs hanging around the main entrance and exit doors to Headquarters Building. He wondered if they were waiting for him. Howard James had told him that two GIs were talking about "what to do with Bluderin" during breakfast earlier in the mess hall. Howard didn't know anything about them, other than their last names being Federer and Akando, the names sewn on their fatigue shirts. He described Federer as being lanky as a starved leopard covered in pimples. Akando was about five-eight, lean, with obvious muscle tone and reddish brown skin. "Somebody doesn't like you," Howard had told him. "They said something about seeing to it that the lieutenant gets his revenge." Howard had offered to help Bluderin in any way he could. The GIs also had made some venomous remarks about black soldiers that did not sit well with Howard, who was black. Bluderin looked down at the GIs again. Howard's descriptions fit. He took the secret route—the tunnel—out of the base to the exit at Bismarck, which conviently was located only three blocks away from his apartment.

Approaching his apartment building, Bluderin stopped to look at its surroundings. The cathedral nearest his apartment, the Heilig-Kreuz-Münster, was built in the early 1300s. It was a grand example of Gothic architecture. An array of gargoyles along the eaves of the building overlooked the cathedral grounds and streets like stern, swine-wolf sentries. When Bluderin first noticed them, he thought they were evil. He was used to having these types of fears when it came to churches. However, when it rained, he saw how the gargoyles regurgitated streams of rain water away from the building's tan gray, exterior stone walls. He had read that gargoyles were long believed to ward off demons, but he came to dismiss that concept in favor of their architectural function.

The apartment was simple: a kitchenette with a living room, a bedroom, and a bathroom with no tub but a shower stall. The dwelling was a renovated cellar unit below a clothing store for women. Bluderin entered it, wiping the soles and heels of his combat boots on a throw-rug imprinted with a rendering of an apple orchard. He sat down on a 1950s deep-blue, three-cushioned sofa to remove his boots. The high-gloss, black bookcase to his right was overstacked with paperback novels, books of poetry, and German versions of U.S. magazines like *Life* and *Look*. The walls of the living room and kitchen area were distinguished by several Impressionist paintings of rural landscapes—rolling farmlands, dense woodlands, and a river banked with flowery meadows. He had purchased them from local artists.

His abode could also be described by the word *modest*. It was nearly invisible in its subterranean setting. The only aspect of his apartment that could be seen from the street was a small window, largely unnoticed due to thick brown curtains that blocked off any view of the apartment's interior. For the equivalent of twenty bucks a month—supplemented by two cartons of American cigarettes—the private living quarters suited his allocated budget and his passion for privacy. On occasion he could hear the footsteps of sales people or customers in the women's apparel store above him, although the sound was more of a distant shuffle than an interruption.

This place—comprising about two-hundred square feet—offered him a great escape from Hardt Kaserne and being a soldier to becoming a quiet, nonessential citizen in the overall community. At least, that was how he perceived himself. He could not place an emotion on anyone or anything, outside of pleasant interests in paintings and literature. Nothing else moved him. He liked the feeling of being invisible.

Bluderin lived the opposite in the sense that his presence was always noticed, whether in town or on base. He did not know why. He did his best to cultivate a quiet deportment, a kindly but highly reserved persona, but many women found him physically attractive, and men enjoyed his low-key sense of humor. He had broken free of his former taciturn behavior.

He opened a bottle of Pilsner and looked into his sparse closet, picking out some civilian clothes. He chose gray flannel pants, a black shirt, and a brown sweater, an ensemble that would let him blend in with the social landscape. After dressing and gulping down the remainder of his beer, he left the apartment and headed for the public library. He was relieved to know that Ingrid Dannette would not be there tonight, since she had a dinner date with McCandley.

The library was a refuge for Bluderin to avoid other soldiers. Few of them ever came into town, and none of them ever visited the library. He also wanted to dig up more information on Gustav Erdmann. When Bluderin had gone into *The Dark Room*, as it was called, in the cellar of Headquarters Building, his intelligence agent had instructed him to cultivate a relationship with Erdmann. However, she had not told him *why*. She had discussed this request from one side of a screened confessional booth configuration, while he sat on the opposite side, blinded to her physical appearance.

Give orders but never explain them seemed to be a credo in the intelligence community. Getting the job done—the mission accomplished—was the top priority. Bluderin believed that his personal safety was not even on the agenda. It was on his. Erdmann already had warned him to be careful, to watch his back, but Bluderin was not sure he could trust the German. *Why would he care about me* was a question he needed to answer.

Two

-◄o►-

Bluderin placed his half-liter mug of Pilsner on the Hungarian oak bar. When visiting the Gasthaus for the first time, he had commented to Gustav on how much better the beer tasted in a clay mug than it did in a glass or bottle. Erdmann had explained to him that the clay enriches the effervescence of beer, while a glass or bottle seems to dilute it. "The clay lets the beer breathe a little better," he had said.

It was early—only five in the afternoon—and the Gasthaus was empty save Bluderin and Gustav, along with a couple of professors conversing remotely at a corner table. Gus refilled Bluderin's mug and placed it back on the bar, along with a small gray envelope. Bluderin casually picked up the envelope and concealed it in an inside pocket of his tweed sports jacket. His intelligence contact on base had told him that a woman would meet him—either at the Gasthaus or his apartment—to take the envelope. He was not permitted to open it.

Delivering the envelope to its intended recipient was Bluderin's first TDY assignment. Gustav had hinted that this exercise likely could be a test case, having no authentic purpose other than seeing if it could be carried through without any interruptions or nuances. Bluderin had been informed by his agent on base that the intelligence community does not like any glitches when it comes to completing assignments. "Everything needs to be lean and clean, smooth as silk," she had said.

Since the Gasthaus soon would be busy, Gustav removed his blazer, hung it on a hook behind the bar, rolled up the sleeves of his white shirt, and straightened his blue necktie. In preparing for a few guests who usually arrived earlier than most, he poured beer into several mugs. His gray, slicked-back hair, light blue eyes, and strong, mug-handling forearms were in picturesque harmony to his surroundings, like a conductor at a concert. With his wrists having developed welts of diplomacy, he was a legend at the tap. It took just one easy, sweeping motion for him to fill a mug with a half-inch head of foam, not a drop spilled. The head, Gus had explained to Bluderin, was his personal symbol for a profit margin.

"Would you like a little cognac?" he asked Bluderin.

"Thank you, Gus, but not right now. The cards never seem to come my way when I drink anything stronger than beer."

Bluderin was waiting for Eddie and Tulla Grau and Hans Kliebert to make an appearance so they could play some poker, five-card draw or stud. Playing cards was a simple way for him to mix in with other patrons of the Gasthaus. He did not want to be noticed for doing anything unusual. He once had drawn unwanted and awkward attention to himself by sitting in a regular patron's chair, and he was chastised quite sternly by the regulars. He made sure never to repeat the act. After all, they were citizens and he was merely a visitor with "temporary" status.

"You have an interesting clientele, Gus."

"You think so?" Gus dried his hands with a towel, and then inspected them for cleanliness. "In what way?"

"When I first started coming here, you were the only one who would talk with me. I was an outsider to the regulars, a presence they preferred to ignore. Now, many of them are friendly and conversant."

"Sure they are. You're a nice, unassuming young man, John. It just took a little time for them to get to know you. You see, there have been a number of GIs who have come in here over the years and caused commotion—often becoming loud and obnoxious—even belligerent. I've had to throw some of them out and file reports on their disruptive behavior to the commanding officers at Hardt and Bismarck. Apparently word got out about my Gasthaus on both bases not to patronize my establishment, that it was not worth the bother. So now I have only a few GIs coming in, respectful ones like you. It's better that way. Besides, there's not much here for most GIs. They're far better off going to a place like Regina's Nightclub, where they might get lucky with a loose and sexy Fraülein looking for a good time."

Bluderin was beginning to understand why Erdmann valued him. Since he was a "quiet GI" who dressed in traditional German attire, his personality was well suited for TDY missions. No one would suspect him of doing anything out of the ordinary. Bluderin's ability to help decode messages could also come in handy for Gus, as he had mentioned when they first met.

Karin Erdmann, Gus's daughter, came into the Gasthaus from its back entrance. She tied on an apron and washed her hands. She kissed her father on the cheek and smiled coyly at Bluderin. Her pure white skin was adorned with splotches of tiny freckles about the same color as her dark brown hair.

Bluderin smiled back at her and winked. She grinned sheepishly, her cheeks turning a shade of red from shyness or embarrassment.

Karin seemed to be timid with everyone, including her boyfriend, Jürgen Treuge. At sixteen, she was finishing höhere Schule, or high school, and preparing to attend the University of Education Schwäbisch Gmünd, or Pädagogische Hochschule, commonly known as PH. When Karin left to wait on a table, Gus leaned toward Bluderin.

"One thing certain about this place," Gus said, "is that nothing ever goes on unnoticed. There's no such thing as keeping a secret around here. Take our mutual acquaintance, Wiley Couch, for example. He left here one evening—just one time—with a farm girl who is known for her easiness, shall we say, and now Couch is rumored to be a womanizer. They still like him, but you have to be careful of what you do and say. They're a good group of regular folks, but they love to gossip."

"I understand," Bluderin said. "They're no different from the people in my home town. I wonder what happened to my card players. They usually arrive early."

"Oh, they'll be here, don't worry about that. I haven't seen them miss a Thursday yet. Do you have any new jokes or word games, by the way? You always seem to have one or two to share with me. My customers get a kick out of your funny stories."

"My stories?" Bluderin was amused. "I overheard most of them through soldiers at Hardt. I may embellish them a little, add a little more humor or local color, just for the hell of it."

"Well, they like them," Gus said. "I think it's because they show how foolish or imperfect Americans can be, how they can screw things up, just like Germans—no better, no worse."

"They're all fictitious, or I think they are. Some of the guys who told the stories or jokes actually may have had similar experiences. Since the population at Hardt Kaserne and its military dependents is like a microcosm of all America, any of the stories or jokes I repeat here could have happened."

"Whether they're real experiences or made up makes no difference," Gus said. "On that note, I need your help. Do you have any political quips or word tricks hidden away in your brain? I could really use one when I meet with my fellow town consulate members tomorrow."

Gustav Erdmann was a *Meister* or *Onkel*—a senior figure or favorite uncle—who was highly regarded in Schwäbisch Gmünd. His public stature and reverence went well beyond the confines of his Gasthaus. He had held public office by having served on the town consulate and public housing committee for the past twenty years.

"Let me give it some thought," Bluderin said. "I don't have much interest in politics, so I don't pay close attention to anything politically related."

"You must have heard a few blips that involve politics," Gus said. "You've got a mind like a steel trap. Tell me one before the place gets busy."

Coincidentally, Bluderin had been playing with anagrams, acrostics, and other word games of late. One of his exercises did pertain to politics.

"I'm afraid I can't help you unless your consulate members are fluent in English. Even then, they may not get the word game."

"Try it on me," Gus said. "What have you got?"

"I play with words a lot," Bluderin said. "Do you know what an anagram is?"

"Sure I do. It's the rearranging of letters in a word or phrase to make a new word or phrase. We used them sometimes in secret communications during the war."

Bluderin did not know exactly what Gustav did during the war, but he had learned at the library that the man was considered a communications expert.

"Fine," Bluderin said. "What do *politicians* do that's in their name?"

Gus took out a pad and pencil from beneath the bar and began scribbling letters from the word "politicians" in various arrangements. He raised his disheveled eyebrows and tapped the pencil on his lips as he pondered over the letters he had made on the pad. The look of amusement on his lips soon turned into a frown.

"I give up," he said. What's the answer to your riddle?"

"Politicians *solicit pain*," Bluderin said.

"I'll be damned," Gus said, looking at Bluderin with what

appeared to be a curious expression. "Very clever, young man." His grayish blue eyes looked into Bluderin's, and his lips were still, as though he were in serious thought. "How true as well. All politicians solicit pain to win people's attention. However, it's what the politicians do with their attention that can be good or evil. FDR and Hitler serve as prime examples in that regard."

From what Bluderin could gather from listening to Gus talk about politics, he was something along the order of a socialist democrat. Indeed, that was how Gus had described his political philosophy, although the term struck Bluderin as being something of an oxymoron. Gus tried to explain that he believed in free enterprise, in building wealth through the use of one's intellect and ambition. He acknowledged that America prospers as a result of the incentives and rewards associated with inventiveness, productivity, vision, and entrepreneurship, among other characteristics. However, he also believed that such virtues could be better placed in a society that provided health care, education, and protection of the environment for all its citizens.

As a Gasthaus owner, Gustav Erdmann was an entrepreneur who had no problem with making money. But he also donated a good portion of his earnings—about fifteen percent—to an association dedicated to the reunification of East and West Germany. The association had been founded by a tiny minority of West Germans, with most citizens believing that reunification would never—*could never*—happen. Gus believed differently and told Bluderin that the U.S. would help reunify the country in due time. However, he did not think he would live long enough to see it happen.

"Gus, do you really like running a pub?" Bluderin asked. "Maybe you should have gotten more deeply involved in politics and risen up the ladder."

"No, the timing is not right. I'm too old. The next generation— not mine—will benefit from the cause I'm pledged to."

"Mind if I sit next to you, Mr. Bluderin?" Jürgen Treuge asked, surprising Bluderin from behind.

Bluderin had not seen Karin's boyfriend for a few weeks, and he did not miss him. Jürgen's deep blue eyes and thin eyebrows conveyed a tone of arrogance, and the way he folded his arms in front of his chest gave off a posture of defensive hubris. His parents had certainly spoiled their curly blond pride and joy. Bluderin often wondered what Karin saw in the guy.

"I assume you're waiting for Karin to get off work."

"I'm hoping to take her to the movies later," Jürgen said. "For now, I'm just keeping an eye on you."

"What are you talking about?"

"Karin has been flirting with you," Jürgen said. "I have to keep you two at a distance from each other."

"You're paranoid," Bluderin said. "To Karin, I'm simply a tolerable GI who stops in here on occasion to chat with her dad and play cards."

"Karin has eyes for you," Jürgen insisted. "In fact, when I returned from the Bundeswehr last week, she told me about a good-looking, nice American guy who comes in here. From what little I know of you, having seen you here but once or twice, you're the one who fits that description."

"It wasn't me. I'm sure about that."

"She said it was a GI who was polite and reserved and spoke German well."

"There are other GIs who speak German," Bluderin said. "In fact, I think it was Wiley Couch whom Karin was talking about. He comes in here on a routine basis, more often than I do, and he loves to flirt with the ladies. I bet he's occasionally tried to steal a kiss from Karin."

"Couch? You've got to be kidding me." Jürgen grinned, revealing an overbite. "Couch is funny. He's a regular guy and I consider him a friend. But he's way too loud and crude for Karin. He swears too much and tells dirty jokes. You're the one, I'm afraid."

"Look, Jürgen, you needn't worry about me. Karin is way too young and naïve for me to have any romantic interest in. Besides, I'm friends with her father, and I would do nothing to spoil that friendship."

Bluderin had just discovered a good way to desert Jürgen, whose presence was starting to annoy him. Hans Kliebert and Eddie and Tulla Grau had arrived. Bluderin joined them at their table. As Karin delivered their beer, Eddie opened a new deck of cards.

The tall, robust Kliebert and the short, stout Grau couple were an interesting trio in the Gasthaus political arena. Hans Kliebert's politics were similar to Gustav Erdmann's, while Eddie and Tulla Grau were monarchists. In their opinion, Germany would have so much more elegance and prestige if it had royalty at the head of state—someone like Otto von Bismarck, but in a position more like the Queen of England. Bluderin found it odd how this couple, who were on the lower rung of middle class, would prefer a privileged monarch over an elected official.

He also found it strange that the trio lived together, in the same apartment, situated above the grocery store where Eddie Grau worked. On several occasions, Bluderin had noticed Hans stroking Tulla's thigh under the table while Eddie, apparently oblivious or not concerned about their behavior, continued to play cards without saying anything. Bluderin understood that while this living arrangement would make sense economically, with all three pitching in on expenses, could there also be a sexual accord among this *ménage a trois*?

Tulla undid the top two buttons of her blouse and wiped her forehead. Hans had aroused her. She gently removed his hand from her thigh and tried to focus her attention on the hand she'd been dealt. Tulla was a buxom woman in her late forties. Now that her blouse was more opened, it was easy to see her considerable cleavage above her white-laced bra.

"I'll open with a mark," Bluderin said. He wondered how Eddie could read his cards, since his Irish Donegal cap was tilted severely downward in the front, covering his eyes.

"Can you see your cards?" Bluderin asked.

"I can see them just fine," Eddie said. "Don't you worry. I know that a good card player can make an educated guess about what's in an opponent's hand by how the opponent moves his eyes. I'm not giving anything away."

"Truth of the matter is, he has to disguise his negligible forehead," Hans Kliebert said, although his own looks were nothing to brag about. Hans had an incredibly large forehead, and his baldness made it look even more out of proportion. "Poor Eduard doesn't realize that it's his nose that gives him away. Whenever he's been dealt a good hand, that long, narrow nose of his flares out and beams an innocuous red."

"The nose glows," Tulla said.

"Are we going to play cards," Eddie said, starting to whine, "or are we going to discuss my quirks all evening?"

Hans reached below the table again, caressing Tulla's thigh. She parted her legs this time and raised her dress to accommodate him.

"I fold" she said, placing her cards in a stack beneath the remainder of the deck.

Hans saw Bluderin's call with a mark.

"Karin, could you bring us another round, please?" Bluderin asked.

"None for me," Eddie said. "John, I'll see your mark and raise you two." His nose was flared and red.

Vera Luchterhand, an eighteen-year old Fräulein notorious for her promiscuity, approached the table. A wave of perfume, like a combination of cognac and lilac, settled in the air. She rubbed the base of Bluderin's neck and kissed him on the cheek. She then walked up to the bar and did the same to Jürgen Treuge. He hugged her waist and blew into her ear.

"You're being naughty, Jürgen. Karin won't like that," Vera said.

Gus poured her a cognac. She paid for it with money Bluderin had given her and returned to the table.

"Who's winning?" she asked.

"Eduard has won the majority of hands so far," Hans Kliebert said, "and it may stay that way. I'm calling it a night."

"Me too," Tulla said. Her round, chubby face flushed red, and her hazel eyes watered amid pink veins. She was bombed.

"Let me join you for a couple of hands," Jürgen said, approaching the table. "Maybe I'll have newcomer's luck."

After Hans and Tulla left, Vera sat down between Bluderin and Jürgen. Her skirt had risen close to her panties as she rubbed the shoulders of both men. Neither of them paid her much attention. It wasn't that Vera was unattractive. She was pretty, in a comely nymphet way. Her short, dark blonde hair curved around her ears, setting off her faux silver earrings, and her body was taut, muscular from her neck to her feet, like a swimmer's, probably resulting from her farmwork. However, her reputation preceded her. Jürgen would flirt with her a little, but it was known that his only romantic interest was Karin. Bluderin was afraid he'd contact some kind of venereal disease from her.

"Jürgen, Eddie, thanks for the game. Vera, take care." Bluderin excused himself from the table.

On his way out of the Gasthaus he bumped into a petite, elegant woman in a tight, black miniskirt ending at mid thigh. The coat she was holding fell to the floor as she strived to keep her balance. She wore long, shiny, black-leather boots nearly up to her knees. Her straight, black hair glimmered past her shoulders, nearly half-way down her back. Her eyes were green, the deepest jade, and beamed with an obvious intelligence.

"Forgive my clumsiness," Bluderin said, retrieving the woman's coat. "I did not see you coming."

"No problem, love," she said. "No harm done. You didn't forget about our date tonight, did you? Now if you did, *that* would be harmful."

That was the cue. The words "harm" and "date" were the keys. Bluderin knew he was to meet a woman this evening, but he had no idea she would be so exquisite. He held her coat open as she slid into it. It was a fitted, brown-leather coat, accentuating her tiny waist and firm hips.

"How could I possibly forget about a date with you?" he said, lightly touching her left cheek and smiling. "You're luminescent."

"Luminescent? I like that," she said. "How flattering."

The woman stood on her toes to kiss Bluderin and whisper her name. After briefly introducing her as Leda to Eddie and Jürgen, then Karin and Gus, they left the Gasthaus.

Jürgen will have no more anxieties about my designs on Karin, Bluderin was assured, having seen him stare at Leda in likely admiration or lust. Whatever it was, she had his full attention.

Leda had captured eveyone's attention at the Gasthaus. So much for going unnoticed, Bluderin thought. He would have to ask Gustav what the patrons thought of him after tonight. He noticed that their eyes were all focused on Leda, so he hoped his own presence would be inconsequential. Then again, like Wiley Couch, he could be branded as a womanizer forever more.

As they made their way to Bluderin's apartment, he saw a soft light surrounding Leda's face. The luminescence he had referred to in the Gasthaus was no hyperbole. Leda Beschwörung outclassed him, but in a good way, that is, making him feel good and worthy, the best he'd felt in a long time.

Leda told him a little bit about herself as they walked. She was born in England and studied art history at Munich, followed by earning a master's degree in political science at Columbia in New York. She began her career in intelligence at the age of twenty-four, two years ago.

Although she was petite, about five-two and maybe a hundred pounds, the disciplined curve of her waist, her sculpted hips, the firm definition of her ass and legs, and the way her jade eyes invaded his, accompanied by a confident smile, collectively exuded a powerful, demanding presence.

"Would you like me to call a cab?"

Bluderin was about to remove the envelope from his sports jacket when she stopped him.

"Aren't you going to invite me in?" she asked. Her kiss was moist and sweet, controlled, and concentrated. "We need to get to know each other."

The intelligence contact had not mentioned a potential liaison being in the works, but he was not going to turn down the possibility of getting to know Leda Beschwörung more intimately. Her eyes drew him toward her like an electric magnet.

They sat on his couch sipping tea. Leda described her upbringing in western England, in a city called Cheltenham. Her father was German and had worked in an espionage capacity for the British during the war. He was now a professor of mathematics at the University of Gloucestershire. Leda's mother was a nurse.

Bluderin felt a mysterious connection with Leda, since his mother was born and raised in Cheltenham, having met his father there during the war. And, oddly enough, Bluderin had grown up next door to Karl Schlovein, a former German officer and spy for the United States. To add a finishing touch to these coincidences, Karl's wife was a nurse.

"You only have one photograph displayed in your apartment,"

Leda said. "I recognize you, of course, but who is the other guy? He looks like he could be your older brother."

"James Curry," Bluderin said. "I was designated to be his replacement at Hardt Kaserne."

"Did you two form a special bond?"

"We saved each other," Bluderin said. "As crazy as it may seem, I was sent to Germany to work as a clerk and interpreter. Don't ask me how I passed the army's test in German. It was a fluke. I arrived at Hardt Kaserne with a German vocabulary of maybe two hundred words and a handful of idioms. The words, for the most part, were those I heard my grandfather use, especially when the man was drinking his homemade *Apfel Schnapps*."

"How did you pull it off?" Leda asked. "How were you able to do your job?"

"Curry made *absolutely* sure that I learned the language: damned well and damned fast. He was anxious to get out of the army and go to law school, and he was upset over the possibility that he might get extended because I was not up to the job."

"How long a time did you have to transition into Curry's job?"

"Thirty days," Bluderin said, "and I can still hear his voice. It went something like this: 'Listen, you fucking goof, I'm due out of here in thirty days and *you* are not going to screw me up. Get it? If you do, so help me I'll do everything I can to make sure you're reassigned—to Vietnam—where you'll be blown up by land mines. Now, like I say, I've got thirty more dreadful days in this man's army and you'll be taking one hell of a crash course in German. We're going into town, and we're staying there, every chance we get, morning through night. And we're going to be speaking nothing but German. And you're gonna talk and listen, listen and talk, read and write, write and read, all fucking day, every day, day in and day out, for the next goddamn month, until you know how to shit in German. Am I making myself clear?' In short and in essence, I will not forget James Curry for the rest of my life."

"It obviously worked."

"Curry was insanely persistent and compulsive as my mentor, and I was just as persistent and compulsive as his student, all for the right reasons. In thirty days he was on a plane bound for the States, and I was translating documents and interpreting between German and U.S. Army officials with what I was told was a strong degree of competence."

"I'm impressed," Leda said. Sipping her tea, she opened a book of poetry, *Neue Gedichte: Anderer Teil*, by the German poet Rilke, that had been at the top of a stack of books on the black-lacquered bookcase.

"What's this?" she asked, finding a handwritten note in the book.

"It's nothing," he said, feeling invaded. "I was playing around with words. I tried to write an English version, mostly a transliteration, of the last two stanzas of Rilke's poem "Archaischer Torso Apollo" or "Archaic Torso of Apollo.""

"I know the poem," she said. "It's about a headless statue of the ancient Greek god of light, healing, music, poetry, male beauty, and who knows what else." She read Bluderin's translation aloud.

> *Other this stone would stand deformed and curt*
> *under the shoulders' invisible plunge*
> *and not glisten like wild beasts' fur;*
>
> *and not burst forth from all its contours*
> *like a star: for there is no place*
> *that does not see you. You must change your life.*

"You must change your life. *Du mußt dein Leben ändern*," Leda said. "There are many English translations of that poem, all different to varying degrees, but that last line is always the same. It is what makes the poem profound. It is something you must do."

He did not know how to respond to Leda's comment. He sat dumbfounded, confused over what she meant. After all, he had changed his life. He had been talking since he arrived at Hardt Kaserne, although the voice that he heard when he spoke was not his.

Leda squeezed his hands. They embraced instinctively in a gentle yet intense kiss, their lips and tongues linked.

"I'm going to teach you what most women like," she said. "We're going to go slow, and you're going to listen very carefully to everything I tell you and follow my instructions explicitly. Similar but of course in a different way from James Curry, you will find these lessons to your advantage for the rest of your life. Are you willing to obey me? It won't be as difficult as learning a new language."

He devoted consummate attention to her every word. From her eyes to her ears, along her neck, he was completely absorbed in her guidance. Her light brown nipples stood at attention as he caressed and kissed them, worshipping their softness and solidity. Her pubic area was trimmed to a small and sparse, exacting triangle.

"I shave for personal hygiene and preference," she said. "It's also more sensual to me."

He listened to her words throughout the evening . . . *softer, now a little harder, up a little, there, yes!* as he kissed, nibbled, and licked deeply into her vaginal opening. She glistened with a warm swell, a testament of her being pleasured.

As their sessions progressed, Leda stopped telling Bluderin what to do. He knew. He could sense her needs by her body's responses. He could *feel* her telling him what to do. She screamed and squeezed his buttocks as he mounted and entered her again.

It was not just sex. They transcended from the clinical to the passionate as the night moved into early morning. They slept until the sun's brightest rays broke through the brown curtains and awakened them. After Leda showered and dressed, she placed the small gray envelope in a secretly lined pocket of her coat.

As Leda and Bluderin walked to the train station, he pointed out that it must have rained during the night. The sun had formed a rainbow, its lower part predominantly purple and gold. He watched the rainbow fade as they approached the train station.

Since they had both been ordered not to communicate with each other unless directed otherwise by the agency, they did not know if they would ever see each other again.

As they kissed good-bye, Leda's final words to him were, "I know what you're thinking, John, and I'm thinking the same thing. It was damned good, wasn't it?"

Bluderin was flooded with unanswerable questions. The gray envelope, followed by a lesson in sex: were the two incidents connected? Was Leda preparing him for an assignment that could involve a female spy? What was his next TDY assignment going to be? All he knew was that his future was not for him to decide. He was a drafted GI, to be used for whatever purposes his superiors chose. His only hope was to get through this tour of duty in one piece. His adversaries had different ideas.

Three

◄o►

April 1967

Leaving his apartment to follow a path that would lead him along a sheep farm on the eastern side of Schwäbisch Gmünd, Bluderin felt a cleansing sensation, a clearing in his lungs, from the fresh spring air. He had been given his second TDY assignment. He wasn't sure how he felt about it, but at least it would be something different. His work at Hardt Kaserne had become routine, a series of processing documents on the field activities of Batteries B and C. The Pershing missiles were lowered according to schedule, with preventive maintenance performed, then made upright again, the warheads pointing toward Moscow. Other duties consisted of writing the procedures associated with court-martials. Most of the cases were about GIs disobeying the orders of an officer, showing up for duty under the influence of alcohol or drugs, or fighting with other soldiers. Most of the fights were racially motivated. In short, there was a continual wave of misconduct by the soldiers stationed at Hardt Kaserne.

Bluderin came to the highest point in the path, overlooking the Rems Valley. He stopped and sat on a stone wall to observe the pastoral surroundings. The sun sat like a lemon amid the rolling green horizon, sprinkled with newly leafed trees of various species, including cherry, oak, maples, and European white birch. A redolence of hay and farm animals crept into his nostrils.

What appeared to be a German shepherd with a large, whitish head and brindled body barked and danced among an ever-rambling flock of thirty or more sheep. A shepherd sat on a boulder, his staff held closely beside his head, the crook leaning out like an extended, third eye. The crook was immobile while the front of the shepherd's shirt undulated in the breeze. Bluderin waved to him, and he waved back, motioning for Bluderin to join him.

Bluderin's intelligence agent on base had forewarned him about the shepherd. The man spoke in metaphors and used imagery in much of his speech. He was told to listen carefully to everything the shepherd said and interpret his wording with a more practical understanding. He had no clue what the agent meant.

"*Guten tag.* Lovely day. I'm John Bluderin."

"*Sicherlich.* I am Günter Mann." His shirt and pants were a faded shade of brown, each with occasional pinhead holes. His hands were grass-stained, and mud circled the outline of his sandals.

The moment of silence between the two prompted Bluderin to study the shepherd's face: laced with diminutive, silver hairs across the forehead and an unkempt beard of bluish gray. Protruding eyebrows of the same color obscured his eyes to an extent, although Bluderin could tell that they were an olive shade of green. His nose was broad and long, intelligent looking, as if it could smell things a mile away. Bluderin was convinced that, if reincarnation were a possibility, Günter either had been a lion in a previous life or would be one in the next. He appeared to be in his fifties, but his clothes probably made him look older than he was.

"I'm glad you stopped by, son. Occasional company can be a gift to solitude."

That was the cue: the key was *gift*, followed by *solitude*.

"Care for an American cigarette?"

Bluderin reached in his pocket to retrieve a pack. He offered it to Günter, who accepted it, looked inside the pack, and briefly took out a key before replacing it.

The key was to the back door of Bluderin's apartment. His landlord had not given him the key, since the door always was intentionally locked and not to be used except as a fire escape. It could be unlocked from inside the apartment. So Bluderin only had the key to the side door. However, Gustav Erdmann had given him this key to deliver to Günter. From what seemed like a sixth sense of analysis or suspicion, Bluderin had tested the key on the back door. It worked. Apparently the agency wanted free access to his apartment without his knowledge.

Günter removed a cigarette, lit it, and placed the pack in a flapped pocket of his woolen shirt. He dragged on the cigarette, looked up at Bluderin, and smiled. His teeth were a pinkish white, like a child's fingernails.

"As you are now, I too was once young and handsome," Günter said. "I lived in Berlin at the time. Like most young men during the war, I had a lot of questions about my fate and the madness of my country. Tell me, in this day and age, what are your questions?"

"I don't know what you mean," Bluderin said.

"Questions of a human nature. Questions about your future, your purpose in life. I thought you might be looking for answers. I've had a good number of people come to me over the years, seeking such answers. I'm looked upon as some sort of mystic or soothsayer, having insight into questions that transcend human knowledge by communicating with divine spirits. Of course, I could be deceiving myself."

Bluderin was certain that curiosity played a factor in people approaching Günter for any spiritual or visionary guidance.

"You do look like a Biblical figure, tending to your flock of sheep and meditating, perhaps having séances with deities or the dead."

"I have no answers for you," Günter said.

"I didn't ask for any," Bluderin said.

"You were looking."

"Aren't we all?"

"I'll tell you what," Günter said. "Maybe this will help. I knew a woman, whom I married, when I was not much older than you. She had radiant, caramel hair, amber-sun eyes, and she moved as gracefully as a gliding swan. She gave me answers that were framed in questions. That was over a quarter of a century ago, before the Nazis took her away."

"And you still think about her?" Bluderin asked.

"I see her every day," Günter said. "I see her in the sky. We let each other know our thoughts, and then she fades away."

"After all these years, you still relive that relationship?"

"One experience in your life can compose eternity," Günter answered. "It is at this time in your life—from your late teens to early twenties—when the center of your self crystallizes. Everything else from that point forward will be nothing more than a manifestation of that center."

"I suppose everyone, at one time or another, believes that his or her life is in disarray, that there is a place or time that will form the basis of what one becomes."

"Not a *place*," Günter said. "A *time*, indeed, wherein your psychic core is conceived. For me, the eternal experience I described to you is why I spend my time in solitude."

"I'll have to think about what you said. It will take a while for me to understand."

"It is a premise to *accept* more than *understand*," Günter said. He opened a thermos and poured black coffee into a gray cup. "Which way are you headed?"

Bluderin pointed in the direction and described the meandering route he was taking: a long, roundabout path eventually making its way back to the center of Schwäbisch Gmünd. Günter seemed to be listening to him as if he were taking mental notes.

"If you're going in that direction, I suggest that you take repose at an evening café called Oasis. You should meet a lady who works there several evenings a week. I suggest that you become friends with her, learn from her. She is intuitive and smart, about ten years your senior, I'm guessing. She is also pleasing, easy to look at, if that matters to you. However, be aware of her sensitivities. She has many."

"I will look for the café along the way."

"Good. Now, in parting, I ask you to remember this: *In all things we do not know, there is light.*"

Again, Bluderin had no idea what Günter was talking about. The shepherd's language was too erudite, too poetic, for him to assimilate. His understanding of Günter's advice was fragmented at best.

"I will remember your words," Bluderin said.

"I have spoken enough for one day."

Bluderin and Günter shook hands. With his most recent mission as a courier now accomplished, Bluderin continued on his walk.

When he reached the tiny, easternmost village area of Schwäbisch Gmünd, he was in need of nourishment. The village grocery was closed, but down the road across the street he saw the Oasis café sign. He decided to take Günter's advice.

Oasis appeared to be more of a private club than a Gasthaus. The café was on the army's list as an off-limits establishment, but Bluderin figured he could pass as a European. The café's floor, a deep shade of cherry, looked as if it had seven or eight coats of varnish. The floor was also enhanced, or brightened, with multicolored Oriental throw rugs. Blood-red leather swivel chairs surrounded black, wrought-iron tables with glass tops. Brass wall lanterns, each emitting only ten or fifteen watts, beamed like little stars on the glossy, gray walls. There was only one couple in the lounge, a man and a woman. Bluderin could hear their near-whispering voices, their Swabian dialect, as they held hands. Unnoticed by the couple's sole attention to each other, he walked quietly past them to the bar's entrance. The bar was otherwise walled off from the lounge by a four-foot high partition.

He took a seat at the polished granite counter. A tall, svelte blonde woman appeared from a back room. Her hair was arranged in what Bluderin recognized as the latest trend in southern Germany. It was cut to neck length, styled meticulously with bangs on the forehead and curls around the ears, each lobe having one diamond stud in them.

"Guten abend, Fraülein," he said, and ordered a cup of tea with lemon and a glass of cognac.

The lady's smooth, delicate white hands gently placed Bluderin's order in front of him. Her deep blue eyes set off her cherubic-like face, with a geometrically perfect nose and full, ruby-like lips. Her make-up complimented, more than accentuated, her exotic features with a tint of mascara and ever-so-thin coating of lipstick. Her presence inspired him to recall a quotation by Goethe. Bluderin believed he was living the moment: *Thinking is more interesting than knowing, but less interesting than looking.*

"Would you like a sandwich as well? We have some fresh cold cuts from the delicatessen. Perhaps a salami and cheese with mustard on pumpernickel? Some lettuce and tomato?"

"You must have read my mind. I've been walking for most of the day and am famished."

The woman walked back to the little room behind the bar and repeated the order to someone. She then went into the lounge, attending to the romantic couple and another couple who had just arrived. Bluderin could see a complete view of her from this angle. Her form-fitting red cocktail dress revealed her long, shapely legs, and her black high heels emphasized her toned calves. It pained him to take his eyes off her ass.

A shorter, rotund woman came out of the little room behind the bar and delivered Bluderin's sandwich. He thanked her, and she wished him *guten Appetit* before retreating into the back room, apparently a small kitchen.

"How is your sandwich?" the blonde one asked.

"Just what I needed," he said. "It couldn't be better."

"We have a very simple menu here," she said. "Mostly sandwiches and soups, a light salad or coleslaw, and fresh fruit. Frau Müller purchases the food from the local grocery, delicatessen, bakery, and farms on each day that we're opened for business, so we have a *fresh reputation.*" She smiled at Bluderin when he grinned, signaling perhaps that he had caught her pun.

"Is Frau Müller the lady who made my sandwich?" he asked.

"She owns the Oasis. I only work here part time, three evenings a week, to help Frau Müller and augment my salary as a telephone operator."

"You must know a number of languages to qualify for that job."

"Oh, I know some," she said. "You seem to as well. Your German is quite good, but you're American, aren't you?"

Bluderin became a little nervous over her comment. He was afraid the woman might report him to army or municipal officials for patronizing the café. However, he decided he'd better admit to it and watch her reaction.

"I try to speak German as correctly as I possibly can, but I suppose I still have an accent, like most Germans do when they speak English. I noticed an accent with you as well. I cannot place it, but you're not a native German either, are you?"

"I'm surprised you picked up on that. Not many people do. I'm Norwegian," she said.

She then began speaking in English, describing the circumstances that led her to Schwäbisch Gmünd. She had spent time in Denmark,

Spain, England, France, Italy, and last but not least in Germany—
first in Berlin, then in Schwäbisch Gmünd. Her diction was nearly
flawless, outside of a few words that hinted of a European accent.

"I hope you don't mind my asking, but I'm curious," Bluderin
said. "How many languages do you know?"

"I guess you could say I'm conversant in seven. Norwegian, of
course, which is actually a Germanic language, closely related to
Swedish and Danish, so I don't count those, then English, German,
Spanish, French, Italian, and Russian."

"I envy you," Bluderin said.

The lady appeared to ignore his admiration by not saying anything,
but her smile told him that she appreciated the compliment.

"When you've lived in various European countries, languages
tend to come to one easily, especially with the countries being so
relatively close together."

Her explanation of learning languages by living in different
European countries definitely made sense, with the exception of
Russian.

"Did you live in Russia as well?"

"I visited Moscow once, for a month, as part of an academic
program," she said. "I studied the Russian language in a more
formal setting, at a university. Russian and English were my primary
concentrations, or majors as you call them in the States, in earning
my baccalaureate."

She turned her attention to two men dressed in dark blue suits
who had taken seats at the opposite side of the bar. Their white
shirts stood out in contrast to their maroon ties. As they ordered
drinks and sandwiches, Bluderin was able to ascertain that they
spoke a different dialect of German; he guessed it was Bavarian.
After serving their drinks and giving the food order to Frau Müller,
the Norwegian returned to Bluderin and poured him another glass
of cognac.

He noticed a small, golden broach, about the size of a quarter but oblong in shape, pinned to her dress, above the left breast, toward her shoulder. The word "Solveig" was engraved in the broach, and the letters were augmented with diamond chips.

"May I assume Solveig is your name?" he asked.

"Solveig Evensen. However, other than being simply a name the word 'Solveig' has another meaning."

"I'm John Bluderin," he said, extending his hand.

She nodded politely but did not shake hands with him.

"So tell me, what else does Solveig mean?"

"I'm not going to tell you," she said, "and quit looking down my dress."

Bluderin watched Frau Müller and Solveig embrace. He was embarrassed. He had only briefly, for a mere second, looked down at Solveig's cleavage, admiring her graceful curves. He did not mean to be so bold, so forward, and so obvious. After all, he had just met the woman. Damn it, he thought, she's probably telling Frau Müller about my unseemly behavior.

He could see that the way Solveig touched Frau Müller was more than just a mild act of endearment. It was more intimate, more of an exchange of emotions. He remembered that Günter had warned him of Solveig's sensitivities.

Bluderin quietly sipped the remainder of the cognac, thinking back to his one night with Leda Beschwörung. She had awakened his sensuality in such a way that he began to look at all women in more depth. That he had a lust for certain women was not the point. Even women to whom he was not sexually attracted still made him think about their sexuality in an attempt to get to know them more comprehensively as human beings.

It was time to leave. He had not meant to, but he had caused enough damage for one evening.

"I would like to pay up," he said, "and please forgive me, Solveig, for being so rude, for my uncouth behavior. It was not intentional. I'm truly sorry."

He felt his face pulsate as he pulled some bills from his wallet. Just then the man of the romantic couple in the lounge called Solveig over so he could cash out. Bluderin caught another glimpse of Solveig's long, smooth legs and forced himself to look in another direction, toward the two men at the bar. He could see that they were leering at her as well. It was hard not to, although he hoped that he did not impart the same lecherous smiles that these men did as they whispered to each other.

"I can see that you are embarrassed," Solveig said as she took Bluderin's money. She poured another ounce of cognac into his glass. "Here, have one on the house before you go. I'm sorry for making you feel so uncomfortable. When I think about the situation again, your eyes were merely instinctive, a natural reaction for a man who may be attracted to a woman. You did not leer at me, not like those two men behind me. You more or less stole a glimpse, shall we say? My terse response was an overreaction. Let's let it go."

Bluderin stared into his tea and cognac, still feeling foolish, but relieved that Solveig had accepted his behavior for what it was.

"Thank you for understanding," he said. "Günter warned me about your sensitivities. I should have known better."

When the two men at the bar asked for their check, Solveig told Bluderin to wait and talk with her some more.

Maybe his so-called glimpse was dimwitted, but these two men literally were undressing Solveig with their eyes as they settled their bill, leaving a generous tip.

"So who is Günter?" she asked. "Am I supposed to know him?"

"He is a man I met during my walk," Bluderin said. "He lives on a farm about four or five kilometers west of here. He tends to a flock of sheep, along with his big dog with a whitish head, a German shepherd."

"So *that* is the Günter you're referring to. I never knew his name."

"But do you know him?" Bluderin asked. "He seems to know you."

"I have seen him several times, whenever I drive Frau Müller out to visit him, but she never told me his name. She believes that Günter is a remarkable visionary, so she goes to him for spiritual guidance while I wait in the car. She calls him *The Prophet*, like in Kahlil Gibran's novel. I never heard her call him Günter. Frau Müller finds him comforting. She suffers from bouts of depression, not often, about two or three times a year. It is during those times when I take her to see Günter. What did he say to you?"

"He advised me to take a rest at the Oasis," Bluderin said. "He suggested that you and I become friends. He talked in parables of a kind, describing images I could not understand. He said something about light being in all things, even ignorance. No, that wasn't it. Let me think." Bluderin looked into her eyes. "*In all things we do not know, there is light.* Those were his exact words. Do they make any sense to you?"

"Günter is a strange man," Solveig said. "I mentioned to Frau Müller that I was not sure I trusted him, but she refuses to listen to me. She worships him, I think, and he does seem to bring her comfort, so I let the matter go. Let him be her prophet, as long as he's harmless."

There was something unnatural going on with Solveig, Bluderin believed, but he could not ascertain what it was. It was as though her occasional smile protected, rather than exuded, her true feelings, but he had learned earlier not to intrude any further. *Be aware of her sensitivities*, he reminded himself.

"Whether Günter is a true prophet or merely a harmless eccentric is something we'll probably never know," he said, "if it makes any difference." He looked at Solveig's hands as she poured a little more tea into his cup. Like Leda Beschwörung, Solveig had incredibly elegant hands, but with longer fingers.

"What are you looking at?" she asked him, in a tone that rang of curiosity more than annoyance.

"Your rings," Bluderin said. "How they decorate your elegance. All little golden rings of diamond, ruby, jade, and sapphire."

"My one extravagance," she said. "As you may know, Schwäbisch Gmünd is highly regarded for its fine jewelry. My passion for rings began here."

Someone, likely Frau Müller in the kitchen, had turned on a stereo. Music started coming from that direction. *On my own, would I wander through this wonderland alone …*

"Do you like Johnny Mathis?" Solveig asked him.

"I believe I know the lyrics to most of his songs. 'The Twelfth of Never' is my favorite."

"Mine as well," she said. "His voice is mysterious, yet soothing. He's probably my favorite singer, although I love all kinds of music, especially singing, from Gregorian chants to the latest Beatles songs. Music is everything."

She seemed to be opening up to him now. He had hoped that he gained some of her trust. He was interested in her and wanted to get to know her more personally. Günter was right. He could learn a lot from Solveig. Of course, the sexual aspect of her presence could not be ignored. He simply had to place it in context of the whole human being.

"Stop in again," she said.

"I'll see you this coming Tuesday."

"Oasis is closed on Tuesday," Solveig said. "It's also a day off from my telephone job."

He didn't know if she was stalling him or giving him an opportunity, but he decided to ask her out.

"It's a lovely time of the year to walk," he said. "Perhaps I could meet you here. Would you like to go for a walk and have dinner later?" He was almost sure that she would turn him down, but he could not stop himself from trying. Her charm was too compelling. She was worth the risk.

"I love to walk," she said. "It is great exercise, and you get to see all kinds of things you overlook when driving. I walked routinely with Frau Müller until her knees gave in. I'm afraid to walk alone, especially in the late afternoon or early evening, after I spotted a man following me one time. You'll protect me, won't you?"

"I'll be privileged to accompany you," Bluderin said. "I'm sure you know the area better than I and could show me some of its beautiful settings. That is, if Frau Müller doesn't mind being left alone for a while."

"It is nice of you to think of her. Believe me, Frau Müller will not mind at all. Her sister from Stuttgart will be paying her a visit on Tuesday. They can spend some personal time together without having to pay any attention to me. They're very close. Besides, if Günter is a prophet, I would not want to refute his prophesy."

"I would never undermine the advice of a prophet. So Tuesday it is," Bluderin said, kissing Solveig's left hand lightly. "See you then."

Her hand seemed to chill when he bestowed the token of affection. Her lips quivered and her eyes blinked in what he thought was surprise or fear.

"I'm sorry," he said. "I was only meaning to be polite and respectful. It was nice meeting you."

"Don't be sorry," she said. "You're very kind. See you on Tuesday."

On the way back to his apartment, Bluderin could not stop thinking about Solveig Evensen. If she were a lesbian, would a simple kiss on the hand mortify her? She was definitely hiding something; her reaction to his touch told him that. He wanted to assure Solveig that she could trust him completely, that he would respect her wishes at all times. She was a person for whom he already felt a certain reverence, although he did not know why.

The dualism of Bluderin's first two TDY assignments struck him as being uncanny: first the gray envelope and Leda, followed by sex instructions, and secondly the rear-entrance key to his apartment and Günter, followed by meeting Solveig, whose psyche seemed to mirror his.

He thought it was all orchestrated until she agreed to go out with him. Something between them clicked, he was sure. He could feel it. It was as though they needed to protect each other from harm and deception, that their interdependence was not contrived but indispensable to their survival.

Four

-◄o►-

While most GIs stationed at Hardt Kaserne had little to no interest in Schwäbisch Gmünd, Bluderin had read some history about the area to get a feel for the town's cultural evolution. When he and Solveig decided to take a coffee break from their hike, she asked him how long Schwäbisch Gmünd had been in existence.

"The first settlement in the area was around the second century A.D., when Roman soldiers moved into the nearby Limes," he said. "The area became known as Schwäbisch Gmünd in the twelfth century, founded as a Free Imperial City, until it became part of Württemberg in 1803."

Solveig told him that she admired the architectural masterpieces and the town's policy on land use.

"More than eighty percent of the population resides in or very close to the center of town," she said. "The intention is to preserve as much property as possible for pastoral uses, or wildlife and forestry."

What impressed Bluderin about the town's center was its cleanliness. The cobblestone streets surrounding and spreading out of the Marktplatz were so immaculate that they glittered in sunlight. The windows of various commercial buildings were washed so frequently he couldn't find a speck of dust on them.

"I find it fascinating how the people walk in a quick tempo

during the week and slow down to more of a meditative pace on weekends, especially Sundays," Solveig said.

"I've noticed that as well," Bluderin said. "Families cling together for their Sunday walks. Many of them are on their way to religious services at one of the cathedrals, I imagine."

As they made their way through the Gmünder Market Square, a young German man greeted Bluderin, saying that he hoped to see him at practice later in the day. At five-four and with smooth, soft skin and flaxen hair, he looked much more like a boy than a man.

"I'm taking today off," Bluderin told him. "I'll see you there next week."

On their way to Mutlangen Strasse, Solveig asked Bluderin what the conversation with the German was about.

"We take karate classes together," he said. "He's one of several high school kids—two boys and a girl—taking in the art."

"I'm surprised," she said. "I cannot believe that you would harm anyone. You seem too gentle to be a fighter."

"I would never start a fight," he said. "I practice karate as a means of self defense."

"It's so violent."

"Karate is a striking art," he said. "It does use punches, kicks, knee and elbow strikes, and open-handed techniques such as knife-hands. However, karate also teaches the practicioner, or karateka, about self-discipline. The strict training also supports my creative efforts."

"What creative efforts? And how so?"

"I'll tell you about them later," he said, "after we've finished hiking."

At one of the high points in Mutlangen, Solveig pointed out various features of the Schwäbisch Mountains to Bluderin, including the three peaks known as the Drei Kaiserberge, or Three Emperor Mountains. The light-blue, early spring air was at work, turning the mountains and hills into deep and dark, as well as light and bright, shades of green, with black streams riddling among the trees at a distance, resembling a circuitous roadmap from the Middle Ages.

They went into a section of woods designated as a bird sanctuary. Solveig introduced Bluderin to a forest guide there, an ornithologist named Wolfgang Parler.

"Wolfgang is a descendent of the earlier Parlers, a famous family of architects who came to Schwäbisch Gmünd in the 1300s to design and build the town's Gothic cathedrals."

"I'm honored," Bluderin said. "I'm humbled by your ancestors' architectural genius."

"I appreciate your comment, but let's talk about the genius of nature instead," Wolfgang replied.

With the diligence and enthusiasm of a scientist who loves his job, Wolfgang's walnut eyes gleamed happily as he described a number of birds as they appeared, darting from tree to tree or skirting along a brook. Their distinctive chirps and whistles composed a melody of species-distinctive overtures. Wolfgang's high-pitched voice rose even higher when he pointed out a white stork, the national bird of West Germany. He also identified and described the features and habits of a black grouse, great spotted woodpecker, Eurasian wryneck, black-tiled godwit, song thrush, winter wren, and warblers. Solveig and John told him how charmed they felt by the serenity around them, with birdsong, the sky of leaves, the roguish squirrels, and gurgling brooks all contributing to an inner sense of peace. Wolfgang meekly hung his head as though they had awarded him an Olympic gold medal. His thin, sinewy frame and quick gestures were like those of a sixteen-year-old, but his curly gray head and deep wrinkles revealed that he was closer to sixty.

As they left the sanctuary, heading toward the Oasis, Bluderin mentioned to Solveig how the influence of nature seemed to have a profound effect on the people living in the region. They must have greeted nearly a hundred people along their walk, and they all seemed content, mesmerized, as if they were living a dream.

"It's hard to imagine all the bloodshed from the war that took place here twenty-odd years ago," Bluderin said. "The transition from Nazism to a congruous landscape of peace is beyond my ability to understand."

"An evolution from charades to celebrations, from meaningless to meaningful," Solveig said. "John, I'm going to run upstairs for a minute to check on Frau Müller and her sister before we head off to Josef's. Please warm up your Volkswagen so the drive will be more pleasant."

The car's heater quickly rid the early evening chill. They sat in Josef's Gasthaus on the eastern outskirts of Schwäbisch Gmünd, close to the neighboring town of Aalen, and reflected on their long walk. A young girl, whom Bluderin guessed was thirteen or fourteen, set two half-liter mugs of beer on their table. Solveig removed a pencil from her purse and made two small lines on a cardboard coaster.

"What are you doing?" Bluderin asked.

"Keeping track of the drinks we have," she said, "so we'll know how much to pay when we leave. It's a common practice in this Gasthaus, as well as others. Have you not been here before?"

"Just once, and it was not a good experience."

"Really? Why is that?"

"It's a rather dishonorable story."

"Tell me. We've all done dumb things."

"I suppose we have. Okay, if you want to know. I was with an acquaintence who had hooked up with a girl from one of the farms in Aalen. He was trying to set me up with the girl's sister, but I resisted his encouragement. Later on, however, the beer got the best of me. Before I knew it, the four of us were in his car, heading for their parent's farm. After we got there, we went inside one of the barns, equipped with a bundle of blankets. As we began to embrace the girls and get more intimate, they both started talking rather loudly about making babies. It could have been the alcohol talking for them, but I was getting scared. Then we noticed that someone had turned on the lights in the farmhouse. Making babies and confronting the girls' parents was the last thing he and I wanted, so we quickly refastened our pants and jumped into his car. As we sped out of the driveway, an older man, apparently the girls' father, had opened the back door of the farmhouse and walked hurriedly in the direction of the barn. I have not let beer tell me what to do since."

Solveig signaled to the young girl for two more beers as Bluderin finished his story.

"At least you guys were sober enough to realize the potential consequences of your intended actions," she said. "That's more than others have done. There are quite a few children around here who were sired by American soldiers who left the scene, shall we say, upon hearing the pregnant news of their girlfriends."

Bluderin smiled at Solveig's usage of the term *pregnant news*, and he thought it quite fitting. He retrieved a small pad from his sports jacket and jotted down the expression.

"Are you a writer?" she asked. "I noticed you writing things in your pad today."

Bluderin was surprised that she had observed this behavior, as he had only taken two or three notes the entire day. "I think about being a writer," he said, "but at this point I've composed nothing but scratch marks, notes on things I've seen or heard that make an impression."

"I don't think writing is anything you can rush, John. It must take time for a number of observations or feelings to gel before they can serve as a basis for a poem or story."

"A valid point," he said, "and, of course, you have to live first—live out or experience episodes worthy of examination—before you can create anything worthwhile."

"Well, if you're not a writer yet, you look the part," she said, "with your gray sports jacket and black turtle-neck sweater. Clothes like Hemingway or Steinbeck would wear."

"I'm influenced by them," he admitted. "They are both very high on my list of idols."

"They should be, as should Günter Grass and Herman Hesse. Have you read *Cat and Mouse* or *Siddhartha*?"

"I have, and I admire those novels, but I could never emulate the authors. Grass and Hesse both reach way back into their childhoods in their writings to arrive at the meaning of existence. I cannot remember anything worthwhile about my childhood."

"Oh come now, you must remember something."

"There is nothing memorable about it." Bluderin was getting a little frustrated about how the conservation was gearing toward him. He was determined to change the direction, to learn more about Solveig.

"I can't remember a thing. When I try, everything becomes nebulous. Sometimes I doubt that I ever existed before I came to Germany. What about you? Tell me about your childhood."

"I suppose nothing about your childhood matters to you right now," she said. "That's something we have in common."

He looked intently at the cat's eye ring on her right middle finger. It stood out from the other rings and seemed to be looking at him as if it had a pupil of its own.

"I assume you are comfortable with yourself," he said, "despite you erasing your childhood."

"Perhaps not in relation to any specific set of social mores, but to contentment."

The cat's eye seemed to be showing Bluderin Solveig's personal philosophy: that life is more fulfilling when you forego a feeling of selfness. You are free, then, from yourself—perhaps the only kind of freedom there is.

"What I propose, John, is that we are a couple of harmless but heartless souls."

"I'll drink to that, Solveig, if I can get another beer."

Bluderin looked around the room in search of the young girl who had been serving them, but she was nowhere to be found. Instead, he saw an older man behind the bar who, according to Solveig, was Josef Westoff, the Gasthaus owner and grandfather of the young girl.

"John, I don't want to make you feel uneasy, but the owner does not allow GIs in his establishment. Don't take it personally. Josef doesn't even know you. His resentment has to do with the war."

"The Vietnam War? I'm against it as well."

"No, although he thinks that war is unjust. I'm referring to World War II."

"*That war* is over."

"No war is ever over," Solveig said as Josef approached their table.

"Guten abend, Josef. This is John Bluderin, a friend of mine from England."

"What can I do for you?" Josef asked abruptly. The rotund, wide-faced man who was probably in his seventies looked troubled, and his hands quivered ever-so-slightly.

After Solveig ordered two more beers, Josef limped back to the bar. His arms moved awkwardly, working against each other, and his elbows collided against a shelf of liquor bottles and glasses. Several items fell to the floor and broke into pieces.

"Josef doesn't believe you," Bluderin said. "As I mentioned, I've been here once before, several months ago, when I unintentionally met up with Wiley Couch, a fellow GI with whom I shared the farm girl experience. Josef never waited on us though, and we were here for only half an hour. I don't believe he remembers me."

"It was foolish of me to deceive him, John. I should have said that you were an American friend."

"Well, apparently he already knows." Bluderin felt himself getting tense, and there was nothing he could do to ease the uneasiness.

Josef carefully placed Solveig's beer on the cardboard coaster and dropped Bluderin's beer in front on him, spilling some.

"Josef, I'm sorry for lying to you about my friend. He is an American. Perhaps we should go."

"No, no, don . . . don't go," Josef stammered. "Please stay. I will be back in a minute."

Josef hobbled off and climbed a stairway leading to the second floor of the Gasthaus. Bluderin watched the older man as he winced, holding the stair rail with one hand and gripping his right knee with the other.

"Please accept my apology, John. I had no idea that Josef would be so rude. He is by nature a very courteous man."

"I had no problem the first time I came here. In fact, Couch comes here often. It's his favorite Gasthaus. Even though it's off limits, Josef has never asked him to leave the premises."

"I don't know Couch personally, but I know who he is," Solveig said. "I have seen him here on several occasions with Jürgen Treuge. I actually thought Couch was German. Regardless, if Josef is willing to serve someone as boisterous as Wiley Couch, he certainly should be able to tolerate someone who is, let's say, somewhat more refined."

"*Somewhat?*" Bluderin smiled, thinking that "somewhat" was as close to a compliment as he would get from Solveig tonight.

"Solveig, John, forgive me for being so rude. My behavior was impulsive."

"It was wrong of me to come here, Josef," Bluderin said. "I know your establishment is off limits to GIs."

"You are welcomed here," Josef said. "Since you are Solveig's friend, I am sure that you are a nice young man. He reached for Bluderin's hand and gave it a firm shake. "May I join you two for a minute?"

"Please do," Solveig said. "You'll be busy when the party begins."

"Thank you. Yes, families will be coming in shortly and running me ragged." He placed his right hand over Bluderin's. "You have honest hands, John. Large and strong, yet calm. Let me tell you a story." He reached under his sweater and took out a photograph of a little girl. He placed it on the table, in front of Bluderin.

"What do you think?" he asked.

Bluderin studied the black-and-white photograph of a child in a white dress. She appeared to be around nine or ten years old and held a white Bible against her chest. "Lovely child," he remarked. "Such fine, soft hair, lighter than air . . ."

"I don't want to shock you, John, but I need to say something. During the war, many months before it happened, most of us German civilians knew what the outcome was going to be. Hitler was in trouble from a number of perspectives. Defeat was inevitable. About a year before the war ended, a group of American soldiers came into town. Five of them broke into my house. They were behaving strangely, yelling and stamping their feet, possessed with the stare of madmen. Two of them aimed their rifles at me while the others shouted out for Nazis. I said that no one outside of my family was in the house, but they did not believe me.

"One of the soldiers went upstairs and returned, pushing my wife and children in front of him. 'This is all,' he said to the others.

"The two soldiers pointing their weapons at me finally lowered them. One of them approached me, demanding food and liquor. I went into the kitchen and started getting out some cheese and bread. The biggest one—a sergeant, I believe—pushed me aside. He and the others helped themselves. They took all I had.

"The soldier who discovered wine in the cellar during his search placed six bottles, the last of my supply, into a burlap bag. The sergeant was not interested in the wine. He took a bottle of whiskey out of his coat pocket and began drinking from it. The others drank the wine. They were all drunk. They were about to leave when the sergeant said that he wasn't finished with us yet.

"I went dizzy with anxiety. One soldier whacked the butt of his rifle across my son's face, then tied him up and kicked him into a corner of the living room. The sergeant grabbed my wife and, despite all the resistance she could muster, he ripped off her clothes. I jumped on the sergeant, choking him with all my might until another soldier smashed an empty bottle across the side of my face. Blood gushed out of my ear and nose. I fainted.

"How long it was I'm still unsure, when the Jewish family that had been hiding in a secret tunnel off the basement came upstairs to help. The wife, her eyes filled with tears, was cleaning my face and covering my head with homemade bandages. Every part of my head was sore. It was difficult to raise my eyebrows. I had lost sight in my left eye. The vision in that eye has never returned.

"Gradually, I was able to see with my one good eye. My son was now untied and crying frantically. My wife was standing in back of the Jewish wife, shaking, wearing a blanket. Her dress was on the floor in a ragged, blue heap. As for my daughter—"

"I'm afraid to ask," Bluderin said.

"And I would be afraid to tell you, except that I have to. It will help you understand my wrath for American soldiers. These soldiers were not satisfied with the damage they had inflicted on my wife, my son, and me. Oh, no. That wasn't enough. They raped my daughter as well. The youngest one of them, who closely resembled you except for a look in his eye that was pure evil, ripped off my daughter's dress and raped her. Even in my unconscious state, I could hear her crying. Her screams have never left my ears. Your resemblance to the soldier was what triggered my anger today."

"My God," Bluderin and Solveig said at the same time. They sat attentively, looking at Josef, Solveig stroking his forearm, waiting to see if Josef had anything else to say.

"My daughter was passed out, convulsing on the floor, bleeding profusely. The husband of the Jewish family was a physician, and he did all he could to help heal my daughter. Yet she succumbed the following day. The doctor could not stop the hemorrhaging.

"That happened twenty-three years ago last month. I still have nightmares about it, but in the course of time I gathered a few wits about me."

Bluderin sat, momentarily frozen, picturing Josef's story in his mind. He could not speak. The silence spoke for him. The fact that the girl's rapist looked like him was nauseating, and the fact that he had a "look-alike uncle" who fought in Germany during the war made him want to vomit. This uncle, his father's youngest brother and an alcoholic, had jumped off a bridge to his death ten years ago.

Bluderin had never heard of any misconduct by American soldiers during World War II. He had heard plenty about the murders of Jews by the millions. Their plight was far worse, of course, but the loss of millions of lives did nothing to ease Josef's pain. Widespread killing does nothing to relieve the impact of one single loss of life, especially that of a child.

Solveig reached across the table for Bluderin's hand.

"Josef does not want you to feel remorse," she said. "You hadn't even been born yet. He only wanted you to know why he behaved the way he did. Impulse brings out the best and worst of us, I'm afraid."

Josef left the table, but the image of a little girl, with blood heaving out of her genitals in an angry stream, would not leave Bluderin's mind. He thought back to his conversation with Günter. *In all things we do not know, there is light.* The light that Günter sees is his young wife in the sky when he talks with her. There seemed to be no light for Josef, only a stilled black creek filling his heart.

"You have a sympathetic face," Solveig said. "Such sad,

contemplative eyes—blue in expression as well as color. If people only knew what a surreptitious bastard you are, they would be less inclined to accept you."

"That's *our secret*," he whispered. "Don't go sharing it with anyone else."

Solveig looked slowly around the room, commenting on the costumes the some of the patrons wore.

Bluderin heard footsteps close behind him. A girl who appeared to be about a year or two younger than he smiled at him as she passed their table. He returned the smile and, when he lifted his mug, the girl began to giggle.

"Seems you have an admirer," Solveig said. "You devil."

"A cute one, too. Not a shred of your gorgeous presence, Solveig, but nonetheless pretty in an innocent, pubescent sort of way. A fragile-light bud on its way to blossom."

"I must admit, he has elegantly toned legs."

"*He?*" Bluderin looked again at the slim figure seated at a table about twenty feet away. Thin, firm, and hairless legs were revealed to mid thigh. "Are you sure?"

"Absolutely. Beyond that clear, rose-colored, smooth complexion, the silky brown hair, and the tender hazel eyes beats the heart of a seventeen-year-old boy."

"What about her breasts?"

"*His*. Probably a bra stuffed with foam or tissue paper."

Bluderin waved to the girl—or boy—and blew her a kiss. In return, she smiled and raised her sweater, flashing him several times. Her girlish breasts were real—small, each about the diameter of a tennis ball and nearly as round—and her nipples jutted out, pink and proud.

"You are wrong for once, goddess," he said. "She just flashed me, and let me tell you something: her breasts are as real as any I have ever seen."

"Hmmm . . . maybe he's on hormones now. I will have to ask Frau Müller. She knows his family quite well, and the boy's mother once told her that he wants to be a girl. I do know that the boy has been going to a psychiatrist. Maybe he is undergoing therapy and drugs to make a transition to female."

"May be the best thing for him," Bluderin said. "He appears to be an attractive girl in every sense of the word except, I suppose, where his legs join at a small bulge."

"Why *small*?" Solveig laughed.

"Well, I just assumed—"

"You're infatuated, aren't you?"

"Not at all. Intrigued, to some degree, but hardly infatuated. His hands are as feminine as yours. I think nature played a trick on him, some sort of genetic mistake."

"Are you gay, John?"

"Certainly not."

"But you do find him attractive."

"In terms of his femininity. If anything, I'm exposing my heterosexual preference. Quite candidly, he appears more feminine than some real girls."

"I must agree," Solveig said. "He is, in a sense, femininely exotic. Erotic as well. You surprise me, John. You are more acceptive and mature than I had thought. I was almost certain you were going to say something disparaging."

"What type of party are we about to witness?" Bluderin asked, trying to change the subject.

"It's a masquerade party of sorts," she said. "I'm not sure of its significance. The Germans in this part of the country celebrate thirty-four holidays a year. I get confused. This particular party follows the *Maibaum* or maypole activities held a few days ago. I will warn you, though, that people can get carried away on such occasions—especially in this place, where most everyone seems to be related, like one big, extended family. If the boy gets a little tipsy, he could lose his inhibitions and make a move on you. He feels protected here."

"If that happens, I may have to leave," Bluderin said.

"Don't be so panicky, John. He's not going to lunge at you, just tease. Most people dance a lot at these parties. The boy has his eye on you. I know how he is . . . I've seen him at parties before. He'll come up and ask you to dance, and he'll throw his arms around you and give you a kiss at the end of the dance."

"Maybe we better go. Do you mind?"

"You're frightened of him."

"I accept the boy for what he is, I have no problems with that. I simply do not wish to be subjected to his ways."

"Calm down. He will not do anything perverse, I guarantee you. He'll just flirt with you a little. After all, it's a party. It's all in fun."

"If you insist on staying," Bluderin said, "I suppose I had better start some serious drinking."

"Me too," Solveig said. "I don't go out much."

Bluderin looked again at the girl-boy. He was sitting on a man's lap, and the man was kissing the boy's neck and stroking his thigh. One old woman, whom Solveig described as the Village Matriarch, was dressed in black as a witch. She was playfully poking her broom at others; the broom was painted in vibrant shades of blue, red, and orange.

Many of the party-goers, including the girl-boy, were wearing large buttons with the words *Flower Power* imprinted on them in a pscheldelic script, with each letter in the two words having a different, flower-toned color. The buttons were evidently a way of expressing all-around peace and love as well as opposition to the war in Vietnam.

Musicians were setting up their instruments on a small stage. Three of them were tuning their guitars while a fourth one assembled

his drum set. Soon they began their entertainment with a Rolling
Stones number.

I can't get no satisfaction . . .

Two girls who could not have been more than fourteen danced
from table to table, kissing men for a sip of their beer. Their innocent
flirtations were met with wholesome, robust affection, burly hugs in
appropriate places. The girl-boy lured Bluderin onto the dance floor.
The musicians, obviously amused by the unusual couple, rushed to
play an Elvis Presley song, "Can't Help Falling in Love."

Take my hand, take my whole life too
For I can't help falling in love with you.

The girl-boy wrapped her arms around Bluderin's neck and
pulled his head down for a kiss. Bluderin was trying to think of a
way to excuse himself when a stranger came to his rescue, cutting
in to dance with the girl-boy.

Bluderin returned to the table, relieved, and quietly observed
the crowd. After several other dances, the girl-boy reappeared, this
time sitting on Solveig's lap and giving her a hug. After exchanging
some rather intimate stroking with this mysteriously sexy creature,
Solveig caught Bluderin's attention.

"I'm perfectly smashed," she said. "You better take me home."

"Have one dance with me before we leave."

She rested her head on his chest, circled her arms around his
waist, and nearly fell asleep as they danced slowly to a popular
Beatles' tune. *Listen, do you want to know a secret . . .*

Little did he know that her secret would be his amulet.

Five

◄○►

Bluderin lifted his sore head from the futon's hard wooden arm. His ear was swollen from the pressure of having rested it against the wood, and the remainder of his body was cramped from having slept in a fetal position on the confining piece of furniture. He eyed the surroundings of Solveig's living room. She was a minimalist. A stuffed, red-leather chair and an oak table for the stereo and record albums were the only other pieces of furniture in the room. The freshly painted, ivory walls were bare with the exception of one painting, an Impressionist rendering of the Drei Kaiserberge. He vaguely recalled helping her upstairs late last night, as she had difficulty stepping. He drifted in and out of dreams when he tried to relive the incident in his mind. She was inebriated and giddy, calling Bluderin her knight in shining armor. "Save me, Sir Lancelot!" she had wailed repeatedly in jest as he guided her into the apartment.

Sunlight shivered along the floor, marked with blue shadows. His brain throbbed at the invasion of light. He had stopped drinking at Josef's before Solveig had, and by the time he took her home he had regained a few chords of sobriety.

She had given him a pill to take before he went to sleep, saying that it would make him sleep soundly, promising him that he would wake up feeling clear-headed and full of energy. It did not work. His stomach swayed as he stood up. He managed to float his way to the kitchen sink. He turned on the faucet and drowned his head in the rushing cold water. The throbbing faded as he dried himself and combed his hair.

He felt an urgent need to pee. There were several doors in the kitchen and living room, but he did not know which one led to a bathroom. He opened the nearest one, discovering a bedroom. Two naked women slept coverless, their legs and arms entwined. Solveig was one of them, but who was the other? It was not Frau Müller. He had learned last night that Frau Müller had her own apartment, across the hall from Solveig's. This other woman had black, wavy hair, cut short, and a strong, muscular body. Apparently Solveig's lover, the woman raised her head and stared at Bluderin.

He had never before seen eyes like hers. At first he thought they were blue, but they were violet. Did her thick, dark eyebrows affect the color of her eyes? No, even her lips were violet, but a deeper shade, more like purple.

"You! Solveig said you would be gone by morning. What do you think you are doing?"

Words were hard to come by. After concentrating for a few seconds he managed to utter, "Looking for the bathroom."

The woman stared at him, her violet eyes focused on his with a dead-serious glare. Slowly, she raised her eyebrows, as if her mood had taken another turn.

"You poor guy. You're a mess, aren't you? The bathroom is at the end of the hallway." She pointed the way. "We share it with Frau Müller. Join me in the kitchen when you're finished. I'll be making breakfast."

The cold cranberry juice proved to be the elixir of life. Even the mild throbbing had ceased, and his vision became more acute. He studied the woman's movements. She seemed to have no sense of modesty. She stood nearly naked, wearing only a nearly transparent, pale gray teddy as she prepared some scrambled eggs.

"Thank you for saving my life. The juice sparked my recovery."

"Solveig told me she had given you a pill so you could sleep well. It works for her but obviously it is not for you. I don't care for the medicine, either. I get bad side effects—an enormous headache."

"It's somewhat awkward, but I think it's time we introduce ourselves. I'm John Bluderin, Solveig's new friend, I guess you could say."

"Monika Müller," she said. "Frau Müller's niece. We have the same surname because my mother married a man whose last name was also Müller. I accompanied my mother on the drive from Stuttgart yesterday. I did not tell Solveig I was coming because I wanted to surprise her. I am an old friend of hers, which you no doubt already know."

Bluderin sat down at the kitchen table. The sound of the coffee percolator, the smell of freshly cut apples and pears, the crackling of bacon, and the stirring of eggs were appealing. Monica's biceps hardened as she removed the cast iron skillet from the stove and placed it on the counter.

"You're making an awful lot of breakfast."

"You can use a good, hearty breakfast," she said. "Solveig said you two skipped dinner last night after your long hike. Drinking on an empty stomach is not good. Besides, I enjoy cooking for people, especially breakfast."

"You're so maternal, Monika," Solveig said, appearing from the bedroom. She was wearing a pink bathrobe that ended at her feet. She had another robe slung over her arm. "Here, my dear, put something on, for God's sake. You're being quite the exhibitionist."

"I was so busy taking care of your friend that I overlooked how skimpily dressed I was," Monika said. "Not that it matters much. Mr. Bluderin had a bird's eye view of us *au naturel* earlier this morning."

"Yes, and it was lovely," Bluderin said.

Solveig looked deeply into his eyes, and he did the same to her.

So incredibly beautiful, he thought, so inviting, and so unrequited.

"Now you know what I am," she said to him.

"I had a premonition before this morning. Not that I mind—"

"You shouldn't," Monika interrupted. "You've no right to."

"I didn't mean it that way," Bluderin said, realizing how immediately defensive Monika was becoming. "Those were a poor choice of words. What I mean, Solveig, is that I had a feeling about your sexuality when we first met, and it doesn't matter. I like you. I enjoy your company, even though we feel differently about each other in terms of sex. I believe in you as you are, and I'm grateful to your friend, Monika. She reinvigorated me back to life this morning. I had ill effects from the pill."

"I'm sorry about that," she said. "They work for me. I'm feeling great this morning."

The German coffee was splendid, darker and more robust than the coffee Bluderin was used to on base. He knew that the eggs were fresh before he tasted them, a result of Frau Müller's daily shopping. The entire meal, with freshly baked rye bread and incredibly lean bacon, was fortifying. The fruit was an uplifting dessert.

"So my sexuality does not bother you?" Solveig asked Bluderin.

He looked at her and winked, trying to cast an aura of insouciance. She had never deceived him, never led him on or promised to be physically intimate with him, so why should he feel offended?

"You and Monika are both very attractive and charming. From a greedy perspective, I suppose I feel abandoned by your sexual preference. However, I do wonder if there is a difference between what a person is and does. Nonetheless, I respect your sexual orientation, whatever it is."

"As we do yours," Monika said, placing a hand on his cheek

and winking at him. "To be frank, I swing both ways. It's so much better, or more limitless, to be bisexual. Solveig doesn't, to the best of my knowledge, have any male lovers, but I do. It's the best of both worlds—so divinely expansive and fulfilling. Besides that, you double your opportunities for intimacy, shall we say?"

Bluderin was not sure how to respond to Monika's point of view, and Solveig said nothing. Monika looked at Bluderin with what seemed to be an intense curiosity.

"I suppose being bisexual provides a path for all kinds of relationships," he finally said.

"I enjoy what bisexuality isn't," Monika said. "*Confining.* And just in case you're wondering, the answer is yes. I could do you."

"Stop it, Monika" Solveig said. "You can be such a slut."

"I see your point, Monika," Bluderin said. "Thank you for breakfast, by the way. It was absolutely perfect. The eggs had a distinctive seasoning that I could not identify. I feel like a new man."

"Lavender," Solveig said. "Monika flavors almost everything with the plant. That's why her eyes are so violet. They used to be blue."

"Deep down inside, you could be bisexual," Monika said to Bluderin, ignoring Solveig's comment.

"Not in the least. I've never been physically attracted to a man."

"Except for boys who look like girls," Solveig said. "You were occasionally checking out that girlish boy last night."

"The boy was ninety percent girl," Bluderin said. "It was you whose lap he or she was sitting on, as you stroked his thighs and kissed his ears."

"That sounds quite interesting," Monika said. "Wish I had been there."

As Monika excused herself, Solveig stood behind Bluderin and rubbed his neck. Her fingers worked magic on him, easing the tension in his muscles.

"You still like me, John?"

"Of course I do."

"I'm not sure I would be the way I am," she said, "if I did not suffer from sexual abuse when I was a child. I may tell you about it sometime, but not yet."

"When you're ready," Bluderin said. "Whatever you are, you're still a goddess."

No wonder Solveg avoids thinking about her childhood, Bluderin thought—she was robbed of it—she never had one, only a cloud of fear and violence.

"And you're a fool," she said. "Let me change, and we'll go for a short walk before we leave for work."

Bluderin observed both women in the bedroom as they took off their sleepwear and changed into casual slacks and a sweater for Monika, and a navy blue dress for Solveig. The graceful movements of Solveig and Monika seemed to create a soft music, something like Chopin's Nocturne in D flat. Their silhouettes were contemplative, complementing each other. Bluderin imagined what it would be like to live with these women. It could be fun, he mused, especially if Solveig expanded her sexuality like Monika. Yet in reality, he thought, it would never work out. There would be problems with such a ménage a trois. He could already see a little jealousy in Solveig, although he could not understand why. She did not want him. Maybe she just wanted Monika all to herself.

He thought that if he took a European out when his army tour was over, he would go it alone. He would find a simple job, something to get by on, and test his talent in writing. He would have an occasional lover, no doubt. Leda Beschwörung had changed him so that he could not go for long without the intimacy of a woman. Still, the change in him did not mean that he could no longer remain a stranger, holding back his innermost feelings, not giving it all away.

Monika returned to the living room, closing the bedroom door behind her. She came up to Bluderin and placed a silver ring with a black opal gem on his right pinky finger. "Give it to Gustav Erdmann," she said. "He'll understand." She then kissed Bluderin good-bye, saying she had to go next door and drive her mother back to Stuttgart.

Bluderin removed the ring and put it in his pants pocket. He wondered if Monika knew of his intelligence assignments, or if she simply wanted Gustav to have the ring, for whatever reason. How did she know that he knew Gustav? Something was not making any sense. None of his intelligence contacts had said anything about a ring.

"I'm ready to go," Solveig said, breaking Bluderin's thoughts. "Are you?"

"As ready as I'll ever be. You smell really good, by the way."

"I do? What do I smell like?"

"A fierce sweetness. Juniper, maybe. Juniper dressed in radiance."

"Be careful of what you say, Mr. Bluderin," she said, kissing him on the cheek. "You could turn a queer girl straight."

Although he was sure Solveig was bluffing him, it was pleasing to think about the fantasy and its will to endure.

Six

◄○►

Private Daniel Akando looked cautiously outside the guard shack before reaching into the back of his pants and pulling out a flask of whiskey. He gulped several times, wincing from the stinging sensation the whiskey made in his throat. He placed the flask back inside the seat of his pants and put on his field jacket, zipping it up and straightening it out. Akando then stepped out of the shack, which was just large enough to provide shelter from rain or snow for one guard on duty. With an M-14 lodged over his right shoulder, he walked three paces toward the entrance and exit gates of Hardt Kaserne. The shoulders of his field jacket, as well as his entire wardrobe of fatigues, were marked with shadows of PFC stripes and strands of thread that at one time had been sewn into the outer edges of the stripes. The litany of promotions and demotions from buck private to Specialist 4 to buck private had made its way back and forth at least three times over the past six years.

When sober, Akando was an outstanding soldier. His technical knowledge and skills as a missile technician were widely respected. He easily could have made warrant officer, based on his expertise. However, his episodes of poor behavior typically led to demotion. AWOL, drunk and disorderly, late for duty, insubordination, and who knows what else had contributed to his agitated military career.

Guard duty was not a bad assignment. The rotation of two hours on and four hours off for two days was not all that stressful, and one of the perks of the assignment was that the guards could check out GIs' wives when they inspected their IDs upon their entering the base. Most of the women came to shop at the PX or commissary, while a few of them arrived to join their husbands at the NCO or Officers Clubs.

The women had an ample choice of whatever GI they desired, and there were hundreds of strong, virile young men at their beck and call. Akando's Native American good looks—his deep brown eyes, prominent nose, and cinnamon complexion—may have been appealing to some of the women, but his well known temper, bolstered by alcohol, frightened them. They ignored his come-ons or invitations as best they could. Even Private Jim Scully's wife, a cute little blonde rumored to have had sex with dozens of GIs before the army sent her packing back to the States, paid no attention to Akando's flirtatious, blinking eyes, and crazed smiles.

Looking out of the gate, Akando jumped when a horn beeped behind him.

"Damn it, Bluderin. You scared the shit out of me. I never heard you coming."

"Sorry to bother you," Bluderin said. "but you are on guard duty, for God's sake."

"Don't tell me how to do my job," Akando said in a demanding voice. "Don't piss me off. I can make it hard on you to leave the base."

"Danny, I can smell the booze on your breath." Bluderin offered him a couple of life savers. "Suck on these before Lieutenant Getz brings out another guard to relieve you."

Akando took the minted candy and shuffled his way to open the exit half of the gate. Bluderin watched every move that Danny made. He was ready to kick open the car door if Akando tried to hurt him, but maybe the life savers had pacified him for the time being.

"Tell me, Bluderin," Akando said as the Volkswagen came closer, "what do you have going for you?"

Bluderin felt repulsed by Akando's indignant, sarcastic smile, as if he had something that could get him in trouble. He knew better. Unlike Danny, he had done nothing that the army would find offensive. He was as straight-laced as anyone on base.

"I'm good at my job, as you are at yours," Bluderin said. "The only difference is I keep my nose clean."

Danny grinned widely as he inspected the back seat of Bluderin's car. He was looking for contraband. He walked in front of the Volkswagen and opened the trunk. It was empty except for two cartons of cigarettes. Akando had been instructed to be on the lookout for hashish, which was becoming ubiquitous on base.

"I ought to let Lieutenant Getz know about the cigarettes," Akando said. "No sense in telling *Candy Ass*. You're his golden boy."

"I buy two cartons of cigarettes a month, as rationed and permitted," Bluderin said. "Smoke them, give them away, whatever. It's all perfectly legal, unlike the flask of booze in the crack of your ass."

"Jesus," Danny muttered, "is it that noticeable, even with my field jacket on?"

Bluderin was not sure if Akando had a flask hidden in his pants, but he took an educated guess. How else could the guy have liquor on his breath, he reasoned. Although the guards had been given instructions to search every automobile for hashish, Bluderin was tired of Danny giving him a hard time.

"How long you gone for?" Akando asked. "Rumor is there's going to be an alert tonight."

"I'll be back long before then," Bluderin said. "I need to finish the latest court-martial report for Captain McCandley."

"Stupid bastard, that Calvin Federer," Akando said. "He used to be my buddy. I can't believe he tried to kill a taxi driver, especially with only a month to go on his enlistment. The asshole would be home by now. Instead, he'll be locked up in Mannheim for who knows how long."

"The brass hasn't determined the sentence yet," Bluderin said, "but it will be for a long time." From a selfish perspective, he was relieved that he didn't have to worry about Federer any more. He was confident that he could handle Akando if he tried anything on his own. Defending himself against both Federer and Akando could have been a lot more challenging.

The taxi driver nearly died from the knife wound to his neck. Federer's lawyer said that his client's behavior was based on substance abuse, so he was pleading for a reduced sentence and treatment for Federer's drug dependency. The lawyer might have a case, Bluderin thought. Since Federer was a medic, he had access to an extensive supply of drugs.

"Look, Danny, I've got to go."

"What's your hurry? Places to go, people to see?"

"Without much time to do it in. See you later."

"Hey, hold on for one minute," Akando said. "How about fixing me up with some babe like you did for *Candy Ass*? I'll be off of restriction in a few more weeks, and if I had a nice honey to keep me busy I wouldn't drink as much."

"Fix you up? You've got to be kidding," Bluderin said. "Just a few drinks, and who knows what you'd do to a woman? I remember you pulling Rosalind's skirt down at the PX the last time you were on one of your binges. You terrified the poor woman."

"I was just having fun. That's the Indian in me." Akando laughed out loud, then looked at Bluderin with a solemn expression. "You know why I get crazy when I'm drinking? 'Cause I ain't gotten laid in over a year."

"I can't help you with your problems," Bluderin said. "I'm just a clerk, not a shrink. Get some counseling for your alcohol abuse. As for getting laid, you can always go to the Dreifarbenhaus, the brothel in Stuttgart, like some of the guys around here do."

"The brothel sucks," Akando said. "The girls just lie down and wait for you to do your thing. Some of them even read a magazine or newspaper while you go about your business. That's no fun."

Bluderin was losing his patience with Akando. Hooking him up with a German girl would be the dumbest thing he could do.

"Danny, will you get out of the way? I'm running late."

"So will you do it, then? Fix me up with a sexy honey?"

Bluderin had to do something to appease Akando. Danny would not let him go without getting an answer, and the answer of *no freaking way* would not work. Bluderin knew that the only thing you can do in such a situation is lie—tell him what he wants to hear.

"Listen, Danny, if I set you up with a girl—and I'm not saying I can—you better be a complete gentleman. You do anything wrong, and I will make sure your ass is had. Believe me, Captain McCandley will make sure of it, too."

"I'm not going to do anything weird, John. Honest, I'll be polite and respectful. God knows how long I'd be put away in Mannheim for doing anything bad to a German girl. Hell, I'd be serving more time than Federer."

"You better not forget that," Bluderin said. "I'll see what I can do when you're off restriction. Just remember, I'm not making any promises."

Bluderin drove out of Hardt Kaserne toward downtown Schwäbisch Gmünd. He did not know what to do with Danny Akando. The guy was dangerous. He was sure of that. Akando's belligerent episodes on base would only amplify in a different setting—especially one surrounded by voices he did not understand and where drinking beer was more of a potion for camaraderie than fuel for venting pent-up anger, as it was at the Enlisted Men's Club. Akando had been thrown out of the EM Club, or taken away by the MPs, twice for starting fights over the past year. Akando's new focus, or concentration, on trying to get closer to Bluderin meant nothing but trouble.

It was an odd moment when Bluderin handed the opal-gemmed silver ring to Gustav Erdmann. The German looked puzzled as he studied the ring, rubbing the opal. Gustav, whose fingers were noticeably thinner than Bluderin's, was able to wear the piece on his ring finger.

"So how did you meet Monika Müller?"

"Through Solveig Evensen," Bluderin said. "Do you know her?"

"I met Solveig through Frau Müller," Gus said. "She—Frau Müller, that is—and I go back a long way. Her husband died around the same time my wife did. My wife had apprenticed for Johann— Frau Müller's husband—in learning how to make jewelry. She had made this ring and had given it to Johann Müller as a token of appreciation for his mentoring her in the craft."

"I'm perplexed why Monika gave it to me to give to you," Bluderin said. "Why didn't she or Frau Müller give it to you directly?"

"I don't know. Monika does not come into town very often, and memories from the ring are bittersweet. Frau Müller could have kept it. I never asked for it or even brought up the subject. Yet I suppose returning the ring was something Frau Müller wanted to do, and going through you would be less painful. You don't share the memories that she and I do."

"I don't understand how Frau Müller and Monika drew the connection between us," Bluderin said. "Well, I did mention your name to Solveig once—"

"Women talk a lot more than we do," Gus said. "Especially when it comes down to who knows who, relationships, that sort of thing. Speaking of relationships, are you special friends with Solveig?"

"Just friends," Bluderin said, "although there is something special about Solveig, don't you think?"

"All I know is that she is beautiful and very kind to Frau Müller, who could not manage the Oasis on her own. Here, have a beer on me. I appreciate your returning the ring. It's quite a surprise."

As Bluderin sipped his beer, Wiley Couch and Jürgen Treuge walked into the Gasthaus. They were counting money. After they finished, each took a share of the money, and they shook hands.

"Gus, give Bluderin another beer," Couch said. "Give him a cognac as well. He looks like he could use it."

"No cognac, but thanks for the beer, Wiley."

"You like cognac."

"McCandley wants me back on base tonight, sober." Bluderin leaned over to Couch and spoke in a whisper so that Jürgen could not hear him. "Rumor is that there will be an alert tonight at Hardt— either that, or there's going to be a search for hashish."

Couch looked worried upon hearing the news. His lips quivered sporadically. Bluderin was not sure why, but the mention of hashish certainly got a rise out of Couch. The prospect of Couch dealing in hash was possible, maybe even probable, as the guy always had a ton of money on him. Bluderin speculated that Couch and Jürgen could be partnering on the sale of hashish to Germans and GIs.

"For once I'm glad to be stationed in Göppingen," Couch said. "We're a small unit, so the brass there leaves us alone." He ordered another beer and cognac for him and Jürgen. "So you won't be playing cards with Hans, Eddie, and Tulla tonight?"

"I'll be gone before they get here," Bluderin said.

"I'll take your place, in that case," Couch said. "Have another beer."

"I have to get going."

"Why are you in such an anxious mood today?" Couch asked. "Is the potential alert or search bothering you?"

"I was driving out of Hardt Kaserne, and Danny Akando was on guard duty. He kept on bugging me, trying to threaten me unless I hook him up with a German girl."

"Don't tell me you took the asshole seriously."

"I would never do anything like that for Akando," Bluderin said. "No girl in her right mind would ever go near the guy. He's crazy. Who knows what he might do?"

"Ignore the asshole, John, and if he gives you any other shit, let me know. I'll sic my guys on him. I'm friends with some of the city boys—GIs from Chicago, New York, Los Angeles—he won't want to mess with them again, I guarantee you."

Bluderin knew who Couch was talking about, even though he never mentioned names. One of the city boys had approached him to see if he were interested in buying some hash. It was becoming obvious that this group of GIs was distributing hashish to other GIs at Hardt Kaserne, and he wanted nothing to do with the matter.

"You have an awful lot of money on you," Bluderin said, "enough to make the brass ask questions. I advise you to play it safe. Things are heating up on base."

"I'm trimming all that down," Couch said, "now that I've got my divorce problem settled."

"I never knew you were married."

"It wasn't something I wanted to talk about," Couch said. "Anyway, paying the bitch off took a lot of stress out of me. Now that we've settled, she's planning to marry another guy soon. Good for her, I guess. I want nothing to do with her anymore. It's one hell of an expense to get rid of a wife, but it's worth it. I do feel a little sorry for the dumb bastard she's marrying, though. He has no idea of what's he's getting into. She'll be loving and passionate with him for about a month, then she'll turn completely cold, like frozen tundra. I'm not being bitter—it's just the simple and sad truth. I was husband number two, and husband number one had the same experience with her that I did."

Bluderin reflected on what Couch had said, the description of his former wife influencing him to recall the one-line fling of bitterness by Chekhov: *If you are afraid of loneliness, don't marry.* "If you have any other ideas on how to handle Akando, let me know," Bluderin said. "The guy disturbs me."

"I'll take care of the matter," Couch said. "The guys I do business with at Hardt make good money, thanks to me. They'll make sure that Danny Akando sees the light."

"You sure of that?"

"I'm certain," Couch said. "Akando threatened me once, too. He wanted a piece of my business. I told my partners about his threat and—funny thing—next time I saw Akando he was in bad shape. Looked like he'd been hit with a wrecking ball. Scrapes, bumps, and bruises all over his body. One big pink and purplish black eye."

Bluderin was reluctant about Couch's offer to take care of Akando. He did not want to incite any further physical damage to him. He just wanted to keep the guy at bay.

"I don't think you need to go to that extreme," Bluderin said. "Outside of his technical astuteness, Akando has no credibility with senior NCOs nor the brass. Danny is more of a pain in the ass than anything else."

"Sure he is. He's sex-starved, lonely as hell, like ninety-nine percent of the GIs stationed here. So what are we supposed to do just because we made some inroads with the German community? Run a fucking lonely hearts club?"

"No," Bluderin said, "especially not for a psychopath like Akando. It's weird how booze turns him into a maniac. I always thought the notion about alcohol making Indians crazy was nothing more than prejudice, but it rings true for him."

"Tell you what," Couch said. "We'll take a different approach. I'll have one of my partners give Danny a little hashish and a bottle of whiskey, explain to him that he's paid his dues, took his beating like a trooper, and there are no hard feelings. That way, Akando can create his own demise."

"He'll likely buy the stuff anyway, even if you don't give it to him. Still, I hate to contribute to the guy's problems."

"You have nothing to do with it," Couch said. "It's my way of making peace with Danny Akando."

"That's your decision. I've got to go."

"Back to Hardt?"

"I was intending to stop at the Oasis, but I spent too much time here."

"You like that seductive dyke, Solveig? You hot on her?"

"Solveig said she knew about the boisterous Wiley Couch," Bluderin said. "How did you know that she and I are friends?"

"Word gets around," Couch said. "A buddy of mine saw you two together at Josef's. He said both of you were having a good time, playing with the transsexual faggot, dancing the night away. Anyway, I don't give a shit who you hang with—that's your own business. I'm just curious."

"We're friends. It's a platonic relationship, as you can well imagine. Solveig is an interesting person. She has shown me a lot of the country and forests in southern Germany and has introduced me to a whole new world of people."

"Nothing wrong with getting to know the old world, especially if you're planning to take a European out like me."

"I've thought about it," Bluderin said. "I'll have to investigate what my opportunities are before making a decision. If I can't find any here, I'll go back to the States and enter college."

"You are the literary type. I suppose education is the way for you to go, but it's not for me. I'm already lining up a job as a bartender—at Josef's, matter of fact—when I get out."

Bluderin ordered drinks for Couch and Jürgen, since they had already paid for two of his.

Jürgen was on the phone, making several calls. Bluderin overheard him explaining to his friends that he recently completed his obligation in the Bundeswehr and was planning a party to celebrate the occasion. His parents were away on business in Switzerland, so he had the house all to himself.

"Are you going to the party? It's this coming Saturday," Couch told Bluderin.

"I wasn't invited. Jürgen doesn't like me."

"That's not true," Couch said. "Not after he saw you with the little brunette. The woman impressed him so much that he no longer feels he has to worry about Karin and you getting together. In fact, he told me to make sure to invite you. Some fine-looking Fraüleinen will be there, and these girls like guys in the *right way*. Should be a lot of fun."

"Karin is a nice kid, very sweet, but I've never had any romantic interest in her."

"You may not find her sexy, but I wouldn't mind getting in her panties."

"Come on, Wiley. She just turned seventeen—not that she's *that young*, but Karin is way too innocent for you."

"I can overcome that barrier," Couch said. He looked over at Karin, caught her attention, and winked at her. "Show her the way, and she could be a passionate little number."

"Jürgen would kill you."

"You have to understand, John, I've been around here longer than you. I'll take it really slow with Karin and eventually win her over. What's more, I'll get Jürgen to thank me for doing it."

"I seriously doubt that," Bluderin said.

Jürgen returned to the bar, bringing Karin with him. "Thanks for the drink, John. Did Wiley tell you about my party this Saturday? Are you coming?"

"I should have the day off," Bluderin said. "I hope to make it."

When Bluderin left the Gasthaus, Jürgen and Karin went right behind him. They were on their way to a movie. Couch had left to pick up his recent girlfriend and join them. The latest sensation in town, *One Million Years B.C.*, staring Raquel Welch, was set supposedly in the time of cavemen. Solveig and Bluderin had seen it together, and the loosely held plot and absence of dialogue was sustained by Welch in her role as "Loana the Fair One." She played out various action scenes, fighting dinosaurs and enemy cavemen, wearing nothing but a prehistoric animal-skin bikini. Not much of a film, but Bluderin and Solveig agreed that looking at Raquel Welch for an hour and forty minutes was worth the price of the tickets. Solveig had told Bluderin that the movie version they saw was about ten minutes longer than the one released in the U.S. Apparently the American movie directors thought that some of the original scenes were too risqué, so they edited out some clips. Solveig found this tidbit of news to be hilarious.

As he drove back to the base, Bluderin thought some more about the opal and silver ring he had given to Gustav. The German had been less than candid with him about the meaning or history associated with the ring. When was in his possession, Bluderin had noticed that the opal could be lifted, or opened, that it had a minuscule hinge and clip beneath its setting. When the opal was unlatched, the silver part of the ring revealed a delicate, hollowed-out area where a symbol had been etched. Bluderin was not sure of the symbol's meaning, and he had no luck in researching the matter. He thought at first that it could be a symbol for German reunification, but Germany had not been divided at the time Gus's wife made the ring, so his hunch made little sense unless the symbol had been etched in after the war.

What else could it be? Gus never mentioned that the gem could be carefully opened, and none of Bluderin's other intelligence contacts had said a word about the ring.

He understood that his role in intelligence activities was at the bottom of the heap, that he was simply a courier or errand boy, but all the other times he performed the role his intelligence contacts at least had told him *what* item or items he was to receive, *from whom*, and *who to give it to*. This latest assignment, or lack of one, was imbedded in mystery.

Perhaps there was a message in his apartment regarding the ring. By the time he was due to return to the apartment—after the alert or search initiative had run its course—he would have been away from it for five days. He would have to see if there were any messages or cues about the ring waiting for him upon his return. If not, he thought that ignorance was bliss unless he was being duped or the agency did not trust him.

Seven

◄○►

Bluderin parked in the cobblestone driveway behind the Oasis building. He looked up at the moonlit hills' grayish blue blankets instead of their daily, dense forest green and could smell the rain that had recently ended. He climbed the outside stairs to Solveig's apartment. Two quick taps on the door, followed by a third tap after ten seconds, was the code they had devised.

"What are you doing here at this hour? You scared me." Solveig scolded him in a nervous whisper. She held a copy of Steinbeck's *The Red Pony* in her hands.

He could see that she was alarmed by his eight-hours-early arrival. "Forgive me for barging in on you," he said. "I know we were not supposed to meet until morning, but I wanted to see you before I went to my apartment. I was surprised to find the café closed."

"Of course it's closed. Do you know what time it is?" Solveig frowned.

"You must have just closed it."

"An hour ago." She looked at her watch. The thin, golden band was braided, resembling nautical twine. The time was marked by two red dots over a navy blue circle. "Closer to two hours."

"I was at Jürgen Treuge's party," he said. "I had a few drinks and lost track of time. I'm sorry. I'll be on my way."

She looked at Bluderin, pouted, breathed deeply, and took

hold of his hands, bringing him toward her. "You're not driving anywhere—not after drinking. Please, come inside." She led him into the kitchen, where she poured him a cup of tea. As she leaned over the counter, her left breast emerged from her oversized tee shirt, the disclosed flesh a golden white, alight, like an early morning sun.

"Enjoying the book?" he asked.

"I like everything Steinbeck writes," she said. "His adventures in the western United States are fascinating to me as a European, living where all the land is more or less cultivated or claimed. Steinbeck has a different sense of life's meaning, always dreaming of creating one's own world from a new frontier. And his characters, my God. They are as unforgettable as much as disheveled."

"His characters are not so different from those around here," Bluderin said. "Some of the folks who frequent Gustav's are like those described in *Cannery Row*."

"Obstensibly," Solveig said. "From how you've described some of them—like Eddie and Tulla Grau—I know what you mean."

Bluderin sat on the futon, glimpsing over a women's fashion magazine, the only thing available in print. Solveig resumed reading *The Red Pony*. Bored with the magazine, he went over to the stereo and looked through a stack of albums. He came across a recording of Wagner's "Liebestod, or "Death-Love," from the opera *Tristan und Isolde*, and played it, turning the volume down low so he would not disturb Solveig's reading. He had seen the opera in Chicago several years ago and was emotionally moved by the masterpiece, especially by the ironic manner in which the antagonists, Tristan and Isolde, announced their love for each other. The music had almost lulled him to sleep when he heard Solveig's voice.

"We can talk now. I've finished reading for the night."

"I read the story in my early teens," he said. "I remember the first hard lesson—the love and loss Jody felt when his pony died."

"Any one love—or any one loss—is the first, in the sense that they're not like any other," Solveig said.

He was staring at her with an intense focus aimed deeply into her eyes.

"Why did you come here tonight?"

"I think you know."

"It won't work," she said in a resigned tone.

"Günter said it will," he reminded her. "*In all things we do not know, there is light.*"

"Günter doesn't know what he's talking about."

"He may be a lunatic, for all we know," he said, stretching on the futon and resting his head on a cushion. He could not stop yawning. "I need to sleep."

"You can sleep on one side of the bed," she said. "It's much more comfortable than the futon. I'll sleep on the other side when I've finished my tea, but don't get any ideas."

"It's up to you, not me," he said.

He went into the bedroom, took off his clothes, folded them, and placed them on the bureau. He lay on the bed, beneath the covers, drifting off to a semiconscious state of sleep. He had fallen asleep, or so he thought, until the quiet squeak of the opening door awakened him.

Solveig stood in the doorway, bathed in moonlight. He admired the outline of her body, her upper half shadowed under the white silk tee shirt. He was taken with the narrowing curve of her waist, the firm tone of her legs, her skin looking smoother than in his dreams—and her child-like smile and sensitive, intelligent eyes—in all, beauty too real and too deep to comprehend. Since he had first met her at the Oasis, where he had embarrassed himself, he tried in all earnestness to avoid staring at her. Now he had given up. He moved to the foot of the bed.

"Care for a cigarette, goddess?" He knew that Solveig did not smoke as a rule, but she admitted that sometimes before going to bed she would have a cigarette.

She closed the door and walked slowly toward the bed. She held her hands out in front of her chest until she found Bluderin's. He guided her to the bed and placed an ashtray between them. She lit a cigarette, took several drags, and crushed it out. She then got under the covers and lay down, her backside facing him. He lay down as well, with his backside facing hers.

He heard her strong heartbeat and, sensing her nervous tension, kept completely still. After listening to her breathing for what seemed like ten to twenty minutes, she turned to him, and he rolled over, on his back. She laid a hand on his smooth and hairless, chiseled chest. Her hand then touched his shoulders and lips.

With as much sensitivity as he could find, he kissed her lightly but with an urgent passion on the lips. He kissed her again, instinctively remembering Leda Beschwörung's advice on how most women like to be kissed. Leda had also instructed him on how most lesbians like to be touched. He gave thoughtful consideration to Solveig's responses as he caressed her neck and shoulders, slowly lowering his loving attention to her breasts and midriff.

She ran her fingers through his hair, around his neck, and back to his head, urging it downward. Bluderin kissed and licked around her golden mons, circling his tongue in and around her vaginal opening. She raised her knees and spread her legs to accommodate him. He worshiped the world between her legs, her universe of erotic pleasure. She pulled him into her further and shuddered when he found the genesis to her zone. The trembling excitement of her breathing, rising and falling, rippled under her soft screaming. Her opulent responses formed a night pond over his lips. Her smell was intoxicating, exploding his id.

After she settled from her peak of orgasm, his attention returned to her breasts and lips. Sensing her reluctance for anything more, not penetration, he lay beside her, with one arm around her shoulders. He kissed her hands and closed his eyes.

"I'm sorry, John. I'm not ready yet."

"I think I'm beginning to understand," he said.

"Would it be okay for me to stay here and sleep with you?" Solveig asked. "Or would that be too frustrating?"

"Please stay," he said.

"You won't mind? I won't drive you crazy?"

"If you don't stay, I'll have to go."

Bluderin stroked her back as she nudged into his side. The soft roundness of her magnificent derriere, along with her hands finishing him off, was something he desperately needed.

"God, that felt good."

"It's the least I could do," she said. "I wanted to give you some kind of release. You certainly took care of me."

He slept lightly, slipping in and out of consciousness. He wondered if Solveig would take the next step with him. Not for a while, he thought, and maybe never. But if she could go on, what would happen? His mind rolled back further than it had in a long time. He was back in Ohio, at grade school age. Gretchen, his kid sister, was playing with a doll. The doll's name was Betty, and Gretchen was taking it to school for show-and-tell.

The doll was the state-of-the-art in its day. Betty walked, talked, cried, and winked. He remembered his parents telling all the neighbors about the doll: the face was made of porcelain, its hair was real, human hair, its clothes were handmade, and it "came alive" via friction. He watched his sister play. She came running over to him, showing him the doll. The doll winked, and Gretchen mistakenly dropped it. The doll's face was chipped. Bluderin picked up the doll, and for hours he and his mother tried to mend the face, but none of the glue nor anything else they had could keep the chink of face where it belonged. He weaved into sleep, dreaming of the doll, then Solveig, back and forth, until the morning sun made its way into the bedroom.

Solveig already had risen out of bed, he noticed, as his sleepy eyes adjusted to the light. He could smell coffee and toast as he dressed and joined her in the kitchen. She was dressed in black. A black turtleneck sweater and black-leather slacks, along with shiny black-leather ankle boots, stood in contrast to the long, thin golden necklace holding a small peace symbol medallion between her breasts.

"Wow, you look stunning," he said, and kissed her firmly on the lips. She kissed him back.

"These are the only country clothes I have," she said. "With the exception of hiking shorts and a few other garments, everything else I own are dresses or skirts and blouses. So today I'll have to make do as the lady in black. When I first gave my vacation notice to the phone company manager, I was not sure where I was going, and you weren't sure you could get a five-day leave. Sometime after you received permission, Monika called and suggested that we take a drive toward Düsseldorf, where we can stop in and visit some friends. I may buy some other casual clothing in Düsseldorf. The city is known for its leading fashion trends."

Bluderin thought it strange how Captain McCandley had turned down his request for a leave, saying the timing was not good, and then reversed his decision the following day. He had given no explanation of why he changed his mind, and Bluderin was not about to ask for one. He was free to get away with Solveig. That was all that mattered.

It would be a long drive to Düsseldorf, a port in North Rhine-Westphalia located approximately three-hundred fifty kilometers, or two-hundred ten miles, northwest of Schwäbisch Gmünd. The two gentlemen they were going to visit, Walter Lebrecht and Klaus Griesinger, were delighted to hear the news. They had asked Solveig to visit them on many occasions, but she never seemed to have the time.

"Stay on this road for the next hundred kilometers," she said. "Actually, Walter and Klaus live about thirty kilometers south of Düsseldorf, closer to Soligen."

"Got it," Bluderin said, checking the odometer.

"You're going to like Walter and Klaus," she said. "They're gay—I don't know if it is necessary to tell you that, but I thought it best not to have you caught off guard. They're a nice couple, although they do tend to bicker on occasion. It's funny to watch them argue and make up. They remind me of traditional couples who have been married for a long time. They're so *cute* in that way. "

Bluderin listened as she continued talking about Walter and Klaus. He knew a little about their destination—Soligen—that it was known as the "City of Blades" because of the knives made there. He also remembered Solveig saying that there were a number of mountain trails in the area.

"What do Walter and Klaus for a living?"

Solveig smiled into the windshield. "That's a common question which, in this case, has an interesting answer. Walter is a writer and part-time professor of literature. He is also a world traveler."

"He makes enough money to afford such luxuries?"

"Walter does not have to worry about money. He earned a fortune through his business dealings with Reinhold Würth, who is known as *The Screw King,* since he is the owner of a wholesale screw company." She winked at Bluderin when she said that. "The name Würth may not carry the cachet of Porsche, but the company is one of Germany's biggest postwar success stories."

"Interesting," Bluderin said, "and Klaus?"

"Klaus is a helpless eccentric." Solveig grinned. "He is all emotion—his heart does all the thinking for him, in place of his brain. Walter met him at a tavern that caters to gay men. I imagine that Klaus would have wound up as an alcoholic nomad or the like if Walter hadn't come to his rescue. It is difficult to say what

Klaus' interests are, as there seems to be many. He is an artist of ethereal stature. His paintings, in my opinion, are eccentric, abstract landscape evolutions. I don't believe that Klaus has ever tried to sell any of his paintings—he's never had a showing. He also collects and deals in antiques—mostly pottery, glassware, and silverware, those types of things. *Small things*, he calls them."

"Has Walter published anything?"

"Lots of magazine articles and two novels. I don't know how well the novels fared."

"With money being no objective for him, he probably doesn't care, unless he is after fame."

"He writes his novels under a nom de plume, so I doubt if he craves fame. He writes whatever he feels like writing, regardless of the potential market value of any article or book."

"Must be nice to be so independent," Bluderin said.

The summer air had painted the northwest countryside into a darker green. The trees were thriving, the water within them enriching an abundance of leaves.

"I've been looking forward to this vacation," she said. "I had wanted to get away—to take a break from my telephone and Oasis duties—for the past year, but I could not get away. Leaving Frau Müller on her own to run the Oasis was a major obstacle until Monika offered to take my place for the week. I jumped at the opportunity."

They stopped at a gas station and got out of the car while the attendant refilled the tank and cleaned the windshield.

"Look at the sky, John. It is so marvelous at this altitude."

Although the sun hadn't gone down yet, the moon was nevertheless visible, looking surreal, with aquamarine rivers riddling through it while a white, spraying halo surrounded the moon's circumference. Bluderin gazed at the Daliesque image, subconsciously comparing it to an Ohio moon, a fire-reflecting tan and plum arc along the

Maumee River. That river—once an important part of his life, as he drove the Boston Whaler around the river's nooks and crannies, occasionally casting out a fishing line—was now insignificant. He enjoyed being away from the river, away from its growing industrial stench.

Solveig pointed to a road on the left. "It's a sharp turn, from memory," she said.

Bluderin downshifted the Volkswagen into second gear, leaning heavily on his left side as he managed the curve. Coming out of it, he accelerated, moving onto a straight, narrow road with trees spaced closely together on both sides. It was dark overhead, with a round opening stenciled in the distance.

Solveig seemed to be mesmerized by the leafy ceiling they found themselves under. Her eyes were locked on the blue-and-white clearing. As they came out of the naturally formed tunnel, the air opened, affording them a grand vision of valleys on both sides of the road. Solveig pointed to a statue of Lorelei in the Rhine River.

"It's a copy of a larger Lorelei statue located in Sankt Goarshausen," she said. She described Lorelei as a legendary nymph of the Rhine who lured sailors to shipwreck on her rock by singing the most beautiful song they ever heard, a creation from a Klemons Brentano poem.

"We're almost there, John. See that large, timber-frame and stone, Tudor-styled house toward the left, way up on the hill? That's where Walter and Klaus live."

"They must have quite a view from that vantage point."

"It is spectacular. Walter says he can see Belgium from his second-floor study. I remember looking out of the large window in that room, pointing to a strange phenomenon off in the distance. It looked like a large, white whale with a jagged head. Walter told me it was the white cliffs of Dover, but I think he was joking. He can be such a tease."

Bluderin was now looking out of the same window, and the view was indeed stupendous. Gigantic trees looked more like a garden of leaves, buildings were the size of dice, and ponds were teardrops. The Rhine River looked like a long, narrow stream. Since it was an immensely clear day, Bluderin could see the phenomenon Solveig had described, and it reminded him of a painting, actually a print of a painting, that hung in his parents' living room. The painting was of the white cliffs of Dover, his mother had told him, but his knowledge of geography, and certainly topography, was too insignificant to know if he were looking at white cliffs or clouds. He had no idea whether or not Walter had been bluffing Solveig.

A giant of a man placed one hand on Bluderin's shoulder and pointed out certain aspects of the view with his other. His white beard was clipped to short whiskers, and the white hair on his head looked as light as cotton. His blue eyes were never still; they seemed to pulsate every time he spoke.

"What do you think of the view, Mr. Bluderin?"

"It's so inspirational. Divine, perhaps, is a better word. It is a writer's Muse."

"You're very perceptive," Walter said. "As you can see, I have only a few writing tools in my study—a dictionary, a Bible, a typewriter, a couple of writing pads, and some pens and pencils. It may seem odd that I don't have a thesaurus, but whenever I need inspiration or specific information—such as a particular word or image—I look out this window and meditate. After a while, whatever it was I needed comes to mind."

"I can almost feel how that's possible," Bluderin said.

Klaus was shouting from downstairs. "Walter, you old goat, where are you? I've been slaving away."

"Come with me," Walter said. "Klaus has prepared supper— with Solveig's help, no doubt."

Klaus pulled out a chair for Bluderin to sit and returned to the kitchen to finish carving a stuffed, roasted chicken. Walter poured wine from a bottle of Riesling into four large, stemmed glasses. Klaus was right behind Walter, placing the platter of chicken on the table, along with stuffing, mashed potatoes, gravy, and asparagus. Round-shouldered and incredibly thin, Klaus stood at five foot seven and weighed around one-hundred thirty pounds, a mere shadow of Walter's six foot seven, three-hundred pound frame. Klaus seemed to dance and twirl, instead of simply walk, back and forth from the kitchen to the dining room. As Solveig had described to Bluderin during their drive, Klaus loved doting on people and being a host.

When they had finished dining, Walter opened another bottle of Riesling and poured into everyone's glasses. He performed this act with authority, twisting the bottle away from each glass, thereby not spilling a drop.

"John, you are so handsome! You could be an actor or politician with those looks," Klaus said.

"Klaus, I think you're hallucinating," Bluderin said. "Either that, or you've been drinking a lot more than we have."

Klaus giggled, gently touching Solveig's and Bluderin's forearms as he moved to sit between them. Walter sat at the opposite end of the table.

"Walter, don't you think Mr. Bluderin is a gorgeous, fabulous-looking young man?"

A minute passed, and then a low, thoughtful voice surfaced. "I would concur, by Western standards, and he also has a kind, quiet presence."

Bluderin was ill-at-ease from all the attention he was getting. He looked to Solveig for solace. She smiled at him and removed a sapphire and silver ring from her thumb. She placed it on his left pinky finger.

"Solveig, you agree with us, don't you, dear?" Klaus asked.

"I never gave it much thought," she said. She grinned widely at

Klaus and Walter. "But since you've asked I would say—he is awfully masculine-looking—that I am intrigued with his eyes. They are so clear and glassy, reflective, like blue mirrors."

"It may not sound like it, but coming from Solveig, that's quite a compliment," Klaus said to Bluderin. "She is *so* fussy. But enough of that. I suppose we've picked on you enough."

"I'm glad you are finished with me," Bluderin said.

After helping Klaus clear the table, Solveig went over to Bluderin and sat on his lap. He placed his arms around her waist. Walter poured some more wine and asked if anyone would like dessert.

"Maybe some coffee," Solveig said. She placed a hand on Bluderin's neck and whispered in his ear. "We have a way to go before we find a hotel, so let's not drink any more wine, okay?"

"Excuse me for intruding," Walter said, "but why not have some more wine and relax? You are staying here for the evening, I assume. Surely you'll be more comfortable here than in a small hotel room."

"That's very thoughtful of you," Solveig said. "I think you were reading my mind."

"I thought it was understood that you'd be spending the night here," Walter said.

"I wasn't sure."

"Solveig, you should know better, a dear friend like you."

Bluderin was relieved to hear that the sleeping arrangements were settled. It had been a long day, and after another glass or two of wine he would be numb.

"Walter, Solveig told me that you've had a couple of novels published," Bluderin said. "Are you working on another one?"

"I have one at my publishers, and I'm working on another story," Walter said. "Whether it turns out to be a novel or not, I'm unsure. We'll see where it goes."

Bluderin was again mystified how Walter's eyes grew and shrunk, running deeply into their sockets and then nearly out of them, as he spoke. He looked like a man possessed by a high intellectual spirit, with a deep curiosity about everything.

Solveig excused herself. "I'm ready to pass out," she said. "I hope you don't mind."

"Of course not," Walter said. "Do whatever pleases you, my dear. Pleasant dreams."

Solveig kissed Walter and Klaus good-night and whispered a few words to Bluderin.

"I'll see you in a bit," he said, "after Walter and I have finished talking."

"I'm turning in as well," Klaus said. "Good night, all. Nice meeting you, John, *you handsome savage.*"

"Klaus can never let it go." Walter sighed and led Bluderin into his library. Floor-to-ceiling book shelves had been secured to all four walls, and they were all filled with books.

"Here is a copy of my second novel," he said. "I no longer like the first one." Walter inscribed his nom de plume, Martin Winterer, on the title page of *The Invisible Soldier of Dresden.*

Bluderin thanked him for the present. Reading the flaps of the dust jacket, he learned that the novel was about a black American soldier who kept a German woman and her infant from starvation during World War II. Whenever his squad made the rounds in town to search houses for Nazis, the soldier gave the woman food. He never said anything to her, and she never said anything other than acknowledging his kindness. The war ended, but the impression of the soldier stayed in the woman's mind to the day she died. To Bluderin's awe, there was a sealed envelope tucked away in the back cover of the book. It was addressed to him.

He concluded that Walter could also be an intelligence agent, among his other accomplishments, and perhaps the reason McCandley had changed his mind about his taking leave. However, he had never told McCandley where he was going, other that saying he might take a day trip to Düsseldorf. He had never mentioned Solveig. The damned intelligence community was full of surprises, and he was becoming more aware every day that he was a pawn under their control. He would see what was in the envelope after Walter went to bed.

"In reading the summary, the story seems to endure hope," Bluderin said. "I think you're something of a romanticist."

"Not really. There is plenty of bloodshed, famine, and death in the story. Not unlike my first novel, as Solveig would tell you. She thought it was depressing and morbid."

"But there appears to be romance in this one," Bluderin said.

"A romance, perhaps, although it is unfulfilled. Or maybe not—maybe it is one of the few times a romance sustains itself. A romance wherein the bodies never touch each other, a romance without words, except for a few words of gratitude."

"You are unique in writing about a black soldier in World War II," Bluderin said. "I can't think of any war novel I ever read where a black soldier is a significant character."

"Writers have written about black soldiers in wartime," Walter said, "but most unobtrusively, perhaps due to a lack of experience with blacks. Homosexual soldiers are also rarely mentioned, but there have been plenty, believe me. The idea for the book came to me when one of my students asked me what blacks, in particular, have done to massacre countries the way whites have?"

"Nothing that I know of," Bluderin said. "But, on another level—*today*—there are a lot of race riots taking place in cities throughout the United States."

"So I read in the papers," Walter said. "The blacks have good reason to be mad, but I do not think rioting will resolve any problems. I've also read about the quagmire in Vietnam, and that the U.S. Army is sending blacks out to the front lines while holding whites back. Is this true?"

"I don't know. I have heard similar remarks. The black soldiers I'm stationed with are treated the same as white soldiers. I think the army is essentially color-blind. There have been race-oriented fights among the soldiers themselves. I've recorded them in court-martial proceedings. Those are personal dislikes, however, and have nothing to do with the army per se."

"That's good to hear. By the way, the ring Solveig gave you tonight—do you know what it means?

"I was taken by surprise," Bluderin said. "I didn't know how to respond."

"She gave you the ring for touching her soul," Walter said. "The gesture means that—whatever becomes of you two—she wants you to know you have touched her in this way. Think of that whenever you look at the ring. If you ever feel the same way toward her, give her a present in kind."

"I will," Bluderin said. "Thank you."

The two men shook hands and bid each other good night.

Bluderin went upstairs and carefully opened the door to the guest bedroom. The room was void of any sound except for Solveig's soft, sleepy breathing. He crept through the bedroom into the guest bathroom, closed the door, and turned on the lights. Opening the envelope with care, he withdrew and unfolded the sheets of paper. The first page provided a set of instructions on how to decode Walter's message.

Walter had disclosed some alarming and wildly insightful information. Lebrecht belonged to a secretive organization he referred to as Vereinigten Frieden, or United Peace, although the name of the organization changed frequently to avoid consistent identification. Its goal was to "ensure peace by keeping both sides honest." Vereingten Frieden had planted moles in both KGB and CIA units. If one side was planning mischief, the other side would be so informed. The idea was to compromise each agency's plans so that neither would have the upper hand. The intended effect was to create a stalemate, to freeze any potential attacks from either the Soviet Union or the United States. If Vereingten Frieden favored anyone, it was the United States, since the Soviets were sure to bomb West Germany first, long before attacking the United States on its own turf.

Bluderin was dumbfounded to learn what Walter knew about him and the intelligence orders he had been assigned thus far. The pages quivered in his hands as he decoded the message.

The gray envelope he had delivered to Leda Beschwörung contained a message stating that the agency had started "missing things" since Bluderin's duties commenced. He was not yet a suspect for taking anything, but the "coincidence" was noted. Vereingten Frieden was unable to determine who was supposed to be the ultimate recipient of the message.

Leda Beschwörung was described as a dedicated agent, and the agency's instructions were her only priority—anything else was dispensable. The lesson in sex was thought to be a verification of Bluderin's sexual orientation. The agency was suspicious that he could be homosexual, since he kept to himself and avoided the nightclubs that catered to GIs looking for girls. The fact that his best and likely only friend on base was Howard James—an army cook and freelance artist who could nearly pass as a double for the actor Sidney Poitier—a man with a brilliantly wide forehead who looked like he ate with his eyes—further aroused their suspicions. Leda Beschwörung, however, had put that issue to sleep when she reported that Bluderin was an "eager heterosexual" with a healthy appetite for women. *The fucking agency is warped*, Bluderin thought, when he read that the agency thought that he and Howard James could be gay. Howard, for that matter, had been counting the days until his wife, Diane, would join him in Germany. He was madly in love with her, could not stop talking about her. Bluderin also looked forward to Diane's arrival so Howard could get back to other topics of conversation with him.

The key he had delivered to Günter Mann, as he suspected, was intended for agency members to enter his apartment as they saw fit. Walter advised him that agents would be searching the apartment periodically to discover what Bluderin was reading, writing, eating, drinking, and whatever else.

Walter noted that Solveig Evensen was the one person he could trust. She had worked for the American agency in Berlin as an interpreter, translating documents from Russian or German into English. She had resigned from the position several years ago. The departure was amicable, but Solveig wanted nothing more to do with the agency. She had had enough of their sleuthlike behavior.

The opal ring that Monika Müller had given him to deliver to Gustav Erdmann was a signal that Bluderin and Solveig Evensen had formed a friendship, a platonic one through which they shared mutual interests. He learned that the symbol etched into the ring meant that their relationship was based on their interests in literature, nature, and music. Monika was an agent based in Stuttgart, although recently she had submitted her resignation.

Gustav Erdmann was described as a good, honorable man. He liked Bluderin and would treat him like a son or nephew, but he had to be careful about showing any partiality to the agency. He would always be direct and honest with them. Walter noted that Gustav wanted to see him in five days, at five p.m., after he reported back to Hardt Kaserne.

At the end of the message, Walter advised him to make a note of every interaction with the agency from every possible angle. He had assumed, and rightly so, that Bluderin was a dedicated American. Nonetheless, the agency would be watching his behavior. To get updated information on what the agency thought of him, Walter told him to meet with Peter Vanderwerken, an entrepreneur, craftsman, builder, and artist living in Schwäbisch Gmünd.

With the exception of the page describing how to decode the message, Bluderin folded the rest of the papers back into the envelope and placed it in the book. He tore the one page into miniature pieces and flushed them down the toilet. He suspected that the agency knew he was in Düsseldorf or Soligen and probably visiting Walter Lebrecht and receiving a message. He was not going to make it easy for them to read it. He had memorized the code, so if the agency pressured him he could translate the message. He knew he couldn't destroy the whole message—the agency likely would search his apartment for it. If they didn't find a message, suspicions about him would only magnify.

He felt helpless, out of his league. He wondered if the agency were preparing him for more difficult assignments or if it were using him as a possible scapegoat for some other cause. He had thought he was so fortunate in being sent to Germany instead of Vietnam. After reading Walter's message, he realized that he was living in a fishbowl with a borescope shoved hard up his ass and through his ears, looking for flaws in his heart and mind. They might find a lot of weird shit about me, he thought, but they will also see that I am a dedicated soldier and servant of the agency.

Bluderin removed his clothes and crawled under the blankets, giving Solveig a quick kiss between her neck and shoulder before pulling the covers up and going to sleep. *I have to trust you*, he said to her in his dreams, *you are my only hope*.

When they awakened, he kissed her again. She smiled glowingly at him.

"I was not fully asleep when you kissed me last night," she said, "but I was physically and mentally exhausted. You made me feel special, both desired and respected. You also proved to be a sleeping potion. I slept through the night with pleasant dreams."

"As Walter had wished," he said. "You had a similar effect on me."

His sense of comfort was short-lived, however, when he questioned why Gustav Erdmann wanted to see him in exactly five days, at five in the afternoon, after he returned to Schwäbisch Gmünd.

Eight

◄○►

Hans Kliebert sat, scratching his chin, eyeing three fives, a duce, and a seven. Without much fanfare he started the bidding with two marks. Hans was a stoical German. He was in his late fifties, one would guess since, when in his mid thirties, he served as a mechanic in the Luftwaffe during World War II. As he waited for the others to bid, he looked expressionless. The quiet nature of Hans' disposition seemed to be unintentional. Even when he won a hand, he simply gathered the money and waited for the next set of cards to be dealt.

Hans once had told Bluderin that there was no mystery in his life. He simply had done whatever he had been told to do since the day he was born. He never elected to do anything on his own. He never married because no woman ever asked him, and he was not about to take the initiative. The only time Bluderin could detect the slightest smile from Hans was when he stroked Tulla's knee or thigh.

"I'll see your bid," Tulla said, adding two more marks to the center of the table. She stacked her cards and ran her fingers along the edges. Two pair—eights and tens, accompanied by a nine—usually stood a fair chance. She sipped her beer and, like Hans, was relatively expressionless, although her cleavage was perspiring.

Eddie Grau, whose eyes were invisible as ever under his cap, had a full house—three aces, two nines. He matched the bid, then raised it two more marks, the most allowed by unanimous decision of the players. The end of his nose was inflamed and red as a tomato.

Bluderin placed his cards—a hand of four queens and a lone ace—face down in front of him. "I'll see your bid, Eddie, and raise you two."

The card players' table was surrounded in silence. Bluderin was known for his conservative approach to the game. He sometimes matched a bid but hardly ever raised one. Apparently Tulla and Hans were convinced that his hand was better than theirs, since they folded.

"Karin, bring us another round, please," Bluderin said. As Karin set four new mugs of beer on the table, Eddie Grau's nose looked like it had grown a half-inch. Bluderin was sure that Eddie had a good hand—his nose always gave it away, of course—but not a royal or straight flush. That's what it would take to beat him unless, by a very long shot, Eddie had four kings. Bluderin had one ace, so he knew four aces were out.

"Let me pay for this round of drinks," Eddie said.

"You don't need to do that," Bluderin said. "I ordered it."

"That's quite all right," Eddie replied. "You'll be paying for it anyway, indirectly that is, after I win this hand. How about it if I bump you five?"

"Two is the limit." Hans reminded Eddie.

"You and Tulla already folded," Eddie said. "So the limit will be decided by John and me." He pointed at Bluderin. "I would like to raise you five marks."

Bluderin moaned softly, not wanting to raise the agreed-upon limit, but Eddie was very persistent. He had already thrown five more marks into the pot. "Okay, Eddie," he said. "I'll call your hand."

"I was hoping that you would bump me another five, so I could bump you back." Eddie placed his full house, face up, on the table with an authoritative gesture. Raising the lid of his cap, his eyes were no longer invisible. "Read them and weep," he said.

"Quite a hand, Eddie," Bluderin said. Indeed, it was damned close, he thought, knowing that if he had Eddie's hand he probably—no, definitely—would have played the hand to its end. The mathematics would have been on his side. Although Bluderin knew he had Eddie beat, he hesitated to lay out his four queens. Eddie needed the money more than he did, but it would be another ten days before Bluderin would get paid again.

His dilemma was exceptionally aggravating because he had not wanted to be here. He would have preferred being with Solveig first, followed by reading at his apartment or in the library, but he showed up because of the note Walter Lebrecht had given him. Gustav hadn't said anything, but Bluderin anticipated that another assignment was in the works. As he deliberated over what to do with Eddie, he felt a hand smack him on the back of his neck.

"What are you waiting for, Bluderin?" Couch said. "Show Eddie your cards and take the pot. I need a favor, real bad."

"I wish you would mind your own business," Bluderin said before laying our his four queens in front of Eddie. "Sorry, my friend, you usually beat me when it comes down to the two of us, but not today."

Eddie looked at Bluderin's cards as though he were in a state of shock. He grabbed his chest and grimaced. "Four whores—I'll be damned."

"You still did okay tonight, as a whole," Bluderin said. "Karin, bring us another round, if you will, before I leave with Couch for who knows where."

Eddie Grau remained stupefied as Karin placed a beer in front of him. Still, he managed to behave like a gentleman, clicking mugs with Bluderin, who shook Eddie's hand respectfully before giving his attention to Couch.

"What is it, Wiley? You're jumping up and down like you need to take a wicked piss."

"The Mercedes blew a gasket yesterday," he said. "Literally. I had to get it towed to a mechanic in Aalen, near Josef's Gasthaus, the closest place to where the car died. The trouble is, I cannot get it back until I pay for the repair. First, I need a ride to Siegfried Kaufmann's house, so I can pick up some money he owes me, then I need a ride to Aalen so I can pick up the car. The garage owner said he'll be open until ten tonight, so if he's done with the car we have plenty of time to get it."

"Your Mercedes is all set, Couch," Hans said. "I finished the job late this afternoon. I didn't know it was your car."

"And I never knew where you worked," Couch said. "Thanks for the good news, Hans. I'll be on the road again, as long as I can pay for the repair."

"Let me settle up with Gus before we go," Bluderin said.

He gave Gus enough money to pay his bill and give the card players another round. He noticed that Vera Luchterhand had taken his place at the table. She looked more fashionable than usual. A see-through white blouse displayed her firm, braless bosom, and her hair was adorned with platinum streaks. Vera must have had a manicure recently, Bluderin assumed, as her pink fingernails gleamed when she shuffled the cards. He left a tip for Karin as well.

"You're very generous," Gus said. He lowered his voice to a whisper. "I put a small, wooden box in the trunk of your car. Here are the instructions on what to do with it."

Bluderin saw that the note was wrapped under his change, a ten-mark bill. As he took the bill and tucked it away in his wallet he heard Gus say *nice ring* in a voice that seemed more surprised than anything else. Bluderin could not understand why. The silver ring with a sapphire stone was not something that would draw one's attention. Its genderless design was one of smooth simplicity.

"It's a present from Solveig Evensen," he said. "She gave it to me, in appreciation, I guess, for driving her all around Soligen and Düsseldorf. I wouldn't let her pay for any gas."

Bluderin did not know why he felt obliged to explain the circumstances behind the ring to Gustav, but overall it would be better to be upfront with him—sort of—without getting into the matter of having touched Solveig's soul. It was not a good idea to be less than candid with any intelligence contact. Yet he wasn't candid with some of them. There were a few agents he didn't trust. What concerned him more at the moment, however, was that he was itching to know what was inside the wooden box. He would have to play it cool until he had finished helping Couch and returned to his apartment.

He was depressed that he could not be with Solveig tonight. Since his return from leave, he had been overloaded with work at Hardt Kaserne. USAREUR alerts were occurring more frequently, based on the growing disturbance in Czechoslovakia over that country's internal struggles and its decaying relationship with the Soviet Bloc. Those disturbances had quieted down recently—at least temporarily—so Bluderin had the evening off. Still, he could not see Solveig. She was in Norway.

She had been working at Oasis on the evening she and Bluderin returned from their trip. Frau Müller told her that her aunt was on the phone with an important message. In taking the call, Solveig's aunt, Jora Bjornsen, informed her that her father had died. An avid fisherman, Knut Evensen had been at sea when his boat, a modest trawler, collided into a much larger boat, an old, fifty-foot long fishing schooner. Knut Evensen had fallen overboard. His trawler, which had been in need of repair, disintegrated and sank upon impact. Four days after the accident, students from Molde University College discovered the corpse of what was later identified as Knut Evensen. The body had been washed ashore to a low point near the

Molde Fjord, an inlet of the Norwegian Sea. Bluderin considered how, given the fact that Knut Evensen had molested his daughter many times—*until Janne, Solveig's mother, committed suicide after catching her husband in the act*—she may have felt relieved upon hearing the news. A sense of freedom, an inward peace, a spiritual awakening that she had been given a new life, could have risen within her.

The telephone company had granted Solveig a generous three-week leave of bereavement with pay so she could travel to Molde and take care of affairs. Knut Evensen had left a modest savings account and a cottage on the coast of Molde. Jara Bjornsen had made damned sure, through numerous threats, that his will bequeathed all of his belongings to Solveig.

Monika Müller was once again taking Solveig's place at the Oasis. The last time Bluderin checked in with Monika, she had not heard from Solveig. Her lack of communication with Frau Müller and Monika made him wonder about Solveig, what state of mind she was in, how she was coping with the demise of her perpetrator—that pedophiliac monster whose estate was now in her hands.

Bluderin's contemplation of Solveig was disrupted when Karin Erdmann gently nudged his arm.

"Since you're driving Couch over to Siegfried Kaufmann's house, could you take me with you? I'm friends with Heidi, Siegfried's sister, and I need to talk with her."

Bluderin, who thought that Karin was supposed to work at the Gasthaus until closing time, turned to Gustav for approval. The old German looked like something was troubling him. Bluderin sensed angst between Gustav and his daughter.

"It may be a good idea for Karin to take a break," Gus said. "She's upset. She and Jürgen had a nasty argument last night, and they're not speaking to each other. Maybe a visit with Heidi Kaufmann will lift her spirits."

Karin walked into the room behind the bar to get her coat and purse and two bottles of Riesling.

The coincidence of helping Couch and Karin at the same time bothered Bluderin. He did not trust Couch when it came to Karin. It occurred to him that Couch could be the cause behind the difficulties Jürgen and Karin were having.

It seemed that Gustav shared those feelings, since he had deliberated over permitting Karin to leave the Gasthaus.

"Gus, we'll be happy to take Karin along with us," Couch said. "We'll do what we can to cheer her up."

Gustav did not acknowledge Couch's comment. Instead, he looked toward Bluderin for a reply.

"I'll watch over her," Bluderin said. He accompanied Karin and Couch out of the Gasthaus.

Unlocking a gray, metal box stowed beneath his bed, Siegfried Kaufmann removed a band of four-thousand marks. The lines on his forehead creased in concentration beneath his tight blond curls. He counted the money once again before giving it to Couch.

"We're all square now, Wiley," Siegfried said. "I've settled up with Jürgen as well. No more deals. I quit. I don't want to get in trouble."

"That's fine by me," Couch said. "I can't get any more American cigarettes anyway. My supply source is heading back to the States, so the game is over. At least I have enough money to get the Mercedes back."

"I would think so," Siegfried said. "That's a lot of money. I bet your mechanic's bill won't be a third of that."

When Couch, Siegfried, and Bluderin returned to the living room, Karin and Heidi were sitting on the floor, drinking wine and listening to a Beatles' album, *Revolver*. Karin sunk her head in her hands and pressed on her ears when the song "Eleanor Rigby" played.

*Eleanor Rigby picks up the rice in the church where a wedding
has been
Lives in a dream
Waits at the window, wearing the face that she keeps in a jar
by the door
Who is it for?*

"What's the matter with Karin?" Siegfried asked. "Why is she so
melancholy? For as long as I've known her—and it's been for quite
some time, since we were five-year-olds—she has always been quiet
but calm, a shy but self-confident girl."

"Fucked if I know," Couch said, lying through his teeth, in
Bluderin's opinion.

"She broke up with Jürgen," Bluderin said. "I don't know whether
the breakup idea was hers or his."

"That's hard to believe," Siegfried said. "Karin and Jürgen have
been an item for three years. I expected them to get married at some
point, probably after Karin earned her teaching degree. I will talk
to her later. In the meantime, let's have some cognac to celebrate
the end of my adventure with my dubious business partner, Wiley
Couch."

Everyone sat on the floor of the living room, drinking wine,
beer, or cognac—or some combination thereof—and sharing a pipe
of hashish. Heidi's blonde hair, puffy pink cheeks, and girly giggles
were was in stark contrast to Karin's brunette hair, brown-freckled
cheeks, and solemn expression.

Siegfried had brought out his guitar and began playing it, singing
in unison with Donavan's recording of "Catch the Wind."

*In the chilly hours and minutes
Of uncertainty, I want to be
In the warm hold of your loving mind.*

Couch placed an arm around Karin and whispered something about her getting bombed and forgetting all about Jürgen.

"I know what you're thinking, Wiley," Karin said, "and it is not funny."

"Tell me, dear lady, what was I thinking?" Couch asked.

"You think I'm in complete disrepair because Jürgen had sex with Vera. Well, I wouldn't mind if the asshole catches syphilis, but that's beside the point. I know he's been with other women because I said I would not have sex with him until we were married. What upsets me is that he actually likes—*has feelings for*—that tramp. On top of that, Vera had the audacity to come into my father's Gasthaus tonight and act as if nothing unusual happened."

Bluderin listened carefully to Karin. He vaguely remembered being so innocent, once believing that he would have made love to only one woman, after he was graduated from college, had gotten a job as a teacher, and married. What was he thinking? The events of the past year had done more than diminish the possibilities of a monogamous life. His being drafted into the army, and his subsequent assignments, had destroyed even the memory of innocence.

"What actually kills me is that I think he has fallen in love with that slut. Can you imagine? She's had sex with nearly every available male in Schwäbisch Gmünd, and suddenly she's the girl of his dreams."

"One man's shipwreck is another man's dreamboat," Couch said, trying to put a new spin on an old cliché. "You never know. Don't go blaming yourself."

Karin finished drinking her third glass of cognac.

Couch poured her another.

Bluderin noticed how her eyes blurred from the drinking, and how her previously gloomy lips had transformed into a faint smile.

Heidi kissed Karin on the cheek and told her that things were going to get better, that maybe she would find her soul mate at the Pädagogische Hochschule.

"I need some time before I can even think of another relationship," Karin said. "Ever since we started going out, Jürgen told me how he wanted a virtuous woman, a virgin, someone who would know him and only him. And now this—incredible. He used to watch me like an armed guard. In fact, he was petrified of you, John, merely because I said you were good looking." She wiped her eyes with tissue paper.

A wide smile usurped Couch's face. He kissed Karin on the forehead and pinched her cheeks. "Now, now, little girl, take it easy. You simply made a mistake in choosing the wrong man. You need someone who understands you."

Karin ignored Couch's comment and finished her fourth drink. Her brown eyes were glazed, but her speech showed no signs of inebriation.

"I'm surprised at how much liquor you can hold," Bluderin said. "Tell me when you've had enough. I should be taking you home soon."

"Don't worry about me," Karin said. "My father taught me how to hold my liquor." She hissed at Couch. "He also taught me how to eschew horny, lecherous curs like you. Wipe that grin off your face, Smiley Wiley. It looks stupid."

Couch let go with a near-echoing belch, stuck his tongue out at Karin, and got up to grab another beer from the kitchen.

"Is Couch mad at me? I didn't mean to be cruel, but I suppose I was," Karin said to Bluderin.

"He deserves everything you said."

Heidi nodded in agreement. "He's trying to get you drunk so he can seduce you. I'm sure you know that."

"He's so blatant," Karin said. "Sex to him must be like playing cards. When you've finished playing, you shake hands, say 'thanks for the game,' and move on."

"Couch is not a difficult read, to make an understatement,"

Heidi said. "But he doesn't mean anything to you. What about Jürgen? Does he still matter?"

"I don't know," Karin said.

It was clear to Bluderin that the two young women had grown up together. They seemed to foster sincerity and care for each other, like sisters.

While still relatively sober, Siegfried told Bluderin that he would take Couch over to Aalen to retrieve his Mercedes. They would be back within the hour.

"All things must pass," Heidi said, stroking Karin's back. "That's simply the way it is."

Bluderin felt a sharp pain in the back of his head. He was not sure if it came from the liquor or from what Heidi had said. He saw an image of a woman for a second; the pain cleared as the image faded.

"I agree with Heidi," he said. "We come and go. Since our lives are not permanent, how can any relationship in our lives be permanent? I have tried to live with this philosophy. Once you accept it, you feel a clearing. Don't get helplessly involved or make things overly important, and the most intense experience can pass by without a personal sense of tragedy."

"That's a rather narrow perspective," Heidi said. "Karin is a very spiritual person. She is not afraid to give of herself entirely to someone or to some cause. If she suffers pain along the way, that's part of the journey. What is life, if you suffer no pain? Pain is the difference between what things are and what they might have been."

Siegfried had told Bluderin that Heidi was a philosophy major, and Bluderin wondered what philosopher Heidi was paraphrasing. No one came to mind, although he remembered having read a similar sentiment from William Hazlitt, the British essayist.

"You may have a valid point, Heidi, as long you see things as they are," Bluderin said. "I do think, however, that one can deceive oneself when one sees what he or she wants to see instead of what's there. The subsequent distortion, or pain, therefore evolves from self-deception."

Siegfried and Couch had returned from Aalen, and Couch was in a good mood. He loved having his precious Mercedes back, and the bill was only five-hundred marks. He he had plenty of cash left to celebrate.

"It's time to play," he announced.

With Couch having bet Siegfried twenty marks that he could beat him in arm wrestling, they sat at the kitchen table and commenced their battle.

Bluderin assumed that Siegfried Kaufmann would win. He was an athlete, a local soccer player of high regard. Bluderin was humbled by having played soccer with Siegfried and other German players. They *lived* the game, much like American kids who played baseball. It was also apparent that Siegfried lifted weights; his biceps and wrists looked as hard as iron.

Yet, as the struggle continued, Couch remarkably was holding his own. His somewhat flabby biceps wiggled and his face was blood-blue, fused in sweat.

Their arms twisted back and forth for a good fifteen minutes until Siegfried gave it a final go, pushing Couch's wrist within an inch of the table's surface. Couch's eyes seemed to disappear into the back of his head and, with a cavernous grunt, he pushed Siegfried's arm back until they were in a dead heat again. With both men deadlocked and exhausted, they decided to call it a draw.

"You're much stronger than I thought," Siegfried said.

"I thought you had me there for a minute." Couch breathed heavily.

Bluderin was impressed that an overweight guy like Couch, who avoided exercise in any form, could give Siegfried a run for his money. Couch has tremendous willpower, Bluderin acknowledged, a sheer instinct far stronger than any physical prowess.

Karin rested her head on the kitchen table, her right hand loosely holding a glass of cognac. Bluderin shook her shoulders to get her attention.

"Come on, kid. Time to take you home. Let's go."

"Just a second." Karin's lips quivered. She made a beeline for the bathroom.

Couch let out a hearty laugh and began making a series of belching sounds.

Bluderin was irritated. "That's enough, Couch. Have a little pity."

"Don't act like you're concerned, because you're not," Couch said. "I know Karin is all fucked up in the head tonight, but politeness is exactly what she doesn't need. She's got to lighten up, forget about it all, get a grip. She needs a good fuck."

Bluderin did not know how to respond to Couch's comments. He agreed that Karin needed to pull herself together, but taking advantage of her drunken condition would be both cruel and repercussive. She needed some time to think things over.

Couch gave Bluderin a pat on the shoulder and affectionately squeezed his neck. "You want to take her home, or should I?"

"I'll drive her home. I told Gustav I would watch out for her."

Karin returned to the kitchen, looking a little relieved. "I feel better now."

"Grab your coat," Bluderin said. "I'm taking you home."

"No, you're not. You're no fun. I want Couch to take me home." Karin walked over to Couch and sat on his lap, wrapping her arms around his neck and kissing him. He reached under her skirt and began massaging her thighs.

Bluderin lit a cigarette and sat back, watching Karin and Couch. He reflected over their embrace: maybe what everyone needs to make things go easier is to get laid by someone strange every now and then. Could it be that simple? He was not about to let Karin find out—not tonight, anyway.

"Come on, Karin. I promised your father I would take care of you."

"Go with John," Heidi said, giving Karin a good-bye kiss before going into her bedroom.

Couch surprised Bluderin with his cooperation. "Gustav Erdmann is not a man to dishonor or mess with," he said. "Let John take you home. I don't trust myself."

After returning Karin to her father, who was not pleased with his daughter's inebriated state, Bluderin drove to his apartment.

He parked the car, unlocked the hood, and took out the wooden box. He briefly examined its contents and carried it into his apartment. His heart skipped a beat when he opened the door. The bathroom light was on. Bluderin quietly took off his shoes and, as he removed the Luger from the wooden box, he tiptoed in his socks to the wall outside the bathroom. He waited, listening to the toilet flush, and he waited again as water ran into the bathroom sink. When the water stopped running and the bathroom door started to open, Bluderin held the automatic pistol, the nine-millimeter caliber, in front of him, ready to fire. Although the apartment was dim—he hadn't turned on any lights—he immediately recognized the lithe, graceful silhouette.

"Leda Beschwörung—what are you doing here?"

"Oh my God." She stood motionless. "You scared the breath out of me."

"As you did me," Bluderin said, putting his arms at ease, with the Luger pointed toward the floor.

It was obvious to Bluderin that the key he had left with Günter found its way into Leda's hands. Yet no one had informed him that Leda would be arriving for the Luger. Nothing in Gustav's notes gave any indication, no mention of Leda Beschwörung nor anyone else. The only thing mentioned in the notes was that someone would be contacting him to obtain the Luger.

After making tea for the two of them, Bluderin questioned Leda about the Luger handoff. She said she was required to have the gun with her for her next assignment, although she currently had no idea what the assignment was going to be. He did not believe her. As for her cunning appearance tonight, she said that she had not wanted him to know she was coming. She had wanted it to be a surprise. It certainly was.

Leda and Bluderin resumed their discussion of Rilke from their first time together. The poem they studied this time was from Rilke's book *Das Buch der Bilder,* translated to *This Book of Paintings.* The poem "Eingang," or "Initiation," in particular struck them as a thought-provoking theme to share. Several lines in the poem seemed to weld their psyches together:

> *Slowly you raise a shadowy black tree*
> *and fix it on the sky: slender, alone.*
> *And you have made the world. And it shall grow*
> *and ripen as a word, unspoken, still.*

When they went to bed they embraced without conversing. They both knew what they wanted, and their lovemaking did all the talking for them. It spoke of the need to hold and be held, the need to fulfill urgency, and the need to give and receive. Despite everything—the unanswered questions and the mysterious character of their relationship—they had, at some point, made a connection. Regardless, Bluderin believed from Walter Lebrecht's note that the agency was all that mattered to Leda. The sex only made the assignments with Leda more pleasant—a nice frill, like an embroided white border on a scarlet dress—a dress designed to kill, if that's what the agency ordered.

Nine

◄○►

On the way to pick up his laundry next to the PX, Bluderin was possessed by Dylan Thomas' poem, "Fern Hill." He could not shake it from his mind, no matter how hard he tried. The last three lines of the poem in particular roared through him repeatedly in their demanding cadence.

> *Oh as I was young and easy in the mercy of his means*
> *Time held me green and dying*
> *Though I sang in my chains like the sea.*

It might have been the final sentencing for Calvin Federer that made Bluderin escape into the poem. Being locked up in Mannheim for five years was justifiable punishment, but the craven look in Federer's eyes—something like outcast Adam might have given Paradise—was an image Bluderin wanted to erase. Another GI, Nelson McCombs, had received the same sentence as Federer for running out of Regina's Nightclub with a bottle of liquor stuffed under his shirt. McCombs had not physically violated anyone, and he had cooperated fully with both the German police and U.S. military authorities.

Did prejudice play a hand in McCombs' sentencing, since he was black and Federer white? Was the army indeed color-blind, as

Bluderin had told Walter Lebrecht? He had written a memorandum to Captain McCandley on behalf of Nelson McCombs, appealing for a reduced sentence for the GI. McCandley agreed with Bluderin's logic. He said he would see to it that the sentence got reduced to one year. With any luck, McCombs could be released on good behavior within six months.

Bluderin stopped momentarily at a coffee shop on base. There were only five small tables in the dining area, each one able to accommodate three or four chairs. As he took a seat he reopened a violet envelope and reread the invitation composed on violet stationery. It was a note from Gretchen Vanderwerken, asking him to accompany her to her cousin's wedding.

Gretchen was the girl whom McCandley and his recent fiancé, Ingrid Dannette, had introduced him to. The niece looked like a subdued, darker version of her aunt's lighter and more mature pulchritude. Much to his surprise, he had already seen the girl at karate practices. They hadn't talked, but they recognized each other when they were introduced.

On their first date, as arranged by McCandley and Ingrid, they went to a movie. Bluderin was not pleased with the setup aspect of the arrangement, and his displeasure could have affected the way he overlooked Gretchen's charming presence.

She was an athletic, brown-haired and brown-eyed girl of eighteen, soon to attend the University of Munich. He also learned that she was a devout Catholic, something she reflected upon after their seeing *A Man for All Seasons*. She greatly admired Sir Thomas More as a man of conscience who remained true to his principles and religion despite enormous pressure from the royalty to do otherwise.

Several days after their date, Gretchen had mailed Bluderin a note that included Robert Whittington's observation of Thomas More in 1520: *"More is a man of an angel's wit and singular learning;*

I know not his fellow. For where is the man of that gentleness, lowliness, and affability? And, as to time requires, a man of marvelous mirth and pastimes, and sometimes of steadfast gravity. A man for all seasons." Bluderin was not religious, but he shared Gretchen's admiration of More as a man who could not be compromised.

They went on two other dates—*on their own volition*—and enjoyed each other's company. She reminded him of his youngest sister, also named Gretchen. The platonic relationship could have lasted longer. It was unrestrained, as they both dated other people, but Gretchen had left to attend the university, and they hadn't kept in touch.

The wedding reception was to be held at Josef's Gasthaus, actually in a large tent behind the Gasthaus, overlooking a lake. Bluderin smiled dreamily, remembering the girl-boy and other strange characters wearing large, colorful *Flower Power* buttons at the party he and Solveig had attended.

"Are you going to pay your bill or just walk out of here?" The laundry clerk tapped Bluderin on the shoulder with a pencil.

"Oh, I'm sorry," he said. "I wasn't paying attention."

"No kidding," she said, "Why were you so preoccupied?"

"Of course I do—need to pay you," he said, handing her the money. He noticed her green eyes, flecked with yellow, behind the octagonal, titanium-framed glasses. Although he had never spoken with the woman at any length, he knew quite a bit about her—that is, what GIs said about her. The laundry clerk's name was Aarika Taar, but nearly everyone called her Riki. The gossip was that she had married a GI, had three children (one of whom was stillborn) during her marriage, and had gotten divorced a couple of years ago. She was known to read a lot, and she spoke fine English with a British accent. Many of the GIs at Hardt Kaserne thought she was snobbish. She did not hesitate to correct their grammar when they talked to her.

"You're not going to tell me what had your utmost attention?" she asked.

Her question, framed a second time using different words, intruded his sense of privacy. "I wasn't thinking of anything in particular," he said. "Just random thoughts."

"Tell me."

Her nosiness was petulant. He would have to set her back, gently.

"One thought was about a smart but prying woman who works in the laundry at Hardt Kaserne."

Aarika Taar brought her pencil to her lips and smiled after listening to Bluderin's wry comment. "I should charge you a few extra dollars for your ill-conceived remark," she said. "Or better still, you can buy me a book from the store down the hall. I've been dying to read Hesse's *Magister Ludi—The Glass Bead Game* in English. I read the first edition, called *Das Glasperlenspiel*, several years ago. I wonder what liberties the translators took."

"The Hesse phenomenon," Bluderin said. "He's captured the spirit of people in our generation. I have the book in my car. I've finished reading it, so I'll drop it off here before I leave the base."

"Perfect," Aarika said. "By the way, I saved your poem from drowning in the wash."

Bluderin was disconcerted that Aarika had discovered something about him that he did not want known. He was not confident about his writing ability, and he certainly did not know this woman well enough to share his innermost thoughts.

"It's not a poem," he said. "It's just some notes on a pastoral setting I observed."

"Forgive me for *prying*," she said, emphasizing a word he had used to describe her, "but notes usually do not rhyme."

"It may be the start of something that is not finished."

"I recognized the area you wrote about. It is where Günter Mann tends to his sheep."

They talked about Günter and his prophet-like persona, his séances with deities, and his rambling flock of sheep. As he grabbed his laundry, Aarika or Riki—she had no preference to what Bluderin called her—offered to take him to one of her favorite places where she meditates. She noted that her "hideaway" included a waterfall surrounded by birds and trees, nestled away in woods not far from Günter's field.

"It is a secret place," she said. "If I take you there, you cannot tell anyone where it is."

A sixth sense cut into his consciousness. He decided it would not be a good idea to be alone with this woman.

"I would like to bring Howard and Diane James along," he said, avoiding her tendancy to control the invitation. "Howard is an excellent Impressionist painter who could be inspired by the scene."

"I've talked with Howard and Diane on occasion, when they come in here," Riki said. "They are a nice, soft-spoken couple. I've also seen Howard's painting of the Martplatz in Schwäbisch Gmünd. I agree, the man is immensely talented. However, let me give some thought to the idea of inviting Howard and Diane before I make a decision."

After leaving the Hesse book with Riki, Bluderin started his car and contemplated over her motives in offering to show him her special place. Although she was an intelligent and attractive woman, he had little interest in her. His only personal interest was in finding out when Solveig would be returning from Norway. She had been gone for over a month.

He stopped at the gate and was irritated to see Danny Akando on guard duty. *Again.*

"Why are you still pulling guard duty?"

"Where are you going?" Akando asked, ignoring the question. "To see a girlfriend?"

"I don't have a girlfriend."

"You lie," Akando said. "Where are you going?"

"It's none of your business, but I don't have any plans."

"Then why are you wearing a coat and tie?"

"I'm going to church," Bluderin said, "to attend a baptism."

"I'll be off duty in another hour," Akando said. "Take me with you, Blud. *Please.* You promised to hook me up with a babe."

Besides the fact that Akando once conspired with Calvin Federer to harm him physically, Bluderin despised being called Blud, especially when it was pronounced "blood' instead rhyming with *mood*. He often thought if he took a European out he would change the spelling of his last name to Blüderin, ensuring that the long u would be recognized.

"Akando, get off my case. I know all about what you and Federer were planning to do to me. And you expect me to do you a favor?" He waved Akando off and drove out of the gate. "Stay out of my way, punk."

"I'll be on the lookout for you," Akando said. "You'll get yours."

Just like the previous time with Akando on guard duty, the guy was like a hornet that would not leave him alone until he passed the hilly road alongside Günter's pasture. The grass was inflamed with sunlight, and the sky was amethyst. In the low hum of the Volkswagen, his thoughts drifted to another time and place. He had to escape from Akando's latest threat.

He envisioned a young girl with straw-blonde hair, indigo eyes, and wind-blown cheeks, standing beside a bright autumn maple. The image began to shape into an identifiable face but faded away. He stopped at a traffic light. Off to the Vanderwerken house, he reminded himself.

Peter Vanderwerken being as wealthy as Walter Lebrecht, a member of Vereingten Friedan, Ingrid Dannette's brother-in-law, and Gretchen's father were all too intricate for Bluderin to accept as mere coincidences. He needed to connect the dots to what he considered a strategic pattern among Vanderwerken, Lebrecht, Ingrid, and possibly McCandley. They were all trying to control him.

As they sat in the Vanderwerken living room, Peter updated Bluderin on some recent events. The only intelligence news he had to share—and it was critical—was that a soldier stationed at Hardt Kaserne was suspected of being an informant to the Soviets. Peter had no idea who the suspect was. When Bluderin inquired about the Luger assignment, Peter said it could be used when approaching the suspect.

"The shit is getting deeper," he said.

His other news was more personal. He had sold a farm he speculated on to a British gentleman who wanted to turn the place into a bed-and-breakfast establishment. Peter had sold the farm for three times the amount he had paid for it. To take advantage of the situation, he intended to take a year off and travel throughout Europe and the United States. He was planning to show his sculptures in various countries.

"In essence, I will try to do nothing," he said. His voice was so low-toned that Bluderin could hear its vibrations.

"You're not the type of person who just hangs around," Bluderin said. "Ingrid always keeps me up to date on your projects."

"Oh, my sister-in-law," Peter said, scratching his thick black and gray beard. He took off his wire-rimmed glasses to clean them. His mahogany eyes twitched. "Ingrid is kind. She is forever telling Johanna what a good husband I am. What a good deal she got. *Most of the time.* I do slip up on occasion."

Bluderin asked for Peter's advice on what to wear to the wedding. He intended to buy a new suit, shirt, and tie. He wanted to look like a traditional, common German.

Peter pointed to several watercolored paintings on a side wall, one of which showed a man in a suit. He suggested that something similar to that image—a light gray suit—was what Bluderin needed.

Bluderin walked up closely to the artwork to get a better view. He studied the other paintings as well.

"Tell me what you think of the paintings—and be honest. I need the input."

"They remind me of Andrew Wyeth's work."

"Funny you should say that," Peter said. "I always thought I was a better sculptor than painter, but a month or so ago I was looking through an art magazine. The issue had copies of ten Andrew Wyeth paintings. I could see the similarities, so I understand your comment. Johanna thought my paintings were as good as Wyeth's, but I don't believe it. Yet I do regard my paintings more seriously now."

"Many people know about your sculpture," Bluderin said, "but not your paintings. Have you ever had a show? Ever tried to sell any?"

"I don't think I could sell my paintings and still paint."

"Most artists do both," Bluderin said. "They have little choice."

"Some scrape by, I suppose," Peter said. "The wealthy artists—whether a Wyeth or a Warhol—are accepted geniuses and extremely talented. But such artists are too wealthy and famous to be artists any longer. Instead, they depict signatures. They embrace taste."

Bluderin was surprised at Peter's attitude. "You sell sculpture. What's the difference?"

"I'm no scholar on the subject," Peter said. "To me, sculpting is something one makes, much like a table or chair. With respect to paintings, I cannot see how an artist—impassioned, angry, hungry to grow his vision—can continue being an artist when he is rolling in piles of money."

"Famous artists continue to paint," Bluderin said. "That's all I know."

"Yes, but as I've tried to say, they become trademarks. I believe an artist must be neglected, crying out of his soul for eternal beauty, to arrive at the summit of his talent."

Bluderin did not take Peter's words lightly. The man was intense, with an energy that ignited his eyes. What made him so searching, so longing for infinity? What makes an artist? Is it misery? Does one have to be rooted in a problem, or be mad at life, to create?

Johanna Vanderwerken entered the living room, carrying a black metal tray. Her long blonde hair was tied in a large bun, and her glasses magnified her sky-blue eyes. Her ample breasts and full, flowery red apron gave her a matronly disposition. She served Peter and Bluderin beer in high-relief, cobalt blue steins with silver paintings of Frederick Barbarossa, the red-bearded German king and emperor of the Holy Roman Empire in the eleventh century. Johanna appeared to be about twenty years younger than Peter, but from what Bluderin could see the difference in age did not matter. The two seemed to blend naturally, like green and gold.

"You should come to our house to freshen up and change for the wedding, John," Johanna said. "We've added another bathroom, in the wing reserved for guests. It's Peter's latest pride and joy."

Peter lit a pipe, and the smoke swirled around his bald head. He looked intently at the portrait of his wife above the fireplace mantel.

"I didn't realize the wedding was this coming Saturday, my love. I thought it was still a couple more weeks away."

"Peter, I told you about the date I don't know how many times. You're so absent-minded, darling."

"More preoccupied than absent-minded," Peter said, "if there's a difference. Well, there is not much for me to do, other than pull a suit out of the closet. What are we giving the couple?"

"The sculpture you made for them. Don't you remember?"

"Oh, that's nothing. It's very *tiny*," he told Bluderin.

"We're also going to be giving them a dozen of the wine glasses you made."

"Ah, marvelous idea."

"It was your idea, my husband, not mine."

Bluderin was intrigued by this husband-and-wife dialogue. Peter was something of an eccentric genius, and Johanna was continually picking up after him, more or less keeping him in tune with reality. Despite Walter Lebrecht's suggestion, Bluderin did not think he could trust Peter on intelligence matters—he would likely overlook or forget important details.

When Johanna left the room, Peter looked again at her portrait. "When I painted Johanna ten years ago, I believed I really knew her face. Now she looks so different, don't you think? Not in age so much, but in the light around her eyes. Did she look like the portrait at one time? Or could it be that I painted an image of how I felt about her at the time? Yes and no to all these questions. One thing matters: something that has happened is still happening."

"I don't understand," Bluderin said.

"You can't," Peter said. "Nothing ever happens to you: things occur but you have no inner reaction, no deep approval or desires. You do not look at or within something; you look *around* it. When you are alone, thinking of someone, do you accurately recall the face? Do you remember the person's distinct expressions?"

"Maybe not with a full degree of accuracy," Bluderin said, "but I distinctly remember the voice and everything that was said."

"That's what I'm talking about," Peter said. "Nothing stuns you. Nothing matters enough for you to absorb the full essence of a person."

With the exception of Solveig Evensen, Peter may have something, Bluderin thought. He had heard the comment before— that nothing mattered to him—but he was tired of Peter's analysis. Walter Lebrecht was a much nicer guy.

"If I do not get heavily involved with people, it is because I don't want to."

"What you are involved in is what you are," Peter said.

"I don't decide what to get involved in. Others do that for me."

"Just a pair of eyes, looking through binoculars from the wrong end?" Peter said.

"Let's talk about something else."

"Yes, gentlemen, that is a superb idea," Johanna said, returning from the kitchen with two more steins of beer.

Peter seemed to be confused over Johanna's remark. His wife never interrupted a conversation between him and a male guest. She only listened. Now she seemed perturbed with Peter, as if his treatment of Bluderin were unwarranted.

Johanna kissed her husband lightly on the forehead. "Now, if you gentlemen would excuse me, I have to prepare dinner. Gretchen should be arriving any minute."

Peter still seemed bewildered by his wife's earlier comment. He scratched his bald head and looked out the window with a forlorn expression.

Heaven help us if someone besides Peter has an idea, Bluderin thought. "Women can think, too," he said. "You do believe that Johanna can have her own ideas, don't you?"

"All right," he said. "Let's try to be nice."

Bluderin heard Gretchen's voice in the kitchen as she spoke to her mother before joining him and her father in the living room.

She did not appear to be the same person Bluderin remembered. She seemed noticeably more at ease as she bent over to kiss her father. When Bluderin stood, she kissed him with her hands around his ears. It was a forthright kiss, something she had never done to him before. She had changed from a quiet, disciplined girl to a more active, liberated presence. Her former page-boy hair style had transformed into long, straight hair falling well below her shoulders. Her shiny brown hair and eyes still enhanced her flawless, ivory complexion, but her innocent fragility had been replaced with a more confident smile and manner. She was wearing a white blouse—with, quite obviously, no bra—along with faded, tight-fitting blue jeans. Gold anklets set off her brown leather sandals.

"It is a beautiful surprise, seeing you," Bluderin said. "You seem to be wearing college well. You look happy and fit."

"The university atmosphere does something to people," she said. "In my case it provokes me to question my outlook on life. It will be interesting to see where it all goes."

Peter Vanderwerken sighed at his daughter's comment but said nothing.

Gretchen's voice was lower than what Bluderin had remembered. As she talked with him and her father, she subconsciously, or so it seemed, unfastened the top three buttons of her blouse. Bluderin could not help but notice a protruding nipple, brown and pink.

"Have you acquired many new friends at the university?" he asked her.

"Only a few, but I have become very close to them." She rested her chin on her hands and looked directly at Bluderin. "Let's go for a walk outside. It will be another half-hour before the lamb is fully cooked."

"Go ahead without me," Peter said. "I'm going to bring in some logs and start a fire. I feel an evening chill coming on."

Bluderin and Gretchen sat on a stone wall near a bed of *Blaue Blumen*, or blue flowers.

"The German author Novalis used blue flowers as a symbol for desire and love," Gretchen said.

"As well as striving for the infinite and unreachable," he said.

She described her new university friends. One was three years her senior, a medical student, and the way Gretchen described him made it quite evident that they were lovers. Two of her other friends were girls—students of history and political science. She had not decided on a major yet.

"We talked about the war in Vietnam in our political science class," she said. "What do you think of it?"

"It is the most needless and senseless waste of young lives," Bluderin said. "Sadly, many soldiers have been killed without ever experiencing the comfort of a woman's loving touch. And for *what?*"

"It's so awful," she said. "Of course, Germany's war history is steeped in the most unforgivable murder of millions, so I cannot be self-righteous about America's role in Vietnam. But if you are so much against the war, why did you join the army?"

"I did not *join* the army," Bluderin said. "I was drafted—ordered by the government—into the army. It was mandatory. I did not have any say in the matter. My only other choices were to go to prison or exile to Canada."

"That's preposterous," Gretchen said. "I could understand a mandatory draft if America were defending itself against a formidable enemy. A small country like Vietnam poses no such threat. It's ridiculous to have invaded it. The Americans could have learned something from the French for once. If they did, they would not have had to sacrifice one soldier's life."

"It was a matter of luck that I was sent to Germany," he said. "Otherwise, I don't know what I would have done."

"You mean you would have gone to jail or escape to Canada?"

"I had thought about it many times. I probably would have gone to Vietnam—more out of a sense of guilt, with so many other soldiers being sent there. My life is no more valuable than theirs."

"So you are not a man for all seasons?" Gretchen asked him, alluding to the movie they had seen together. "You are not the ultimate man of conscience, willing to die for your principles?"

"I'm no Sir Thomas More, if that's what you're thinking," Bluderin said. "I am a man of chance, I suppose you could say."

"You are a man of fate," she said. "When you were drafted, fate worked on your behalf."

Bluderin noticed Johanna waving at them from the house.

"Dinner is ready," Gretchen said. "Let's go and eat. Then I will show you two dresses. I'm not sure which one I will wear to the wedding. I would like to have your opinion."

"You want *my* opinion?" Bluderin asked. "I don't know anything about fashion."

"You know what you like. Since you will be my escort at the wedding, I want you to like what you see."

One dress was black, the other a silver shade of blue. Gretchen undressed in front of him. She was built as solidly as a featherweight.

"Have you had any time at school to practice karate?" he asked.

"Three days a week," she said. "I have to, to think clearly."

The black dress was elegant, held up by thin spaghetti straps. It hugged her frame tightly to where it ended, an inch or two below the knees. The light blue dress was more revealing, showing her cleavage and ending at mid thigh.

"You prefer the blue one," Gretchen said. "Your eyes say it all."

"I wonder how formal this wedding is going to be. If it's like a Catholic wedding mass, the black dress would be more appropriate."

"It's going to be a civil ceremony, not a religious one," she said. "The bride is going to be wearing a 'mini' gown. It's shorter than my blue dress."

"Then the blue dress it is," he said. "I'm looking forward to the occasion."

She blew him a kiss and walked toward him. "Let's go out tonight. There's a band playing at the Pädagogische Hochschule. They do a lot of songs by the Beatles, the Rolling Stones, and Bob Dylan." She kissed Bluderin on the lips and smiled. "Who knows

what will happen? If you behave, I may show you something I
learned at the university."

With Solveig having been gone for over a month and without
him having heard a word from her, he would be elated to discover
what Gretchen had learned. She had grown into a definitive free
spirit. She was lulled in green sleep, adrift in her new feelings and
dreams of universal wholeness. She had become her own woman.

He could not become his own man until he was free of the
army's and agency's hold on him. The only time he felt totally free
was when he was with Solveig Evensen. Where was she? What had
happened to his psyche's salvation?

Ten

---◄○►---

May 1967

Bluderin tried to follow Peter Vanderwerken's car to the wedding, but he could not maintain the speed—the quick downshifting and accelerating out of curves—with which Peter maneuvered his Porsche. Bluderin's Volkswagen stood no chance of trailing the superior performance vehicle. It soon disappeared.

"Your father is a mad man behind the wheel. He must know that there is no way I can keep up with him in this old bug."

"He likes to maximize the engineering features of the car," Gretchen said. "My father terrifies me when he's driving. I won't go anywhere with him unless he promises to drive more slowly. I don't know how my mother stands it, but she seems to take it all in stride."

It was a picture-perfect day for a wedding. The sky was an endless mass of solid sapphire, with only a trace or two of the slightest clouds. The trees glimmered in sunlight, enriched with warmth yet providing a cool, cleansing feel to the air. Bluderin glanced over at Gretchen and smiled.

She looked elegant in her blue dress and simple, delicate-looking white sandals. A thin, golden necklace with a ruby resting on her chest set off her toned, athletic body. Her long, brown hair hung gracefully around her back and shoulders while her strong legs made her dress appear even more delicate and lighter than it actually was. Ruby lipstick and gold earrings set off her porcelain skin.

It was easy being with Gretchen. She was sexy and sweet. She was also very bright, but her conversations were, for the most part, light-hearted and easy going. He was not accustomed to being with such a self-confident young woman.

He was puzzled when he arrived in Aalen and saw Peter's car parked at Josef's Gasthaus. He became more confused when Gretchen told him to park next to the Porsche.

"I thought there was going to be a wedding ceremony first— maybe in a church nearby—before the reception," he said.

"The wedding ceremony will be held here as well as the reception," Gretchen said. "It will be a civil ceremony, as I told you—officiated by what the States call a justice of the peace."

Bluderin and Gretchen walked into the tent behind the Gasthaus. It was decorated in long crepe paper stripes of black, red, and gold along the tent's ceiling and walls. All the tables were covered with white table cloths, each one having a magnum of champagne on its center. A waiter approached them and said that the actual wedding ceremony would take place very soon inside the Gasthaus, followed by the reception in the tent.

As Bluderin and Gretchen walked into the Gasthaus, they noticed her father greeting the bride and groom. Since they both had relatives from Sweden attending the wedding—and since both were fluent in Swedish—Peter saluted them in the language. It was the only Swedish he knew, Gretchen told Bluderin. He had been practicing exactly what to say, just for this occasion.

Two elderly people, whom Bluderin learned were the bride's paternal grandparents, approached Peter, addressing him in Swedish. Peter recoiled nervously, asking the couple if they spoke German, explaining that he only knew a few words in Swedish. The couple laughed, affectionately patting Peter's hands, and resumed their conversation in German.

"I told you that you would only get yourself in trouble, pretending to know Swedish," Johanna said to her husband.

Gretchen only smiled over the mini fiasco, saying that she could not understand why her father had to "show off" all the time. For such a brilliant man, with all his creativity and entrepreneurial savvy, she told Bluderin that Peter always needed to prove that he was more learned and accomplished than everyone else.

"There is still something of a little boy in him," she said.

The bride, Clara Dannette, unlike any other Bluderin had seen before—all of whom had worn more traditional wedding gowns—was quintessentially beautiful in her modern attire. Her mini gown, as Gretchen described it, was more of a subdued gold than pure white. A tiara of miniature red roses encircled the top of her head, followed by a chain of miniature yellow roses flowing along her blonde tresses to her tiny waist. As Gretchen introduced Bluderin to the bride and groom, he could not help but notice how the bride's smile—exuding a sensuous warmth with an intriguing mystery behind it—reminded him of Solveig Evensen's charming ways. Like Solveig, the bride's beauty was immense. He could understand why the groom could not take his eyes off her.

"God, she is lovely," Peter Vanderwerken said as the bride and groom left to meet with the official who would be marrying them. "She will *own* her husband, if she doesn't already."

The groom, Wolfgang Parler, was tall—about six-foot five, Bluderin guessed—and remarkably thin. Bluderin wondered if the groom were related to the Wolfgang Parler he had met with Solveig during their walk in the bird sanctuary. The other Wolfgang Parler had a much less imposing physique and was a good thirty years older than the groom. With his almost flaxen hair cropped neatly above his ears and in his black tuxedo, stark white shirt, and silk white bow tie, Wolfgang the groom stood in absolute silence behind his bride. He appeared to be more of a dedicated bodyguard than a husband-to-be.

Gretchen mentioned that Wolfgang was a civil engineer, a fact that prompted Bluderin to ask her if this Wolfgang Parler was related to the Wolfgang Parler he knew as an ornithologist. Gretchen knew both Wolfgang Parlers and had asked them if they were related. They had given her the same answer: they were not related as far as they knew, and that if they were, the familial ties were so distant it did not matter.

Bluderin looked around the Gasthaus as the civil official joined the bride and groom's hands together. Outside of the Vanderwerkens, McCandley, and Ingrid, he did not recognize any of the other guests. The civil official was soft spoken, saying something about Clara and Wolfgang growing together in their own singularities while bonding in reflection of each other's light and life. He then pronounced the groom and bride as husband and wife.

Bluderin waited for more formalities, but that was it. It seemed to him that the ceremony was innocuous, even a little superficial, taking from tradition but without much depth or detail. Yet, it was gentle and brief, and the crowd quickly departed outside to the reception tent.

Peter Vanderwerken poured champagne into the glasses at the table. Peter, Johanna, Bluderin, Gretchen, McCandley, and Ingrid were all assigned to the same table. McCandley mentioned to Bluderin that he and Ingrid could stay only for half an hour, as they had an appointment with a priest in preparation for their own wedding. They were planning to be married in the Heilig-Kreuz-Münster and intended to have a very small wedding of twenty or so guests.

Bluderin learned from Gretchen that Ingrid had been married once before, as had McCandley, so their wedding would have a decidedly more reserved and serious tone than the one taking place today. It occurred to Bluderin that, with both of them having had failed marriages, McCandley and Ingrid would likely be extremely committed to making their marriage work. After their wedding, which was to take place in a month, they already had made plans to go to the States for a three-week honeymoon. That way, they would have enough time for McCandley to introduce Ingrid to his family and for Ingrid to get a little taste of life in America.

After all the wedding guests rose to toast the newlyweds, Gretchen took Bluderin by the hand and led him onto the dance floor. A band of six musicians played their instruments—a piano, two guitars, a horn, an accordion, and a set of drums. They began playing classic German wedding music.

"I can't dance to this type of stuff," Bluderin said. "I have no idea what to do."

"Just relax and follow my lead," Gretchen said. "The floor is quite crowded. No one will notice how you dance. You're only another German guy at the wedding."

It did not take long, however, for everybody on the dance floor to start dancing all together, in unison. They formed a circle, each person standing behind another, holding onto the one in front of them by the waist. Bluderin began to enjoy the frivolity of the crowd. He vaguely recalled a similar type of dance back in the States—the "bunny hop" or something like that—where the dancers moved about in a circle, hopping behind each other. The newlyweds danced together in the center of the circle while the other dancers revolved around them.

After several rotations the bride left the center of the circle and took her father's hand so she could dance with him. The groom followed suit and took his mother's hand. This sort of dancing exchange went on until every guest had an opportunity to dance with the bride or groom. It appealed to Bluderin as nice symbol of the interactions between marriage and community.

When the band took a break, the wedding guests returned to their tables. Bluderin ordered six glasses of cognac. Ingrid and McCandley thanked him for the drink, then excused themselves for their meeting with the priest.

"Now that my boss is gone, I can relax," Bluderin said. "You know, these German weddings are a lot of fun."

"It is only a shadow of a traditional German wedding," Gretchen said, "but it is fun, I agree. I must say, though, that the hors d'oeuvres do not do it for me. I'm going to need something more substantial."

"We can have dinner in the Gasthaus later," Bluderin said. "Josef's has a simple German supper menu."

"Terrific," she said. "In the meantime, just look at all the faces at this party. It's a very happy wedding." She left the table when a man, some distant relative, she had said, approached her and asked her to dance.

"Not all weddings are so happy," Johanna said to Bluderin. "My wedding, for example, was quite intense. The overall mood was somber because my parents thought I was too young."

"That wasn't exactly the reason," Peter said. "Many girls married younger than Johanna at the time." He squeezed Bluderin's elbow and spoke in his vibrating-low tone. "Johanna and I had to deal with a lot of pressure. Her parents were strict Catholics and sick over Johanna 'living in sin' with me before we married. Also, they did think I was too old for their lovely daughter, this naiad of the Rhine."

According to Johanna, her parents became more accepting of their marriage through time, especially when Ingrid had gotten divorced. Bluderin noticed that, although Johanna and Ingrid had been polite and cordial with each other during the reception, it was clear that they were not close. Ingrid had spent more time talking with Peter than she did with Johanna. There seemed to be some disagreement about how Ingrid had her first marriage annulled so she could marry in the church again. Johanna thought rather callously that Ingrid had paid off the priest for the annulment.

There was something else going on with Johanna, Bluderin believed, other than her questioning Ingrid's behavior regarding the divorce. Could it have to do with her husband? Bluderin and Johanna danced, her breasts pressing against his ribs as she wrapped her arms around his waist. Her womanhood—the soft curvature of her back to the small roundness of her belly, and the scent of her hair beneath his chin—commanded instinctual attention.

"You know what I need," she said, "and I can feel you getting aroused."

It was easy to be attracted to Johanna. She had a beauty that was quite similar to Ingrid's, but Johanna did not take the time and effort to be as made-up or as fashionable as her sister.

"I'm not the right person," he said.

"I know it seems complicated," she said, "but my needs are no different from any other woman's. We could make it simple."

"It's wrong," Bluderin said. "You're married, and I respect your husband."

"Peter understands my dilemma," she said. "He accepts getting old as gracefully as anyone I've ever known. He realizes that I'm a lot younger than he is and that my sexual needs are still very much alive. He hates to see me frustrated."

"I don't know," Bluderin said. "I do not want to ruin our friendship. I'm not sure I could give you what you need. My sense of guilt could overtake my ability to perform."

Johanna inserted a knee between Bluderin's legs and raised her thigh.

"I don't think you will have any problem," she said. "Peter told me that, if I do take on a lover, he would prefer him to be someone like you, a lot younger, and someone who will be leaving here in another year or so, someone with whom I could never get emotionally involved."

Bluderin was at a loss for words. He had never experienced what one could call altruistic sex, or charitable sex, for a friend.

"Johanna, I need some time to think about it. I may need to speak with Peter. I don't want to make it difficult, but I do not want to deceive anyone."

"I don't think Peter would be keen on discussing the matter," she said. "He will be aware if we have a rendezvous once a month or so, but he doesn't want to confront the issue. Maybe we ought to forget about it."

"I'm sorry," he said.

Johanna looked at him sympathetically. "No wonder Americans are in such a state of angst. The men and women are all afraid of each other. You feel guilty if you're aroused and guilty if you're not."

"I know," Bluderin said, taking Johanna's arm and heading back to their table. She rested her head on his shoulder.

"Forgive me, John. I did not mean to intimidate you. I got at Peter for doing so the other day."

Although the reception had come to a close, Peter Vanderwerken ordered another bottle of champagne. "I haven't had such a good time in quite a while," he said. "Let's go back to the Gasthaus and find Gretchen. She said for us to join her when you two had finished dancing. Another band is getting ready to play for the regular patrons. Let's stay a while longer, Johanna."

"I'm not sure that's a good idea," she said.

"There is nothing to worry about," Peter assured her. "I've already retained a driver to take the car home with another driver following him. I'll call for a taxi to take us home when we've had enough. You've nothing to worry about."

After Bluderin and the Vanderwerkens met Gretchen and took a table in the Gasthaus, a booming voice filled the room.

"Give this table a drink on me!" Wiley Couch appeared, accompanied by Karin Erdmann. "Fancy meeting you here, John."

After introducing Couch and Karin to the Vanderwerken family, Bluderin turned down Couch's offer of a beer and opted for a coffee. He would have to drive Gretchen home eventually, and he wanted to be sure he was sober. Solveig had warned him that if he were caught driving while intoxicated there would be hell to pay. The German system carried very strict penalties for drunk drivers. He was sure that the army would carry out such punishment even further. Manheim was not to be on his agenda.

Couch looked different from his usual appearance. He was well groomed and wore a white shirt with a tie and sports jacket. Had Karin influenced him to clean up his act? Couch leaned over Bluderin and spoke in a near whisper.

"Karin and I are becoming an item," he said. "It's been good so far, and Gustav seems to be accepting the situation. Can't you see how good it's been for Karin? See how she's smiling again? There is nothing like fucking on a regular basis to straighten the head out. Hell, you've got to admit that she looks better—no more of that tightness around the mouth. No more drooping eyes."

Bluderin conceded that Karin looked much better than the last time he had seen her. It looked like her breasts had grown—either that, or she no longer tried to minimize their natural effect. She had also applied some makeup. Her lips looked fuller and her eyes brighter, making her appearance more vivid and pleasing.

"So, besides rescuing Karin from her misery, what else have you been up to?"

"Slowly drinking the day away," Couch said. "We've been visiting some friends. We even went over to see Jürgen Treuge and his ever-ready girlfriend, Vera Luchterhand. They seem to be hitting it off. I guess a slut is just the thing some guys need."

"If their relationship works for them, I suppose it's good," Bluderin said.

"I saw your car outside. Can you drop us off at Gustav's later? I've been taking a taxi for most the day, since I've been drinking. Goddamn taxi drivers—those pricks are robbers."

"If you can wait a while. Gretchen and I are going to order dinner. The wedding reception only offered hors d'oeuvres."

"That's fine. We're in no rush, are we Karin? Let's dance."

Bluderin tried to understand the nature of their relationship. He watched Couch and Karin dance, caressing each other with light kisses. Couch was no longer a boisterous oaf. He held Karin gently as they glided across the floor. He seemed to have grown considerate of her, and she in turn no longer appeared too timid to express her sensual side. Bluderin could find no reason behind this evolving couple, but then he questioned why there had to be any reason.

Gretchen nuzzled Bluderin's neck, and he turned to kiss her softly on the lips. She held his head in place and returned his kiss with more pressure. The band played its version of "Unchained Melody."

> *Oh, my love, my darling,*
> *I've hungered for your touch a long, lonely time . . .*

Although Peter Vanderwerken paid no attention to Gretchen and Bluderin, Johanna Vanderwerken smiled at their embrace.

After the band finished its first set for the evening, the Vanderwerkens left for home, and Bluderin and Gretchen finished their abundant Wiener Schnitzel dinner. It was time to drive Couch and Karin to Gustav's. However, Karin and Gretchen wanted to listen to the first few songs in the band's second set.

As the band reunited, it launched into a more lively repertoire than its first set, beginning with their rendition of the Rolling Stones'

"(I Can't Get No) Satisfaction." They hadn't finished half of the song when they stopped playing. All the musicians' eyes focused on the main door to the Gasthaus. Bluderin and Couch turned around to look for the cause to the sudden quiet: Danny Akando, in uniform, no less. *Shit. Absolute shit.*

Bluderin closely observed Akando's body to see if he could detect anything that could be used as a weapon. He thought he saw the tips of blades sticking out from under the cuffs of Akando's fatigue shirt.

"How in hell did he find this place?" Bluderin asked Couch.

"How you doing, studs?" Danny Akando forced a wide grin, apparently aware that Couch and Bluderin were feeling helpless.

Couch rubbed his eyes in disbelief, making a futile attempt to sober up.

"Come on, Blud! Say hello to your fellow GI. What's the matter? You ashamed of me? And don't speak Kraut to me. It makes me nervous."

"Take a seat," Bluderin said, offering Akando a chair. He waited to see how Akando moved, so he could evade an attack.

"I'd rather stand for now," Akando said.

Bluderin quickly explained the situation about Akando to Gretchen. She listened carefully as he described Akando's psychotic personality. With her knowledge and practice of karate, Gretchen told Bluderin not to worry about her. She was confident that she could defend herself.

"If he comes near me, I'll kick him in the nuts so hard he won't be able to move for a week," Gretchen said, holding Bluderin's hand and joining him in observing Akando's behavior.

Akando ordered a glass of vodka from Josef, but the older man ignored the GI, evidently pretending not to understand a word he said.

Akando shrugged his shoulders, then sat down at the table next to Couch, opposite Bluderin.

Bluderin and Gretchen placed their feet on two of the table's legs, preparing to use the table to counter any attack.

"Gee, guys, all I want is a little fun."

Couch grabbed Akando by the neck, staring into his eyes. "Listen up, Danny boy. We'll make it easy on you. We're leaving now, and you are leaving with us. We are all going to walk out of here peacefully. One false move and my fat ass will be all over you. And don't think for a second that I can't take you out."

"Okay, Couch," Akando said. "You're a regular guy, not like Bluderin. I don't like it here anyway. The pussy is all spoken for."

Bluderin, Couch, and Akando stood up. Couch told Karin and Gretchen that he and Bluderin would escort Akando back to the base and return to pick them up. As he leaned over to kiss Karin good-bye, Akando freed himself from Couch's grip and headed into the crowd that had been watching them.

Before Bluderin knew what happened, he heard the pop of a bottle breaking—like a shot from a cannon—followed by shattered glass and torrents of screams. Josef Westoff was lying on the floor, face down, with broken remainders of a bottle of cognac beside his head.

Bluderin drove his elbows hard into Akando's head and neck. His left fist began bleeding when he struck Akando's mouth, breaking a tooth. Akando backed into the table where Karin and Gretchen sat, his mouth open, gaping for air. Gretchen struck Akando with a couple of lightning-fast kicks to the groin. Akando fell to the floor, his mouth bleeding considerably. He gripped his knees to protect his crotch. Couch had gotten some rope and used it to bind Akando from his ankles to his neck.

"Call the MPs," Couch said to the crowd, giving instructions on how to make the call. "Call the German police as well."

"Call for an ambulance," Bluderin said.

"We better get the fuck out of here," Couch said. "The MPs will hang our asses, too, just for being here."

Bluderin ignored a curve and nearly drove into a field on the back road leading to Schwäbisch Gmünd. Gretchen and Karin begged him to slow down.

"Sorry, ladies. I just wanted to get out of sight from the police as soon as possible."

They could hear sirens but saw nothing. A while later they felt the effects of the calm *after* the storm.

"No matter what Akando tells the police, the guys at Josef's will back us," Couch said. "The story is that we were invited to the wedding earlier in the day—all very legit. As we were leaving the reception with our girlfriends, we were shocked to see Akando come into the Gasthaus. After Akando attacked Josef, we contained him and went to find a doctor. Our girlfriends knew where the closest doctor lived, but with it being a weekend and the doctor probably home, no one had his unlisted home number."

As Bluderin glanced in the rearview mirror, he noticed Karin cuddled with Couch and unhooking his belt.

"How in hell did Danny ever find us?" Couch asked.

"Damned if I know," Bluderin said. "I've been in Aalen since ten this morning. Gretchen invited me to the wedding—the bride is her cousin."

Karin's lips nibbled at the head of Couch's penis. "He must have seen Karin and me getting into a taxi and followed us," Couch said excitedly, as he stroked Karin's hair and breathed deeply.

Bluderin's palms sweated on the steering wheel. "You know, Couch, Akando is going to tell the MPs all kinds of shit."

Couch did not say a word for several minutes. It was apparent that he had ejaculated into Karin's mouth. Gretchen opened the window next to her and covered her mouth. She was giggling hysterically but trying to keep quiet. Bluderin noticed Gretchen and began laughing to himself. What is the best way to forget about a horrifying event, such as assaulting an old man, he thought. *Get a blow job, of course. It makes everything better.*

"Don't worry about Akando," Couch said. "My story is bullshit, but the other patrons will vouch for me. Your story is essentially the truth."

"I suppose," Bluderin said. "McCandley was at the wedding with Ingrid, who incidentally happens to be Gretchen's aunt, so you'll have to modify your story. What about Josef?"

"He was standing up and a woman was cleaning his face when we left," Couch said. "Josef will be all right. He'll get over it. He'll also get some money from the army for Akando attacking him."

A headache circled Bluderin's brain, pinching it like a sphere of arrowheads. He tried to respond to Couch's comment, tried to tell him how Josef had suffered trauma from U.S. soldiers twenty-odd years ago, but he could not find the words.

"I worry about Josef," he said.

"Don't sweat it," Couch said. "I'm sure Josef has seen worse things in his life than what happened to him today. He'll get over it, as I told you."

"I don't know." Bluderin glanced over at Gretchen, who finally had stopped giggling. "There are some things people never get over." How ironically awful, he thought. *Josef got whacked on the head again by another American soldier while I never saw it coming—me, a GI who resembles the soldier who raped his daughter.*

"Did you see any blades under the cuffs of Akando's shirt when you struck him or tied him up?" Bluderin asked, looking first at Gretchen then in the review mirror at Couch.

"They looked like bracelets," Gretchen said. "I noticed them when Akando was crouched down on the floor, protecting his crotch."

"I saw them, too," Couch said. "I think the goon was intending to use them on us—like brass knuckles."

Bluderin stopped the car in front of Gustav's Gasthaus.

"You two coming in for a drink?" Couch asked.

""I have to drive Gretchen home," Bluderin said, "and I'm sure McCandley will want to talk with me when he hears about the assault."

It was not something he was looking forward to. The intelligence enigma with the Luger, and now Akando's behavior, had put his mind in disarray. There was no way out. *The shit is getting deeper*, as Peter Vanderwerken had told him.

Eleven

<figure>◄○►</figure>

Bluderin measured the distance from the peak of his army cap to his eyebrows—exactly the the width of his three middle fingers—militarily correct. He removed a few specks of dust from his Class-A jacket with a strip of scotch tape. His shoes shone like black glass against the oak flooring.

With his clipboard, pad, and pen in hand, he walked down the first-floor corridor of Headquarters Building to Lieutenant Getz's office. He knocked on the door and waited for Getz to respond.

"Sorry to keep you waiting, Specialist Bluderin, but I was in the middle of writing some final notes for the hearing. I didn't want to lose my train of thought."

Lieutenant Howard Getz was slim, about six-two and one hundred sixty pounds. He had such a small head that his thick-lensed, black-framed glasses appeared to cover the upper half of his face.

"You have something you wanted to ask me, sir?"

"I need to clarify a few matters with you, Specialist Bluderin, but first I would like to ask you how the old German man, Josef Westoff, is doing. Have you found out anything about his condition?"

The formality of Getz's affected speech pattern with enlisted men was legendary on base. Howard James could impersonate Getz with an impeccable resonance, so well that GIs would beg him for a rendition.

"It was questionable at first, sir, whether Josef would be here today. He should be. I talked with Josef's doctor in Aalen. He said that the wound to the head was not serious. There was no eye damage, but Josef did undergo four stitches immediately below his right eyebrow."

The lieutenant poured himself some coffee, stood erect, paced around his office, and looked out the window. He addressed Bluderin with his back turned to him.

"So I guess Private Akando is within a fraction of an inch of being lucky. If eye damage were inflicted, we would have a lot more serious case on our hands."

"It is still a serious offense, sir. Look at what happened to Nelson McCombs. He was locked away in Mannheim for six months, and he assaulted no one."

"McCombs is back on base now, thanks to Captain McCandley," Getz said. "I understand that you had something to do with convincing the captain to reduce McCombs' sentence. I respect that."

Getz's comment made Bluderin suspicious. Why was the lieutenant complimenting him?

"Let's get back to the reason I requested your presence. Private Akando swears you can testify that Josef was holding a bottle when he tripped, his injured knees giving out, making him fall to the floor and cut himself."

Bluderin was disturbed with the way Getz was questioning him. It seemed that the lieutenant was trying to make him embellish his original statement. That was not about to happen.

"As I wrote in my statement, sir, I attended a wedding at Josef's premises on the day that Daniel Akando came into the Gasthaus. I entered my date's telephone number and home address into the record. William McCandley and his fiancé, Ingrid Dannette, also attended the wedding, as stated in my affidavit."

"*William* McCandley, not *Captain* McCandley, is it?"

"It was a *civilian* affair, sir. No disrespect intended."

"I tried to get in touch with Gretchen Vanderwerken," Getz said, "but she has returned to school in Munich. However, her parents signed a statement that you attended the wedding with them and their daughter."

Getz seemed to be taking a different track now. Bluderin was not sure what the lieutenant's intentions were, other than to confuse him.

"So you already have several witnesses verifying my presence, sir. You can also contact Specialist Wiley Couch in Göppingen. He and his girlfriend were leaving the Gasthaus at the same time Gretchen and I were."

Getz stared at Bluderin and listened carefully. His brown eyes widened under his glasses like rippling, polluted lakes.

"Yes, Akando said that Specialist Couch was also at Josef's. You and Couch wouldn't be siding up together now, would you?"

Back to square one, Bluderin thought. It was time for the good lieutenant to get his own *non sequitur.*

"No, sir. You know that Private Akando has a history of getting into trouble." His comment seemed to annoy Getz.

"Tell me, Specialist Bluderin, what do Private Akando's previous mistakes or misdoings have to do with this incident at Josef's Gasthaus?"

Bluderin felt that it was time to become more proactive with Getz. "Akando fabricated his story, hoping to get off the hook for his actions. Look at his military record, sir. I'm no psychologist, but Private Akando is mentally unstable. He needs help."

The lieutenant appeared to be frustrated. He paced around his office, again addressing Bluderin with his back turned to him.

"I'm not denying the fact that Akando could use some professional counseling, and I would press you more about the details of your whereabouts that evening, except that you are well covered. I doubt I could make a dent on Akando's behalf. Besides, Josef's Gasthaus is off-limits, another factor that makes the whole ordeal rather messy. If I were to get into the off-limits approach, I would only be opening up Pandora's box. I have no desire to get you and Specialist Couch in trouble, and certainly not Captain McCandley."

"Yes, sir," Bluderin said.

"Don't take it so casually, Specialist Bluderin. I have been the defense counsel on two previous court-martial cases, as you well know, and I won both. That's good for my record. Serving as counsel at court martial hearings is supposed to be a captain's billet, but with the shortage of captains I'm picking up the slack. The Akando case is extremely important to me."

"Why, sir, if you don't mind my asking?"

"If I win this one—or more specifically, if I save Akando from being sentenced to Mannheim—it could be another positive factor in my being promoted to captain. Talk to your German friends. Convince them that the incident was partially an accident. Maybe Akando did trip Josef, but it was by mistake. Understand? Josef will be compensated for his injury. The army will be fair and upstanding in that regard."

"How can I do that?"

Getz leaned over and rested his elbows on his desk. He looked up at Bluderin with a stern intensity. Although Bluderin was sure the lieutenant was trying to intimidate him, he also sensed that Getz had a little fear in his eyes.

"I want Akando *free* of the assault charge. I'm going to deal straight with you, Specialist Bluderin. Akando told me about Specialist Couch's dealing in hashish and cigarettes. If I expose Couch, he will need more counseling that Akando does. You could be implicated as well."

Bluderin was not threatened by the lieutenant's posturing. He had done absolutely nothing illegal, but he did not want Couch to be court-martialed, whether he deserved it or not. It would be difficult to prove anything against Couch anyway, since he had stopped dealing in hashish and cigarettes altogether. Bluderin thought he would take a low-key, non-committal response to Getz's comment.

"I have nothing to say, sir."

"Interpret things my way, Specialist Bluderin."

Bluderin decided to take an offensive turn in this cat-and-mouse dialogue. "I cannot do that, sir. The potential repercussions from consciously misinterpreting statements by German citizens would far exceed anything that you could try to pin on me."

Getz squinted at Bluderin and covered his lips with an index finger.

Bluderin's gut instinct told him that the lieutenant wasn't going to say another word until he said something else first. It may be time to throw the lieutenant a bone, he thought.

"I really do not know what happened in the altercation between Private Akando and Josef Westoff. From what I gathered in questioning some of the patrons at Josef's, no one actually *saw* an attack. They all stated that they heard the sound of glass breaking and saw Josef lying on the floor, bleeding. They concluded that Private Akando must have attacked Josef, since the private was standing over Josef with part of the same bottle that struck Josef still in his hands."

"*No one saw the attack.* That is an important point, Specialist Bluderin, one that could help me win this case."

"Good," Bluderin said. "If you're successful, I humbly suggest that Akando no longer be assigned to guard duty."

Getz removed his glasses to clean them. He grinned widely at Bluderin as he placed them back on.

"We'll see. By the way, you wouldn't know how Akando got all those bruises, would you? He said they came from you and your girlfriend."

"The statements I took from the patrons were all in accord, that they contained Private Akando until the MPs arrived. I'm not drawing any conclusions as to what they did or how they contained him."

"You better hope I win this case," the lieutenant said. "I'm finished questioning you. See you at the hearing."

Bluderin was not impressed with the way Getz was trying to scare him. Maybe I ought to set the lieutenant back a few steps, he thought, and make him a little nervous.

"Yes, sir. Incidentally, I'm surprised that you have not already heard, but McCandley is no longer a captain. He was promoted to major earlier this morning. He called to tell me the good news and, of course, I gave him my warmest congratulations."

Without saying another word, Bluderin had made his point. Getz looked drained. Major McCandley already had been appointed to serve on the evaluation committee regarding Getz's promotion. Now, the major would be chairing the committee.

As Bluderin entered the court-martial lobby, he saw Josef, several of his patrons, and—oddly enough—Peter and Johanna Vanderwerken. He wondered what the Vanderwerkens were doing there. Were they to testify that he and their daughter had attended the wedding with them? What Getz must have not read or overlooked was that McCandley had entered a statement about who sat at his table during the wedding reception. Since McCandley and Bluderin were wedding guests, the off-limits factor did not apply to them. They had been invited to the wedding by German citizens. McCandley had conducted some research and confirmed his recollection that their presence at the wedding was all perfectly legal and appropriate.

Bluderin approached Josef and the Vanderwerkins, shaking their hands. They were friendly to him, even Josef, which pleased him immensely. Peter whispered that he was in attendance to see how the army was going to handle Akando. The Vanderwerkens already had told Lieutenant Getz about their being at the wedding with Bluderin and Gretchen. What Getz did not mention to Bluderin—but Peter now did—was that the Vanderwerkens stated that, although they left the wedding reception before Bluderin and Gretchen, he and their daughter returned to their house shortly afterwards. The "shortly afterwards" period was actually three or four hours later. Bluderin did not want the Vanderwerkens to commit perjury, but "shortly afterwards" was a relative term and could be taken any number of ways. The fact was, after Gretchen called her parents to say she would be spending the night at Bluderin's apartment, the Vanderwerkens asked Bluderin if he would stay overnight at their house instead. They worried about Gretchen's safety. Bluderin agreed when Gretchen said that her parents had no problem with them sharing the same bedroom. However, the Vanderwerkens were fast asleep by the time he and Gretchen had arrived.

"You don't look like a soldier," Josef said, wearing a white bandage over his right eye. "Even in uniform, you look too gentle to be a soldier."

"I'm thankful that you don't hold anything against me, Josef. I'm truly sorry for what happened. It must have been traumatic for you, given what you experienced during the war. Déjà vu was the last thing on earth you needed."

"I could never be mad at you, John. You have always been very kind and respectful to me. I'm directing my bitterness at the source—that psychotic GI who, from what my lawyer told me, has an extensive record of violence and other misbehavior. He hurts the U.S. Army's image. You would think he'd be discharged and sent home."

Bluderin heard some motion in back of him, and he turned to see Lieutenant Getz and Danny Akando enter the courtroom. Bluderin did not realize that he and Gretchen had hurt Akando as much as they did. They guy had bruises all over his neck and face, and he walked rather gingerly, perhaps because of Gretchen's attack on his scrotum. The girl sure knew how to take care of herself.

"It looks as though the hearing is about to begin," Bluderin said. "I wonder why they haven't called for me. They always call me into the courtroom before the proceedings."

"They may not need an interpreter in this case," Josef said.

"Really? I'm surprised. Why?" Bluderin sensed that something was wrong. Had Getz disqualified him from doing his job?

"My lawyer speaks excellent English," Josef said. "Also, there is a legal technicality regarding the case. My place, as you know, is off-limits to GIs. According to proper procedure, I should have notified the German police the second I saw Private Akando anywhere near the Gasthaus. The police would respond immediately, notifying the MPs about the situation along the way. Private Akando's counsel is arguing that I waited too long to call the police. My lawyer is arguing that I was assaulted before I could get to the phone."

"It's my fault," Bluderin said. "Couch and I were going to escort Akando back to Hardt Kaserne when he broke free of Couch's grip and attacked you."

There was a riveting irony to this scenario. In researching the meaning of Solveig's name at the library last evening, Bluderin also had discovered, out of curiosity when thinking about the court martial, that *Akando* meant *ambush*.

"John, I know you and Couch were trying to keep the peace. You wanted to get Akando out of the Gasthaus before he did anything stupid. Things did not turn out that way. At any rate, because of legal technicalities and other issues, both sides are trying to reach an agreement."

"They better not let Akando completely off the hook," Bluderin said. "That would not be fair, not with all the legal precedents having been set with other GI-German altercations long before this one."

"It is not likely that he will get off without some punishment," Josef said. "He was in an off-limits establishment. That is one offense that is going to stick. Both sides concur with that fact."

Lieutenant Getz, Danny Akando, and Josef's attorney walked into the lobby. Akando had a wide smirk on his face. He tried to withdraw the expression upon Lieutenant Getz's prompting, and he made an effort to look serious and scared when he saw Josef Westhoff. Akando extended a hand toward Josef and murmured that he was sorry for what happened, but Josef waved him off. Getz escorted Akando out of the building.

Akando's punishment was extremely mild, in Bluderin's opinion. He was confined to army territory for ninety days—that was it. If Akando were to escape from the confines of the base or field operations maneuvering grounds, he would be sent to Mannheim for two years.

The German lawyer informed Josef about the settlement. All of his medical bills would be paid for by the army, the army would also pay his lawyer's fees, and Josef was to receive a check for punitive damages for an undisclosed amount within thirty days.

Peter Vanderwerken later told Bluderin that the army originally was trying to settle for five-hundred dollars, but Josef's lawyer negotiated successfully for ten thousand. Bluderin doubted Peter knew what the amount was because part of the settlement agreement included the entreaty that the amount was not to be disclosed. It again amazed Bluderin that Walter Lebrecht had any faith in Peter's ability to handle intelligence information.

Whatever the amount was, Josef agreed to the settlement and left the lobby, shaking Bluderin's hand on his way out. Bluderin also said good-bye to the Vanderwerkens, who invited him to dinner. They told him to let him know when he would be available.

He knew it would not be today. He first had to write a document about the settlement before he could leave the base. He was about to go into the courtroom when Lieutenant Getz stopped him in the lobby.

"Sorry if I made you nervous earlier today, Specialist Bluderin. I was on a mission." Getz was apparently pleased with the outcome of the case.

"It's no matter, sir. You were doing your job."

"Well, let's put the issue to sleep. It's all over now. I believe Akando has learned a lesson he will never forget."

"I'm sure he did," Bluderin lied. He did not want to discuss anything further with the lieutenant. "Best of luck on your promotion hearing."

Getz smiled at Bluderin and punched him gently on the shoulder. He knew that Bluderin had a solid working relationship with Major McCandley and perhaps a little influence. It was likely Getz was thinking that it couldn't hurt to be cordial to the clerk.

The settlement document was easy to prepare. It consisted of three pages, simply recording the terms of the settlement for an undisclosed sum and Akando's confinement to base and field operations.

After filing the records, Bluderin drove out of Hardt Kaserne and headed for the Gmünder Market Square. Peter Vanderwerken had told him about a little jewelry store owned by Lieb Born, an Austrian man who made all the jewelry in the shop. Beautiful stuff, Peter had said, but the guy did not make a lot of money, so he was always willing to negotiate.

Monika Müller had told him that Solveig would be returning to her apartment at the Oasis very soon. He was not sure if she had already arrived, but he wanted to have a present for her when she did.

As he entered the shop, he noticed how the Austrian's glasses magnified the wrinkles on his eyelids. The man appeared to be setting a diamond into a gold band. His eyes looked over his glasses as he greeted Bluderin.

"May I help you, son? I'll be with you in a minute, after I secure this setting."

"Please, take your time."

Bluderin looked into a bulletproof glass case, secured with stainless steel edges and locks, at a wide assortment of rings for ladies. There were numerous styles, varying in what he guessed were ancient to avant-garde designs—made with tooled and enameled gold, adorned with rubies and emeralds, others set with jargons and pearls, silver rings set with turquoise and chalcedony. They were exquisite and expensive. He could not afford any of them, even if he were able to negotiate fifty percent off their list price.

A less expensive assortment of rings, crescents, lockets, small brooches, bracelets, and necklaces were displayed in another glass case.

The jeweler unlocked it and winked at Bluderin. His eyes again looked over his glasses below a mass of unkempt, gray hair that reminded Bluderin of Einstein.

"See anything here that appeals to your eyes and budget?"

"They are all appealing to the eye," Bluderin said, "and much more in line with my budget than those in the other case. I don't know what to get her. All the jewelry I've seen her wear seems to exude simplicity and elegance, if that makes any sense—nothing too ornate or romantic."

The Austrian winked at Bluderin with a fatherly gesture. "As for simplicity and elegance, let's take a look."

Although Bluderin intended to buy a ring for Solveig, the jeweler picked up a necklace with some kind of jeweler's instrument or tool that looked like a long pair of tweezers. He held the necklace in the light of a table lamp. A semi-transparent, bronze-colored stone hung from a thinly crafted, silver chain. The stone was principally brownish gold in color, but it also held flecks of red, blue, green, and black within its translucent surface.

"Interesting. What kind of stone is it?" Bluderin asked.

"Amber," the jeweler said. "Amber is not technically a stone. It is a fossil resin, something like sap from trees that turns rock-hard over a long period of time. This piece could be centuries old, for all I know."

Bluderin held the piece of amber in his hand and thought about Solveig Evensen. He was enamored of the piece. It seemed to emit sunlight, as though it had captured a ray of sun as it hardened into a stone-like density. The flecks within it reminded him of Solveig in the sense that, like the piece of amber, she had a smooth, outward beauty and an inward mystery of experience that made her complex, sophisticated, troubled, and with an inner strength he much admired.

"Years ago, I purchased more than fifty pieces of amber from a fellow jeweler who escaped to Austria from his home in Katowice, Poland, during the war. He desperately needed money, and I was intrigued by the luminosity of the amber. I had never worked with this material until I bought it. This piece is one of my favorites. I'm proud of what I did with it, but it has problems. If you think your girlfriend would like it, I'll sell it to you for a very cheap price. If she does not like it, you can always return it for a ring but, as you can see, the rings are more expensive."

Bluderin examined the amber once again, along with the fine silver chain. The Austrian was a superb craftsman, as Peter had said. The necklace was an article of perfection.

"I don't see any problems with it."

"When I cut the amber into its present shape—that of a droplet of water, as I call it—I had to trim the upper end into a very thin slot, to fit the tip of the amber into its holder. Amber can be brittle. If you strike it against a hard surface, like a kitchen counter, it is liable to crack."

Bluderin again thought about Solveig. Like the amber, she too was brittle, with brittle meaning *fragile*, holding in the angst of her molested childhood that, if she delved too deeply into it, could shatter her otherwise controlled persona.

"The lady takes good care of her jewelry," Bluderin said. "I will advise her of its brittleness."

"I have it listed for three hundred marks. You can have it for two hundred."

Realizing that he could have the necklace for the equivalent of only a little over fifty dollars, Bluderin quickly took out his wallet and paid the Austrian before he could change his mind. After giving Bluderin his change, the jeweler folded the necklace and placed it in a white-cushioned, silver-colored box, then wrapped the box in green felt.

As he left the jewelry shop, Bluderin imagined Solveig wearing the necklace with her short black dress. It occurred to him that, if he and she eventually were to go their separate ways, she would always have a symbol of what he thought of her, how he adored her sensuous, gentle, and brave character. Wondering what Solveig felt about the events regarding her leave of absence, a stanza from Rilke's poem "Erinnerung," or "Memory" crept into the ridges of his mind.

> *As you wait, awaiting the one*
> *to make your finite life grow:*
> *the mighty, the uncommon,*
> *the awakening of stone,*
> *the depths to be opened below.*

He drove to the Oasis, hoping that Solveig would be there and that the closeness between them was still alive. Then again, her dealing with so many issues back in Norway could have changed her sentiments toward him in ways he could never understand. He hoped not. She was the water to his survival.

Twelve

◄○►

A jolt of blood skipped through Bluderin's arteries when he saw Solveig Evensen at the Oasis. The second he opened the door to the café, she ran into the lounge to greet him, wrapping her arms around his neck and planting a long, moist kiss on his lips.

His hands trembled on the sides of her waist; her intimate greeting made his head dizzy and weightless. He was overcome with her responsive warmth, the golden complexion of her skin, and her uninhibited, lavender-scented smile.

"It seems like a year since I last saw you," he said. "When did you get back?"

She leaned her head on his chest as she spoke, her soft blonde hair tickling his nose. "This morning. I had to request an extension in my bereavement leave so I could complete the legal process regarding the will. It hasn't been a year, John—only six weeks."

"It felt like forever," he said. "I'm surprised you're not taking the day off to recuperate from your lengthy return trip."

"The journey from Molde, by ferry and train, to Schwäbisch Gmünd was stressful," she said. "The North Sea had no mercy yesterday, bouncing the boat around like a rubber ball. I had no choice but to work today. Monika and Frau Müller had to leave. Come. I'll tell you about it."

There was no one else in the café, so he figured they would

have plenty of time to talk without her attention being diverted to customers. She poured champagne into two stemmed glasses, and they drank a toast to their reunion.

Solveig had accomplished a lot during her stay in Molde. After she and her aunt, Jora Bjornsen, had arranged for Knut Evensen's cremation and memorial service, Solveig was able to liquidate all of her father's assets, including his cottage on the coast of Molde for what she described as *a handsome sum of money*. Bluderin was interested to know how "handsome" the sum was, but he was not going to inquire into her personal business. Instead, he listened thoughtfully to her description of how relieved she felt, *like Hercules unchained*, as she phrased it, in putting all the bitterness and belongings associated with her father behind her. She looked like she had undergone an emotional rebirth.

He placed the little box wrapped in green felt on the bar. "Welcome back, goddess." He kissed Solveig's hand and looked deeply into her dense blue eyes.

She unwrapped the package with great care, making sure to keep the green felt intact without making a tear. After gently lifting the silver lid off the box, she looked at the amber tucked into the tufted, white-silk lining. She removed the necklace from the box and held the amber piece up, directly under a ceiling light. She had not yet said a word.

He worried that amber was not to her liking, since he had never noticed any among her collection of jewelry.

"John, it's lovely—elegant and simple, yet complex and intriguing. I love the miniature bits of twigs or minerals—or whatever they are—inside the stone."

He did not tell her that amber was not technically a stone, although she probably already knew.

Solveig directed her voice toward the small kitchen behind the bar. "Aunt Jora, I want you to meet a friend of mine."

A woman of Solveig's height but a good twenty pounds heavier, whose once blonde hair had turned silvery white, came out of the kitchen. Her soft, visibly veined hands shook Bluderin's with a strong grip as Solveig introduced them. Jora Bjornsen looked like a woman who had seen much in her life—the proverbial good, bad, and ugly—and took it all in stride. She had an endearing smile, and her silver-blue eyes shone in wisdom's light. When Solveig showed her the necklace, Jora winked at Bluderin.

"Solveig, your friend likes you very, very much," she said. Jora spoke in *Hochdeutsche*; her voice was rhythmic and gentle, pleasing to the ear. She excused herself and returned to the kitchen, saying that she could see that Bluderin was hungry. She would make him a sandwich.

Solveig accompanied her aunt into the kitchen. When she returned to the bar, she was wearing the necklace. The amber set off her black dress and added depth to her golden skin.

"Where did you find it?" she asked him.

When he described the location of the jewelry shop, she recognized it immediately. She had been there several times, she said. On one such occasion she had purchased a red garnet ring with a sterling silver band.

"The Austrian jeweler, Lieb Born, comes in here on occasion," she said. "I'm baffled that I've never seen anything in his shop made of amber."

"I suspect the reason you never saw any is because you're always shopping for rings more than anything else," he said. "The jeweler told me it would be too easy for amber rings to crack, since rings come into contact with hard surfaces much more frequently than necklaces or earrings."

"Amber is fragile, is that what he meant?" Solveig brought the amber close to her lips and blew on it softly.

"I told Herr Lieb that you take good care of your jewelry," he said. "I'm sure it will last forever, like your infinite beauty."

"Stop it." She faked a pout and held his hand. "You can be goofy at times, but I appreciate the attention. You make me feel special."

Their conversation drew to a close when six people walked into the café—two at the bar and four in the lounge.

"Why do people always come in here an hour before closing?" Solveig whispered to Bluderin.

When Jora Bjornsen served Bluderin his sandwich, Solveig suggested that he take it to her apartment. He thought that was a good idea. He would not be able to talk with Solveig since she was busy, and he would have some privacy to write or read while he waited for her. He also needed to give more thought to some of the things she had said.

She had told him that Monika Müller had taken her mother and Frau Müller with her on a two-week vacation to a resort in Corsica overlooking the Ligurian Sea. The resort was owned by one of Monika's lovers, a Frenchman who, with his wife, apparently had a ménage a trois understanding with Monika. In the meantime, Solveig and her aunt would manage the Oasis.

Jora Bjornsen was staying in Frau Müller's apartment. Bluderin, of course, thought that was a splendid idea, so he could be alone with Solveig without interfering with Jora's privacy or she interfering with theirs.

Solveig also had told him that her relationship with Monika had cooled off. It was a mutual decision, with Monika deliberating whether or not to accept her lovers' invitation to live with them in Corsica.

All of this was fine with Bluderin until Solveig told him that she, too, would be leaving Schwäbisch Gmünd, probably within a month or two. She planned on going away for good. She had been offered telephone operator positions in Belgium and England. However, she had not yet made any decisions regarding the matter. She was bored with being a telephone operator; she wanted to do something more challenging. Bluderin felt a fluid thickness, like a stream of kelp, run down his throat when Solveig told him of her intentions.

She had told him that she thought about their relationship during her stay in Molde. She had learned something from their love-making. It had transformed her, but it was not Bluderin—on his own, meaning simply as a man—who had changed her. It was the *endearment of intimacy* he bestowed, as she called it, that moved her, taken her to where she latently had wanted to go. Now, to acclimate to her new identity, she needed to be alone for a while. He could not understand her sentiment.

"I have to become comfortable with who I am," she had said. "I need to know fully what is in my heart before I can go forward. And I need time to heal. "

Bluderin had told Solveig that he wanted to visit her, wherever she went, when he was relieved of active duty. She responded that she would be ready to see him again when the time came, but first he had to promise her that he would continue his education.

They recognized they had "difficulties" to resolve in determining the future path of their relationship. Age was one of them, with their being ten years apart. It was not the number of years that mattered, however, but their *accent in time*. He needed to become more educated. She was investigating the feasibility of becoming a language teacher at the high-school level, a position that would enable her to apply the academic credentials she already had earned.

"We are a mistake in time," she had said.

He did not accept her suggestion. He sat down on the futon and tried to clear his head of Solveig's plans. The whole idea was maddening.

Leaning back with a notebook and pen in his hands, his mind drifted to trees and fields, lakes, castles, and animals, especially birds. One element of his mind focused on a section of a forest he and Solveig had visited. Standing near a tree-lined pond, he was fascinated by an old tree stump nestled in the midst of maple saplings. His hand moved slowly as he wrote, engaged in the tree stump.

Somewhere below your weathered stance
roots drift in a sluice of water, broken,
going away.

I awake like a thought, spirited
by your vacant presence,
bodiless as motes of air.

An intense following of green,
breathing omnipresence, scatters
like secrets rapt in quiet.

Trees shift, twisted from the rape
of each day, clutched
to the pearl-covered palm of sky
(but it is you who truly remains
the world's core and muted bond).

What will happen? Will
white petals dress your grave?
Will deer form a path, their striding
rhythm a pulse for the gone?

I ask to exist. I whisper names:
"wind's shoe, water-heart,"
and believe the dead are listening.

He read the verse over several times and, without much thinking, named it "The Vacant Presence." He did not know what he thought of the poem, or if it were indeed a poem. He was not sure if he liked it, but it seemed to be telling him something he needed to know.

The notebook and pen fell to the floor. He lay down on the futon and closed his eyes. The events surrounding the court martial hearing, the risk in choosing the amber necklace, and the intensity of seeing Solveig lilted him into sleep with phosphorescent dreams. Images of Solveig appeared intermittently amid unrelated dreams of his future as a college student, followed by disturbances about how he could make a living.

Writing poems was the only thing he wanted to do, but the thought of making a living by writing poetry was idiotic. Teaching was a possibility, but he was not thrilled with the idea.

He found himself in Shaker Heights, Ohio, in his uncle's insurance office. He was sitting in front of a large, oak desk, in back of which was a wall of gray, metal filing cabinets. Pictures of his uncle's wife and kids were on both sides of the desktop. A name plate bearing "Walter W. Williamson" was placed prominently on the front edge of the desk. Framed licenses and various certificates covered the walls on both sides of the desk, along with a plaque. Walter Williamson's personal motto or proverb was inscribed on the plaque: "I never met a man who did not sell."

Bluderin was not sure if the statement was imbedded in his uncle's personal philosophy or an act of self-defense. Yet the words did ring of an overriding truth: everyone is a peddler. We all sell something, whether it's religion, law, medicine, motherhood, sex, talent, or anything else. He wondered what he could sell to make a living. Selling real estate or insurance was definitely out of the picture. He did not deem those career choices trustworthy. He could identify no career in which he thought he could be happy—a definitive and unquestionable fact—unless he changed his personality. He did not believe he could do that, change himself to a point where he could convince himself he liked a job that he knew he hated. Yet he had no choice. Since he would need to make a living, he would have to play charades.

The thought of grooming his hair and wearing a white shirt and tie made him feel weak. The only compromise to writing poetry would be to write novels and see them turned into films. After accomplishing that most unlikely scenario, he could then retire, rich and famous, and devote the remainder of his life to writing poetry. He could go anywhere and observe whatever interested him. Poems would emerge out of those observations.

He went into Solveig's bedroom to look out the window at the mountain slope. He gave some more thought to taking a European out. If Solveig decided she did not want him living with her, he would remain in Germany. He could find some kind of nocturnal job, such as a janitor or watchman, and write during the day. He could estrange himself from society in a country like Germany or Belgium. Unlike the U.S., nothing would be expected of him here. He would not have the burden of rising to his family's expectations. People in Germany or Belgium would expect nothing of him other than what they saw. People do not expect much of anything out of a foreigner or expatriate.

Returning to the futon, he considered going to a university in Germany, perhaps the Pädagogische Hochschule, where he could study to become a teacher. However, he could not formulate his thoughts any further when he heard footsteps ascending the stairs.

Solveig came into the apartment, carrying a couple of record albums and a bottle of Riesling. As Bluderin followed her into the kitchen, she reached high into a cupboard for two wine glasses. Her legs grew to mid-thigh in her reach. Bluderin kissed her lightly on the back of her neck.

"How was the quiet, John? Were you able to write?"

"I wrote something, but I'm not sure if it is anything meaningful. I also started rereading Günter Grass' *Cat and Mouse* but fell asleep. I think Joachim Mahlke's protruding Adam's apple and the screwdriver bobbing between his shoulder blades were a little too much for me to digest in my bereft state of mind."

"The Great Mahlke—he is one conspicuous character," Solveig said. "Everything about him is uproarious." She told Bluderin to take the book with him, so he could finish reading it at Hardt Kaserne during work breaks.

As they sat, sipping wine and listening to Brahms' Symphony Number Two, conducted by Herbert Von Karajan, Solveig talked some more about coming to grips with the awful memories of her father during her time in Molde. She had evolved from a highly troubled girl who once considered having a clitoridectomy to curb her sexual desire into the freedom of a sensuous, glamorous woman who was pleased to explore the fine essence of her sexuality. She leaned against Bluderin and kissed his neck and ear. He held his arm around her and cherished her loving gestures.

"Let me see what you wrote today."

Her request frightened him. He was unsure of the poem's value and skeptical about what Solveig would think of it. She was intellectually mature. She had learned more, knew a lot more languages and, from what he had ascertained through their conversations, had read as much or more than he had. He was not so much concerned about whether she liked the poem—that would be a matter of taste. What worried him was the possibility that she could find the poem naïve or juvenile. With mixed feelings he decided to let her read the piece. First, however, he would excuse himself to take a shower.

"Just a minute," she said before he headed for the bathroom. She went into her bedroom and returned with a pair of hair shears, a razor, and some shaving cream. She asked him to trim the hair around his genitals as well as his face.

"Anything for you," he said, and left for the bathroom. When he got into the shower, he lathered his pubic hair. The razor was sharper than he realized and, before long, he rid his pubic area and testicles completely of any signs of hair. As he looked at his appearance in the mirror, he felt younger and incredibly aroused.

Solveig was removing her dress when he entered the bedroom. She smiled at him, noticing his inspired state.

"I like what you wrote," she said. "It confirmed something within me, linking life and death with infinity. We could very well be soul mates. Let me give you a soul-kiss before I shower."

Their tongues entwined, gently wrestling with each other, and they felt their hearts beating rapidly in unison. She then removed the rest of her clothes, threw on a nightgown, and disappeared into the hallway. He went into the living room to turn on the stereo and play an album of Chopin's nocturnes. He returned to the bedroom and waited for her.

When she stepped into the bedroom and removed her nightgown, he noticed that she had shaved her mons so thoroughly that the pink, inner lips of her vagina were clearly visible. Her nudity gleamed from within as she stood near the bed.

As they kissed, their presence turned into many presences, each one growing in intimacy and desire. It was at this time, in the most erotic and spiritual moments in life, when their hands created energy through touch, when a temperature reckoned of dandelion texture and simplicity. Transfixed, they were stars in the bell light of their passions. Nothing could touch them, other than their selves.

He would attend to her all night, not leaving an iota of her skin without the anointing worship of his lips. She responded in a similar way, tasting the warmth of his rigid manhood and later screaming a newly discovered octave when she felt him move inside her.

"What do you think of heterosexuality, now that you have

experienced it with me, in light of the suffering you endured as a young girl?" he asked her in the morning.

"I think how the same physical act can be so violent, ruthless, and ugly in one context, and yet so beautiful and life-affirming, a means to achieve nirvana, in another."

"It was sheer nirvana for me," he said. "I've never before experienced anything remotely close to how we made love."

"Was I as good as Gretchen Vanderwerken?"

Her question stunned him. She did not seem to be upset at all, but she was definitely interested.

"How do you know about Gretchen?"

"I've known the Vanderwerkens for several years. I met them through Walter Lebrecht and Klaus Griesinger who, as you know, are good friends with Peter Vanderwerken. *Very good friends, especially Klaus*," Solveig said. "I suspect that Peter and Klaus are having an affair."

Bluderin winced when his mind's eye created an image of Peter getting it on with Klaus. It was not pretty.

"That could explain his sexual disinterest in Johanna," he said.

"When I talked with Johanna on the phone today, she told me about the wedding and your attendance. She also told me about her propositioning you. She thought, understandably, that my friendship with you was platonic. I informed her otherwise and set her up with a nice man, an Oasis customer, a widower who is lonely and starving for a woman's touch."

He was pleased to hear what Solveig had done for Johanna. He had avoided seeing the Vanderwerkens because of her.

"I hope Johanna finds fulfillment," he said. "She's a good woman."

"You never answered my question," she reminded him, playfully pinching his nipples. "Tell me. I need to know. How do I compare?"

Her sense of competition amused him, and he was flattered. "Solveig, there is no comparison," he said. "Gretchen and I are completely different people. The sex was a physical release, a one-time opportunistic swing, for both of us. We knew that. There were no pretenses being made."

She seemed comforted by his answer. "According to Johanna, Gretchen told her the same thing." She rolled over, sat on top of Bluderin, and guided him into her. He was sore, but her moist softness was irresistible. He watched the amber necklace as she rode him slowly, up and down, squeezing him with her vaginal muscles. The amber swung slowly from one breast to the other, back and forth, like a pendulum clock. Her eyes watered as she let go with a shivering orgasm.

"I never knew how much I wanted this," she said. "I was in denial for such a long time."

Bluderin realized that he also had been in denial about not having any genuine feelings.

"I was convinced that nobody could ever get near me, that I was simply playing a game," he said. "I was sure that nobody could touch my soul. I was wrong."

She had cracked his psychological shell, much like the cracking of an egg, and he knew he could not get it back again. In a similar way, she had broken out of her glass bubble of denial and was learning how to live with her newly developed persona. How was he going to handle her absence? What would become of her? He rubbed the sapphire and silver ring she had given him against her amber necklace. They had touched each other's soul. Would their feelings for each other be enough to give them strength on their own?

It would have to be that way. She was creating a new life. He was going to be facing challenges that would test him more than he could ever believe.

Thirteen

—◄○►—

The departure of Solveig Evensen spurred an avalanche of emptiness in Bluderin's mind. He was angry. Could he could have been one of the reasons she needed to get away? Did the intelligence community make her leave? Or was she being straight with him, that her mission was to build a new life and create a better world on her own terms? Whatever it was, he had to inhale the death of her intimacy. He rubbed the silver and sapphire ring and looked blindly into the sky.

She was in England. Frau Müller had told him that Solveig became certified to teach at the high school level. She recently had taken a position teaching modern languages at the Newlands School, a coed boarding school in East Sussex. Malin Müller, Frau Müller's niece and Monika's younger sister—who could damned near pass as Monika's twin, right down to her lavender eyes—had replaced Solveig at the Oasis.

He had hoped to avoid Malin, Frau Müller, and the Oasis altogether, as the café only reinforced the thud of Solveig's absence. Yet he would have to stop in there at least once a week to see if there was a letter waiting for him. Solveig had already sent him one, describing her apartment near the school's campus, how she loved having a fireplace, and what fun it was to observe her new surroundings and students. It is enriching, she had written, and she described the practice of teaching as her healer. She ended the letter calling Bluderin her *literarisch und lieblich Seele*, meaning *literary and lovely soul*. He did not know what to make of that term of endearment, but it helped him take a pause from his psychological abyss.

To numb the misery of dealing with his loss, he began running long distances. He always ran alone, and he realized that feeling 'the loneliness of the long distance runner' to curb the loneliness he felt when thinking about her could be an exercise in paradoxical futility. Outwardly that could be the case, but inwardly (or *intowardly*, as he called it, inventing a new word), the running eased the pain caused by her absence and relaxed his nerves. He was averaging ten miles a day.

It was during one of those runs when he witnessed the annihilation of Daniel Akando. He had been running on a path toward Aalen that ran parallel to a road, about thirty feet away. There was a short clearing of trees he had approached when he heard a car coming toward the clearing. He discovered that the car was an army jeep. As it sped past the clearing, he ran out to the road and watched the jeep soaring away. It looked like it was about to go airborne when a human figure dressed in tightly fitted, camouflaged fatigues appeared from the woods and aimed a gun at the jeep. When Bluderin heard the distinct, muffled sound of a Luger, he ducked and crawled back to the path. He had no idea who was driving the jeep, but he reversed the direction of his run and headed back to Hardt Kaserne.

He kept reflecting on the image of the figure at the edge of the road, firing the Luger. He could not determine if the figure was shooting at the driver or the jeep. It had been dusk when the shooting took place, making it difficult for him to see things clearly. He could not see the color of the shooter's skin or hair. The head seemed to be covered with a mask, a smooth form-fitting mask, as though it were made of a black nylon stocking. The body he watched appeared and disappeared within a second or two. It leapt high, back into the woods, strong and graceful as a deer.

He knew someone who could move in a similar way—Leda Beschwörung. The shape of the figure, petite and firm, and the disciplined swiftness and smoothness of its movements were identical to hers. Yet that would be impossible, he reasoned. When he had last seen Leda—*the evening when he delivered the Luger to her*—she said that she was going to be assigned to Berlin. She would no longer be working in southern Germany.

Maybe she had lied to him, to throw him off guard, in case something like this 'incident' happened in Schwäbisch Gmünd. Yet how on earth would she know that a GI would steal a jeep and drive on that particular road at that particular hour? It made no sense, and it didn't matter. Whether the shooter was Leda or not, he knew nothing. He never saw any jeep tearing down the road, never saw a shooter or heard a shot, never felt an impact from any car crashing.

By the time he had gotten back to Hardt Kaserne, everyone was talking about Akando. The most consistent story among the troops was that Akando had hot-wired the jeep. When he had driven up to the gate, he told the guard on duty that he had orders to go to Göppingen. When the guard asked to see the paperwork, Akando struck him in the face with an empty bottle of whiskey, the same tactic he used to assault Josef Westoff.

Word spread around Hardt Kaserne that Danny had been intoxicated and drugged. He had sped out of the gate toward Aalen, weaving between lanes before he swerved onto a hill on the left-hand side of the road. The jeep spun around, slid back onto the road, busted through a fence bordering a cliff, and went off the cliff, crashing down into a valley. The vehicle landed upside down, launching Akando about fifty feet away into a rocky stream.

The MPs had assumed that this scenario was what happened, judging from the tire marks on the hill, road, and fence. Akando's body was decapitated, and part of his severed right leg was found under the steering wheel. Before Danny's court-martial meeting, Bluderin bitterly remembered telling Lieutenant Getz that Akando needed psychiatric help. Getz did not care about trying to help Akando. The lieutenant simply wanted to win his case.

The day after Akando's death, Bluderin translated the MPs' account of the accident for the German police, who had arrived at the accident scene the same time as the MPs. What surprised him most was that there was an addendum to the MPs' report, a statement taken from Wiley Couch and Jürgen Treuge. They were in Couch's Mercedes on their way to Josef's Gasthaus and stopped at the scene before the police arrived. Couch and Treuge's statement was nearly identical to that of the MPs. They had not actually seen the accident, but they noticed the skid marks on the road and the broken fence. When they got out of the car to see what happened, they looked down into the valley and saw the jeep on fire. They had observed no one else near the scene of the accident until the police arrived.

Bluderin tried to forget about the accident as he sat on a large boulder overlooking valleys and mountainous hills. The Drei Kaiserberge consisted of three mountains called the Hohenstaufen, Rechberge, and Stuifen. Bluderin, Riki Taar, and Howard and Diane James were picnicking on the Hohenstaufen, situated close to the ruins of an ancestral castle, a reminder of the Staufer Emperors period. Howard was painting an Impressionistic rendering of the Rems Valley. The canvas and oil paints had his devout attention. His wide forehead was as still as a statue while his arms moved deftly, like those of a boxer sparring. His massive hands, the color of peanut butter with deep pink fingernails, made delicate, intricate strokes on the canvas. As he played with shades of blue, red, and yellow, his forehead wrinkled vertically. He gray eyes were locked, as if he had already seen the image he was painting, with the canvas simply being a medium to transfer his vision. Diane, Riki, and Bluderin were being quiet so they would not disturb him.

Diane was knitting what was to become a baby's yellow sweater. Her thin fingers moved like a classical guitarist's as she knitted while observing the evolution of her husband's creation. Her lucid, ecru eyes cast an aura, a radiance that shone along her India ink curls and on her full, ruby smile.

Bluderin wondered if her internal beauty rose outwardly because of her euphoric mood. She recently had learned that she was pregnant, telling Riki and Bluderin how God had blessed her and Howard. Diane was a devout Christian, and a silver necklace with a large, golden crucifix stood out from her brown skin and navy blue sweater and white blouse.

Bluderin and Riki decided to go for a walk so they could talk without disturbing Howard or Diane. He had been ambivalent about accepting Riki's invitation to the picnic. He was not interested in developing a relationship with her, but he was also bored. Having nothing else to do, he had accepted Riki's invitation, primarily because she had invited Howard and Diane.

Riki was dressed differently from a traditional Fraülein. She wore a bright orange sweater, blue jeans, and sneakers. Her attire reminded him of American girls back home, something which she may have intended. They stopped along their walk to observe the movements of a waterfall spilling into a stream.

"This is my place," she said. "I come here often, sometimes with my children. Kane likes to fish in the stream, Eve likes to pick wildflowers, and I come here for the quiet and the problems it takes me away from."

Bluderin could sense sadness in Riki's eyes and voice. He understood that she had it tough. It was a challenge to provide for her children on her salary, although her stepfather and mother had custody of the children. They lived with her parents, while she lived in a small, three-room apartment several blocks away from them. It was better that way—less arguments with her parents—especially her stepfather, she mentioned.

"I'm sure you already know some things about me," she said. "GIs love to gossip. They're worse than the nosy old ladies in my apartment building who watch everything I do."

"I've noticed quite a few of them flirting with you in the laundry," Bluderin said, "as well as in the library, when you're working there."

"You know what they're after," she said. "They only want sex, and they certainly don't have a lot of women on base to choose from."

Bluderin did not believe that all the GIs on base wanted sex—and nothing else—from Riki. Some of them seemed to be genuinely interested in her. He was going to tell her so, but she began telling him about her upbringing.

Her biological father, with whom she had a great relationship, died when she was nine. She and her stepfather never got get along. She was always a nuisance to him, and he paid no attention to her. However, her stepfather did enjoy her children, and he helped take good care of them. Riki gave her parents money each month to help provide for Eve and Kane.

"Men would be disappointed with me if I did offer myself to them," she said. "When I had my third baby, Kane, the nuns who delivered him performed a Cesarean section and butchered my abdomen. It is marked with a lot of ugly scars. The nuns did it on purpose. They said I was a slut when I was a teenager. That is why, if I do have sex, it has to be at night with the lights off."

"How awful," he said. Why was she telling him such personal information when he barely knew her? He guessed she needed to vent whatever was bothering her at the moment. He felt like he was a priest hearing confession.

"That's why my husband left me. He could not stand the sight of my scars."

Riki sat down on the grass and looked off into the distance. Bluderin sat down next to her and gave her a comforting hug. Riki's legs were long and slender. Her bright auburn hair, hollow cheeks, and virescent eyes set off her skin, a light shade of peach.

"I'm sure there are men who would not give your scars a second thought," he said. "You are an intelligent and attractive woman. Accentuate your positive traits. You could be charming if you weren't so defensive. I've seen a good number of GIs put off by your sarcastic remarks."

"I'm sorry for bothering you with ranting over my morbid past, John. Tell me about yourself."

There was nothing he wanted to tell her. "There isn't much to say. I haven't done anything noteworthy."

"You don't share much with anyone, do you? With the exception of Howard James, I've never seen you socialize with other GIs. Why is that? Is it because you're both damned good-looking, like Poitier and Redford, with well bred manners?" She winked at him after making the comment.

"We share common interests," he said. "Not many GIs want to talk about art and literature."

"Have you written anything lately?" she asked.

He recalled her having discovered the rough draft of a poem in his laundry. "Just a few notes. I don't feel inspired to write." He had not written a thing since Solveig had left for England.

As they stood up to rejoin Howard and Diane, she grabbed him by the waist and pulled him toward her. She kissed him hard on the lips and stroked his back.

"Tell me you love me," she said. "You don't have to mean it. Just say it."

He could not talk when she drew him closer, kissing him deeply.

His hands ran down her vertebrae. She was incredibly thin, causing him to think she could be anorectic. She had not eaten anything when they picnicked. She was also definitely neurotic. How in hell could he say he loved her when they had only spent an hour alone together? What would she do if he didn't say it?

"You don't have to say anything," she said. "Just hold me."

The off-emerald gleam of Riki's eyes disturbed him. He looked at her with a pretense of affection. Of course he could not say that he loved her, but somehow, through her openness and tender touch—in her insane way—she breathed in his mind, her face intricately clear. Yet he was scared over how dangerous this woman could be. He had made a mistake in accepting the picnic invitation.

"It is getting late, Riki. We ought to go. I'm sure Howard and Diane want to get back to their apartment."

She opened his right hand and placed a ring in its palm. Bluderin was astonished to see the silver ring with the black opal gem. It was the same ring that Monika Müller had handed him to give to Gustav Erdmann. His intelligence contact on base had informed him that someone would be delivering a ring for him to give to Günter Mann. He had no idea that Ricki was in on intelligence matters and would be the person to deliver the ring. He placed it on his right pinky finger since the left one already had a ring on it, the silver and sapphire one that Solveig had given him. Was he passing along messages copied on tiny pieces of microfiche hidden beneath the gem? He knew nothing; he was just an errand boy.

Howard had finished the painting. As it is with Impressionist works, the picture looked a little fuzzy or haphazard when viewed up close, but it took on an amazing clarity when you stepped back a few feet and looked at it again. Its likeness to the Rems Valley was undeniable.

"The chiaroscuro effects of the painting are stunning," Bluderin said.

"The depths of light are remarkable. How did you do that?" Riki asked.

"Plein-air paintings often have that quality," Howard said, smiling at their compliments.

Diane was beaming in pride of her husband's talent. Her huge ecru eyes looked at him as she sighed, her open smile showing a perfect set of teeth, the whitest Bluderin had ever seen.

They walked in the direction of Hardt Kaserne. Riki was silent, not saying a word, just looking at Bluderin intermittently and smiling crookedly, her lips elusively hidden against her teeth.

Howard and Diane crossed the street onto the road leading to their apartment. The James couple had absolutely loved the views from the mountain, and Riki said she would take them to other places that were just as inspiring as the view from the Hohenstaufen.

"Let's look at our schedules and see when we can do this again," she said.

Riki then took off in another direction, toward her parents' apartment, saying she was going to have dinner with her children. Bluderin offered to see her home, but she declined his gesture, saying she did not want her parents to observe her with another GI, not yet.

After Riki and Bluderin went their separate ways, he heard a car beep. Wiley Couch drove his Mercedes onto the shoulder of the road. He was with Jürgen Treuge.

"We're on our way to Bavaria, to a town called Nördlingen. Care to come along?" Couch asked.

The burly, black-haired Couch and the blond, slender Treuge looked as if they were understudies for Laurel and Hardy. The common bond in their distinctly different ebony and cyanic eyes was the gleam of alcohol.

"I'd like to, but I have to work in the morning," Bluderin said.

"So do I," Couch said. "We'll be back tonight, although it will probably be late—after midnight. Don't worry. You won't turn into a pumpkin."

"What's in Nördlingen?" Bluderin asked. "Is it worth losing sleep over?"

"It's an interesting place," Jürgen said. "The town is located in the middle of a giant meteorite crater called the Nördlinger Ries. It is also one of only three towns in Germany with a completely established city wall."

Jürgen's short description stirred Bluderin's interest. As he took a back seat in the car, Jürgen handed him a beer. Opening the flip-top bottle of Weißbier, he took a healthy sip and appreciated the way it quenched his thirst. It was strange seeing Couch and Jürgen still hanging around together. It was not so long ago when Jürgen had been incredibly protective of Karin Erdmann, always watching her to make sure that no man got too close to her. Then Vera Luchterhand has her way with him, Couch comes along and grabs Karin for his own, and Jürgen seems to be overjoyed with the way things turned out. Was there any accounting for friendship?

Jürgen offered Bluderin a drink from his bottle of Steinhäger. Bluderin thought how the fragrance of the gin's juniper berries reminded him of Solveig. Christ, he missed that woman.

"Thanks, Jürgen, but I'll pass," he said. "So tell me, why are we going to Nördlingen? I'm sure it's not the crater or city wall that's attracting you, Wiley."

"A pub, of course," Couch said. "It's located just outside of town, about a quarter mile before you get to Nördlingen. The pub is rustic, a renovated barn, but let me tell you something about it. Jürgen and I went out there last week, and the place was buzzing with stellar babes. We met a girl named Winifride there whom I want you to meet. She's a real sweetheart, and she looks like a centerfold right out of *Playboy*. Jürgen and I didn't score with her, probably because we got a little too drunk and let it slip that we had steady girlfriends. I think she'd go for you, though. Jürgen and I were building you up. We told Winifride that you were a really good-looking guy from a wealthy family, and that you were very thoughtful and polite."

"Thanks, I guess," Bluderin said. "There's nothing like a girl having false expectations of me before I meet her. Why did you bother to do that?"

"So you have can have a gorgeous babe to bonk when you take your European out," Couch said.

"What makes you think I'm doing that?"

Couch looked in the rearview mirror at Bluderin and shook his head. "It's only a matter of common sense, John. I mean, shit, how can you even be *thinking* of going back to the States with the blacks rioting in every major city, with the hippies and other war protestors busting heads with the police and National Guard, and with LBJ escalating the war in Vietnam? Face it, the whole country is burning up. It's going down like the Titanic."

Bluderin believed that all the issues Couch was talking about would settle down, but he had made a point. "Maybe you're right. I don't know what I'm going to do. I could go to school in Europe."

"Now you're thinking right," Couch said. "You could hang out with Jürgen and me."

Couch's proposition did not appeal to him. There had to be better alternatives to drinking his life away. Luckily, Couch's driving was fine. He knew how to pace himself.

"I'm surprised to see you two palling around again."

"Why is that?" Jürgen asked.

"The situation with Karin Erdmann," Bluderin said.

Jürgen laughed and gulped down a swig of Steinhäger. "Wiley and I have it all figured out and squared away, don't we, Couch? We're both happy with how things turned out. With Karin, Couch had his first virgin, and I've got a girl who could suck the marrow out of my bones. Have you seen Vera lately, John? She looks terrific—

new hairdo and stylish makeup, and she's lost weight through diet and exercise—she's as svelte as a top model. She says I'm the best she's ever had. I tell you, Vera worships every inch of me."

"Is that a fact?" Bluderin said. Jürgen was being an arrogant little prick.

"You better believe it." Jürgen continued bragging. "Vera will do whatever I ask her to, whenever and wherever."

"That's right," Couch said. "Jürgen has Vera trained just the way he wants her."

Couch was taking Jürgen for a ride in more ways than one, and the guy didn't have a clue. When they had first met, Bluderin thought that Couch could be manipulative, that there was something Machiavellian about him. Jürgen being Couch's puppet proved that his premonition had validity.

"I always thought Vera could be quite attractive," Bluderin said. "Before you showed an interested in her, Jürgen, she wasn't taking care of herself all that well."

"Karin has changed, too," Couch said. "She dolls herself up, and you and Gretchen saw how well we get along. She was a little slow on the take with sex in the beginning, but now she loves to fuck. I can't get over it. Blow jobs, sixty-nines, around the world—anything I want, anytime. I have to be one of the most satisfied guys on the planet."

Bluderin could not help but smile when he recalled the image of Karin performing fellatio on Couch in the back seat of his Volkswagen, while Gretchen giggled uncontrollably, pinching her nose closed and covering her mouth.

"If things are so good for the both of you, why are you Casanovas bumming around, going over to Nördlingen on the hunt for women?"

"We're not really looking for women," Jürgen said. "We're just in the mood to drive around and take in a little fun."

"That's about it," Couch said. "As for Karin and Vera, you've got to take a break once in a while. Too much of a good thing can spoil you."

Couch pulled the Mercedes off to the side of the road so Jürgen could get out and pee in the bushes.

"He's really funny about Vera," Bluderin said.

"What do you mean?" Couch asked. "Vera is being good to him. Don't knock it. He's getting more action than you."

"I don't doubt that for a minute."

"What is it with you, John? You want nothing but the best, and the best aren't around any more, with Gretchen in Munich and the beautiful dyke in England?"

"I don't know," Bluderin said. "I guess I'm not ambitious about women."

"You will be," Couch said. "I don't know if Winifride is going to be at the Gasthaus tonight, but if she is you'll be hooked. She is just as beautiful as Solveig, but she likes guys. Her smile will make you melt, and she can be really funny. She tells great stories."

Bluderin knew that Couch was prone to exaggeration, but with Solveig gone, it would be nice to meet someone new, to ease the pain of his loneliness.

Winifride was not in the Gasthaus.

"Shit," Couch said. "You missed out. Jürgen, get us some beer. I'll find us a table."

Bluderin thought that he would go to Nördlingen on his own in a few weeks to see the meteorite crater and city wall. He would have no history lesson tonight.

Jürgen brought over the beer, along with three girls he invited to join their table. They were all young, somewhere from fifteen to eighteen, and the way they talked—*with teehees and ha has*—made them seem even younger.

"We had a nice drive over here. Pretty country," Bluderin said to the girl next to him.

Her name was Helga, and her pubescent face with red cheeks and thin, breastless frame made her look child-like.

She had a child-sized voice. "Yes," she said. "We like it here. We're close to nature. I don't ever want to leave."

They did not know what else to say to each other. Bluderin thought about what the girl had said, but he could find no natural response. He thought he would offer her some insight, from an American's point of view, on Germany.

"Germans take good care of their country. I have never seen trash of any kind—not even a napkin or bottle—anywhere near the woodlands or fields where I often walk or run. The rivers and lakes are likewise impeccably clean. When I think about the rivers back home, many of them are polluted, brown and stilled. Nature takes a second seat to industry in the States."

She smiled at him but looked blanked in her silent response, kicking her feet up and down and fidgeting in her chair.

Couch went outside to the patio. He looked pale, so Bluderin followed him out to see if he was all right.

"Something wrong, Wiley? Are you okay?"

Couch lit a cigar and sat on a stone bench, staring into the wide, rolling field where German dressage horses were meandering about and drinking from a round, man-made pond.

"Fuck," he said. "The thing with Akando bothers me. See, I had a guy give him a bottle of whiskey and some hashish on the day he stole the jeep and killed himself. What's more, I've got a problem with Karin that we need to resolve. Funny, I'm starting to get a conscience. It sucks."

"Anything I can do to help?"

"I'll tell you about it some other time, when Karin and I make a decision."

It was strange to see Couch worry. He typically didn't let give a shit about anything.

Couch took a hit of Steinhäger and swallowed quickly, grimacing. "I'm trying to come to grips with the fact that my carelessness has gone too far," he said. "It's time for me to become accountable for my actions."

Bluderin inferred what the problem was: Karin was pregnant. He also guessed that the decision she and Couch had to make was whether she would have the baby or get an abortion. He wondered how Gustav would react to the situation, how it would affect his pride in Karin. She recently had gained admission to the Pädagogische Hochschule. Would she give up or postpone her desire to become a teacher? Or would she have an abortion right away and move on with her plans for school? It is one of those profound minutes, he thought, that no matter what you decide, the impact of your decision will remain with you for the rest of your life.

He wasn't allowed to make any decisions. He looked at the opal ring on his right hand. He was afraid to open the latch. The agency would know if he did. Someone had covered it with a clear resin—it could have been fingernail polish, for all he knew. What did the agency want from him? Something was going on, his sixth sense told him, and it had to do with Aarika Tarr. It would be better to be lonely than to be with her, but he didn't have that option.

Howard James had taught him how to look for a code in his paintings. The code could be a warning or a prayer. In the painting of the Rems Valley that Howard had painted earlier in the day, Bluderin was able to decipher the code: *she is evil.*

Fourteen

◄○►

April 1968

The cold war was in a heat wave. A potential uprising against Soviet rule had created tension on military bases throughout Euruope. The strain was as dense and malleable as lead, heated to its molten state, spitting out of dark nebulae.

The political reforms demanded by the Czech leadership and rejected by the Soviet hierarchy stood as the major reason for the 4th Battalion, 41st Artillery, to be on alert. A motion by the Soviet Union to invade Czechoslovakia was at the forefront.

If the Soviets decided to infiltrate Czechoslovakia, how would the United States react? Bluderin did not know, but he did know where the Pershing missile warheads were aimed. McCandley had said that if the United States were to go to war against the Soviets, the battle could make Vietnam look like a game of hide-and-seek. "We could be knocking on Armageddon's door," he had said.

Things had quieted down, at least temporarily, and Bluderin left Hardt Kaserne for the day to fulfill some errands. He sat at a small, round table in the Steuben café and ordered coffee. He glanced at the headline stories in the *Rems-Zeitung,* the regional daily newspaper, and looked further down the page to paragraphs describing bodies sunk in rice paddies. The news made his bones feel hollow, absent of blood. He leaned back in his chair, turning the pages, and stared at a photograph of Viet Cong soldiers splayed all over a dirt road. Yet some politicians back home were insisting that there was no war in Vietnam. The matter was only a conflict, soon to be resolved. Sure, he thought, and Hitler was a nice guy, deep down.

As Bluderin sipped the strong coffee, he eavesdropped on a conversation a group of teenagers were having. One of the boys, a skinny, dark-haired kid whose nose looked like it had been battered to look like the shape of the state of New Hampshire, read aloud from an article about race riots in the United States. Washington DC, Baltimore, Detroit, New York, Berkeley, and Chicago, among other cities, were all ablaze, paralyzed with arson, shootings, and vandalism. LBJ had ordered troops into the cities. The police, the National Guard, and military reserve units were doing whatever they could to prevent the rioters from causing further damage.

Martin Luther King, Jr., had been assassinated. Bluderin first had heard about it on radio earlier in the morning. As the kid held the paper up to turn the page, a photograph of Dr. King amid other photographs of inflamed buildings from somewhere in urban America was on display. The buildings were surrounded in black smoke. A chill crawled up Bluderin's spine. He was used to reading about freedom marches, draft-card burnings, and various demonstrations protesting the Vietnam War, but he could not fathom the violence spreading throughout the country. It was not something Martin Luther King ever would have wanted to see, no way.

He thought about some of the black soldiers stationed at Hardt Kaserne: McCombs, Baker, Aaron, Cosby, Cooper, and of course his good friend, Howard James. He wondered what they were all thinking. Even the army newspaper, *Stars and Stripes*, would not be able to ignore reporting about the riots, although the coverage undoubtedly would be brief. The publication always tried to paint a rosy picture of life back home.

He worried especially about Howard, who was a thoughtful and sensitive man. His home town, Philadelphia, had not been struck by the race riots as viciously as other cities, but it had been struck. The "City of Brotherly Love" was not immune to violence. There was little doubt in his mind that Howard was drawing a portrait of Dr. King at this very minute. He would have to connect with Howard after completing his chore and assignment for the day.

First he had to bring a table and four chairs over to Riki Taar's apartment and deliver the opal ring to Günter. McCandley had asked him to transport the furniture as a favor to Ingrid Dannette. Since Ingrid would be moving into a larger apartment with McCandley, she had sold her old dining set to Riki. Bluderin did not want to accept McCandley's request, but there was nothing he could do about it. It would not be smart to deny his superior officer a favor.

He had managed to fit two of the chairs in the trunk of his Volkswagen and the other two on the back seats. He secured the table upside down on the roof of the car and held it tight with rope. Since he could not open the car doors under this arranagement, he crawled through the window space on the passenger's side and rolled over until he was able to sit upright behind the steering wheel.

Despite the inconvenience, he had gotten back out of the car to have some German coffee and stretch his cramped legs. He had shoved the front seats forward to fit the chairs behind them. His legs had been squeezed against the steering wheel. He would have to take the longer route to Riki's apartment to avoid sharp turns.

When the German kids saw him climbing back into the car, the one with the New Hampshire nose told him that if he wanted a mobile home he should have gotten a Volkswagen bus.

"I don't need any smart-assed kid telling me what to do," Bluderin said. "Lugging this stuff around is enough of a hassle. Aren't you guys late for school?"

Apparently they were. They looked at their watches and began sprinting down the road.

When Riki and he had finished moving the table and chairs into her apartment, she asked him if he would like something to drink. He wanted to decline her offer but decided to accept it. He had to be polite. Riki and Ingrid were friendly, and with McCandley being aware of the relationship, political expedience was required.

"I never turn down the thoughtfulness of a nice German lady," he said.

"I made a fresh batch of iced tea this morning," she said. "I'm not German, by the way. I'm Hungarian. I came here during the revolution in 1956. I was ten."

When Ricki poured iced tea into two glasses, he noticed what looked like the tips of steel blades on her wrists, just like the blades he had seen on Akando before he assaulted Josef. What was it with these knife-bracelets? Was it a fad he had overlooked? Or were they weapons, as Couch had suggested, like brass knuckles?

"I remember the Hungarian Revolution," he said. "I was around the same age. A half-dozen Hungarian refugee kids enrolled at my school. They were happy to be there."

"I wish we had made it to the U.S.," she said, "but Germany was as far as we got. Life sure would have been different for me if we had gone to America."

"We're all victims of fate," he said. "That's why I'm here today."

"My father died during the revolution," she said. "That marked the first blow of my victimizations. Dad was a musician, a violinist who also played the lute. He was a member of an orchestra in Budapest. He was a very sincere and gentle man, and he had a Spartan-like frugality, but with unbridled generosity toward me. He read to me every day, and I sang with him when he played the lute. I think my mother was jealous of our relationship, feeling that she had been left out."

"Quite a drastic change for a child," he said, "to have your whole life uprooted, soon after you lost your father."

"After we arrived in Germany, my mother began dating a man. He was a large and muscular man—a steel worker—and I was afraid of him. He did not want to marry my mother because of me. I was a burden. Still, my mother pleaded with the man to marry her. She told him that she would work to support me. She finally convinced him, but my situation degraded further after they married. I was an unwanted child."

"Did you eventually come to an understanding with him?" Bluderin asked. He did not see any evil in this woman, despite Howard's forewarning.

"Things only worsened. After my mother had a child with him—a boy—he purchased a town house. My bedroom was in the cellar, although there were spare bedrooms on the second floor. My stepfather and mother and their child lived upstairs, where it was warm and comfortable. The cellar was damp, and I caught more than my share of colds, but I was afraid to say anything. I didn't want to anger him."

"Did he ever harm you?" Bluderin wondered if Riki had been molested, like Solveig.

"As long as I did well in school and behaved myself, I was tolerated. Luckily, I loved school. It was so much better than being home. My teachers were encouraging, and I was at the top of the class."

"I'm not making light of your situation, but being tolerated is better than being sexually abused," Bluderin said, again thinking of Solveig.

Riki looked at him and frowned, as though she had been hurt by what he had said. He wanted to leave, but he realized he had gotten to her and thought he could gain some insight on the evil that Howard had signaled.

"It was my *husband* who took care of the sexual abuse," she said. "I met him the summer after my high school graduation. I was swimming at the public lake on the northeastern side of Schwäbisch Gmünd, near Mutlangen. He kept looking at me. He even followed me when I got out of the lake and sat down on a blanket next to my mother and stepbrother. He introduced himself to my mother and was charming. I translated what he said for my mother.

"She liked Allen the second saw him. She thought he was handsome, courteous, and in all likelihood from a wealthy family. Upon my mother's invitations, he visited the house frequently. Even my stepfather invited him back."

Bluderin felt something eerie going on with Riki. She began speaking at an accelerated pace and with a higher pitch.

"I did not want to go out on dates with the man. Although I went out with boys from high school, he—Allen Williams—was ten years older than they were. Nevertheless, my mother insisted that I date him. I think it was her way of getting me out of the house and into a better situation. Since my mother thought he was well off, she would no longer need to feel guilty if I married him."

"She probably had your best interests in mind," Bluderin said, "and it would free her conscience."

"He didn't have any money to speak of. When I got pregnant, he wanted to marry me. He spoke to my mother about the situation, and she told me that I had to marry him—that I had no choice."

"The guy was doing the honorable thing," Bluderin said. "He must have cared about you."

"You don't know anything about it," she said.

"Tell me." He could almost feel the anxiety bounce off her eyes.

"I tried very hard to adjust to marriage and was managing fairly well. I cooperated with whatever demands he had and, with his army wage and benefits and my working part-time, we provided a decent, modest living for the family. After the dreadful experience of losing my second baby at childbirth and getting morbidly scarred when delivering my third, I began going to an American doctor, an army captain stationed at the military hospital in Stuttgart. He was an excellent and understanding physician, and he performed surgery on my abdomen to make my scars less obtrusive and unsightly."

She threw her empty glass on the floor, and Bluderin jumped back.

"The scars still repulsed my husband, so much that he would only have sexual intercourse with my back turned to him. One day he bought home some sex toys and told me to play with them, to build up my vaginal muscles. I obeyed him, and he was pleased with the results, the improved movement and pressure when he fucked me."

"There's something you're not telling me," he said.

Her hands shook, and her virescent eyes turned black as onyx. "Before long, he was bringing other soldiers home to have sex with me. I must have made a lot of money for him because he bought a new Mercedes a few months after I began servicing other GIs. Two years after he began *this little business*, as he called it, he filed for divorce."

Something did not seem right to Bluderin. Why were her children living with her parents and not her? When McCandley had asked him for the favor, he inadvertently mentioned that Riki had told Ingrid to get the money for the furniture from her parents. Riki's ex-husband mailed child-support and alimony payments to them each month, so they had money to pay for the dining set. Riki was troubled, McCandley had said, and Ingrid was trying to help her. Ingrid would let her have the furniture for free.

Bluderin suspected that the local social agency may have taken custody of Riki's children and turned it over to her parents. Riki did see her children every day, but her stepfather did not let her stay in the house for more than an hour. Whatever it was, she was not being straight with him.

"Have you ever met a good man?" he asked her.

"I've met some nice GIs at Hardt Kaserne. There was one extremely kind man named Victor with whom I spent a good deal of time. When he was released from active duty, he studied engineering in Ulm and continued seeing me. We would take long walks together, often with my children, whom he adored. He would play a guitar and sing to them. The reason we never married is that he was impotent. He offered to marry me and said I could have a lover, but I refused to live under those circumstances."

"I'd like to stay and talk," Bluderin said, "but I've got another task to complete.'"

She looked depressed but asked him for a good-bye kiss. As she rested her head on his chest, Bluderin glanced into her bedroom and noticed some apparatus—parts of chains and shackles—on the floor, sticking out from under the bedspread. He wondered if she was sexually deviant. It would not surprise him, but he said nothing. He wanted to be on his way.

Bluderin knew next to nothing about sadomasochism, other than what Leda Beschwörung had told him. She had said that sadomasochistic sex was not an uncommon fetish in Germany. She advised him to avoid this type of deviance unless he completely trusted his sexual partner. Bluderin had said that he thought the fetish was perverse and demeaning. He wanted nothing to do with it. He was happy to leave the apartment.

After he had given Günter a pack of cigarettes with the ring inside it, the shepherd in turn gave Bluderin two small envelopes to deliver—a gray one to Gustav Erdmann and a yellow one to Aarika Taar. Damn it, he thought, I cannot keep away from that woman . . . whenever I think I'm done with her, I get another fucking assignment, *involving her.*

Günter spoke in his ethereal manner, using metaphors and allusions. If not a soothsayer, he assuredly was a philosophical man.

"If you want to become whole, you must withstand the trial of your soul."

Was the shepherd imparting wisdom, or was he giving him a warning? Bluderin was confused. As he prepared to get on his way, Günter left him with some final, parting words.

"The one you overlook will look out for you." Günter looked at the sky and began speaking to his long-deceased wife.

Before returning to Hardt Kaserne, Bluderin decided to stop at Gustav Erdmann's Gasthaus and give Gus the gray envelope. He wanted to have a beer or two anyway, to contemplate what he was going to say to Howard James. It was not going to be easy.

Gustav appeared to be in a somber mood as he poured Bluderin a beer and removed the envelope Bluderin had hidden beneath a coaster. There was no one else at the bar. Eddie, Tulla, and Hans were seated at their card table, being the only other patrons in the Gasthaus.

Gus announced that he had to leave for half an hour. He asked Hans to take care of any customers in his absence.

Bluderin went over to the card table and sat down.

"John, are you okay?" Eddie Grau asked. "We haven't seen you for some time. We've missed you at cards." His Irish Donegal cap was tilted downward as usual. He wore his cap that way so often that Bluderin had forgotten the color—or shape—of Eddie's eyes.

"I'm fine." Bluderin assured him. "My work at Hardt Kaserne has kept me from socializing in town over the past few weeks."

"We all thought you gave up drinking," Tulla said.

"Not at all, although I have cut back considerably. This past month has been especially dry. I've been working long hours. The Soviet and Czech disputes have us on our toes."

Bluderin dealt the cards. He noticed Eddie's sour expression, as if something was troubling him. His nose was inflamed, and he hadn't yet looked at his cards. Tulla also looked upset. Her cheeks were puffed and reddened, as if she had been crying. She must have had a box-worth of facial tissue in her cleavage, and the pink veins along the whites of her light blue eyes stood out. Hans was as stoical as ever, but more silent than usual and scratching his large, bald head.

"What's going on?" Bluderin asked. "Did someone die?"

"We are all dying," Hans said, "but that's not the point. It's to do with Karin."

Bluderin gently grabbed Eddie's forearm. "What's wrong with Karin?" he asked. "Is she ill?"

"It is nothing that concerns you," Eddie said.

"Of course it concerns me. I care very much about Gus and Karin."

"There is nothing that any of us can do about it," Hans said.

"Tell me," Bluderin said. "As a friend, I have a right to know."

"An accident," Eddie said.

"Is she in the hospital?" Bluderin asked.

"It's not the kind of accident that you're imagining," Eddie said. "It was an accident of behavior. Karin is pregnant."

"Oh, I see," Bluderin said. She must be going through a hell of a time, he thought. She already had been accepted to matriculate at the Pädagogische Hochschule.

"Your buddy Wiley Couch knocked her up," Eddie said. "She was a virgin until she hooked up with him. After Karin told him about the pregnancy, he disappeared."

"Gustav is pretty upset," Tulla said. "He does not know what to do about the situation. Karin wants to talk with Couch before reaching any decision, but no one knows where he is. I think he's gone for good."

Bluderin knew that, if Couch had any conscience at all, he would take some responsibility for getting Karin pregnant. He must have known that she was too naïve to go on birth control before getting sexually intimate with him. Hell, all she wanted to do at the time was forget about her breakup with Jürgen. *Some fucking way to forget about a boyfriend,* he thought sarcastically.

"John, what in hell is the matter with Couch?" Tulla asked. "Doesn't he care about Karin? What does he think she is? That it was all her fault?"

"Well, I don't know—"

Tulla cut Bluderin's response short and launched into an attack. "He doesn't give a damn, and you don't either. What is it with you Americans? Do you think we're all inferior? That you can come over here and take what you damn well please without the slightest respect?"

"You know better," Bluderin said.

Tulla wiped her teary eyes with a white tissue, sniffled, and took a deep breath. "Maybe I went overboard, John, but I can't control myself. Where is Couch? He's probably getting drunk somewhere right now, laughing about the whole matter like it's all one big joke."

Bluderin would have agreed with Tulla at one time, but after talking with Couch in Nördlingen, he began to respect him. He probably was still thinking how to sort things out.

"I think you're underestimating Couch," he said. "He is not as heartless as you think. I'm sure he's been giving a lot of thought to Karin."

Bluderin's words could not have come at a better time. Wiley Couch walked into the Gasthaus and appeared slightly inebriated as he approached the table.

"You know I have more balls than to run away," he said. "Karin and I are getting married. We told Gustav about our decision. Gus wanted to talk with Karin alone before he reacts to our plans. They're still talking."

"Why did you take so long to tell Gustav?" Tulla asked Couch, staring at him suspiciously.

"Karin and I first had to work things out between *us*, not Gustav. I respect his fatherly concern, but he was not our priority. The first priority was for Karin and me to talk things through. Don't you get it?"

"It took you long enough," Tulla said.

"You won't give it up, will you?" Couch shook his head impatiently and walked over to Tulla. "I appreciate your concern for Karin," he said, "but we've worked it all out. Over the last few days, I applied for a European out and got it approved. Karin and I also filed for a marriage license."

Karin and Gustav returned to the Gasthaus as Couch finished talking to Tulla. He gently lifted Karin up and twirled her around. She kissed Couch and waved to her friends at the card table, giving them a wide smile.

Bluderin bought everyone in the Gasthaus a drink to celebrate the wedding revelation. Even Gustav had a drink to acknowledge the occasion—whether he liked it or not didn't matter. He had resigned himself to accept his daughter's wishes.

Couch slapped the back of Bluderin's neck. "So, you bastard, you won't take a European out with me, will you? Well, if I have to go it alone, that's what I'll do. What do you have to say about that?"

"It's tremendous, Wiley. I'm happy for you."

"Tremendous or tremulous? You're a sly one with words."

"It's good," Bluderin said. "Give me some credit. I've been here betting on your honor. I think Hans, Eddie, and especially Tulla all thought you were a goner."

"I know. I heard part of the conversation. Anyway, it's a done deal."

The wedding was going to be in a week, and other plans were being made. Gustav had a vacant apartment in one of the several buildings he owned. Karin and Couch could live there for free, Gus offered, on the proviso that Karin follow through with her plans to attend the teacher's college. She promised her father that she would, and she would retain a nanny to care for the baby when she was at class.

Couch's mother had made plans to fulfill that role, at least for six months. She already had booked a flight. According to the school's schedule, Karin would complete her first session before she had the baby. Couch was going to attend the local technical academy for occupational training. He intended to become an electrician, and through the GI Bill he would receive a monthly stipend. He would also work part time at the Gasthaus. Bluderin thought that the whole scenario was wonderfully pragmatic.

Couch was having a grand time, sitting down at the card table, telling jokes, and drinking beer with Karin sitting on his lap. It was just his luck to have a father-in-law who owned a Gasthaus.

Karin said she looked forward to having the baby. An abortion had never been an alternative. Bluderin felt sure that she would be a great mother.

"John, I want you to be my best man," Couch said. "It's going to be a small, quiet civil ceremony. All you have to do is sign a couple of papers as witness."

"I'll be happy to," Bluderin said. "What about a present? What would you and Karin like?"

"You can sell me your Volkswagen before you leave," Couch said. "Either that, or get a European out and go into business with me. We could do some damage."

"I'll sell you the car really cheap, so Karin can drive back and forth to school."

"That's cool," Couch said. "We appreciate it."

Bluderin got up to leave. He felt loose and queasy from the beer and cognac he had consumed too quickly. It was time to talk with Howard James. He had been putting it off too long.

When he walked into the mess hall, Howard and his cooking crew had just finished cleaning the kitchen for the day. Bluderin noticed a clipboard on one of the tables and went over to look at it. Howard always kept a clipboard and sketch pad close at hand.

Bluderin studied the portrait of Martin Luther King that Howard had drawn using an artist's pencil. Howard had caught the essence of King's persona, an expression of restraint and determination. The sheer power of peace was evident by the manner in which Howard had drawn King's clear, piercing eyes.

"It is so terrible, what happened to him," Bluderin said.

Howard said nothing in response. He simply picked up the clipboard, removed the sketch pad from it, and showed Bluderin his release papers. Most of the required signatures were already in place on the documents.

"Diane and I are flying home in eight more days," he said.

"What are you going to do?" Bluderin asked. "I remember you saying you had your own business designing store fronts for retail shops in eastern Pennsylvania. Will you be able to reclaim the business when you get home? You must feel a lot of pressure, especially with the baby coming."

Howard's wide forehead gleamed in sweat, and his gray eyes, which usually captivated Bluderin with their intensity, looked astray.

"I'm having difficulty formulating my thoughts," he said. "In Philadelphia, I had worked with people whom I thought fostered respect among all citizens. That may be gone now."

"You have your art," Bluderin said. "You created over fifty paintings during your time here. That may be enough to get you going."

"Enough?" Howard looked at him and shook his head from side

to side. "Not enough for Dr. King. I want to become a community leader, to follow his dream for equal opportunity, for *equality*."

"King was also my hero," Bluderin said.

"Then pray for him," Howard said. "You will need his strength."

Howard and Bluderin sat together at the table and prayed for Martin Luther King and his dream. They recited the lyrics to the overly common "Amazing Grace" song, but it felt right. Nothing else fit the mood.

"A lie cannot live," Bluderin said. "That's one of my favorite quotes from Martin Luther King."

Howard offered his: "Freedom is never voluntarily given by the oppressor; it must be demanded by the oppressed." He then got up to go home to Diane. He was distant in his mannerisms toward Bluderin, who could sense his friend's anger. There was stillness, a cold vibrato, in Howard's voice when he said good-bye. His handshake seemed forced to Bluderin, as if it were noncommittal, a mere formality instead of the warm friendship they once had enjoyed.

Bluderin saw Howard a number of times afterwards, but they never had one of their long talks again. All Howard had told Bluderin was that he was going to fight actively for King's cause. Bluderin wished him well, but Howard left Hardt Kaserne without giving Bluderin his home address, although Bluderin had asked for it several times.

Bluderin often thought about Howard and Diane after their departure. He thought about Howard painting and Diane knitting. Her sweet smile was contagious, but it was mostly Howard—his deep voice, his stories, and his wickedly sharp sense of humor—that stayed in Bluderin's mind, as though Howard's spirit was sewn into his brain. Bluderin knew that, like his loving memory of Solveig Evensen, he had lost another good friend. At the same time, the people he wanted to avoid were getting closer. Every time he took a step forward, he felt he had moved three paces back. In interpreting Günter's words from earlier—*The one you overlook will look out for you*—he was convinced that he would become involved in some kind of conspiracy.

Fifteen

—◄○►—

To say that Vera Luchterhand was good to Jürgen Treuge would not do her justice. She damned near worshipped the guy. Bluderin could not look at them for a minute without Vera massaging Jürgen's neck, lighting his cigarette, flicking dust away from his sports jacket, kissing his earlobe, or performing some other act of endearment. All of these ministrations were annoying to Bluderin, but he had to admit that Vera never before looked so vibrant and sexy. She was wearing a magenta, sequined dress for the wedding, a short one that showed off her tanned, toned legs and smooth, ample cleavage. She had lightened her naturally dark blonde hair, complimenting her pink lipstick as well as her pink fingernails.

Jürgen rolled his eyes back as Vera caressed his shoulders. He looked like a sinner who has seen the light. "It's too bad about Couch getting married," he said.

That was a strange comment to make, Bluderin thought. Both Couch and Karin were happy. Even Gustav was enjoying himself as he walked around the Gasthaus, carrying Wilhelm, commonly known as Willie, a grandnephew who would be turning two years old in another week. Earlier in the day Gus had told Bluderin that getting married was a good influence on Couch and Karin. It gave them stability, he said, calling their union a natural maturing process with a sense of purpose and optimism.

"What makes you say that?" Bluderin said to Jürgen. "I'm happy for them."

"It's not that I don't wish them well," he said. "I do, but it means that my days of hanging around with Couch, getting all fired up on beer and Steinhäger, are over. He was a great drinking buddy."

"It's time for us all to move on to another phase, a new beginning," Bluderin said. "Look at the bright side, Jürgen. Couch indirectly is helping to save your liver. I doubt if either of you will quit drinking, but a little moderation could go a long way."

Speaking of worn-out livers, Bluderin watched Tulla Grau lift Eddie's right arm over her neck while Hans Kliebert grabbed the other arm. The two were nearly carrying Eddie back to their apartment. He had drunk way too much and could barely stand up, a condition that was not typical of his behavior. Although Tulla had said that Eddie was a heavy drinker at one time, he had only two beers on a typical evening. He was more interested in playing cards. The wedding reception, however, had gotten the best of Eddie. Gustav had opened up the Gasthaus for free drinks for a couple of hours to celebrate the wedding, and Eddie had decided to take full advantage of the opportunity.

"John, could you bring me another glass of champagne?" Leda Beschwörung asked. "The bubbly stuff makes me wickedly horny."

"That's encouraging to hear," Bluderin said, smiling at her. "I didn't mean to neglect you, Leda. I should have been paying more attention, but I got sidetracked watching these people. It's interesting to meet so many Erdmann relatives. So far, I've shaken hands with an ex-con, a cardiologist, a professional soccer player, and a prostitute."

Seeing Leda arrive at his apartment earlier in the day nearly had shaken Bluderin out of his wits. She had a deceptive inclination to rattle him with unannounced arrivals. He had assumed that she was working in Berlin, but she told him she had returned to Schwäbisch

Gmünd for another temporary assignment. He had remarked that her appearance was a lovely shock, and he asked her to accompany him to the wedding. She agreed to join him and conveniently had a navy-blue miniskirt and white blouse packed in her suitcase, along with high-heel dress sandals.

When Leda showered before getting dressed, Bluderin had searched through her suitcase and discovered two M67 High-Explosive Fragmentation hand grenades. They were secured in a pine box and cushioned on spongy gray fabric. He was surprised that the box was not locked. He carefully replaced the box and clothing in the precise order and location where Leda had left them.

He wondered if she had already known about the wedding. Maybe she talked with Gustav, he thought, hypothesizing that Gustav played a part in her new assignment. Nevertheless, he played dumb and acted delighted to see Leda again. He was sincerely pleased to see her—that was no act. He missed the magic touch of a woman. He had not been intimate with anyone since Solveig Evensen had left for England months ago. Of course, he had kissed and hugged Aarika Taar, but those gestures were more reactive than proactive, and not without a pang of sympathy.

Everyone who was at Gustav's Gasthaus during Leda's first time there remembered her. It was difficult *not* to remember her, Jürgen had said. Vera had whispered to Bluderin that, although she was not gay, she would not mind "doing" Leda. "She is so damn elegant and classy," Vera said. "She inspires me."

Bluderin tried to forget about his suspicion that Leda may have fired the Luger at Daniel Akando or the jeep he was driving, but he could not remove the image of a lithe figure near the road firing two shots before leaping back into the woods. The whole scenario took all of a few seconds, perhaps, but it stayed in his mind like an embedded sting.

Wiley Couch brought over snifters of cognac for Leda and

Bluderin. As the three raised their glasses in celebration, Couch swallowed the cognac in one toss while Bluderin and Leda sipped a little on theirs.

"Come on, drink up," Couch said. "It's not always going to be on Gus."

Bluderin thought how baseless it was of Couch to be so generous with someone else's generosity. "You've been a legitimate son-in-law for a couple of hours, and you're already at work spending Gustav's hard-earned money."

"Hard-earned, my ass," Couch said. "Gus got away cheap—no huge wedding or fancy reception. Simply a little grog and grub at his own establishment for fifty, maybe sixty, relatives and friends."

"Well, I'm sure you'll prove to be enough of a financial liability down the road," Bluderin said.

Karin came over to join them. She was holding Willy's hand until Couch picked the little boy up and held him in his arms. Willie's little hands tugged at Couch's ear.

"Gustav's grandnephew, Willy, if you don't already know," he said. "He's one. Can you believe I'm going to have a little tyke like this in another year or two?"

"I didn't know you were so keen on fatherhood," Bluderin said. "Of course, given the circumstances, it's only good that you are."

"Here's to parenthood," Leda said, raising her glass. "Love your baby."

"I'll tell you what," Couch said. "I'm going to teach my kid the way of the world long before I learned it."

Gustav walked around the Gasthaus, ringing a brass bell, which meant that the official wedding reception had come to a close. From this point onward, if guests wanted another drink, they would have to pay for it. The timing was perfect, Bluderin thought, as many of the guests had consumed more than they should have. Gus did let the guests know that there was still plenty of food around, as well as coffee, free for the taking. *A Gasthaus owner can never let things get out of control*, Gus once had told Bluderin, and his actions backed up his advice. Within an hour following the bell-ringing, many of the guests had some coffee before saying good-bye and parting ways. The crowd had thinned out considerably after the professional soccer player left with the prostitute.

As Bluderin swirled the glass of cognac, savoring its smell, a pair of hands pinched the sides of his waist, then reached around in front of him and gave a hug.

"Are you ignoring me again?" Leda asked him.

"Of course not." He assured her. "How on earth could I ignore your charm and elegance? Why would I ever want to?"

"You've been very quiet," she said.

He kissed her lightly on the lips. "I was just contemplating a few things, getting philosophical. I was thinking that I could never look forward to the prospect of fatherhood, not at this stage in my life. It's the last thing I'd want."

"You've journeys to make," she said. "You will have many voyages, both geographically and intellectually, before you are ready to settle into a traditional role, such as getting married and having a family. I can sense that about you."

Leda Beschwörung was an enigma to Bluderin. Her always unexpected, rare appearances at his apartment, coming from who knows where, were like a lovely illusion that crystallizes to life. Yet she behaved as though she had never left him. Their intimacy was a continuum of mutual instinct and pleasure, no matter how long they had been separated. Was it because Leda had taught him what to do from the beginning of their relationship, when he had extremely limited, prior sexual experience? He thought it could be. Leda had taught him how to cherish the moment, to never take a woman's intimacy lightly, and to remember it in the spirit and words of Marcus Aurelius: *It loved to happen.*

While Bluderin was grateful for what Leda had taught him, he was also wary of her. She knew too much about him. Although she supposedly had been working in Berlin, she knew about the wedding he had attended with Gretchen Vanderwerken and her parents. She was aware of Daniel Akando's attack on Josef Westoff, the subsequent court-martial proceedings, and Akando's death. She also knew about Bluderin's friendship with Solveig Evensen, but she said her knowledge on that front was limited. How did Leda know about all these events when she was away? Were intelligence contacts keeping her informed of his activities—if so, why?

After they left the reception and returned to his apartment, Leda began questioning him on how he felt about Akando's untimely death. He had eliminated the incident from his mind, he told her.

"It no longer exists," he said. "It's time to move on and complete the remainder of my military obligation and whatever intelligence assignments come my way." Leda would find out no more about his knowledge regarding Akando, no matter how hard she pressed him.

When she appeared satisfied that he knew nothing more about the Akando affair, she began asking him what his impressions of Aarika Taar were.

Knowing that Riki was involved with intelligence work, the question came as no surprise. Bluderin decided to answer her questions nonchalantly on this matter, but with a double entendre. He hoped his answers would prompt Leda to share what she knew about the woman.

"Riki is an attractive, interesting, and obviously intelligent woman. When we went on a picnic with Howard and Diane James, I could see that nature had a deep-seated effect on her. I also felt that, although she and I are the same age—within six months of each other—she acts older than I do. Something about her past may have aged her, but I'm only postulating."

He knew that Leda was way too smart to overlook his tactic to elicit more information about Riki Taar. However, he wanted to make a point: dispensing with information is a two-way street. While Leda was an intelligence agent and he was only an errand boy, he wanted some insight on how to deal with this very strange woman, Riki Taar.

"You know more than you're letting on," she said.

"I told you everything I know, not everything I heard," he said. "I know what GIs say about her, and I know some other things she told me, but I do not know what is true and what isn't. I don't spread rumor or hearsay."

"You're no ordinary army clerk or intelligence assistant," she said. "The information I had read about you before you arrived in Germany was copious. You finished high school in the top five percent of your class, not bad for a kid who took a rigorous curriculum, played three varsity sports, and worked forty hours a week."

"What else do you know about me?" he asked. "I didn't know I was such an interesting subject."

"When I reviewed your military file, I was not surprised to discover that your general testing scores were in the top percentile. You are inordinately bright, an attribute that made you a viable candidate for intelligence work. Your assignments have been limited because you were going to be on active duty in Germany for only nineteen months, and now you have less than three months remaining. It would not be worth the expense to train you for any higher level work."

"Riki is no slouch when it comes to brain power," he said.

"What makes you so inquisitive about her?" she asked. "You never raised any questions about Gustav Erdmann or Günter Mann. I bet you never knew that Solveig Evensen once worked for the U.S. intelligence community, so I can understand why you never asked me anything about her. Let me enlighten you. Five years ago Solveig had taken a position translating Soviet documents. She resigned from the position in good standing. The statement on her personnel record was that she had tired of all the translation work and needed to take a break. She could have the job back whenever she wanted it, but I recently learned that she's teaching at a school in England."

Like Gustav with the black opal ring, Bluderin was convinced that Leda was holding something back. He decided to forego asking any questions about Solveig. His curiosity, if expressed, would only stir further interest about the details of their relationship.

"My knowledge of the relationship between Solveig and you is limited," she said. "I do know that you were good friends, with both of you having an affinity for languages, literature, and music. The fact that the age difference between Solveig and you spans ten years—along with the assumption that Solveig is a lesbian while you're heterosexual—made the intelligence community assume that the relationship was platonic.What else could it be?"

"She was a mentor," he said. "She accepted me without motive. Unlike others with whom I've interacted, Solveig had no schadenfreude."

"We've been pretentious with each other all evening," Leda said. "It's not something either of us is good at or particularly fond of. Let's be straight with each other, as we've been in the past. What do you want to know about Riki Taar?"

Bluderin was not about to jump into a free-for-all, candid discussion with a person of Leda Beschwörung's caliber. She was way too smart for him. He would begin the discussion with a soft approach.

"It confused me why she was a conduit between an intelligence contact and me to deliver the ring to Günter. I've never been one to ask questions about my role in a situation, but I've known Riki, or rather who she was, for over a year before the intelligence connection. I never knew she was in the network."

Leda looked straight into Bluderin's eyes. "She didn't know you were in the network, either. We were running a test on Riki, verifying that she follows our orders without question. We've done the same to you, as well as scores of other intelligence assistants."

That was one way of saying that his allegiance to his country was in question. He was perturbed at the hidden insinuation. He was dedicated to his country and angry that the agency could have suspicions about his loyalty. Still, he had to hold his cool.

"Understood," he said. "I guess what really confused me was that Riki began to take an interest in me personally. She was always indifferent towards me in the past, whenever I picked up my laundry or checked out a book from the library. I could not understand the cause of her recent interest."

"Whatever she did in that respect was on her own accord," Leda said. "I do know that she was in a relationship with a man that ended a few months ago. I suppose you were her next prospect. You can't blame the girl for wanting a man. Believe me, I was advised to get better acquainted with you, but not to the level of our intimacy."

Bluderin did not know what to think. Leda may have been telling the truth about herself, but he was sure that someone in intelligence had advised Riki to take an interest in him and develop a relationship. Maybe how strong that relationship should be was up for grabs, as Leda had implied.

"From what I know, you don't mind being charmed by a woman," Leda said, smiling flirtatiously.

"Normally I don't," he said, "but something about Riki bothers me."

"What may be bothering you is that Riki wants you, but you are not interested in her," she said. "That could make you uncomfortable."

Bluderin listened mindfully to what Leda had said and closely observed her facial expressions and body language. He did not respond to her comment because he felt that she was still holding out on him, not being straightforward, despite her supposed willingness to do so. What was Riki's role in the intelligence community? Was she merely an errand person, like him, or was she something more? There was no way of telling, and Leda was not about to release any further detail.

"Did she tell you about her scars?" she asked him, breaking the silence.

Whenever Leda asked him a question, he was sure that she already knew the answer. He studied her as she raised the teacup to her lips. Her fingernails were manicured to the point of perfection—fully glossed, naturally pink, but the tips were painted with white polish. He would answer her question factually, as precise as her fingernails, and finish it with conjecture.

"Riki told me that her abdominal scars were inflicted on her during the delivery of her third child. I never saw the scars, but she said they had repulsed her husband to the point where he left her and filed for divorce."

"The scars are more psychological than physical," Leda said. "They were grotesque at one time, but an army surgeon did a terrific job in restoring her abdomen. The once large, thick, discolored scars are now fine, slightly whitish lines. I have seen the results when we interviewed her. There is nothing at all repulsive on any part of her body. You would not even notice the incisions unless you looked closely."

Bluderin felt that Leda was being straight regarding Riki Taar. He already had known about the army surgeon's operation to minimize the appearance of scars, but the success of the surgery was questionable. Leda thought it was highly successful, while Riki thought it was an improvement but that her abdomen was still unsightly. Two widely different opinions, but he thought that Leda's was more credible. She withheld information, but she did not outright lie to him. Now he wondered what information Leda wanted from him.

"Her paranoia about the scars could be a factor in why I find her so weird, for lack of a better word," he said. "I sensed angst in her psyche. She can exude a calm exterior, but I think that, if something triggered her emotions, she could erupt in hysteria or physical violence. It's a feeling I have."

"You're very perceptive," Leda said. "Intelligence contacts have been monitoring Riki's behavior periodically over the past three years. Her psychological stability had been in question, but her professional conduct has been exemplary. A psychiatrist who interviewed Riki judged her to be stable. He thought that she was troubled but coping well and making the best of her circumstances—much like any normal person. She has had no history of incidents in exhibiting out-of-control behavior."

"That's reassuring," he said, although he did not share the psychiatrist's opinion. He was in no way qualified to question the evaluation of a mental health professional, but he was going to be careful when dealing with Riki Taar.

"So, you didn't notice anything unusual about Daniel Akando's accident?" she asked. "You were very close to the scene."

Bluderin had been waiting for that bomb to drop, realizing that the shooter was indeed Leda Beschwörung. She had given him some insight about Riki, and now it was time for him to give back. Again, his approach would be slow and unassuming.

"I was out running when I heard the sound of a car roaring along the road beside me. When I ran toward the road to see what was going on, the jeep sped by before I could get a good look at it. I saw it wavering wildly down the road until it disappeared around a curve. I had no idea who was driving the jeep or if there had been an accident. When I returned to Hardt Kaserne, some of the soldiers told me what had happened to Akando. You've obviously read the report I filed about the accident."

He was not going to tell her anything else. She might have seen him as the jeep zoomed by the clearing of the tree-lined road, but he had not necessarily seen her. His comment that he did not recognize the driver was the absolute truth. Whether she believed him or not, he didn't know.

"So you didn't approach the side of the road and notice someone off at a distance, firing a shot toward the jeep?"

Damn, he thought, how do I answer that one? If he denied seeing anything, she would know he was lying.

"I saw the shape of a human figure off in the distance," he said. "It was dusk, so all I noticed was more of a silhouette. Probably a pedestrian, I thought, what else could it be?"

He was determined not to tell her anything else. Who knew what the intelligence community would do to him for being in the wrong place at the wrong time.

"You have twenty-fifteen vision," she said. "Tell me, was the human figure large or small, fat or skinny?"

"It looked small and slender," he said. "I could not tell the person's height from such a distance—about two hundred yards away. If I had to hazard a guess, I would say the guy was around five-six."

He knew that Leda was only five foot two, so his estimate had to be within reason. He used the term "guy" to throw her off. It was an intentional chauvinistic maneuver.

"What makes you think it was a man?"

"Could have been a woman," he said. "I could not distinguish the gender of the figure. I did not notice any breasts, and all I could see of the face was a shadow of a head—no hair, no ears, nothing. I was not giving it much attention. Seemed like just an ordinary citizen walking down the street. I was more concerned about getting back to the base and finding out what was story was behind the jeep."

He knew her small breasts could not have been detectable at

such a distance, and the black nylon mask hid all of her facial features with the exception of her hair, the majority of which was tucked under the collar of her camouflaged shirt.

"Akando had to go," she said. "He was providing Soviet intelligence agents with top-secret information about Pershing missile technology and operations. An agent shot at the jeep's tires to force it to stop. Since we had been informed that Akando was inebriated, we assumed he lost control of the vehicle. We have been tracking Akando, bugging his phone calls and following him around. He was on his way to meet with the opposition on the day he was killed. He was going to join them full time."

It was unbelievable to Bluderin that Leda would share this information with him. He could not imagine Danny Akando being a traitor, but he definitely had expertise that the Soviets would find valuable. Yet Akando had been restricted to the base and field operations grounds so often that Bluderin questioned how the missile technician could have had the opportunity to participate in covert discussions. There were a whole lot of questions Bluderin wanted to ask Leda, but he thought it best to let it go.

The sex they enjoyed before Leda left in the morning, supposedly headed back to Berlin, was bittersweet. They both knew without saying it that it would be their last time together. Bluderin was appreciative of Leda's earnest attention to him, especially in light of his long hiatus in not having a lover. The sexless period away from Solveig had made him anxious and depressed.

The incident with Akando made him question who Leda really was, if her affection was nothing more than a divergence from her intelligence duties. However, he had no doubt that she enjoyed the sex, She once had said that a woman can never really know a man until she goes to bed with him.

Any of the previous times he was intimate with Leda could have been the last, but this time it was for real, a situation that inspired both of them to ensure that each other's needs were met. Maybe one should always think that being intimate with a lover could always be the last time, Bluderin thought. It could deepen the gratitude.

The following morning he stopped at the Oasis on his way to Hardt Kaserne. Frau Müller had a letter from Solveig Evensen for him. It was a short letter but intense in its tone. He read it in the car, parked outside the Oasis, before going to work.

> *Mein literarish und lieblich Seele,*
>
> As I told you when I left for England, I needed to learn how to live with myself. I know you were hurt by my leaving, but I want you to know that I miss you terribly. You were instrumental in helping me recognize or acknowledge my rebirth, as it were, in coming to terms with the wholeness of my being.
>
> I have enjoyed the quietude of my cottage and this quaint school where days pass by with deep significance. There is something so relevant in helping young minds grow.
>
> I believe you have experienced a rebirth as well when you learned to speak out of your heart. I carry a powerful dream in my mind that tells me we may have something special. Could we go further if we wanted to? Do we? Should we?
>
> Your meaning to me is a wonder, a mysterious confirmation that the soul exists. We see each other in our dreams, and that is beautiful.
>
> My next letter will be more down to earth, I assure you, but I wanted you to know that you are hardly forgotten.
>
> *auf Weidersehen fur jetzt, mein gut Freund . . .*

Bluderin's mind was filled with images of Solveig Evensen as he drove into the parking lot at Hardt Kaserne. The letter made him lonely, but he was glad to hear that she had accomplished what she set out to do: find her essence. The letter moved him to think of the first stanza of "The Waking," a villanelle by Theodore Roethke.

> *I wake to sleep, and take my waking slow.*
> *I feel my fate in what I cannot fear.*
> *I learn by going where I have to go.*

We think by feeling. What is there to know? Bluderin kept repeating that line from the poem as he walked into Headquarters Building. His in-basket was overloaded with various requests he had to process. As he shuffled through the papers and placed them in categorical stacks, another line from "The Waking" kept its rhythm in his ears: *What falls away is always. And is near.* It was time to get down to the business at hand as a soldier and forget about his role as an intelligence assistant. When he assumed that role again, he would need all of his senses working at their highest acumen—anything less would jeopardize his safety.

Sixteen

◄○►

Like a spiritual awakening or a cure for the blind, brilliant sunlight filled the air at Hardt Kaserne. The buildings were adorned with small evergreens, like bluish green skirts, trimmed at the window sills. The cobblestone sidewalks reflected bright hues of silver and gold. It was a day meant for walking, Bluderin decided, so he left his Volkswagen on base and followed a wooded path into downtown Schwäbisch Gmünd. The air moved in harmony with his breathing, and his hair lifted and swayed. He would have no more military haircuts. He was looking for signs of golden rabbits and kestrels when a thought zinged through his mind in the form of an eruptive scare.

What provoked him was the realization that he was down to seven more weeks of active duty. He would be gone—out of Germany and back in the States—unless he did something to alter that course. He had applied for and gotten approved to take a European out but, regardless of what he elected to do, he would be a civilian again. The prospect made him simultaneously terrified and elated. The best personal thing the army had done for him was postpone his need to make a decision on what he was going to do for the rest of his life. He was confounded now that he could no longer avoid thinking about it.

In his confused state he saw an image of the Maumee River

in Ohio, a view of it north of his home town of Defiance, closer to Toledo. It was within seeing distance of the Craig Memorial Bridge, one of the few moveable bridges on the interstate highway system. He recalled that the bridge was named in memory of Second Lieutenant Robert Craig, a World War II veteran and recipient of the Medal of Honor. Bluderin was no war hero. The only medal he wanted was one of personal freedom, away from the clouds of danger he could almost smell.

He remembered the enormous cinder-block warehouse full of rope, tackle, nets, engines, and engine parts, among various other products supporting the boating industry. Large capital letters were nailed onto the upper third of the building's main entrance: C.F. MACNAIR, INC. The letters were semicircular, about two feet tall, in bright red plastic. He remembered C.F. McNair, a wealthy boatyard owner who dressed as raggedly, and shaved as often, as a wino or homeless person begging for change. McNair took pride in his docks, which were reinforced with new piers, their tops crowned with white paint. However, the catwalks were never replaced. The old planks were kept deathly serviceable with soakings of linseed oil and blotches of grease from fishermen's boots. Today Bluderin felt as if he were running on those warped catwalks.

Boats made by Chris Craft, Owens, Egg Harbor, Hatteras, Sea Boss, and the like bobbed along the docks, some of them humming in a bubbling spray as their owners prepared to take off. A few sailboats further out on the river wavered around their moorings— sloops, ketches, yawls, and one large schooner named *Madrigal*. He had taken a ride on *Madrigal*, when the skipper sailed the vessel to the mouth of the river and into Lake Erie. His memory took him on that voyage again, passing Horseshoe Island, named for its shape and topped with sand, kelp, and lumps of rubbery grass. Sinking into the anchor of his youth, he remembered no one else. Blank faces, mere oval surfaces of flesh, waited to be complemented with their individual eyes, lips and, most of all, voices, but nothing came. That was, except her: long blonde hair, sky-colored eyes, almost platinum skin with sparse, darker freckles, he vaguely admitted the sense of her name . . . sand, surf, seawall.

Seagulls glided in low circles around the island beyond her face. The name Sarah was printed on the sandy bank, inscribed using a stick of driftwood. He could not get closer, could not go further, to touch her lips or smell her sunburned hair. To discipline his senses and devote them solely to his survival, he would have to let her go. He hadn't yet, but he was getting close.

A long, downward flowing of his dreams returned him to Hardt Kaserne. Soldiers walked around, usually in groups of three or four, with the exception of Staff Sergeant Moody. His wire-like physique moved in a military pace, a parade of one, his hair shaved, the sun reflecting off his scalp. Moody was part of a military cult, an army lifer of twenty-odd years but with a rank only one grade higher than Bluderin's. This was Moody's fourth tour in Germany, with each tour spanning three years. Bluderin was depressingly surprised that Moody knew only a few words of German. "Don't know it, and don't want to learn it," he had told Bluderin. With the exception of field duty, Moody never left the base. His social life was spent entirely at the NCO club.

Although Bluderin thought the Schwäbisch countryside was serenely picturesque, especially in autumn, the only color that appealed to Staff Sergeant Michael Kelly Moody was olive drab, the color of his fatigues. Even when he was in civilian clothes, Moody wore an olive drab shirt with matching pants. Bluderin believed that Moody should have been placed on state-side duty for his entire career since his mind remained as flat as his birthplace, the great Oklahoma plains. He could travel the world and go nowhere. There was nothing Bluderin could learn from him. Being self-contained like Moody would be a curse.

Hardt Kaserne was no longer in sight, but Bluderin could still hear the loud, a cappella singing of some soldiers. He knew who they were—Nelson, McCombs, and Cooper—singing their favorite Motown tunes. Smokey Robinson's "My Girl," was usually the first number they sang when they got together, often followed by Marvin Gaye's "I Heard it Through the Grapevine." On one occasion before he was processed out of Hardt Kaserne, Howard James had joined them to sing spiritual music, most memorably "We Shall Overcome" and "Swing Low, Sweet Chariot." Howard had told him that the latter song was created by Wallis Willis, a Choctaw freedman from Mississippi. The faith in either song would help Bluderin face his upcoming challenge.

Bluderin and other soldiers encouraged their singing—their voices were good and their harmony terrific. At first the trio did not want white soldiers around them when they were at leisure. However, after Bluderin and his assistant, Specialist 4 Joe Tyler, had typed the lyrics to over thirty Motown songs, the singers appreciated their efforts and began to entertain the troops. As time went on, they drew increasingly larger crowds. They even managed to book a paying gig once a month at Rosa's Gasthaus, just east of Hardt Kaserne, in Mutlangen. Many German citizens, especially the young ones, loved to dance to the sound of Motown. In observing those fans—people of every ethnicity and background that one could imagine—Bluderin came to believe that music could unite the world. Solveig had been right about music being everything.

As the singing drifted off in the distance, Bluderin began to see images of his family. His three sisters appeared out of nowhere, wavering in and out of the picture, each independently and then all at once. Two of them already had married their high school sweethearts. The older one had two little girls and the middle sister a baby boy. They were living the life that Bluderin once thought he would live—simple, straightforward lives with nuclear families set out to live better lives than the ones they had experienced growing up. They seemed to be doing fine, being comfortable at the epicenter of the American Dream. Bluderin's youngest sister was still in high school and would doubtlessly follow a path similar to her older sisters. He did not know why he had to be different, why he was so absorbed in developing or inventing an intellectual presence. His sixth sense told him that if he didn't, he would die an untimely death, like Danny Akando.

He passed an elderhostel on his way to the state school of applied arts known as the Staatliche Werkkunstschule Schwäbisch Gmünd. A marble eagle, its wings spread out and upward, launched a stream of water from its mouth. Old men in charcoal suits sat on black iron benches reading day-old newspapers. Two heavyset women, their legs and backs supported by black canes, puttered around a garden. Silk scarves covered their mouths. Only their noses breathed nakedly.

Peter Vanderwerken had told Bluderin about the art school. The institution had a history dating back to 1776, when it was called the Zeichenschule, or school of drawing. Peter recently had said that the school's art gallery was exhibiting some paintings by Emil Eugen Holzhauer. The artist had been born in Schwäbisch Gmünd, but he moved to the United States in 1906, at the age of nineteen. While in Germany, Holzhauer had apprenticed in a silver and metal ware factory where he learned design and modeling during the day. In the evenings he studied art at the Staatliche Werkkunstschule or whatever it was called at the time. In the United States, Holzhauer had taught art at the Chicago Art Institute for twenty-one years. He also taught art at other colleges, primarily in Georgia. He was currently living and teaching in Niceville, Florida.

The gallery was lit naturally by skylights, making the paintings easy to view. The prominent style in Holzhauer's work included heavy lines filled with color and rhythmic, harmonious space. Bluderin could tell by the paintings' subjects that Holzhauer was influenced by scenes from the southeastern United States. It was also apparent that the artist adopted modernist elements of Expressionism and Social Realism, and there was little doubt that the paintings of Cezanne and Van Gogh had a noticeable influence on Holzhauer's work.

Bluderin sat on a wooden bench and dreamed into one of the paintings. He wondered what makes a writer write and a painter paint. It occurred to him that, because most animals surpass human beings in terms of acuity of the senses, painting or writing can be ways to sharpen such acuity and drive one out of depression. Schopenhauer long ago, he had read, recognized art as a possible way to momentarily escape the distress of one's existence. Bluderin studied the painting of a fishing boat careened off a mud-slicked shore in Georgia when something Nietzsche had said came to mind: *"The truth is ugly—we have art in order that we may not be destroyed by truth."*

The moment he turned his attention away from the painting Aarika Taar walked into the gallery. She was wearing a beige turtleneck sweater and carrying a very large canvas bag that hung off her shoulders. Smiling with a strange twitch as she approached Bluderin, her eyes opened like greenish flames turning burgundy. The whites of her eyes were perfectly clear, like the idea of snow, but her pupils were magnetically dark, like the entrance to caves. Barely noticeable freckles danced around her windblown, pinkish face. Her wet palms anointed Bluderin's neck, and her auburn hair brushed against his lips. He glanced downward at her classic Roman nose, like that of Julius Caesar, with a peculiar gray mole barely visible under one nostril. It vanished when she smiled. She smelled like tea and oranges.

"I'm surprised to see you here," she said, raising her voice barely above a whisper.

Bluderin imagined that Riki might have been stalking him. How else would she have known about the art exhibit? He had not seen it publicized anywhere, not in the local papers nor radio stations.

"I'm the one who's surprised," he said.

"You shouldn't be. I've been taking art courses here for the past year and a half. That's why I'm lugging around this huge canvas bag. I have one of my works in progress inside it."

"You never told me that you were studying art," he said. "You never said a word about it, not even when we went picnicking with Howard and Diane."

"I was too timid," she said. "After all, Howard is an accomplished painter, and my fledgling paintings would have made him laugh in pity."

"Howard would have done nothing of the kind," Bluderin said. "He would have encouraged you. He probably could have given you a few good pointers."

"Well, it's a little too late for that, isn't it?" she said. "Besides, my professor is teaching us more avant-garde techniques, not the classic Impressionism that Howard holds so close to his heart. My art professor recommended that we all visit this exhibit since Holzhauer is a highly regarded avant-garde painter."

"I find his paintings interesting," Bluderin said. "I wonder if he was angry when he drew the heavy lines, then joyful when he filled them with color. It's the contrast that brings his paintings to life, in my humble opinion."

"All the outstanding artists I've studied had personal histories of being mad and seeped in melancholy," Riki said. "My professor told us that even the most serene artists were depressed people whose love of light went hand-in-hand with the deepest darkness."

Bluderin considered the possibility that Riki's doctor, the psychiatrist whom Leda Beschwörung had mentioned, recommended that Riki take up painting as therapy for her depression.

"May I see your painting?" he asked.

"I just started it, so there is not much to see" she said. "I'll show you some I have in my apartment. Would you mind driving me home? I dread the thought of carrying this canvas all the way back."

Bluderin did not want to go to Riki's apartment, but he understood how the weight of the stretched canvas and inner frame would be cumbersome.

"I don't have my car with me, but I'll be happy to carry the canvas and see you home."

Riki seemed delighted with his suggestion, and the two left the gallery for the five kilometer walk to her apartment. However, she rejected his next suggestion—that they stop at a Gasthaus along the way and have a couple of beers—because she did not want to be seen drinking. "Drinking makes me dance," she said. "It knocks me off my point of origin."

They elected to take a different path through some woods along the way. The walk would be a kilometer or two longer but more enjoyable. They walked silently along the path, with Riki leading the way since she knew which path to take whenever one diverged in different directions. She stopped when she saw a small pond near some willow trees.

"Don't you feel more alive when you're at peace with nature?" she asked.

"It's meditative," he said, knowing that poems often came out of him after a walk in the woods.

"I have been intrigued with the Japanese view of nature ever since I read my first haiku," she said. "I like the form of haiku and the intent of it—to illustrate the harmony of man and the seasons. The originator of the verse form, Basho, wrote one of my favorites." She quoted it, raising her voice so that it sounded younger. If she were stalking or trying to seduce him, he thought, she was masquerading her intentions by appealing to his interest in poetry.

A cooling breeze—
and the whole sky is filled
with pine tree voices.

Bluderin noticed that the haiku was not in its purest form of seventeen syllables in three lines: five syllables for the first line, seven for the second, and five for the third. However, the meaning of the haiku was more important to him than its form. Even at this moment, with no bird singing, he heard something, the sound of pine.

As they started walking again, they returned to silence. The moist air of the late afternoon was beginning to lift, and a cooling breeze, like the one in the haiku, passed through him. Huge pine trees have many voices, he thought, a delicate voice on each branch.

"Do you know any haiku, John?"

He said he did, and she asked him to share one with her. He remembered one by Tachibana Hokushi, a student of Basho, and he repeated it in his head several times until they approached, appropriately enough, a massive pine tree. He looked upward to the top of the tree and recited it.

Experimenting . . .
I hung the moon on various
branches of the pine.

"A Christmas haiku." Riki smiled at the thought. "I must remember that one for my children."

He had never linked the haiku to Christmas, but he could well understand why she did. He originally had thought of the haiku as a way to show how man plays with nature. He does not do anything *to* nature; he simply moves up and down, left and right, placing the moon on various branches. Nature offers infinite perceptions this way.

"Will you make up a haiku for me?" she asked.

"I don't think I can," he said. "Give me some time to think it over."

He felt awkward and strange. We are in a land of fairy tales, he thought, a man and a woman quoting poems, enjoying nature as they walk hazily toward civilization. He wondered about Riki—how opposite she was from him in so many ways, although their love of nature was a common core unless she was feigning it. He did not believe her when she told him that nature was her mentor, that it held all knowledge. He reasoned that knowledge would be an illusion if one assumed that all thoughts and actions were determined by natural forces that elude one's cognitive grasp.

It was getting dark when they walked out of the woods and looked up at the open sky. Stars were beginning to appear, inspiring him to complete the haiku he was forming. Riki looked up at the sky as he had asked her to before he uttered the following verse.

> *The gift of moonlight*
> *illuminates tips of waves*
> *on the blood-leafed sea.*

Riki threw her arms around Bluderin's waist, pulling him toward her. His arms responded in kind around her thin shoulders. She stared at him for a long moment, as if she were talking to him with her eyes, and kissed him, all in silence. As she looked up at him again, her eyes blinked slowly and her lips quivered. He took hold of her arm, and they commenced walking.

They entered a park close to the Marktplatz and sat down on a stone bench. Riki wanted to wait there until it was darker so she could bring Bluderin to her apartment without her neighbors seeing them.

An elderly woman sat on a bench opposite them. She had

traces of a white moustache and deeply wrinkled features, like the roughened surface of a birch, but softer. She liked to come to the park after having supper, she told Riki and Bluderin. She would sit on the same stone bench for an hour or two each evening, looking for people to talk with. The fifteen-minute walk from her home to the park always did her good, she remarked, helped her shake the arthritis from her feet.

Riki detected a Hungarian accent in the woman's voice and began speaking to her in the language. The woman got up from the bench and came over to sit next to her. She seemed to be happily amused over the younger woman's perception. Thinking more analytically, Bluderin wondered if the older woman could be Riki's grandmother on her biological father's side. Riki had said that the woman accompanied her and her mother out of Hungary to seek refuge in Germany.

He took the occasion to get up and lay on the soft grass. He listened to their incomprehensible chain of syllables, letting their voices lull him to sleep. His dreams were taking him on a surrealistic voyage. He flew over a herd of sheep, over hills and the panting of dogs, as he held a shepherd's staff that reflected starlight. The haikus he and Riki had shared in the woods were printed in the sky by clouds. It was all nonsense, but why was it happening? He knew it would pass, and a line from the Bible crept into his brain. "It came to pass . . ."

Dreams folded inside of each other, and he found himself at Cape Cod, in Provincetown, Massachusetts. A couple walked on the flats, low tide in the bight, as they held hands, half-dressed, wet with salt. All the wanderings of sand and sea left imprints on their shoulders and coated their arms with a white film. Bluderin saw their faces, although he was thousands of miles away, remote as a god. The man's face was unknown, hidden in large by a black beard chopped carelessly, like brush that is whacked with a sickle once or twice a year. But who was *she*? He looked further.

The girl was Bluderin's fear. How absent he was as he stared into the windows of her eyes, immersed in feelings, and saw that she was unable to feel a mote of his presence upon her. How strange, he thought, that when things die—either by physical disappearance or lack of concern—one begins to see what could have been. In the neck-high sun, the couple rested on the sandy beach, his head settled between her breasts. He fell firmly asleep, secure on the pillowed skin, blanketed with the sounds of waves while the woman, Sarah, thought of her life as the minutes passed. Unlike this man, Bluderin could never sleep when he was with Sarah. He was always awake, his heart beating like the taps of deer running from hunters. Bluderin wondered if the strange man knew what he had known: the melody of her soft voice, the pout of her navel in the sun. *Good-bye, Sarah, good-bye forever.*

Coming back to the present, he was drained but felt a new strength coming on. He looked over at Riki and thought of how he had met her unintentionally at the gallery. He had not smelled any paint on her or in the canvas bag. Something was not making any sense.

"John, let's go. It's dark now."

She walked hurriedly, much faster than he, humming a song in her stride. She was so thin she looked like a self-sustaining limb. Her legs marched forward with extremity. Her sense of simplicity, he felt, was tangled in a cage of distress.

They crossed a bridge and took a moment to observe the stream running under it. Riki's inaudible words, her humming song, seemed to trace the movement of the water.

The quiet moment was raped when the blasts of a siren whored through the town. Bluderin immediately recognized the military alert and told Riki he had to get back to Hardt Kaserne. She understood his sense of urgency and kissed him good-bye.

He ran into the center of town until he was able to wave down a taxi. He got into the black Mercedes, and the driver had him back to Hardt Kaserne within minutes. When he checked into the base he felt a sense of relief.

He had not wanted to go into Riki's apartment. He was confused by their relationship. The only certainty he had was that he did not, could not, understand her. She evoked in him an emotional thrust he found paralyzing and frightening. He could not place what it was but, as he dressed into his fatigues, he thought that the alert had done him a favor. He had so little time left in the army, and he wanted to get out of it in one piece. His temples twinged in pain when his sixth sense told him that Riki Taar had other plans.

Seventeen

This is your final assignment, Bluderin had been told. His intelligence contact had said the same thing after she delegated her previous order to him—to deliver the black opal ring, via Riki Taar, to Günter and, in turn, to distribute the gray and yellow envelopes from Günter to Gustav Erdmann and Riki Taar, respectively, *after the fact, when he had already completed it.* What type of game was she playing? The disparity in her use of the term *final assignment* made him recollect what Gustav had warned him about intelligence contacts: "They will lie to you whenever it suits their needs."

Bluderin looked in a blue plastic box with wires inlaid within its cover. He removed two oversized lipstick tubes. Instead of lipstick being inside the tubes, each one housed what appeared to be part of the fuse assembly to a grenade. He had no idea if the grenades Leda Beschwörung had in her suitcase at the apartment contained fuses. He did not recall having seen a striker on the grenades, although the safety pin and striker lever—some called it a safety lever—were intact. This assignment perplexed him, and it was encumbered by the requirement that he deliver the box to Aarika Taar. Why did he have to deal with her again?

He knocked on the door to her apartment and waited. It surprised him to see a black mailbox mounted on the wall next to the door with the name *A. Williams,* not *A. Taar.* He knew that

230

Williams had been her married name; perhaps she had not yet legally changed it back to Taar.

"We have to speak softly," she whispered. "I don't want the neighbors to know I have a man in my apartment."

"I'll be quiet, but why should they care?" he said in a soft voice.

"They do. They're all strict Catholics—and nosy ones, too."

He noticed that Riki had redecorated her living room. The formerly beige walls were covered with coral wallpaper having the texture of burlap. Riki told him that she could hang pictures now, since the landlord would not complain about little holes in the walls if she did not renew her lease. If one brushed the cloth wallpaper where a picture had hung, it would make the hole disappear. Also, if she decided to change pictures from time to time or remove them, no one would be the wiser.

"Where are your paintings?" he asked. "You were going to show me some before the alert went off, when I had to hurry back to Hardt Kaserne."

"Oh," she said, her lips tightening. "Another student at the Staaliche Werkkunstschule has them. He's going to frame them. I never took a class in framing—know nothing about it."

She took the plastic box from him and went to hide it in her bedroom. He could hear her whispering something but dismissed it as anything unusual, thinking she was humming a tune, as she habitually did.

When Riki returned to the living room, she asked him to have tea with her, and he reluctantly accepted the offer. He did not want to be rude, and his contact on base had told him to take note of Riki's behavior and report back to her. He sat on a Venetian red couch as diffused light from street lamps flickered on the shadowy wall. Music was being played in another room—the bedroom, he guessed.

Riki was boiling water in the kitchen, humming in tune with the song from an album by Joan Baez. Riki's voice was faint, but he knew the lyrics to Baez's "Sweet Sir Galahad" song.

It was true that ever since the day
her crazy man had passed away
to the land of poet's pride,
she laughed and talked a lot
with new people on the block
but always at evening time she cried.

He read the titles to some books that were stacked on a small, cherry-wood chest that Riki used for a coffee table. *Narcissus and Goldman* by Hermann Hesse was at the top of the stack, followed by Hesse's *Siddhartha*, *The Prophet* by Kahil Gribran, a German version of *The Tin Drum* by Günter Grass called *Die Blechtrommel*, and Volume One of Hitler's *Mein Kampf*. Why was she reading Hitler?

She served him a cup of tea, then stood with her arms akimbo before him. He was ill at ease from her staring at him, and in a subconscious act of self-defense he removed *Mein Kampf* from the stack and looked through it. He read that the book was the *Volksausgabe*, or People's Edition. Its cover was navy blue beneath an embossed, gold swastika eagle.

"Do you actually read this crap?" he asked her.

"I wanted to look into the mind of one of the most malicious people in all humankind, in all history," she said. "The book can also be studied as a work on political theory or foreign policy. You should read it."

"I've already read enough to make me sick," he said. "I have no desire to study Hitler's major thesis of 'the Jewish peril,' the alleged Jewish conspiracy to gain world ownership. Nor do I need to read about the process by which Hitler became increasingly anti-Semitic and militaristic. It's all insane."

"To each his own," she said, still standing before him. She crossed one leg in front of the other and leaned against her right hip. Her tightly fitted nylon pants folded into an intimate dimple at the crotch. She kept staring at him, making him nervous. The record album changed, and he heard The Doors singing "Light My Fire." He rose from the couch, intending to leave the apartment, but when he stood he felt seriously dizzy. He fell back on the couch, thinking that he was going to faint. Jim Morrison's voice was taking him on a dream, and he began living in the lyrics of the song.

The time to hesitate is through
No time to wallow in the mire
Try now we can only lose
And our love become a funeral pyre
Come on baby, light my fire . . .

Riki went to her bedroom, and he could vaguely hear her talking to someone. He did not know if the person had just come into the apartment or had been there before he arrived. He attempted to rise again but collapsed back on the couch. He heard Riki speaking in a loud voice.

"Elisha, I told you to wear the red panties, not the yellow ones."

He fell into a deep sleep, dreaming wearily of the music, the eloquence of Morrison's eerie voice taking him on a delusional voyage. He saw himself floating in the air with Riki, as if they were seagulls in flight. There was another young woman floating in front of them. He had seen the girl before, but he could not determine when or where. Still, the long, light brown hair, the delicate hands, the thin, toned legs, and especially the small breasts reminded him of someone who was mysteriously erotic.

She was wearing a red, semi-transparent negligee with thin, spaghetti-like shoulder straps. The negligee cupped her small breasts and fitted her form like a latex glove, ending half-way down the globes of her cute little ass.

Riki was wearing a black, strapless, leather mini-dress and a glass-studded choker. Bluderin could see that she was not wearing any panties, as her auburn, silk-like pubic hair was exposed. Riki and the other woman tugged on his penis and pinched his nipples, making them sore. He was stark naked, much to his amazement, and he felt an erection starting to build. His heart was pounding as Riki stroked him and the other woman played with his testicles and inserted a finger into his anus. He tried desperately to escape the illusions he was having, but instinctively he thought that the horrifying dream could be real.

The chill, evening air nipped at his nakedness, a feeling that contrasted with Riki's warm genitalia as she climbed over him and sat on his thighs, her knees straddling his ribs. He heard her loud heartbeat as she lowered herself over his manhood and inserted him into her. She began screaming. He felt her vaginal muscles pulsate against him, then vacuum him into her like a slippery, wet mouth. Her leather skirt rose up to her waist. She leaked all over his groin when he ejaculated inside her.

It was then when he realized he was not dreaming. The drug, serum, or whatever it was that Riki had deposited into his tea seemed to be losing its effect. Bluderin discovered that he was chained to Riki's bedposts. He tried to free himself, but he did not have the strength or ability to do so. Riki pulled her dress up higher as she stood on her knees before turning sideways to get off the bed. Bluderin looked at her abdomen but saw no signs of scars, nothing unsightly or obvious. She either had lied to him or was so delusional that she saw things that did not exist.

She was right about one thing, however. Her vaginal muscles

could work wonders; they were as flexible as fingers. He ex-husband had gotten her to develop an intricate sexual talent. He was extremely demanding, she had said, and she did everything she possibly could to fulfill his carnal demands.

When Riki left for the bathroom, the other girl sat on the bed and cleaned him with a warm washcloth and towel. She then kissed his sex and licked at the shaft until it was rigid again.

"You've got a big one," she said, and winked at him. "It's so long and thick."

Bluderin was sweating with nervousness. All he wanted to do was get out of this crazy mess. Nevertheless, her attentive hands and mouth were exciting him. His instincts would not obey his brain. It was absurd.

"Who are you?" he asked, breathing deeply.

"You don't remember me?" She frowned. She lay on top of him, bringing her mouth to his. Her kiss was wet and passionate, interlocking his tongue with hers. He instinctively went to pat her ass, but his arms could not move more than a few inches.

"Remove these shackles," he said, and faked a smile. "We can have a lot more fun that way."

"I will in a while," she said. "Riki wants to have her way with you one more time before we take the shackles off. Now it's my turn to have a little fun with you. My name is Elisha Amsel, by the way. It's so nice to see you again."

When she took off her negligee and panties, Bluderin recognized who Elisha Amsel was. She was the girl-boy he had danced with when he was with Solveig Evensen at Josef's Gasthaus. That had to be over a year ago. Her breasts had grown larger, from the diameters of tennis balls to those of baseballs. Her hair was a good six inches longer than when he last saw her, and she had lightened it to a softer shade of brown with blonde highlights, but there was no doubt that she was the girl-boy. Elisha was *nearly all girl*. She looked more feminine than Riki, her tiny waist and hips being more refined. Her skin was softer than Riki's, and Elisha did not have a hair on her body. The only hint of a boy was an incredibly small, lily-white bump with a pinkish sac between her legs.

Bluderin lay helpless as Elisha sucked his nipples and rubbed her genitals all over his body until she climaxed. He had never in his life been so out of control or, more pointedly, so completely under other people's control. It was not right, he told himself. He was being held against his will. In essence, he had been raped. He was thinking that perhaps he was feeling what Solveig Evensen felt when she was raped by her father. It was horrible. These women were robbing him of his dignity and humiliating the core of his being, his very soul.

If the situation were reversed, he'd be sent to prison for who knows how long. Still, his instinct for survival told him to befriend the girl-boy, to win her favor and get her to set him free. He had no clue what Riki had in mind for him, and he did not want to find out. Leda Beschwörung had warned him to avoid this type of sexual deviance unless he completely trusted his partner. Riki Taar was the last person he would ever trust, and now she held him captive. The girl-boy was his only hope.

Elisha got off the bed and was leaving the bedroom when he desperately spoke out to her.

"Maybe we can go out some time," he said. "You know, a movie or something."

Elisha smiled and blew him a kiss before she closed the bedroom door, leaving him alone. He listened to his stressful breathing, felt the darkness in the room, and stared at the shapes of trees shadowed on the walls. Once again all of his senses sharpened, and his erection grew with a painful surge. Had Riki slipped an aphrodisiac into his tea as well as a sedative—or something stronger—to put him to sleep?

Riki came into the bedroom again and leaned over him, biting his neck and chest, running her hands along his groin. He could smell the musk of her moist desire. He slid into her effortlessly as she moved back and forth in slow, long strokes. By the expression on her face he did not think she was enjoying the sex but soon she began screaming again, digging her fingernails into his chest. Using the discipline he had acquired through practicing karate, he managed not to climax this time.

Riki was well on her way. She slapped his face and her eyes twitched. Her forehead wrinkled as if she was in pain, but she kept digging harder into his chest and thrusting her pelvis against his.

"I want more. Give me more." She spoke loudly, apparently no longer concerned if the neighbors heard her. "That's it. That's it. Oh my God." She shuddered madly, compulsively, and raised her fists, as if in victory. "Amazing," she said. She looked at him with what Bluderin judged to be a sadistic expression. She spit at him and slapped him hard again on the face. "Why didn't you come, you cold-hearted bastard? Don't I excite you?"

"You and Elisha dried me up," he said, trying to calm her down. "You can see how you excite me. I can't hide that, but I'm out of gas."

She seemed, at least momentarily, satisfied with his excuse and got off him. Her lips were uneven—crooked—and her eyes lit on and off like fireflies.

"You have to possess a stroke of madness to have unusual sexual desires," she said. "We have over-civilized ourselves so much— divorced ourselves from nature—that even our sexual desires are no longer natural. We are moving away from all beginning." Riki spoke incoherently, going into a long polemic about sexual behavior.

Bluderin tried to blur her ranting out of his mind, but she ceaselessly continued rambling on about breaking the fear of psychic metamorphosis through deviant sexual compulsion.

"Did you know that the Führer's paraphilia included defecation?"

she asked him. "Urination as well. And you're freaked out by shackles and chains—what a wimp."

When she finally stopped the insane blabbering, she raised her hands over her head, stretching, as though she were trying to reach the ceiling. She looked at Bluderin with a crazed grin.

"I hope I'm not pregnant," she said.

"You didn't take precautions?" he asked. He thought she said that to cause him further anxiety. When she raped him the first time, he had exploded everything he had into her. He could not control his physiology that time. Now he could.

"I was going to start taking the pill in a couple of days," she said. "I wanted to have my period first. I'm probably not pregnant, but who knows? I ovulate twice a month." She laughed recklessly, seemingly unconcerned, and left the bedroom.

He could hear Riki and Elisha talking. They were getting into an argument; their voices were fraught with angered emotion. Then he heard someone turn on the shower.

Elisha reentered the bedroom, locking the door behind her. She was in street clothes this time, a black knitted tank top and bright red shorts that barely covered her bottom. Her black sandals, which looked as though they had three-inch high heels, made her smooth calves flex with muscle.

She crossed her lips with an index finger, signaling for him to keep quiet. She took a key off the bureau and began unlocking the shackles from his limbs. He rubbed his wrists and ankles as he was freed. He sat up, finding his clothes and shoes on the floor next to the bed. He dressed as quickly as he could and was about to head for the bedroom door when Riki banged on it from the other side.

"You will both be washed in the blood of the lamb," she said, "but only after you are mine."

"We need to escape through the bedroom window," Elisha said.

Riki's apartment was on the second floor of the building, but Bluderin did not have a second's worth of hesitation in preparing to jump out the window. Breaking a leg would better than being attacked by a vicious mad woman. He pushed up the lower pane.

"Follow me out," he said to Elisha. "Throw your shoes to me first, then ease yourself out the window with your feet pointed to the outside wall."

Bluderin hoisted himself onto the window sill, turned so that his hips and legs fell against the outside wall, then kicked himself free as he fell onto the ground, rolling as he had been taught in army training. He dusted himself off, free of dirt and grass, and Elisha tossed out her shoes. He could still hear Riki yelling and pounding on the door.

"Let me in, or you will die, you bastards. I own you."

Elisha hung out the window with her forearms and hands remaining on the window sill. She was panicking, frozen, as though her body would not let her fall.

"Jump, Elisha." Bluderin said. "Kick yourself free, away from the building, and let go. I'm right here."

She did as he told her and landed in his arms and against his chest. He fell back on his butt with her on top of him.

"Let's get a move on," he said. "*Now.*"

The second she had her sandals buckled he grabbed her arm firmly and forced her to run with him.

"Where are we going?" Elisha asked in a trembling voice, running awkwardly in her high heels.

"To my car. It's about two blocks away. I'm getting the fuck out of town, and you're coming with me."

"You don't have to force me," she said. "I want to go with you." Her voice trembled. "I don't want Riki to find me. I'm scared to death."

Soon they were in Bluderin's car and driving toward Aalen, each of them smoking a cigarette, trying to gather their wits. They needed to settle down so they could talk about the *freakingly perilous ordeal* they had just experienced.

"There is a café about three kilometers north," Elisha said. "It's on the right, a place called Die Engel. We can recover there and talk."

Bluderin had heard about the Engel—translated as Angel—but had never been there. The place was reputed to be a hangout for gay and bisexual men and women. He thought of suggesting another place, but he realized that Elisha probably had friends there. Besides, he didn't want to be seen with her anywhere else.

"You are going to tell me everything you know about Aarika Taar and how you and she got together to torment me. Do you understand?"

Elisha nodded in agreement.

He sensed that she could not stop laughing. She was quiet but biting her lips and shaking her head back and forth until she burst out loud in giggles.

"What's so damn funny?"

"I was thinking of how I fell into your strong arms," she said. "I was completely terrified. I thought I was going to break into pieces. When I look back on it, the whole falling and landing thing was kind of sexy. I really liked it when I landed on you and we hit the ground. Your penis was nudging the crack of my ass, and your hands were wrapped around my boobies."

"Sex was the furthest thing from my mind," he said. "After all, I had just escaped ridicule and torture." He noticed that he still had an erection; it would not go away.

"What did Riki put in my tea?" he asked.

She breathed deeply and forced herself to talk. "I'll tell you everything after I've had a drink."

He did not bring the matter up again until he had consumed

two glasses of cognac. Elisha was on her third glass of Steinhäger. Bluderin looked around the cocktail lounge but did not recognize any of the other customers. None of them seemed to notice Elisha either. Maybe they did but were respecting her privacy.

"Tell me what you know," he said. "*Everything.*"

She looked at him, her eyebrows furled, and she took a deep breath. "I've known Riki for approximately one year. We met at a Fasching celebration. Riki was dressed in men's clothing—a tweed sports jacket, white shirt, and gray trousers—while I wore a pink mini-dress and black tights set off by silver-sequined, high heels. Both of us had black masks. Riki's was plain while mine was sequined, like my shoes. As the evening progressed, we began joking about our fanciful appearances—a boy dressed as a girl and a girl dressed as a boy—when she kissed me hard on the lips and pinched my little boobs. The intimate gesture ignited a series of sexual trysts between us. I always went to Riki's apartment for our encounters. She never came to mine. Her neighbors thought nothing of the visits, probably assuming that we were girl friends who likely worked together."

Elisha leaned into the table and placed a hand between his legs.

"What happened during those encounters?" he asked. "You must have enjoyed them. You kept going back."

"Our interludes were simple at first, with Riki taking on a male role and me being the girl. Even when we had normal intercourse—or as close to it as we could get—Riki would be on top of me, leading the way. Later on the relationship moved into sadomasochistic ventures. I would be in bondage, locked in shackles and chains, while Riki would be in total control, performing acts such as dripping hot candle wax onto the most intimate parts of my body and spanking my bottom with a black, bamboo cane. I derived pleasure in my submissive role. It made me feel more 'girly' or feminine."

"What was the purpose of bringing me into your games?" he

asked. "What was I supposed to do?" He felt her hand stroke his unwanted erection.

"We eventually admitted to each other that something was missing in our sexual relationship. We both wanted 'a real man' to join us in our rendezvous. When Riki told me about you, we devised a plan to bring you under our control. You had the temperament and open mindedness, according to Riki, to join us in our games. As time went on, Riki told me that she had described our relationship to you and that you were willing to become an active participant."

"Riki said nothing of the kind. She never even mentioned your name."

"I came to believe you, but it was too late," she said. "When Riki told me to hide in the bedroom when you knocked on the door to the apartment, I should have known something was wrong."

As she continued stroking his thighs and loins, her eyes widened. She licked her lips, and her lipstick spread, making her mouth look erotically ready for him. "I knew that Riki slipped Spanish fly, or cantharides, into your cup of tea, to get you excited." Elisha insisted that she knew nothing about Riki depositing a sleeping pill or the like into his tea.

"I didn't know anything about that until Riki had me help carry you onto her bed. After she told me about the sedative, she said that it was all part of our plan to make you submissive. With the way that you responded to our seductive touches, I thought that you were responding naturally, that you were getting turned on. I had no idea that you were functioning in an illusory state of mind."

He removed her hand from his crotch and held it. She leaned over the table to kiss him, and he let her. He had to. She was providing invaluable information. To urge her on, he believed she needed to trust him and feel desirable.

"I thought you liked what we were doing to you," she said. "After we had our first sexual foray with you, we were preparing for another. It was all supposed to be in good fun. That was until I saw Riki light several candles in the kitchen. What disturbed me were not the candles but two long, newly sharpened knives onto which Riki had poured hot candle wax."

"What was the idea behind the wax?" he asked.

"She said something about cutting you and sealing you at the same time. I was getting scared. When Riki abruptly left the kitchen to shower, I noticed a photograph on the kitchen counter. It was a picture of a woman's abdomen maligned with dark, viscous scars. I also found a note beneath the photograph. The note said, 'He will get his scars and I will own him.' Next to the note I saw a mouthpiece—something like dentures—but with little metal blades instead of teeth. That's when I could feel my hands shake involuntarily. In my paranoid confusion I somehow had the wherewithal to remember having placed the shackle key on Riki's dresser. I was sure your life was in danger, so I hurried into the bedroom, locked the door, and proceeded to set you free."

He was sure that she was telling him the truth. She squeezed his hand and kissed him again. Her henna eyes floated from an orange shade to more of a red one, reflecting off the candle-lit table. Similarly, her soft cheeks flushed red.

"I don't know what to say," he said. "I could be dead or castrated."

"I'm no heroine. I was afraid for myself as well. I think she was going to stab me first. Riki knew I would have nothing to do with violence."

Bluderin signaled to the waiter for another round of drinks. The alcohol was not giving him a high, but it seemed to help stabilize his anxious state of mind. The booze also helped Elisha talk more easily.

"There is a quote in the Bible by Luke—that 'the light of the body is the eye'," she said. "When I looked into Riki's eyes in the kitchen all I saw was the light of darkness. That's when I knew she lost it. Her eyes literally turned black."

Bluderin thought about Elisha's account of what happened. He had also observed Riki's eyes change color—at the art gallery—not to black, but from a shade of emerald to burgundy. However, he had noticed that they did turn black when she spoke about her husband. Why would Riki physically harm him? Her violent scheming made him nauseous. *So much for her fucking psychiatrist's professional opinion.* He gulped down a full shot of cognac. The bizarre and demented episode of the day was manageable only by the influence of alcohol. He ordered another round.

"Are you going to press charges?" Elisha asked him. "I'll back you up, whatever you say."

"I'm not going to do anything about Riki's malicious behavior," he said. "Pressing charges would only prolong my stay in the army."

He did ask for and received Elisha's street address and phone number, just in case Riki decided to accuse *him* of wrongdoing.

"You never know what a nut case is going to do," he said.

"Riki is not going to do a damned thing," she said. "I'll make sure of that. I know other things about her that could get her arrested. She'll ease off. She doesn't want her children to see her behind bars."

Elisha took out a tube of skin cream from her handbag and told Bluderin to rub the cream on his chest where Riki had dug her fingernails. She had noticed that the front of his shirt was marked with splotches of blood.

Bluderin undid a couple of buttons and rubbed his chest with the cream. "Do you need a ride home?" he asked.

"I have a boyfriend sitting at another table off in the corner. I want to talk with him later—that is, unless you want to have some fun with me."

He didn't want to dismiss her outright, but her kinky sexual predilections were nothing he wanted any further exposure to.

"I've had enough excitement and hysteria for one day," he said. "I can't take any more." He did not want to hurt Elisha's feelings—who knows, she might have saved his life, or at least saved him from mutilation—but he did not want to see her again.

"Maybe you'll change your mind after I have surgery to turn into a complete woman. I was born with Klinefelter's syndrome," she said. "While females have an XX chromosomal makeup, and males an XY, mine is XXY, with the Y hardly being detectable. So why not fix my chromosome disorder with a little help from modern medicine?"

"You're probably making the right decision," he said, "if that's what you want and your doctors support you."

"I've been pleased with the results so far," she said. "You didn't mind looking at my body earlier, did you?" Elisha stood, walked over to him, and sat on his lap, pampering him with a soft kiss and placing his hands on her breasts. "I love turning on straight guys. It's great for my ego." She reached inside his pants and pressed under his testicles in a peculiar, almost clinical, way until his erection subsided. "There," she said. "You'll feel much better now."

Elisha then walked over to the three men sitting at the table she had described. One of them, to Bluderin's astonishment, was Joe Tyler, who was holding hands with a dapper-looking guy with a precision-cut moustache and lustrous, black hair, like Omar Sharif at the beginning of *Dr. Zhivago*. Joe Tyler—Bluderin's assistant, a devout Mormon and married man with two little children—apparently had a gay side to him. Joe had his back to him, which made it easy for Bluderin to disappear before they spotted each other.

You never know who you're dealing with, Bluderin thought out loud as he got into his car, finding it hard to believe that Tyler was gay. He always had acted so straight and professional when at Hardt Kaserne. Bluderin now felt that he never *saw* what he was looking at when he worked with Joe Tyler. He wondered if he ever knew anyone for what they were instead of what they pretended to be. Maybe Solveig Evensen, he thought, if I'm lucky, but who knows if I'll ever see her again.

As requested by his agent on base, he would file a report on Riki Taar's behavior. He questioned whether it would do him more harm than good. Diane James' premonition, as signaled in Howard's painting, had proved to be right on—the woman was evil. He felt ill when the thought came to him that Riki Taar was not done with him yet. He wanted her out of his life. She wanted in.

Eighteen

◄○►

Bluderin once again was in *The Dark Room* of Headquarters Building at Hardt Kaserne. He had described in detail to his intelligence contact the near-calamity he experienced through Riki and Elisha. The agent had not yet responded to anything he had said. Since he could not see her face—or any other physical characteristics—he couldn't fathom a guess about what she thought of his testimony.

The confessional booth setup was much like the one at the church he had attended in Defiance. Although the structural design had two sides, the psychological motif had only one. You spilled your guts on one side and waited. Sometimes there would be a comment from the other side; sometimes nothing would come, other than a rote request, such as "Say three Hail Marys" or the like. At least he was confident he would not be directed to any more assignments involving Riki Taar.

"I have listened to you carefully," the woman said in a deep voice, sounding like that of a contralto. "The incident you described was grotesque at best, if not downright criminal. However, you escaped without any physical damage. Since you do not want to press charges—and I can understand why—you can deposit the incident in your experience bank. The agency will not be overly concerned about the perversion."

He could not discern an undercurrent of opinion in the woman's staccato diction. It was detached, as invisible as her physical presence.

"The intent of an intelligence contact to stab—maim or murder—an intelligence colleague is of not immediate concern to the agency. Is that what you're telling me?" he asked.

"The agency has more immediate—more pressing—priorities at the moment," she said. "Riki could say she was just playing with your mind. It would be difficult for us to prove otherwise, and it would require too many resources to investigate your allegations. Those resources need to be applied to a more urgent matter."

"I see," he said. "I assume you're done with me." As he stood to feel his way out of *The Dark Room*, the agent told him to sit down. She wasn't finished with him yet.

"We're missing things," she said. "For one, the person to whom Riki was supposed to deliver the grenades has not yet received them. Riki is a day late in completing her assignment. We've already verified that Leda Beschwörung delivered the box of grenades to Günter Mann, who in turn gave it to Gustav Erdmann. Gustav had, as instructed, personally delivered the box to Riki. We involved Gustav because Riki's neighbors, who would recognize him, would assume that he was performing a civil function as a public official, since he chairs the town's public housing committee. Apparently the grenades are still in Riki's possession."

"That's not good," Bluderin said. "I assure you, I gave Riki the plastic blue box before she drugged me. I know there were grenade fuses inside the lipstick tubes."

"I appreciate your being candid," the agent said. "What else do you know? What has the Vereingten Frieden been telling you? We found out who the mole was, incidentally."

It did not surprise him to hear that the mole had been identified. It was bound to happen. Too much information was being passed around for the agency not to notice secrets being revealed.

"The information I received from Vereingten Frieden came by word of mouth," he said, "so I have no way of determining its accuracy. Messages came to me from Walter Lebrecht through Peter Vanderwerken, as you no doubt already know. Peter has trouble remembering details, a characteristic that makes me skeptical about what he told me."

"Tell me what he told you," the agent said. "We will decide whether the information is worthwhile."

Like Leda Beschwörung, Bluderin was sure that this agent knew all that he knew. The mole probably had told her everything in some kind of informal plea-bargaining agreement. He had heard that the mole would be fired, but that no further action would be taken.

"I was told that the black opal ring Riki passed on to me to give Günter had information hidden under the gem, listing the items that the agency was missing and likely thought had been stolen. The gray envelope I handed over to Gustav Erdmann purportedly contained a message that Riki Taar was a suspect. The yellow envelope I gave to Riki had a contradictory message—that the suspect was a GI."

"What do you think?" the agent asked.

"I'm clueless," he said. "I never opened the ring or the envelopes, so I don't know anything for certain. Also, I don't trust Peter Vanderwerken's account, for reasons I've already described."

"We have an issue," she said. "Riki possibly has both the grenades and fuses hidden away in her apartment. What she may be intending to do with them is the larger question. During her three years as an intelligence contact, Riki has acquired some of the knowledge and skills needed to insert the fuses into the grenades. We will have to check further into her personnel file to determine how much she actually knows about explosives."

Since he could not get a hint of what this invisible agent may be thinking, Bluderin thought he would drop a red herring. "This scenario is way over my head. I'm of no further use to you."

"Don't be so sure about that," she said.

He could finally detect something human—there was a strain in her voice. He had struck a nerve.

"We will get back to you in a day or two," she said. "If Riki knows how to assemble the grenades, we potentially could need you to help us secure them."

"What good can I do?" he asked. "My knowledge of ballistics is severely limited."

"It's your relationship with her that may be useful," she said. "We have all the grenade expertise we need."

"My relationship with Riki is disdainful," he said. "I can't stomach her."

"Listen to me," the agent said. "We don't want your opinion. If we need your assistance, you will have to tell Riki that you want to see her again. You could tell her that you enjoyed your sexual encounter with her and want to do it again. Sure, you got a little freaked out at first because you had never done anything like it before. Now that you've had the time to think it over you've found it incredibly erotic."

"I don't think she'll buy it," he said, "but I'll do whatever you want."

"We placed some money in your desk," she said. "If we decide to use you, you can call Riki and invite her to dinner—a late dinner, a romantic event. That will give us time to search her apartment for the grenades without her neighbors knowing we're there."

Raising an objection to another interaction with Riki Taar would be pointless. You don't argue with intelligence agents. All an objection would do would raise suspicions about *him*.

He thought that the entire scenario about the grenades and fuses was convoluted, but everyting the intelligence community planned or did was weaved in a mass of frivolous complexity. He did not know what was in store for him on his final week of active duty, but his intuition told him that he had not yet completed his *final assignment.*

When he left Hardt Kaserne and arrived at his apartment, he could hear a sound coming from inside it—something like a muffled scream or cry—before he inserted the key in the door. He decided to check the restricted back entrance, the hatchway or cellar door, to the apartment. If it were locked, Leda Beschwörung would be in the apartment, paying another surprise visit. For security purposes, he knew that Leda would have made sure to lock the back door from the inside.

It was not locked. Bluderin carefully opened the door and descended the three large, stone steps to where a series of curtains hung from the ceiling to the floor. The dark, thick layers of curtains, formerly used in theaters, were the only barricade between him and his living quarters. He pulled out a small section of the curtains on the left side, creating an opening about the size of a golf ball, so he could take a look.

Riki Taar stood over Elisha Amsel, who was sitting on the deep-blue sofa. It had rained earlier, and Riki was drenched. Her makeup had washed away, leaving only smudges of mascara and lipstick. She pointed a Luger at Elisha.

There would be no sense in contacting the agency. They would dismiss his observations as another perverted game and not of their concern. It was no game, he knew, but direct criminal assault. It was devastating to see how Riki had taken on the role of a vengeful aggressor since he and Elisha had escaped from her apartment. Elisha should have known better than to approach Riki on her own accord, by herself, since Riki would take revenge on her for freeing him.

"If you try to counter me again, you'll be one dead faggot," Riki said. "I've got a silencer on this weapon, so no one will hear me blow your brains out."

Elisha nodded nervously in agreement. "Please let me go, Riki. The only reason I came to your apartment was to retrieve my lingerie. I want nothing else. Why did you bring me here? Where are we?"

"Your lingerie belongs to me," Riki said. "I own the pink, red, blue, gold, yellow, and white frilly garments—all of them—just like I own you. Now strip down to nothing. I don't want to see a thread on you— and don't give me any more back talk."

Elisha began to take off her blouse. Her hands and fingers shook so much that she had difficulty unfastening the buttons.

"No stalling," Riki said. "What is it now?"

"Right here? I don't even know where I am. Let's go back to your apartment. I'll do whatever you want there. *Anything.*"

Riki pressed the Luger against Elisha's forehead. "You can't be trusted. You'll try to run away. *Now strip.*"

Elisha took off her clothes in awkward, hesitating movements and stacked them on a corner of the couch. "Being naked in such a strange place gives me the creeps. Why won't you tell me where we are?"

"We're in John Bluderin's apartment," Riki said. "As I told my grandmother and children this morning, I'm going to marry him. I want you here as a witness."

Bluderin momentarily closed the curtain. He was terrified of Riki's expression. He could not shake it off. She seemed to be absorbed in confusion and gleams of desperation. He opened a chink of curtain again when he heard her speaking

"My grandmother questioned whether my new man, whom she had seen at the park near the Marktplatz, was for real—whether he was a genuine candidate for a husband, or if he were another figment of my imagination. She said it would be foolish of me to assume that he would marry me, just as it had been foolish of me to get caught in the rainstorm, since everyone knew it was coming by the appearance of fierce, gray clouds. I have no fear of the weather—not the storms in the sky nor the ones in my head. My grandmother feels partially responsible for my occasional careless state of mind. I'm such a dreamer, my grandmother said, much like her deceased son, my father. He and I shared the need to dream as much as the need to breathe."

"After what you did—or tried to do—to Bluderin, he won't come near you, let alone marry you," Elisha said. "What could possibly make you think he would? It's preposterous."

"A woman's intuition," Riki said. "I know what I do to him."

"No doubts at all?" Elisha said. "I've heard you make such bold statements before about two other men you dated. You haven't even dated John."

"I have little doubt," Riki said. "John has enjoyed his time in Germany, and he has given some thought to staying here, but I believe I can convince him to marry me and take me to the United States."

"You're delirious about your own fabrication," Elisha said.

"That's enough. Now, bend over so I can see up your ass. I need something to entertain me while I wait for John."

Elisha did as ordered, and Riki inched the tip of the barrel into her rectum. Elisha whimpered in discomfort when Riki inserted the barrel in further.

"Are you sure he's coming?" Elisha asked. "Or did you bring me here to kill me?"

"You have to understand the darkest aspects of human nature," Riki said. "I left a note for John with his assistant. I explained that I only wanted to have a little fun with him, to impart mystique into our relationship. I said that you must have misinterpreted what I was intending to do. I was going to scare him to heighten his senses and give him an overwhelming orgasm. I wanted him to reach nirvana. When you enter a state of infinite freedom—oblivious to pain, anxiety, and suffering—is when you find your true being, your karma, I told him."

"If he doesn't show up, you'll kill me, won't you, and make it look like he committed the murder?"

"That's one alternative, if he doesn't do as I wish," Riki said.

Riki withdrew the Luger from Elisha's rectum, stepped back, and started to look feeble. She acted as if her senses had dulled and a flood had erupted within her body. Her knees trembled. She gripped her abdomen and sat down on an arm of the couch.

"I'm pregnant," she said, "and I made him make me pregnant. I forced him into it and now I must make him responsible. He will take care of me, I know. That is why I captured him in the first place. You were there simply to increase the excitement. You were part of the plan to make him enjoy sexual submission. You wanted your way with him, but I saw to it that I had my way first, when he filled me with semen. The day after he and you fled the apartment, I contacted you to make sure that you would say he took advantage of me, but you hung up. *I'm going to own you, bitch. You will become my slave, as will John Bluderin.*"

Elisha covered her forehead with her hands and stared at the floor, apparently trying not to cry. "You have completely lost touch with reality," she said. "Why did you do this to yourself? Take advantage of a man, just because he is kind, sensitive, and considerate? How many men have you seduced, only to find yourself being the recipient of off-color comments and other antics of disrespect? If you are pregnant, for God's sake, have the doctor perform a hysterectomy after the delivery. The world does not need any more unloved and unwanted children. *Lord, let us pray . . .*"

Riki put something into her mouth. Bluderin could not tell what it was, but it seemed to make her voice take on a static quality. Her words buzzed when she spoke.

"Lay down on the sofa with your backside toward me," she said. "I have to do this for my children, Kane and Eve. You're right, Elisha. John is a kind man, very polite and respectful. He told me that children were the purest souls on earth. I have seen the way he treats the children of American soldiers at Hardt Kaserne. He frequently buys them ice cream or gives them change for a candy bar. I'm confident that he will relate to my children in a similar way. Especially Eve—she will enchant him. She is the eternal lightness of being, so pretty and with such a vivid imagination."

"I hope your kids will not be disappointed, as in past occurrences, by you raising their hopes with expectations that never happen," Elisha said, her mouth muffled into a sofa cushion.

Riki fiddled with the contraption she had inserted into her mouth, making it click back and forth. Bluderin thought it sounded like pieces of metal snapping against each other. Little red sparks shot out of her mouth when she spoke.

"May there always be sunshine," she said. "*Immer liebe die Sonne.* I taught my daughter the English lyrics to that song."

May there always be sunshine,
May there always be blue skies,
May there always be mummy,
May there always be me.

"It both delights and depresses me to hear Eve sing those lyrics. I love to listen to the lilting gaiety of her voice, but the line "May there always be mummy" is difficult to accept without regret. Mummy is not always around when Eve needs her."

"Please don't hurt me," Elisha said. "I beg you."

Riki turned to one side. Bluderin could see silver blades—like fangs, each one an inch or two in length—extend out of her mouth. He would have to disable her, without her seeing him, before she could harm Elisha. He mentally hummed a mantra, preparing his mind for attack, and formed knife-hands. He would have to strike her with full force on the side of her neck, just below her ear lobe.

It had to be done with one strike only, to stop the blood flow to her brain for less than a second.

If he did it right, she'd be out cold for ten or twenty minutes, plenty of time for Elisha to escape to safety. If he did it wrong—or if he had to strike her more than once—he possibly could kill her.

He got a break when Riki moved to the side of the couch with her back turned toward him. He slid out of his loafers and opened the curtain wider. Riki reached in her slacks and pulled out a knife, a large one. The blade must have been ten inches long.

"You are mine," she said to Elisha and raised the knife over her head. "I think I'll have your genitals for dessert tonight."

Before she could thrust the knife down on Elisha, Bluderin struck her with a knife-hand, immediately below her ear lobe and jawline. She started falling to the floor in a swoop. Her head hit the arm of the sofa on the way down. Bluderin thought the broken fall could have prevented her head from cracking on the concrete floor.

He was out of the apartment before Elisha had seen him, or so he thought. He hid in the vestibule of the Heilig-Kreuz-Münster where he could still see the cellar door to his apartment. He waited for it to open, and it did, with Elisha emerging onto the sidewalk. She walked toward the cathredal and spotted him.

"Thank God you were there," she said. Her skin was whiter than snow, with the exception of a few blue and red blotches that looked like a peculiar rash. "Did you see the size of that knife? She was going to cut me in pieces. How did you stop her? I never saw anything but one of your legs sticking out of the curtains when I jumped up from the couch."

"I used a karate technique," he said. "I hope it works the way I planned."

She rested her head on his chest, and he hugged her and stroked her back to in an attempt to stop her shivering. She spit and heaved into a handkerchief.

"You saved my life," she said. Her eyes were flooded, and eye shadow dripped along her thin, delicate cheeks.

"Quid pro quo, after what you did for me," he said, trying his best to make light of the dire and almost deathly circumstances she had found herself in. "The one you overlook will look out for you."

"What do you mean?" she asked.

"Nothing," he said. "I was just repeating something a prophet said to me."

Elisha took a deep breath. She appeared to be getting her senses back. "What are you waiting for?"

Godot, he thought, but he did not want confuse her with his allusion to Samuel Beckett. "I need to see Riki leave the apartment. I have to make sure I didn't kill her."

"Jesus," she said. "How long do you think she'll be unconscious?"

"If I don't see her coming out in another fifteen or twenty minutes, I'm going to be in deep trouble." He could almost see the headlines in the *Rems-Zeitung*: **GI Kills Pregnant Girlfriend. Transsexual Involved**.

"Do you think I have time to run over to Riki's apartment and get my lingerie?" she asked him.

He laughed out loud and smacked his hand on a column of the vestibule. Elisha had been within a plunge—a microsecond—of getting slaughtered minutes ago, and now her major concern was for her goddamned panties.

"It's not good timing," he said. "When Riki comes to, I'm sure she'll be heading back to her apartment. I have personal items there as well." He didn't want to tell her about the agency missing things.

Elisha looked disappointed. "What can I do about my lingerie? I need to get it back. One of my boyfriends loves the pink set. I'm supposed to meet up with him tonight."

"Hang tough," he said. "I highly suggest that somebody

accompany you to Riki's apartment—but not today. Go with someone who knows how to take care of himself, understand?"

"I will," she said. "I won't go within a kilometer of that woman without protection. I should have known better, after what you went through. I put my life in jeopardy. I've been such a fool."

"We're all fools when it comes to dealing with insanity," he said.

"I better get going," she said. "I'm off to the Engel. I know a guy there who will be my bodyguard when I go to get my lingerie back. He knows karate, like you. I took the Luger, in case you need to know. I couldn't leave it there. Who knows what Riki would do next?"

He didn't want anyting to do with the Luger. If Riki were dead and police found any trace of him on the pistol, he'd be imprisoned for the rest of his life. He thought it probable that Riki had stolen the gun from the agency.

"Go on," he said. "I'll tell you how to turn the Luger over to the authorities after I find out what happened to Riki. I desperately need to know if she recovers. Right now, I'm living on the edge between liberation and collapse."

Elisha left, after kissing him good-bye, saying she was going to treat herself to a new pair of panties and a bra.

I'll give it a full hour, he thought, to see if Riki climbs out of the hatchway. He stood immobile as a cigar store Indian, his eyes locked on the cellar door. The only thing that moved him was the rush of adrenaline.

Nineteen

◄○►

"When are you flying out?" Wiley Couch asked Bluderin. "It must be soon."

"As soon as they let me."

Much to his dismay, Bluderin had no idea when he would be allowed to leave Hardt Kaserne and Schwäbisch Gmünd. He was already processed out of the army—*in technical terms*. He had turned in the required equipment and clothing, and all the necessary documents had been signed off in approval. He was waiting for the final okay from his intelligence contact. She had told him to stay on base until the agency decided what it was going to do with Riki Taar and the missing grenades and fuses. The agency may need his assistance in the matter. Then again, it may not.

He had complained to his agent about being restricted to Hardt Kaserne. He explained to her that he had been invited to dinner by the Vanderwerkens, and he had not yet bid good-bye to his old friend and communications point, Gustav Erdmann. After listening to his plea, the agent allowed him a little more leeway. She decided that he could go into town, but he needed to be available at either the Vanderwerken house or Gustav Erdmann's Gasthaus. If he went elsewhere, he would have to contact her and let her know where he was. The restriction would be demanded of him for only two or three more days. The agent advised him to be patient. That was her way of saying *Don't press me for anything else.*

"Write to me and tell me about all the good shit," Couch said. "The anti-Vietnam War demonstrations, race riots, freedom marches, sit-ins, and of course the feminist movement."

"There are good things going on behind some of those initiatives," Bluderin said. "People are reexamining themselves and their values."

"Believe whatever you want to. I like what I'm doing—going to school and working for Gus three nights a week. It's a good gig for a new start at civilian life. The GI Bill is not a whole lot of money—just a monthly stipend, a hundred eighty bucks—but it helps me pay the bills. Sure would have been nice to have gotten the educational package the World War II vets got. I guess the Vietnam War isn't good enough for those benefits."

"You've got a good start," Bluderin said. "You'll be doing better financially when you learn the ropes of good bartending. You need to get that 'I don't blame you one bit' philosophy down to an art form, like Gustav. You'll get better tips that way."

"I'm working on it," Couch said. "Want another beer?"

"Why not?" Bluderin didn't have much of a choice. It was either drinking beer at Gustav's or hanging around the NCO Club. He was too irritated about his restriction to read or write anything.

"After talking with a couple of car dealers, Gus figured that you sold me the Volkswagen for half of what it was worth," Couch said. "He said your money is no good today. The drinks are on him."

Although Couch had not yet cultivated the demeanor and finesse of an experienced bartender, he looked the part. His shiny black hair was neatly trimmed and combed back. His white shirt, black bow tie, silk vest, and thin, black arm garters gave him a professional bearing. The pupils of his dark eyes had receded, a sign that he may have ceased smoking hashish.

"The price reduction was your wedding present," Bluderin said. "Besides, Karin needed it for school, and I wanted to help. She'll make a great teacher."

Selling the Volkswagen to Couch was also part of Bluderin's plan to increase his stockpile of cash as soon as possible. He already had sold his Grundig radio to Jürgen Treuge, and Jürgen was selling the Dynaco stereo and some record albums for him to Siegfried Kaufmann. Bluderin's intention was to have so little belongings that everything he owned could fit into his army duffel bag. He figured that he could check out of the army with his duffel bag and about seven thousand dollars in cash.

"Something tells me you're not going back to the States," Couch said, seemingly out of the blue.

"What makes you say that?" Bluderin asked. "You can't possibly know what my plans are, since I don't have any."

"You're selling everything at a loss, not just the car. You could have had the army ship the stuff back to the States. It would be worth more over there."

"I need the money for school. The next semester begins in three months."

"If you don't want to talk about it, I'll shut up," Couch said.

Bluderin did not have a clue of where he was going or what he was going to do. He couldn't make any plans until the issue with Riki Taar was resolved. She was holding things up, and the agency was taking its sweet time before making any decisions. He worried that Riki had told her intelligence contact that *he* had the grenades and fuses. That would not be smart, however, as the agency already knew that Gustav Erdmann had delivered the grenades to her, and Gustav's word was solid, his credibility without question. She possibly could have convinced her contact that he still had the fuses, but what good would that do? The fuses were cheap and harmless by themselves.

"You know, John, if you take a European out, I'm going to find out about it. Especially, of course, if you stay in Schwäbisch Gmünd and shack up with Riki Taar."

"What do you know about her?" Bluderin was surprised to hear Couch mention her name. Outside of the picnic with Howard and Diane James, he had never been anywhere socially with Riki.

"Karin and I saw you walking with her. We were going to drive up and say hello, but you seemed so engrossed in your conversation with her that we didn't want to disturb you."

"I made a mistake in agreeing to go on a picnic with her," Bluderin said. "The only thing I want to do to Riki Taar is get her out of my life."

"I could have told you the woman is all fucked up in the head. I've seen her at Hardt Kaserne, working in the laundry shop, dumping on nearly every GI who walks into the place. She's a bitch, plain and simple."

"She's got a few problems," Bluderin said. He did not want to tell Couch anything more about Riki Taar and was mad at himself for what he already had said. Emotion had overcome his intention to remain silent about her.

He ran a finger along the outside of the clay beer mug, drawing invisible pictures. Perhaps going home would be the wisest choice, he thought. His friends from high school, for the most part, would not be in Defiance. They would likely be away at college or else married and making babies. In deliberating the future further he realized that going home was not a viable option. He could not grow there. He could visit his family on occasion, but he needed to create his own world.

He entertained the notion of living like a drifter or would-be troubadour, wandering around Europe and writing about whatever came to mind. He would keep a journal and take notes about his travels. He thought that if he managed his money shrewdly, he could possibly extend his travels and conceivably fund his personal *Wanderjahr*.

Peter Vanderwerken had brought up the subject of travel during dinner at his house. He had described a number of neighborhoods in various cities of France, Italy, and Spain where Ernest Hemingway spent some time, including some hotels where Hemingway, Gertrude Stein, Ezra Pound, and John Dos Passos had stayed. It was uncanny how Peter talked so much about his travels that evening. Bluderin felt that the man was reading his mind.

During the evening, Peter also had given him a book of poems, *Reasons for Moving: Poems,* by Mark Strand, an American poet who at the young age of thirty-four had already earned widespread recognition, primarily at universities, throughout North America and the United Kingdom. Klaus Griesinger had given the book to Peter. During one of Peter's visits to Soligen, Klaus had said that Walter Lebrecht thought Bluderin would enjoy the book.

Bluderin not only liked the poems, he found them immensely relevant. There was one poem in particular, "Keeping Things Whole," that struck his psychic core because he thought he was going to be living in the poem during his *Wanderjahr*. He had memorized it in its entirety.

> *In a field*
> *I am the absence*
> *of field.*
> *This is*
> *always the case.*
> *Wherever I am*
> *I am what is missing.*
>
> *When I walk*
> *I part the air*

and always
the air moves in
to fill the spaces
where my body's been.

We all have reasons
for moving.
I move
to keep things whole.

No matter where his travels took him, Bluderin knew that a rebirth was coming. He could not keep things whole—for himself or anyone else—by staying in Schwäbisch Gmünd or going home. He was so much in thought about the poem and what part of him was left to move on that he did not notice Couch refilling his beer mug.

"I didn't mean to get all over your case before," Couch said. "Whatever your plans are is your business. It's just that Hans, Tulla, and Eddie were talking about you earlier this afternoon. They said you've been a real friend."

"That's nice to hear," Bluderin said. "Where is the trio?"

"They're at a banquet. The mechanic Hans works for is celebrating his seventieth birthday."

Bluderin knew he was going to miss his friends, but it was not worth dwelling on. He needed to address his immediate fate.

"Wiley, I don't know what I'm going to do," he said. "I go up and down like a Yo-Yo every time I weigh my options." The fact that the scenario with Aarika Taar had put him in limbo did not help matters, but he would not mention that obstacle to Couch.

"Why sweat it?" Couch said. "Do whatever the hell you feel like doing. If things don't go the way you hoped, you can always take a break here. Gustav said to tell you that he will always have a room available for you, free of charge. He'd tell you himself, but he's out moderating at a public housing forum."

Bluderin had a feeling that Gustav was out on an assignment for the agency, but he had no basis for his premonition. Still, the agency could need to consult with Gustav on alternative approaches to managing the grenades and fuses situation. It was all a wild guess on his part as to what the agency was thinking, but it had to be doing something. It could not wait around forever.

"I don't know, Couch. I hate to intrude."

"There's no intrusion when you're invited," Couch said. "Who knows, you may find out that this place is right for you. You could always attend the Pädagogische Hochschule, like Karin. She's already told you that the school likes to have a variety of foreign students. An American student probably would be welcomed."

Bluderin had considered attending the university for the past year. After completing the course of study, he thought he could land a position teaching English at a German school or teaching German at an American school. He had listed the possibility of attending the the school as a fallback option. That is, it *was* on his list until Riki Taar and the grenade-fuse dilemma surfaced.

"I have thought about attending PH."

"It could be a cozy deal for you," Couch said.

"I want to do something of value—something I really believe in." Bluderin wanted keep on moving to keep things whole, as Mark Strand wrote in his poem. He could not keep things whole by staying in Schwäbisch Gmünd, thanks to the agency and Riki Taar.

"Do something of value?" Couch said in a bewildered tone. "What the hell are you talking about? Get over that bullshit, John. When are you going to learn? The supermen, the geniuses, the prophets—they're all gone, man—dead as dinosaurs. All anyone can to do now is simply get by. Live the day and have a little fun whenever you can. The socially redeeming shit is out the window."

Bluderin often tried to be more pragmatic like Couch, but he could not accept his fate so readily. There definitely was value to what Couch was doing. The fact that he was going to be a father in four months was an enormous responsibility to take on. Wiley was being far more productive than he was.

Karin came out of the back room and walked up to the bar. She gave Wiley a quick kiss on the cheek, and he patted her ass. They were comfortable with each other already, Bluderin noticed. Karin had her chores, and Couch had his. She made the bed, cooked, washed the dishes, did the laundry, and cleaned the apartment. He took out the garbage, repaired leaking toilets and sinks, gave each room a fresh coat of paint, and upgraded the electrical switches and sockets. Bluderin was amused by how quickly they had settled into a routine.

"See this?" Couch said, placing his hands on Karin's stomach. "She's swelling just the way she's supposed to. Signs that a healthy baby is on the way."

Bluderin could not argue with Couch's down-to-earth attitude. He and Karin were creating life while his mind was instilled on the natural order of the world. He was starting to believe that his purpose in life was to listen to nature and let it guide him to his destiny. He promised himself that whatever he decided to do, he would pursue his life to find its eternal meaning until he was close to the inevitability of death.

Karin poured him another beer since Couch had taken a break to call his mother. She was due to make her appearance in another three weeks, Karin said, and they were making final arrangements. Couch was to pick up his mother at the airport in Munich.

"Have you spoken with her?" Bluderin asked.

"A little," Karin said. "We exchanged pleasantries. She seems very nice. I hope we get along. I really could use her help when the baby comes."

He valued Karin as one of those people who takes life as it comes, for better or worse, and is not concerned about things beyond her control. Her simple hair style, parted in the middle and trimmed just above her shoulders, and her quiet complexion, a soft shade of white enhanced by a natural sprinkling of dark freckles, gave her a charming appearance. Her pregnancy had enlivened her charm with a radiant glow. She smelled like soap that had been marinated in peaches and cream. It was difficult not to like her. Couch softly fondled the nape of her neck when he returned to the bar.

Jürgen Treuge came into the Gasthaus. His thin eyebrows were nearly invisible, making the distance between his eyes and curly blond hair appear longer than it was. He nodded respectfully at Karin and greeted Couch with a handshake. Jürgen exuded a new confidence as he quietly placed his hands on the bar and gave Bluderin the equivalent of two hundred dollars. Whatever Vera Luchterhand was doing to Jürgen was an improvement. He now had a more relaxed disposition, showing none of the defensive posturing when Bluderin had first met him.

Bluderin had hoped that the amount would be more for the stereo Siegfried had bought, along with the albums, but he accepted the money without saying anything. It was better than nothing, and it was quick. He bought Jürgen a beer, and Jürgen ordered a cognac for himself and Bluderin.

"I owe you another forty marks," Jürgen said. "Siegfried's sister, Heidi, bought the rest of the albums, but she wasn't able to pay for them right away. You may have to wait a little bit."

Jürgen explained that Heidi was working part-time as a waitress at Regina's Nightclub. The GIs who frequented the place tipped well, so Heidi would be able to pay him in a day or two.

"Heidi better not mess around with the GIs who go there, unless she wants to catch a disease," Couch said. "I can't tell you the number of guys who caught the clap from Regina's girls. Some of them even got infected with genital herpes. Not good stuff."

Officially, the medics at Hardt Kaserne had said that *the clap* was a common term among GIs for gonorrhea or other sexually transmitted diseases that were treatable.

"She only works there," Jürgen said. "Regina already has let it known that Heidi is a 'hands-off' waitress, a good girl working her way through college. The GIs either behave by Regina's rules or get banned from the place. They won't be giving Heidi a hard time. They have too much to lose—all the available women."

"I'm surprised Vera isn't with you," Bluderin said to Jürgen. "You two have been inseparable."

"Vera is out exercising," Jürgen said. "She plans on running the marathon during Oktoberfest in another four months. She's down to one-hundred pounds of dynamic passion."

"I passed her by a couple of weeks ago when I was out running," Bluderin said. "I didn't recognize her at first, until she waved hello. Vera was never heavy in my opinion, but now the girl is outright sculpted."

He visually recalled Vera Luchterhand in her tight, white running shorts and lyme-colored tank top. Every muscle in her legs shone in a delicate definition, and sweat outlined her highly toned breasts. It intrigued him how Vera had transformed from a compact but nearly curveless farm girl into a vision of seductive elegance. Her new physique reminded him of Leda Beschwörung, whose body had a tenacious way of arousing him.

"John, join me at a table where we can talk in private," Jürgen said, lowering his voice to a whisper. "I don't want Wiley to hear us."

Bluderin was surprised at the suggestion, since Couch was a lot closer to Jürgen than he was. As they took a table and sipped their cognac, Jürgen began offering him a most unusual proposition.

Jürgen and Vera had been experimenting sexually. They had been involved in a threesome on several occasions with another girl in the mix. Jürgen described how great it was to have two girls at the same time.

"It is nothing but sheer ecstacy," he said. "However, as time passed, Vera said it was only fair for her to have a threesome with another guy. After deliberating about it for a few weeks, I came around to her way of thinking. It is only justifiable that she has her way as well. How can I deny her pleasure when she denies me nothing?"

Bluderin was astonished to hear where this conversation was headed. Here was a guy who had been as possessive with Karin as a little kid guarding his favorite cookies. Jürgen didn't want him within twenty feet of Karin. Now, here he was, the same guy, hinting of a threesome with his girlfriend. Bluderin didn't know what to think.

"When I told Vera I might ask you to join us in a threesome, she said that you were a perfect candidate. I thought so as well, especially since you'll soon be back in the States."

"Wow. Let me think about it," Bluderin said. "Believe me, I think Vera is incredibly sexy, but I'm a little nervous about the prospect. I've never done anything like it." He had dismissed the scenario with Riki and Elisha as a threesome, since it was against his will.

"I thought you would like to know that one of our threesome lovers—Gretchen Vanderwerken, when we were in Munich—had told Vera that you knew all the right moves to set a girl on fire."

Bluderin smiled with a little embarrassment at the comment. Again, he was grateful to Leda Beschwörung for having mentored him.

The thought of massaging Vera's tight little ass and driving into her eventually overcame his fickle hesitation. It could be quite sensual—kinky, perhaps, but so what? He knew one thing: he did not want to associate his last sexual experience in Germany with Riki Taar and Elisha Amsel.

They shook hands on the proposal. Bluderin agreed that whenever Vera decided to call it quits he would respect her decision. Jürgen admitted that there was something of a voyeur in him. He confessed that the idea of seeing Vera having sex with another guy was incredibly erotic.

"I understand your voyeurism" Bluderin said. "I share the same impulse."

Leda had described this type of fetish to Bluderin, and he told her that he could be convinced to take part in a threesome if the people and conditions were right. Jürgen had emphasized that the threesome would be entirely about satisfying Vera's needs. Bluderin agreed that it had to be that way.

As they started to leave for Jürgen's house, Gustav Erdmann greeted them at the front door. Having mentioned that he was returning from an errand, he took Bluderin aside, telling Jürgen that he needed to speak alone with Bluderin for a minute.

"Your presence is requested at Hardt Kaserne," Gustav said. "A decision has been made, but I cannot say anything further."

Bluderin knew Gustav well enough to interpret that the German's deadpan expression meant that something quite serious was in the works. Whatever it was, he did not want to face it right away.

"Gus, before I report to Hardt Kaserne, I have to move some final belongings from the apartment. The landlord will be handing the keys over to the new tenant in the morning. Jürgen was going to help me move the stuff." He did not want to lie to Gustav, but the agency had taken a long time to arrive at a decision, and it was not going to prevent him from going to his immediate destination. He was sure that the agency would again make him interact with Riki Taar, and he was pissed. They're lining me up with a fucking lunatic, he thought.

"I'll tell you what," Gus said. "I will explain your situation to the appropriate intelligence personnel. You better be sure that you are on base first thing in the morning, however, or agents will be out looking for you."

"I promise you, I'll be at Hardt Kaserne no later than seven in the morning." It disturbed Bluderin that the agency would be looking for him if he didn't show up. That could only mean that he was being implicated in some way regarding the missing fuses. He had to find out where they were to free himself of suspicion. He was sure that Riki Taar was setting him up for personal ruin.

On the way to their ménage a trios appointment, Bluderin asked Jürgen to make a quick stop at the Oasis. "I need to check my mail," he said. "I have all my personal letters sent there."

He was delighted to see the envelope from Solveig and told Frau Müller that he would stop in again soon with some flowers before leaving the country. He and Solveig had not corresponded for the past nine weeks. He had been the last one to send a letter, and he did not want to send another until he first heard back from her. He did not want to be overbearing. Her lack of communication made him think that she might have a new romantic interest. He would accept that situation if came to be, but it pained him to think about it. He was anxious to read the letter, but he folded the unopened envelope and slid it into a back pocket. He would read it carefully many times over when he was alone and with nothing else on his mind.

Vera Luchterhand was waiting for them. Jürgen had called her from Gustav's to let her know they were on their way. She greeted them with warm, moist kisses. As Bluderin looked her over, it occurred to him that she could be Karin Erdmann's sexual alter ego. Karin's passion seemed to be within, whereas Vera's was visibly apparent. Her black thong panties and half-cup bra accentuated the toned muscles of her petite frame, especially the firmness of her breasts and the little globes of her ass. Her lapis lazuli eyes, as deep as the mineral itself, blinked slowly as she licked her full lips. She tucked her blonde-streaked hair over her ears, and her concave stomach, set off by a thin golden necklace around her hips, drew in tighter as she led them into Jürgen's bedroom. His parents were away in Switzerland again, so they had the house to themselves.

The woman did not know what the word "inhibitions" meant. She stood on the bed, her arms raised as they took off her bra and panties. Her thigh muscles flexed as she spread her legs to expose herself to them. Her pubic hair was shaved completely and replaced with a tattoo in the shape of the letter V, with a snake coiled around each slash or slant of the letter.

"I think it's appropriate, don't you?" she asked.

"In more ways than one," Bluderin said. "It's very eclectic."

She giggled and pulled him onto the bed and told him to lay down, facing her. She took him into her wide, densely wet mouth, her head moving up and down. When she had him ready, she turned to Jürgen and prepared him in the same way.

She mounted Bluderin and rode him as openly and freely as Lady Godiva must have ridden her horse through Coventry. Jürgen stood at bedside, his eyes frozen on Vera and Bluderin's union.

"God, that's so beautiful," he said, his voice cracking.

Bluderin was consumed with lust. He was astonished how this woman could not get enough. She jerked up and down on top of him, lost in heat, every ounce of her jack-hammering him. She screamed in waves when he came inside her, both of them shivering. Vera withdrew from him and leaned over to Jürgen. She grabbed his hand and coaxed him onto the bed.

"It's your turn, baby," she said, smiling as she guided him into her. She was incredibly wet and her nose flared with a sense of urgency. The smell of sex was pungent when Jürgen climaxed almost instantly. He later said that watching Vera and Bluderin almost made him come without even touching himself. His libido went out of control, he told them.

It would be that way—Vera going back and forth, from Bluderin to Jürgen, with her sometimes taking them on both on at once—until the wee hours of the morning. She finally tired, and Bluderin called for a taxi.

The threesome experience had opened up a new understanding of physical passion to Bluderin. It broke the barrier of his puritanical upbringing. Unlike the forced, violent episode with Riki and Elisha, this intimate excursion was one of free will. He wasn't sure what he would think of it later. He would have to let it sink in.

As he sat in the cab, he thought again about moving to keep things whole. There were pieces of himself all over Schwäbisch Gmünd, and it was time for him to start living a new life.

It wasn't love, he knew, when various images of the evening with Vera and Jürgen entered his mind, *but it wasn't bad*. It wasn't remotely close to the depth of emotional exchange he felt with Solveig Evensen—nothing of the kind. However, the venture did give him a new level of maturity and sexual context. It was also a divergence from thinking about what the agency wanted from him. He was calmer and looser now—more clear-headed and sated—to see what they had in mind. He wished that this supposedly final assignment would be as benign as the Vera-Jürgen tryst, but he knew better.

He got out of the cab and stood at the entrance to Hardt Kaserne. He breathed deeply and, applying his discipline in karate, renewed his senses. As he walked forward he could smell the rifle of the guard on duty. He touched the ground and felt its temperature, tasted the moisture in the air, heard crickets off in the distance, and saw the tiniest star in the universe. He continued looking at the star until his sixth sense, the one of survival, kicked in, joining the others. He was ready to take the assignment on, whatever it was, and see it through to its end, whatever the consequences.

Twenty

‹o›

Riki Taar marched determinedly—her long, thin arms swinging back and forth, like revved-up pendulums—as she crossed the courtyard of Hardt Kaserne. Her greenish, amber eyes focused on the main entrance to Headquarters Building. Her presence there had been requested by Major McCandley. It bothered her that the major had offered no explanation in the note that Specialist Tyler brought over to her. Her heart shot up into her throat, emitting electric zips, when she thought that John Bluderin may have filed a report on her.

What could Bluderin have said? That she drugged him, chained him to a bed, and forced him to have intercourse with her? Who would believe that? Would he also implicate Elisha Amsel in the devious rape? None of those possibilities made any sense. Elisha had freed him, after all, and Tyler had said that Bluderin would be coming in to see her later in the day. He was going to invite her to dinner.

Riki was certain that no one else but Elisha knew about their stealth-like entrance into Bluderin's apartment. She had assumed it was her pregnancy that had caused her to faint when she was within a second of stabbing Elisha. After recovering from her blackout, she had returned the key to the agency's quarters, placing it exactly where she found it. If an agent were to search Bluderin's apartment now, he or she would find the blue plastic box with the empty lipstick tubes, proof that the grenade fuses were still in Bluderin's possession.

He would be in a heap of trouble. The agency would turn its attention away from her, toward him. She also knew that the next time Bluderin grabbed a bottle of beer from his refrigerator he'd be dead within the hour. She had opened the flip tops, spilled out an ounce of beer in each bottle, and poured in an odorless liquid mixed with arsenic. Bluderin's death would be an obvious case of suicide. He had known he was suspected of handing top-secret information and materials over to Soviet agents, and he had decided to take his life rather than face the punishment for his misconduct.

Instead of her normally aloof mannerisms, Riki was rattled with excitement. As she approached Headquarters Building, she asked PFC Steve Bunyan if he had any idea of Bluderin's whereabouts. Every syllable of her diction was laden heavily with saliva and expelled with urgency.

"Ask the guard for Specialist 4 Joe Tyler," Bunyan said. "If anyone knows where Bluderin is, it would be Joe."

Riki could not help but glance at the soldier's groin when he spoke. She had heard rumors that every prostitute at the Dreifarbenhaus in Stuttgart fought with each other over whose turn it was to get Bunyan's reputedly enormous cock for their enjoyment. She could see that the rumors had substance. The bulge from Bunyan's groin hung half-way down his thigh. No wonder his sobriquet was "Tripod," she thought, suppressing a grin.

She hesitated before entering Headquarters Building. Her hands shook as she handed McCandley's memo to the guard. After he validated the request, Captain Howard Getz walked over to her.

"May I help you?" he asked. His mud-brown eyes looked twice their size behind his thick-lensed, black-framed glasses.

"Major McCandley requested my presence," Riki said, "but I

was hoping to speak with Specialist Bluderin first. He's leaving soon, as you know, and I wanted to offer him my best wishes. I have a little good-bye present for him." Riki showed Getz a box with two silver Cross pens inside it. She had not bothered to wrap the present, which was not a pair of high-end pens but state-of-the-art, pop-out switch blades.

Getz escorted Riki down the long corridor. He opened the door to the office where Tyler worked and was careful to close the door gently behind him.

"Specialist Tyler, Major McCandley wanted to see Miss Taar, but he was summoned to meet with Colonel Haskins. Could you tell her what the major wanted and escort her back to the main foyer?"

"Yes, sir." When Getz left the office, Tyler poured coffee for Riki and himself.

Her lips quivered as she sipped. "I've forgotten how awful army coffee is," she said. "It has no body or strength. It is essentially tasteless—lukewarm and bland."

Tyler did not respond to her comment. He opened a notebook and flipped through a few pages. "Here it is," he said. "Major McCandley wanted to talk with you about house-sitting for him while he and his wife are in the States for three weeks. He wanted to discuss your responsibilities if you accept his offer. He also said you will need to speak with his wife."

Riki was relieved immensely to hear why McCandley had wanted to talk with her. She had known Ingrid McCandley nee Dannette for five years, and she also knew that the woman had more than a hundred house plants that needed to be taken care of during her absence. Riki would enjoy taking on that responsibility, and she looked forward to staying at the McCandley residence for the three-week duration.

"It will be nice to get away from my nosy neighbors," she said, but Tyler again did not acknowledge her comment.

Her neighbors had become extremely rude to her since the day they saw her screaming at Bluderin and Elisha. Their escape out of a window from her apartment had caught their utmost attention and concern. The neighbors later told Riki that the escapade was ridiculously immature, to the point of being hilarious.

"Please inform the major that I will gladly house-sit for him," Riki said. She took out a notebook from her purse and scribbled down her telephone number and a couple of short sentences, more or less thanking McCandley for the house-sitting opportunity.

Tyler took the note from Riki, inserted it into an envelope, and wrote McCandley's rank and name on the outside. He stood to escort Riki back to the foyer. She resisted his attempts, holding her arms out to fend him off.

"Just a minute," she said. "Captain Getz neglected to tell you that I need to speak with John Bluderin as soon as possible. Since he is your immediate supervisor, I assume you know where he is."

Tyler looked irritated by the way Riki posed her question. He raised his eyebrows and scratched the right side of his shaved head, above his ear. Yet he maintained a professional demeanor.

"I don't know where he is," Tyler said. "He could be in an official meeting getting debriefed before his departure, or he could be working with his replacement officer. Specialist Bluderin no longer has any responsibilities in this office. He has only a couple more days—"

"I know." Riki said. "That's exactly why I need to see him as soon as possible. We're good friends, and I must see him immediately. It's really important."

"I told you he would be coming to see you later in the day," Tyler said. "Don't you remember?"

Riki eyed Tyler suspiciously. He was trying to protect Bluderin from a woman who was out to get him for something—either trouble or money, no doubt. In Tyler's job as an army clerk at Hart Kaserne, she assumed he had heard a lot of stories and read a lot of signed statements about German girls intentionally getting pregnant by GIs as a way to get to the States.

Tyler stretched, spun around in his chair, and looked up at a painting—a portrait of a helmsman at the wheel of an old fishing schooner—an old salt type of character trying to survive a ferocious squall. Having a ragged, white beard, the helmsman was dressed in shiny black foul-weather gear. A sou'wester clung to his head, fastened by a thick chinstrap.

"Please, Specialist Tyler," Riki said, biting her lips. "I understand that you don't know me very well, but I am not out to cause John any trouble. I get terrible migraines, and he has gotten some pills from medics in the past to help me soothe the pain. I have run out of the medicine, and my migraines are on the verge of driving me insane. I feel like my head is going to explode."

Tyler's eyes focused on the painting as he spoke. "I honestly have no idea where Bluderin is. He was here earlier this morning, and I believe he left to interpret at a meeting with the MPs and German police somewhere in town. I think he was also going to introduce his replacement officer to the German police, but I don't know for sure. He doesn't tell me much. He never did. Aside from his saying that he'll be back later on, I can't help you anymore. I'm sorry."

"I'm sorry too, Specialist Tyler," Riki said. "I know you don't trust me, but I am telling the truth. John would want to help me. He is friends with the medic Clayton Quigley. I know him as well. Since John apparently is nowhere to be found, could you contact Quigley and ask him to come here?"

Riki knew Clayton Quigley a lot better than Bluderin did. The medic was on his second tour of duty with the 4th Battalion, 41st Artillery. He had made friends with Riki's husband during the first tour, and he was one of the many soldiers her husband had brought home for her to service. Quigley always had paid Riki's husband in drugs instead of cash. After Riki and her husband had gotten divorced, Quigley continued coming to her apartment for sex in exchange for drugs. Riki had been hooked on various tranquilizers for some time. It was not until Quigley had left upon finishing his first tour when she began weaning herself off medications.

Bluderin had gotten some pills from Quigley to help Riki treat her migraines, but little did he know that she had gotten pills from Quigley to drug him on the day she and Elisha had their way with him. Riki knew that she could get the medicine from Quigley, but she wanted to get the pills through Bluderin. She knew what she would have to do for Quigley now that she was getting the drugs from him directly.

"I would prefer not to call Quigley," Tyler said.

Riki looked at Tyler and gave him an evil grin, grinding her teeth and snarling her lips. "Maybe Mrs. Tyler would like to know more about your relationship with Dieter Klein. Who's the man when you two get together? You're both so little and cute. I love Dieter's moustache, don't you? He reminds me so much of Omar Sharif."

Tyler said nothing in response, but his entire face pulsated, and his shaved head gleamed in a scarlet beads of sweat. He called the medic quarters and asked for Quigley.

Riki was somewhat persuaded that Tyler was telling her the *basic* truth about Bluderin's location, but her intuition still told her that Tyler could have been more specific about where he was. After deliberating the issue for a while, Riki came to believe that Bluderin had never intended to see her, that what he told Tyler was part of a scheme to keep her at a distance. Perhaps he intentionally had not told Tyler where he was so that Tyler would not know, no matter how persistently she begged him for an answer.

"I will sit and wait for Quigley," Riki said. "Then I'll be on my way."

"Fine," Tyler said. "Care for some more coffee? I've got a new pot brewing."

"No, thank you," she said. "I'm appalled how you guys can drink that crap all day." Riki took out an American cigarette from her purse and lit it. She jittered as she took a drag, imagining that everyone at Hardt Kaserne was watching her every move.

Tyler was filling in a supplies requisition form when Sergeant Clayton Quigley walked into the office. He shuffled and danced his way along the office floor and tapped his fingers on Tyler's metal desk. He appeared to be high on some type of medication.

At twenty-nine, Quigley looked a good ten years older, with heavy lines beneath his hazel eyes and on his forehead, beneath the greasy brown hair that he combed back with the exception of a spit curl. The fiery glow in Quigley's eyes seemed to scare Tyler and Riki, especially when the medic once again danced around the office, snapping his fingers and singing a rendition of a Motown song.

"Hey brother, what's going down?" Quigley laid out an opened hand, waiting for Tyler to slap it. Tyler did not react.

"Miss Taar wanted to talk with you before I escort her out of the building. Why don't you two have a chat while I get Captain Getz to sign this requisition slip?"

Quigley strutted over to Riki. He leaned over her, smelled her bright auburn hair, nipped her quickly on the ear, and jumped back, clapping his hands.

"Hey baby, what's happening?"

Riki looked closely into the medic's eyes, thinking that he already had forgotten why Tyler had contacted him. "I was hoping you could give me some pills to incite my period," she said. "I think I'm pregnant."

Quigley pulled at his chin and mumbled incoherently before he made any sense. "Honey child, I'm not sure what I got to make you shake a baby out. Let me give it a think."

Riki sat rigidly quiet, giving Quigley some time to think about what he could do for her.

Quigley slouched against Tyler's desk, resting his chin on one hand while tapping a beat on the desk with the other. His voice began to emulate Otis Redding. *Sittin' on the dock of the bay . . .*

"Can you help me?" she finally asked him.

"There's a possibility, honey. Doctor Quigley always got something up his sleeve—if not there, then in his medicine cabinet. Course you understand, honey, if you wants something you gots to pay for it. I know you dig what I'm getting at. Tit for tat and all that shit, favor for favor or, as you bitches say, give and take."

The idea of having sex with Quigley—*again*—distressed her so much that, by stimulus-response or happenstance, she felt her period coming. She could feel blood oozing down her thighs. At the same time, she felt the jolt of a migraine. Her body shivered as she looked up at Quigley.

"I'll do anything, whatever you want, you know that," she said. She rubbed her temples in an attempt to blunt the pain. She whimpered as she squeezed the top of her nose, between her eyes.

"Don't fret, no sweat. Doctor Quigley understands your dilemma. Now I'm going to go away for a minute. I'll be right back with some goodies for you. You just sit tight, and Doctor Quigley will return with a solution to your problem. And believe me, child, it will perform. Works so good it will clean your innards out and melt your pain into mellow Jell-O."

Quigley jived his way out of the office, snapping his fingers again, singing "My Girl" as he danced down the corridor. Riki stood up for a minute and viewed the painting Tyler previously had looked at for a long time. She took a deep breath and felt that her life was surrounded in a continual, never-ending squall.

Knowing that she was not pregnant seemed to dull some of her pain. She thought that her feeling of superiority over what she had done to Bluderin may have delayed her period for what seemed to be two weeks but was longer. She had been so aggressive with him that she believed *she was the man impregnating him.* It may have been foolish of her to think that she eventually could turn Bluderin into her cuckold, her slave, but she would not let him off the hook. *He will get his,* she promised. If she could not have Bluderin, she wanted to make sure that no one else could.

Quigley strutted back into the office, holding a light green bottle in his right hand. He peered into Riki's eyes, rubbed his crotch up and down, and waved the bottle in front of her.

"Here you go, little lady. Now listen to Doctor Quigley. Take two of these pills every eight hours, and I guarantee you'll be cool as a breeze tickling your nipples. Got it?"

Riki took the semi-transparent bottle and looked inside it at the long white and pink capsules. There was no label on the bottle.

"What are these?" she asked.

"They're pain killers that help reset your bodily functions, sweet lips. Don't sweat it, baby. Doctor Quigley takes them himself, and I feel just fine. You afraid of them pills?"

"I guess so, but if they do what you say, I could really use them."

"That's cool, doll. I'm telling you, inside of two days you'll be feeling better than ever. That's my personal guarantee. Doctor Quigley knows his stuff. Ask any GI."

Riki thanked Quigley for the medicine and asked him to usher her out of Headquarters Building. He told her that she first needed to return the favor.

"Drop your pants and panties, spread your legs, and lean over Tyler's desk," he said. "We're going to make that desk shake and bake with a good hard fucking, sweet bitch. I haven't been in your magic snatch for a month, not since I gave you the barbiturates and cantharides."

Riki looked at Quigley in disgust. She would try to talk her way out of his directive, but he was so high on drugs she worried that he would not be able to understand her.

"I'm bleeding," she said. "My period started just minutes ago. It would not be any good—just sloppy and messy. If you're going to fuck me, why not wait a week so we can both enjoy it?" Riki hoped that her half-assed compliment would be enough for Quigley to leave her alone, at least for the time being.

Quigley strutted around the office again, this time in silence as if he were in deep thought. When she thought she had him convinced to wait, he stood in front of her and dropped his pants.

"Give Doctor Quigley a topper," he said. "Wrap your lips around my hard-on and take all of me in you. I know you give the best blow job this side of the Atlantic."

Riki could not find a way out of the situation. She looked at the painting again and thought about calming the squall. She had performed fellatio on Quigley—only once, in front of her husband—since Quigley usually preferred to take her from behind. She remembered it took only a few minutes to bring him to orgasm.

"Okay. Let's get it done," she said. She went at him in aggressive pursuit, ravishing his penis like a woman who had not eaten for a week. She knew he wouldn't be long.

He did not last a minute, and he deposited only a trickle. Riki thought that the drugs Quigley took could be having a negative effect on his sexual prowess.

At any rate, her expertise had paid off. She had the pills she wanted, and she returned the favor in less than a minute. Quigley was tightening his belt when Tyler returned to the office.

"Are you ready?" Tyler asked Riki. "You've been here too long. Captain Getz already assumed you had left the building."

"I'm all set. Let's go," Riki said. She took hold of Tyler's arm as he led her down the corridor.

Quigley let out a weird laugh—like a solitary loon's tremolo—as he danced his way down the corridor in the opposite direction. He would be screaming much louder in another hour, after the poison Riki had inserted into his groin, by using the blades of her knife-bracelets for injection needles, worked its way into Quigley's nervous system. If the toxin worked the way she had hoped, Quigley would never get another erection.

"Don't worry about your indiscretion with Dieter Klein," Riki said to Tyler. "You've been a help today. My lips are sealed."

Later in the evening, Riki closed the drapes in her bedroom. She was livid that Bluderin had never shown up at the laundry. Why did he tell Tyler he would stop by? She became more convinced that he had intended to deceive her. He was trying to torment her, as she had done to him. *I will have my way with him, even if I have to blow his fucking brains out.*

After she had changed into a nightgown, she went into the kitchen and poured a glass of water. Her migraines had come back with a vengeance, riveting her with convulsing pain, and the cramps from her period were compounding the torture. She proceeded to swallow four pills instead of following Quigley's instructions to take only two.

Riki sat up on her bed and resumed reading the final seven pages of *Mein Kampf.* Within a half-hour she felt weak and lifeless but with an inner calm. She had a dream recalling the episode with John Bluderin and Elisha Amsel. *I will have my way with him and own his ass,* she softly whispered, and the dream repeated itself until she fell into a deep and dark sleep.

There was one negative side-effect a person could have from the pills Quigley had given her. In an extremely rare case, the pills could induce fits of violent behavior. The fits did not last very long—about five minutes each—and they usually went away altogether within an hour. This condition was associated with a person who had taken the medicine as prescribed. There was no record on anyone ever having taken an overdose.

The grenades, their fuses inserted, were ready for use, hidden beneath a pillow she had tucked against her waist. Her hands clutched the pillow in the way that rosary beads are clasped in the hands of a corpse.

Twenty-One

—◄o►—

June 1968

John Bluderin, Leda Beschwörung, and two agents who would not reveal their names sat at a table in a room at the Hotel Einhorn, a twelfth-century building in the old town section of Schwäbisch Gmünd, about two-hundred fifty meters east of the Heilig-Kruz-Münster. Bluderin was getting informed about the strategy the agents intended to use to retrieve the grenades from Riki Taar's apartment. His role was to accompany Leda and follow her instructions. In essence, Leda would be driving the search mission with Bluderin riding shotgun.

If it were not for the potential danger in dealing with explosives, Bluderin would have thought that their strategy was overly intricate to the point of being absurd. Why didn't the agency simply secure the apartment and conduct a thorough, guarded search of the place? The German police would have cooperated with the agency, but the agency was keen on being invisible. If strangers entered the apartment building in broad daylight, the scene could cause serious concern among the neighbors. The once proposed dinner date concept would not work either. Some of the neighbors would still be up. The search had to be conducted very late at night, and it would be best for Riki to be in her apartment so they could restrain her to ensure an impression of reticence in the apartment.

No one had told Bluderin what the two nameless agents were going to do, but he anticipated that they would be ready to implement a back-up plan if things went wrong. When the other three concurred on what the rules and timelines for Bluderin were, they left the hotel room separately, in half-hour intervals. Bluderin was to meet Leda at one in the morning in the vestibule of the Heilig-Kruz-Münster.

True to her impeccable attention to detail, Leda met Bluderin at precisely one o'clock and led him into the apartment building. She silently initiated her search for the missing grenades. Bluderin stood in the bedroom, ready to contain Riki if she awoke before Leda completed her search. Leda had a detection device that would emit a soft, stuttering whistle if she came within three feet of the explosives. The sound could awaken Riki, and Bluderin had to be prepared for that possibility.

Leda searched every square inch of the apartment but Riki's bedroom, thereby deducing that the grenades were somewhere near Riki's bed. Leda removed her shoes and crept into the bedroom in her stockings. Bluderin moved aside as she crawled under the bed. Squirming into the tightly confined area, she saw a pile of clothes cramped in a corner, around the leg of a bedpost. She slowly separated the clothing and, with the help of a penlight, found the grenade box wrapped in a red sweater. Leda headed back out toward the edge of the bed, reaching for a throw rug to buffer the sound of placing the box on the floor. She slid out from under the bed.

Bluderin was amazed that she had managed to crawl under the bed in the first place, as it stood only half a foot off the floor. Leda was happy with her decision not to bring the detection instrument into the bedroom. The device would have sounded off and all hell could have broken loose, disturbing the neighbors and compromising the surreptitious nature of their activities.

It was about four in the morning when Leda and Bluderin

went outside. She guided him behind a hedgerow on the side of the building, directly below Riki's apartment.

Leda recalibrated her detection instrument. Bluderin rose and stood on his knees. He leaned over the hedges and momentarily looked up at the window to Riki's apartment. He could see no signs of activity. The window was still closed and the drapes still drawn. He went back down in a prone position and whispered his observations to Leda. She was preoccupied.

"We have a problem," she said. "Either the detection unit is dysfunctional or we have a couple of duds."

She motioned for him to follow her along the hedgerow. They crawled to a corner of the building and moved onto the other side. They stood and walked briskly for three blocks and, much to Bluderin's discomfort, entered the area of the park where not long ago he had heard Riki speaking in Hungarian to an old woman.

"Move about twenty or thirty yards away from me," Leda said. "I'm going to open the box and inspect its insides. It could be a trap, so there's no reason for both of us to get blown to smithereens."

Leda's expertise on explosives was dimensions better than Bluderin's, so he relocated to an area just outside the Marktplatz where he could still see her. Several street vendors and some merchants were setting up shop for the day's business. It was not yet six in the morning, but the merchants cleaned their storefronts thoroughly every working day before opening their doors. Members of the Schwäbisch Gmünd maintenance crew also had arrived and were sweeping the cobblestone square. When Bluderin recognized a vendor who sold coffee, he walked over to him and purchased two cups. The long, anxiety-ridden night had made him feel mentally exhausted, and he needed the caffeine to stay alert.

When he returned to the spot where he first had been waiting, he saw Leda signaling him to rejoin her. She was speaking into a mobile phone, an IMTS system in which it was no longer necessary to press a button to talk. She got off the phone just as Bluderin handed her a coffee. He could see the grenades in the wooden box, so he thought that everything about their assignment was finished and copacetic.

"They're duds," Leda said. "They look like legitimate grenades, but there is nothing inside them."

They sat on a park bench in silence as Leda reexamined the empty grenades. She unfastened the safety lever and striker on one of them and handed the grenade to Bluderin. He could see that it no primer, power train, detonator, or filler. He realized that the difference in weight between an empty grenade and a loaded one was probably negligible. There was no way—even for an expert like Leda—to feel the difference.

"What do we do now?" he asked.

"We sit here and wait for the phone to buzz," she said. "Our back-up plan is being executed as we speak. The duds really didn't surprise me. That's why we planned for a backup. It's always best to expect the unexpected, especially with an intelligence agent who has gone bad."

Bluderin had not been informed what "Plan B" was about, but he had a hunch that the two agents were hiding somewhere in the building when he and Leda had entered Riki's apartment. He had seen something human move at the end of the hallway. Although it was very dark at the time, there had been enough moonlight to notice motion.

When a couple who looked like husband and wife walked in the direction of the bench, Leda moved closer to Bluderin and kissed him on the cheek. He was surprised by the gesture, but he instantly placed an arm around her shoulders. Leda kissed him again, fully on the lips this time, and spoke softly.

"It's better for them to think we're lovers more than anything else—anything but foreigners, and definitely not spies. Besides, you don't mind snuggling with me, do you?"

"Don't ask questions to answers you already know," he said. "I'm onto you."

The couple greeted them politely as they passed the bench, commenting on what a beautiful summer day it was turning out to be. When they eventually wandered off and out of sight, the mobile phone started buzzing.

"Move over to that other bench about fifty feet away while I talk on the phone."

He was disappointed with her ordering him to leave. It was another way to keep him ignorant of whatever Plan B was. Why the agency had not yet set him free bothered him even more. There was nothing else he could do for them.

A guy who appeared to be a student wearing a Pädagogische Hochschule, or PH, sweatshirt came over to Bluderin and sat down on the bench beside him. He looked to be about the same age as Bluderin—somewhere between nineteen and twenty-one—with long, wavy blond hair ending midway around his shoulders. He also had a long, unkempt beard and an untrimmed, stringy moustache. It was not until he began talking with the student when Bluderin recognized who he was. His presence had changed dramatically since Bluderin had last seen him, about eight or nine months earlier. Siegfried Kaufmann took out his wallet and gave Bluderin four ten-mark bills.

"It's from my sister, Heidi, for the albums," he said. "I was going to give the money to Jürgen, but since I ran into you, why not eliminate the middle man?"

"I appreciate it," Bluderin said. "I'm leaving the country soon. I apologize for not recognizing you when you first sat down."

"I understand," Siegfried said. "After all, the last time we saw each other my hair was so short I had no need to comb it, and I was clean-shaven. I started letting the hair and beard grow when I enrolled at PH."

The majority of German students was following the fashion—*or fashionless*—trends of college students in the United States. Bell-bottomed blue jeans and chambray work shirts were the rage. Siegfried mentioned that he was majoring in music education at the school. Bluderin was not surprised to hear that bit of news, since Siegfried was always fiddling around with a musical instrument. He had been carrying a guitar in a black leather case.

Siegfried was more intent at the moment, however, on playing his radio rather than the guitar, which he noted was a twelve-string Gibson. He turned the radio dial until he found the station he was looking for.

"The disk jockey out of Munich always plays the most recent popular songs by American and English rock stars." Siegfried turned up the volume when the psychedelic pop hit by Scott McKenzie, "San Francisco (Be Sure to Wear Some Flowers in Your Hair)," played.

Bluderin knew that young people throughout Europe had adopted "San Francisco" as an anthem for freedom. The song also had been played widely a few months ago during the Czechoslovakian protests against Soviet rule. That confrontation was still far from being resolved.

Leda came over to them and told Bluderin it was time to join their friends for breakfast at the Hotel Einhorn. He briefly introduced Leda to Siegfried as his girlfriend "Ediltrudis" and held hands with her as they left.

"So it's *Ediltrudis*, is it?" Leda said. "Whatever made you come out with that for a name?"

"It sort of came out subconsciously," he said. "I had to do something to protect your identity, and since the meaning of Ediltrudis is *noble strength*, I thought it was appropriate for this assignment. Also, I didn't want to introduce you as Leda, since I'd told everyone at Gustav's that you were in Berlin. There's no need to raise suspicions in case Siegfried reports to the Gasthaus that he saw me with a woman who was drop-dead gorgeous."

"You're good," she said, "and you definitely know how to charm a woman."

"I learned from the best," he said most seriously. "Now tell me what's going on. Teach me more."

"I'm about to," she said, and began describing the remainder of his assignment. "The two agents have apprehended Riki. She is confined in her apartment, restrained in a strait-jacket and leg irons. The agents captured Riki just before she attempted to throw a grenade out the window toward us. She had already pulled out the safety pin, but one agent managed to wrestle the grenade out of her hands while the other contained Riki's arms with a smothering body-lock. The other agent reinserted the safety pin into the top of the striker lever before both of them forced the strait-jacket over Riki's arms and shoulders. One of the agents found the other grenade on the bed beneath a pillow. Riki apparently liked sleeping with explosives. However, the other grenade was not equipped with the proper fuse assembly. Riki had inserted a different type of fuse, a faster reacting one, but one that doesn't work with M67 fragmentation grenades."

Shit. That means I'm still not off the hook, Bluderin thought— not until they find the right missing fuse. It seemed obvious that, since Riki had possession of one fuse assembly, she would have the other, probably hidden somewhere in her apartment. Knowing that the agency would not buy his logic, he nonetheless acted naïvely.

"Mission accomplished," Bluderin said. "I can go now."

"Not quite," Leda said.

Bluderin had lost his patience, and he was tired of putting up with Leda's "superior than thou" role-playing behavior. His ass was on the line, and she was playing it cool.

"Get it out," he said. "Stop playing games. What am I supposed to do?"

"I'm getting there," Leda said. "Now listen carefully."

The final leg of Bluderin's assignment was to return to Riki Taar's apartment. An agent would be there to remove the leg irons from Riki's ankles. He would help Bluderin place a sweater and blazer over the strait-jacket and help him get Riki dressed into slacks and shoes.

"Your assignment is to escort Riki out of the apartment, holding her close to you as if you were lovers. You are to walk her three blocks to the west, along Parlerstrasse. At the corner of Parlerstrasse and Ziegelgasse the two agents will get out of a black Mercedes and take Riki to the German intelligence authorities in Stuttgart. It will be up to the cooperative German agency to decide what to do with Aarika Taar."

The whole concept made Bluderin nervous as hell. He could understand the agency's mission to be invisible, but there was always a possibility that something could go wrong with the proposed exercise. After all, things had already gone wrong with Leda finding the duds instead of the actual grenades, and they had been within seconds of becoming cold war casualties. Riki may be evil, Bluderin thought, but she's not stupid. He was sure that she would try to find some way to break his grip on her to escape her imposed fate, whatever that was going to be.

"The back-up plan is farcical," he said. "*Nach Canossa gehen.* I feel like I'm being ordered to greet my assassin. Shall I be nice?"

"I will be following Riki and you at a distance. Should anything go wrong, I will take charge of the assignment."

That comment gave Bluderin little comfort. His stomach tightened in tension. It dawned on him that Leda could have a Luger on her person, to be used as a last resort. Shit, he thought, all I want to do is finish this fucking assignment without hearing a shot. If Leda had to shoot Riki, Bluderin knew he could be held captive by the agency for legal purposes for an indefinite period of time.

When he reentered the apartment, Riki Taar was down on her back on the bedroom floor. An agent stood over her. The irises in her eyes looked diffused. She looked like she had been sedated. She did not appear to be frightened, despite the fact that she was gagged and bound.

Getting Riki dressed and ready to go went a lot easier than Bluderin had thought it would. The agent placed one more article of clothing—a red silk scarf—around Riki's neck and mouth to conceal the gag. Bluderin held onto her with both hands gripped around her shoulders as they descended the staircase.

When they stepped out of the main door of the apartment complex, a resident returning to the building asked Bluderin if there was something wrong with Riki, who was breathing heavily on his chest.

"She is not feeling well," he said. "She was heaving all night and has a fever, so I'm taking her to a doctor."

"I'm glad to see someone taking care of her," the woman said. "She doesn't know how to take care of herself. I've never seen anyone else go to the doctors so frequently."

"I understand," Bluderin said. "She has a number of health issues. Well, we best be on our way. We don't want to be late for the appointment." He wanted to get away from the woman before anyone else approached them.

Bluderin and Riki made it down the first two blocks uneventfully. However, about midway through the third block they ran into Elisha Amsel. She was with Dieter Klein, Joe Tyler's body-building lover. Not knowing his name, Bluderin had dubbed him "Omar," like Riki, for his rugged good looks, deep brown, well groomed hair, and carefully trimmed moustache. His debonair mannerisms completed the Sharif likeness.

"We are on our way to this bitch's apartment," Elisha said, pointing to Riki. "I'm taking my lingerie back. Dieter here is my bodyguard, if she was home and wanted to cause trouble. He's got the Luger with him, just in case we needed it. *What are you doing with her, after what she intended to do to you?* You could be with me instead. I'd be much more loving." Elisha kissed him and lifted her mini-skirt to show off her new, chartreuse panties.

"I'm holding her captive until she tells me where she hid something that belongs to me," Bluderin said, "two small silver tubes containing hashish. I paid a lot of money for the stuff."

"I remember her dropping the contents of the tubes into one of her bedposts," Elisha said, "but the stuff looked more like wires than hash to me. She always hides things there—unfastening the decorative knobs, letting things fall down the hollow metal posts, then screwing the knobs back on."

What Elisha said could be the key to my freedom, Bluderin thought. He could have kissed her right there, strange and off-the-wall as she was. *The one you overlook will look out for you. Crazy Günter really was a prophet.*

"I'm taking Riki to a friend's house," he said. "He's going to keep an eye on her until I get my stuff back. I may see you later at her apartment."

"If we're gone before you get there, I'll leave the door unlocked," Elisha said. "Don't worry—I'm not going to be looking inside any bedposts. As for you, Riki—thanks for giving me a key to your place, bitch. Don't you dare call me again."

They went their separate ways, and fortunately the street was otherwise unoccupied. In walking the rest of the block, Bluderin could see the two agents and the black Mercedes off at a distance on the left.

Riki began in earnest to free herself from Bluderin's grip. The calming effects of the sedatives apparently had run their course. She banged her head hard into his chest, striking her chin against his metasternum. Moving to one side to free his chest, Bluderin firmly locked his arms around Riki's neck and squeezed her into a headlock. He dragged her for about twenty steps, keeping her helpless in the headlock. If she tried to force herself free any harder she would break her neck. He walked as hurriedly as he could, given the difficult conditions with Riki trying to wrangle herself free. The agents stood motionless, apparently unwilling or not permitted to offer any assistance.

He gripped Riki's neck tighter, but his arms and hands were sweating and slippery in the warm, humid sun, as was her head and hair. She tried to knee him in the groin, and when he shifted his legs to protect the area, she managed to slip free of his hold. He had a bunch of her hair twisted in his fist, but to no use. She had been wearing a wig. Riki was as bald-headed as Joe Tyler.

The next thing he witnessed was a most bizarre, android-like depiction of duress and assault. A thin blade with jagged edges popped out of Riki's mouth like a spring-loaded stiletto. She took a deep breath and spit out the gag. Other, similar blades jutted out of her arms and chest, cutting through the strait-jacket until she could tear it off. Two smaller blades protruded out of her eyeteeth like a pair of three-inch fangs. She leaped at Bluderin, howling like an abandoned, starving wolf.

He feigned right and sprung left, barely missing her attack and throwing the wig at her eyes. His right sleeve had been torn by one of the blades. He ran toward the agents, figuring he could force them to come to his rescue, but it was too late. She was so close to him he could smell her sweat. Hearing her breathe next to his right ear, he jumped to his left, leaped up, and spun around, landing a karate kick on her chin. A blade shot our of her mouth like a projectile—missing his head by a fraction of an inch.

He turned his back to her and prepared for a reverse kick. He could almost taste her spit when she lunged to his backside and he kicked in reverse. Her howl faded to a cry and he felt her head knock against his ankles. He turned to see what had happened.

Leda stood over Riki, her right shoe pressed hard against Riki's neck. Bluderin presumed what Leda's attack strategy must have been. He knew how high the woman could jump, and she must have jumped five-feet high this time, kicking into Riki's neck or upper back, maybe between her shoulder blades, forcing her to smack her head on the sidewalk. He watched Leda continually kick Riki's forehead to the ground. Her head swelled into a large bump that started to bleed. Leda kept kicking her head until the blades fell out of her mouth. She then knelt down and injected something into Riki's neck.

"She'll be asleep for a couple of hours," Leda said. She cautiously and methodically removed a metallic, meshlike garment that clung tightly, hugging Riki's upper half like a body shirt. Leda kicked Riki over on her backside and removed the garment.

"What is that?" Bluderin asked. He could see that the blades were embedded into the material.

"Combat gear," Leda said. "I liken it to a modern-day shirt of armor. We've been missing one for over a month. Riki was not even on the list of suspects who conceivably could have stolen it. The shirt is made of titanium. The stuff costs a fortune."

"How did she activate the blades?"

"I can't tell you the details," she said. "That's top-secret information. Let's just say that friction plays a part."

Bluderin and Leda stood the shirtless and bald Riki up and carried her the short distance to the Mercedes. The agents were ready to take Riki into their custody. One of them shoved her into the back seat, put a leash around her chest and waist, and got into the back seat next to her, binding them together with a pair of chained handcuffs. The other agent started the car. Within a minute the Mercedes was out of Leda and Bluderin's range of sight.

"What do you think the authorities are going to do with her?" he asked.

"It's difficult to say," Leda said. "She will undergo a series of tests to try to determine the cause for her erratic and dangerous behavior. I don't know how they are going to handle the legal aspect. When the German moving crew cleans out her apartment, we will make sure that one of the crew members is an agent. He will take all the medication from her apartment and deliver it to the authorities in Stuttgart. The medical branch of the German agency will see what kind of influence she might have been under from the drugs. It is highly probable that Riki will be institutionalized, either in a mental hospital or prison, for some time."

"You may want to look into her hollow bedposts before the moving crew comes," Bluderin said. "In case you didn't pick it up electronically, the young woman you saw me talking with is one of Riki's former lovers. She said that Riki hides things in her bedposts all the time. Have an agent unscrew the decorative knobs on the posts and see what she has stored inside them. It wouldn't surprise me if you find the missing fuse assembly."

"Stay here for a minute," Leda said. She ran up a block and went behind a tree. He could see her speaking into the mobile phone.

While Bluderin waited, he thought about the day's life-threatening events, and it wasn't even nine in the morning. He could not understand why, but he felt sad for Riki Taar. Although she had intended to maim his abdomen and injure or kill him with a grenade, he knew that the woman was extremely sick. He thought back to the evening she had raped him. Before he had felt the effects of the drugs, he had asked her whether her legal surname was still Williams—that of her former husband—or Taar. She had replied, "I am what is left of my husband's name." He did not realize at the time that she was making an anagram. She had rearranged the letters in "Williams" to "I am swill," meaning garbage or kitchen refuse—*waste*. Her ex-husband still owned her, and she obeyed his commands religiously. Peter Vanderwerken had tipped Bluderin off that Lieutenant Justin Williams had ordered Riki to kill him. She could not possibly control her behavior, no more than Danny Akando could control his drinking. Demons owned their souls.

Leda walked back toward Bluderin, meeting him halfway. "This is it," she said. "Come with me to an agency office tucked away on a Parlerstrasse side street, and I will file a report on today's activities. After you sign the report and I debrief you, you are free to go. An agent found the other fuse assembly along with other items and information Riki had stolen. We also just discovered that a Soviet agent had offered her a good price for all of it, but Riki was holding out for more money."

"Amazing what you can find in bedposts," Bluderin said. "It's also amazing that the two agents never checked them out."

"It was an oversight," Leda said.

"I can't believe I was a suspect," Bluderin said. "I'm a patriot."

"No one involved with the intelligence community is immune from observation," she replied. "Don't take it personally."

"Surely the agents knew Riki was wearing the armored shirt," he said. "Why didn't they take it off?"

"It was an oversight," she said.

"An oversight my ass, just like the bedposts. She could have killed me. Riki tried to do me in. She's under the spell of her ex-husband, Lieutenant Justin Williams, although she called him Allen. Ever hear of him?"

"I read your testimony about what you told your intelligence contact on base," she said, "but we dismissed the supposed attack as a sexual perversion tactic. However, the agency did not dismiss the possibility that you and Riki could be in collusion for purposes of mutual benefit. When she tried to attack you today, it confirmed what I had been thinking. I knew there was no such collusion. I also got a call from an agent searching your apartment. He found the blue plastic box and lipstick tubes Riki had planted there. He also discovered and removed the beer she had poisoned. Presumably the beer was her final attempt to kill you if nothing else worked. As for Justin Allen Williams, he went by Allen until he received his commission. I guess he thought the name Justin was more suitable for an officer. You needn't worry about him any more. He's imprisoned for killing his second wife. He cut her into little pieces, like stew meat. Surprise surprise, don't you think?"

"I cannot believe what I'm hearing. The agency is as crazy as Riki Taar. You're talking to a guy who had only one goal in mind—to complete his military obligation honorably and get on with his life. I've never had any motive beyond that."

"I believe you," she said. "You did everything as directed. Gustav Erdmann and Günter Mann back you up as well. However, other agents you don't know raised some questions about the strictness of your dedication."

"That doesn't make any sense at all," he said.

"You were not totally candid about all your actions and thoughts."

"In what way was I concealing anything?" he asked. He was frightened and angered that some agents thought he was less than totally dedicated to his assignments, as he was to the army.

"It's what you *did not do* that raised their concerns, John. Take the fact that you did not reveal the note that Walter Lebrecht left for you in his novel."

"No one told me to deliver it to anyone," he said. "As you well know, I kept Walter's note in a folder, along with any other information I received from members of Vereingten Frieden."

"We know, but that's not the point," she said. "The point was that you did not *volunteer* to share the information."

"The army trained me not to volunteer for anything," he said. "I do as I'm told."

"Granted, but the agency thinks differently. There were questions about how candid you were regarding Akando's accident. I'm personally still unsure about that situation, although it's no longer of any concern. There were also questions about your opposition to the conflict in Vietnam. Could your opinion weaken your dedication to duty, it was questioned. And you did deceive Gustav about where you were going before you returned to Hardt Kaserne as ordered."

"The agency's thought process makes the Keystone Kops look brilliant," he said. "As for the sex show, how did you like it? Did it turn you on?"

"I taught you well," she said. "Now, do you want me to process you back to civilian life, or are we going to discuss the agency's methodology forever? None of it matters anymore. However, I want to offer you one last piece of advice. You are not to tell anyone about your experience with the intelligence community. If you do, we'll be knocking on your door. It won't be pleasant."

She did not have to say anything else.

"Let's move on," he said, and he thought back about something Leda had said previously. *You are free to go.* He had been waiting to hear those five words for the past fifty days. He was starting to feel like Hercules unchained, as Solveig Evensen did when her father died. A strong sense of *Gemutlichkeit* filled his veins. His pulse rate seemed to be a tenth of what it had been an hour earlier.

When Bluderin sat in a brown-leather chair in an agency auxiliary office off Parlerstrasse, waiting for Leda to finish writing her report, he picked up the current edition of the *Rems-Zeitung* and began reading it. He noticed that the day's date on the newspaper was June 19, 1968. He remembered celebrating Juneteenth the previous summer with Howard James to commemorate the emancipation of the last remaining slaves in the United States— in the state of Texas in 1865.

It was dismal, Bluderin thought, how this particular Juneteenth anniversary will commemorate the incarceration of Aarika Taar. As he breezed through the *Rems-Zeitung*, he read that race riots and antiwar demonstrations had taken place in virtually every state of the union.

Leda handed her report to Bluderin. He read the document and inscribed his signature in the spaces allocated. It was a brief report, only three pages long, and he discerned Leda's crisp, succinct writing style. It reflected all that he knew about her—lithe, without an ounce of fat, precise, and pointedly factual. That's how she was—*mean and lean*—with the exception of her input on the Akando file, which he thought was *succinctly fabricated.*

"It's been good working with you," she said.

"You're the consummate professional," he replied.

It had taken him a long time to figure it all out, but finally he understood Leda Beschwörung. Everything about their relationship was contrived. She did not grow up in Cheltenham, as she had described, but in Frankfurt. She did earn a master's degree at Columbia, but she also had an M.B.A. from Harvard, an important credential she neglected to mention. Her father was an executive in international finance, not a professor of mathematics. Her interest in Rilke stemmed from her searching his apartment and reading the poetry books before she met him. Her seduction of him—and subsequent sexual mentoring—was simply part of her assignment in training him how to attract women for potential agency assignments. She had never worked in Berlin. Walter Lebrecht had hinted about some of these issues in his note to Bluderin. Gustav Erdmann had given him some other insightful information about Leda. The formal nature of their departure today confirmed his suspicions. She was all business.

"I need to take a train to Stuttgart," Leda said. "Then I'm off to Berlin."

He knew she would not go to Berlin. He did not know why she had to go to Stuttgart, but he guessed it had something to do with

Riki Taar. They left the office with a firm handshake, along with an
uninspired kiss, and headed off in opposite directions.

Bluderin stopped at a florist shop on the way to the Oasis café.
He purchased a bouquet for Frau Müller, as he had promised. When
he resumed walking toward the Oasis he passed the dark green field
where Günter was tending to his sheep. The shepherd apparently saw
Bluderin off in the distance, since he waved at him. Bluderin waved
back and stood silently. He could hear Günter's voice riddling in the
breeze—*Life chooses you.* He inhaled the pastoral setting. The lilting,
green curves of the rolling hills and valleys, the leaping of a German
shepherd over and around a herd of sheep, a shepherd raising his staff
while likely having a séance with his long-departed wife, and black-
and-white spotted cows further off in the background, sprawled
like scattered rugs among the emerald mounds, were all images that
would remain with him for the rest of his life. The picture induced
him to recall a statement by Anaïs Nin: "*The personal life deeply lived
always expands into truths beyond itself.*"

Frau Müller thanked him for the bouquet of multi-colored
flowers. She went into the kitchen to make him a bratwurst and
sauerkraut sandwich on pumpernickel. Malin Müller served him his
lunch, along with a letter from Solveig Evensen. He was surprised
to receive the letter because he had not responded to the previous
one she had sent. The *final assignment* of late had interfered with his
normally time-sensitive responses.

After he bade farewell to Malin and Frau Müller, he casually
walked back into the heart of Schwäbisch Gmünd, near the Heilig-
Kreuz-Münster, where he would pick up his duffel bag at his former
landlord's apartment.

Bluderin already had said his formal good-byes to Gustav
Erdmann, Karin and Couch, and many Gasthaus customers,
especially Eddie and Tulla Grau and Hans Kliebert. He promised
Peter and Johanna Vanderwerken that he would write to them and to

wish their daughter, Gretchen, all the best. He had obtained Walter
Lebrect's mailing address from Peter so he could write to Walter
and thank him for the copy of the Mark Strand book, *Reasons for
Moving: Poems.* He did not see Jürgen Treuge or Vera Luchterhand
after their threesome experience. He thought it best for them all to
attribute the tryst to the whims of impetuous youth.

There were only a handful of army friends to say good-bye to.
Most of them had departed Hardt Kaserne before him, and Major
McCandley was on leave in the States. Bluderin had a feeling that
Specialist Joe Tyler probably was happy to see him go. It was nothing
personal, other than Tyler could be assured that he would no longer
be around to spill the secret about his sexuality. Bluderin still felt a
strange electric shock in his ear, followed by tinnitus, whenever he
thought about Joe Tyler's duplicity.

He boarded a train bound, after numerous stops, to Oostende,
Belgium. He passively looked out the seat window. Soon he was no
longer in Schwäbisch Gmünd. *Auf Wiedersehen, und danke fur der
Aufklarung* was the only thing he said aloud, to no one, about the
town, the army, and the intelligence community, settings that had
seen his age advance from nineteen to twenty-one. *Good-bye for now,
and thank you for the enlightenment.* He had changed his life.

Epilogue

—◄o►—

October 1968

A collage of autumn leaves blanketed the knolls in vivid contrast to the adjacent, stark-white cliffs of the Seven Sisters buffering the shore of the English Channel. He had taken many walks and runs along those small hills in Seaford over the past several months, sometimes going as far as Eastbourne or Brighton. He ran when he was alone and walked when he was with her. Likewise, the runs were windowed in silence while the walks were adrift in ships of conversation.

He recalled some of his experiences over the past two years, but none of them except for the ones with her entered his senses. The people and the places within the vast majority of those experiences had hidden themselves in the dark cave of his mind.

He tried to write something to ooze out vague, amorphous thoughts, but nothing happened. The function of form would not yield. Every image that passed his mind seemed to settle in disinterest or escape into the dross of death.

He turned off the light in the room and dreamed into the fireplace. Patience is a virtue, his lover once told him. *It is an undying ember,* she had said, *that helps us see the radiant, crimson-amber hue of loveliness in its center.* His heart pounded hard against his chest, as though it was trying to burst out of an indefinable fear. Moments later the heartbeat slowed, beating softly, and his mind beat uniformly. He was without influence. His subconscious wing had vanished. He sat at the desk again, a pencil cuffed in his left hand. He moved the tip across the paper. He had no idea what he was writing.

The moon was full, the earth asleep, and he harbored shapes. They rose like vapor, smelled of the sea, and sailed into his mind's eye. A drunkenness of great depth underscored his vision. So: the earth had not lost its time and all of its properties. This room was not the last remaining fact, the only tangible entity in space.

The presence of a goddess filled his eyes. A white flash filled the room like a wave of heat lightning. A woman with light-blonde hair, styled with bangs over the forehead and flowing loosely over her naked shoulders, turned the light back on, went over to him, and began massaging his neck. Her smooth, slender fingers danced in a rhapsody of movement, her white fingernails tapping on his skin as though she were playing the piano.

"Do you like writing in the dark?" she asked.

"It was the only way I could see." He looked at her with a helpless smile.

Her skin was a vibrant gold, darkened from their sunbathing on the channel, smooth as porcelain, and toned from daily swimming and hiking throughout the summer and into the fall. Her flesh was adorned with a strapless brassiere crocheted in white silk, as were her panties. Having recently showered, she smelled of a hint of jasmine. He could never describe to her how he felt when she wrote to him, inviting him to come live with her at her cottage near the campus of the Newlands School, where she taught Spanish, French, and German.

He had been living with her since July, leaving the cottage three days a week to attend classes in the humanities at the University of

Southampton. Their relationship had deepened into a Yin and Yang interaction, influencing each other's dreams and destinies.

"May I see?" she asked.

He picked up the notepad he had been writing on and gave it to her. She read aloud in her soft voice with incredibly articulate diction. He had titled the poem "A Portrait of Air," but it was unquestionably a portrait of her.

Your eyes ever passing rivers,
currents glide to music: language in language,
each letter voiced with direction.

You speak through sounds
where truth is whistled
as a train moves onto its sun.
You talk along these tracks,
pausing on infinite seconds.
The station, the destination, the arrival are all last lines
leading you into the universe:
you bleed in its union. Air is placed
in air: timelessness, space, and communion.

Air is wider where one lives as he dies;
it had rung with drums as you sung
to open these corners: the passionate life
your lips conceive when you begin a story.

The street runs from under you tonight;
it receives your flow like a brain
vulnerable to changing darkness
so steadily uncertain of its presence, becoming
timidly open to circumstance. Being

aware of this silence: the black ground
so still you hear letters falling
from a cracked window.
As you read, a man's fear
is eased in smiles. His presences
begin and end themselves: You are.

But beyond this statement I try,
through the valleys and tenements of stars,
to see you clearly as the lady
who unfolds the day
with a voice that has given back
wind and sun.

He dedicated the poem to her. She looked at him and smiled lovingly, her deep blue eyes gleaming, reflecting off the fireplace. He stood up to embrace her stunning image. The mixture of her gentle being, graceful intelligence, perfect voice, and incredible body of knowledge as well as erotic beauty filled him with an emotion that was mysteriously virginal each time he kissed her.

"What prompted you to write it?"

"You are my Muse, my Erato," he said.

"John, look at me."

He looked at the Nordic shape around her eyes, then into her eyes, and out of nowhere some lines from a Janis Ian song played in his mind.

With hair of spun gold, lips of ruby red,
And eyes as deep as the deepest sea.

He went into the kitchen and poured each of them a glass of Bordeaux. They rejoined in the living room and began their routine, nightly conversation. They would often discuss the meanings of words.

"Did you ever find out what my name means?" she asked.

"I've been wondering about that ever since I first met you," he said, "when you said the name Solveig had a meaning other than simply being a name. So I did a little research. One reference book I looked into informed me that Solveig is a female given name of Old Norse origin. According to the source, its exact meaning is uncertain."

"Is that all you know?"

"I continued researching the subject," he said. "You know how persistent I can be. I discovered that your name consists of two parts, and both parts have different theorized origins. *Sol* in Old Norse could be sun or sun-colored, while *veig* could mean strength. I like to think of the name as *Sunstrength*, although there may be other meanings."

"My mother always said it meant 'house of power,' although I was powerless growing up in my house. I like your interpretation better."

"Another book mentioned that the name meant 'worshipper of the sun,' which is appropriate for my needs, since I worship you."

"You better." She winked at him and smiled warmly. "Remember the famous 'Solveig's Song' in Henrik Ibsen's play, *Peer Gynt*? I think Ibsen may have favored the idea that the name is linked etymologically with the sun."

He loved listening to her. She always said something that expanded his intellect.

"I recently read at the university library that the name could also mean 'way of the sun.' I like the name *Sunway*, but I still question its meaning, or which meaning is the right one."

"All questions are impossible, brighter than sunlight," she said.

* * *

Enjoined like one being instead of two, Solveig Evensen and John Bluderin could feel the depth of each other's soul. Their lovemaking was intensely spiritual, beyond their own comprehension, and they moved in rhythm to a garden of music.

And what am I to do, Bluderin's psychic voyeur and ethereal Doppelgänger who reemerges outside his tour of duty, set against it like a bookend? Although over three thousand miles away in my New York apartment, I can feel the pulse of his brain. He is telling me to answer the eternal question, *what does it all mean*, and so I begin writing a probing response I name *The Blue Wake*. We'll see where it takes me. He has a long way to go.

Author's Notes and Acknowledgements

◄○►

Let me express my appreciation for the following books, poems, and songs. I list them, by authors, and put an asterisk next to those works for which I feel a considerable debt.

Baez, Joan. "Sweet Sir Galahad," from the album *One Day at a Time*. New York: Vanguard Records, 1970. Ms. Baez famously performed the song at Woodstock in 1969. Quoted in Chapter 17.

Donovan. "Catch the Wind." Released as a single by Pye Records in the U.K. and by Hickory Records in the U.S. (Nashville, Tennessee) in 1965. Quoted in Chapter 8.

Doors, The. "Light My Fire" from the album *The Doors*. New York: Elektra, 1967. Quoted in Chapter 17.

*Galvin, Brendan. "The Eternal Silence of These Infinite Spaces Frightens Me," *The Massachusetts Review*, Volume 9, Issue 4. Autumn 1968. Quoted on the preface page. Used with permission of the author.

Garner, Errol. "Misty," a signature song of recording artist Johnny Mathis. New York: Columbia Records, 1959. Alluded to in Chapter 3.

Hokushi, Tachibana. *The Four Seasons, Japanese Haiku.* New York: The Peter Pauper Press, 1958. His haiku, along with one of Basho's, is quoted in Chapter 16.

*Ian, Janis (lyrics and music), "Hair of Spun Gold," Taosongs Two (BMI). All rights reserved. Used by permission. Quoted in the Epilogue.

Jagger, Mick, and Richards, Keith. "(I Can't Get No) Satisfaction," produced by Andrew Loog Oldham. New York: RCA , 1965. Alluded to in Chapters 4 and 10.

Lennon, John, and credited to Lennon/McCartney. "Do You Want to Know a Secret?" from the album *Please Please Me.* Sung by George Harrison. United Kingdom: Parlophone PMG, 1963. Alluded to in Chapter 4.

McCartney, Paul, and credited to Lennon/McCartney. "Eleanor Rigby," from the album *Revolver.* United Kingdom: Parlophone PMG, 1966. United States (Los Angeles): Capitol Records, 1966. Quoted in Chapter 8.

North, Alex (music), and Zaret, Hy (lyrics). "Unchained Melody," originally performed by Todd Duncan. New York: Capitol Records, 1955. Made famous by The Righteous Brothers in 1965. Quoted in Chapter 10.

Ostrovsky, Arkady (music), and Oshanin, Lev (lyrics). "May There Always Be Sunshine." Created in 1962. Performed for the first time in 1963 at the Sopot International Song Festival by Tamara Miansarova.

Phillips, John. "San Francisco (Be Sure to Wear Some Flowers in Your Hair)," performed by Scott McKenzie. United States: Olde Records, 1967. United Kingdom: CBS Records, 1967. Alluded to in Chapter 21.

Redding, Otis, and Cropper, Steve. "(Sittin' On) The Dock of the Bay," from the album *The Dock of the Bay*. Memphis, Tennessee: Stax Records, 1968. Alluded to in Chapter 20.

*Rilke, Rainer Maria. *Neue Gedichte* (New Poems), "Archaischer Torso Apollo" ("Archaic Torso of Apollo"), Germany: Insel Verlag, 1907. Quoted in Chapter 2.

Rilke, Rainer Maria. *Das Buch der Bilder* (This Book of Paintings), "Eingang" ("Initiation"). Germany: Insel Verlag, 1902. Quoted in Chapter 8. From the same book, the poem "Erinnerung"("Memory") is quoted in Chapter 11.

Roethke, Theodore. *The Waking*, "The Waking," New York: Doubleday, 1953. Quoted in Chapter 15.

*Strand, Mark. *Reasons for Moving: Poems*, "Keeping Things Whole," New York: Antheneum, 1968. Used with permission of the author. Quoted in Chapter 19.

Thomas, Dylan. *Deaths and Entrances*, "Fern Hill." United Kingdom: J.M. Dent & Sons, 1946. Quoted in Chapter 9.

Weiss, George David; Peretti, Hugo; and Creatore, Luigi. "Can't Help Falling in Love." Originally recorded by Elvis Presley. New York: RCA, 1961. Quoted in Chapter 4.

About the Author

—◄o►—

Jerry Ackerman was formerly a military analyst, technical writer, reference book editor, teacher, and soldier. His published works include numerous articles, essays, short stories, and poems. A marketing executive specializing in environmentally sustainable solutions since 1993, he lives in the farmhouse he painstakingly restored in Deep River, Connecticut